John Dos Passos

Manhattan Transfer

HOUGHTON MIFFLIN COMPANY · BOSTON

Contents

First Section

I. Ferryslip

Three gulls wheel above the broken boxes, orangerinds, spoiled cabbage heads that heave between the splintered plank walls, the green waves spume under the round bow as the ferry, skidding on the tide, crashes, gulps the broken water, slides, settles slowly into the slip. Handwinches whirl with jingle of chains. Gates fold upwards, feet step out across the crack, men and women press through the manuresmelling wooden tunnel of the ferry-house, crushed and jostling like apples fed down a chute into a press.

THE nurse, holding the basket at arm's length as if it were a bedpan, opened the door to a big dry hot room with greenish distempered walls where in the air tinctured with smells of alcohol and iodoform hung writhing a faint sourish squalling from other baskets along the wall. As she set her basket down she glanced into it with pursed-up lips. The newborn baby squirmed in the cottonwool feebly like a knot of earthworms.

On the ferry there was an old man playing the violin. He had a monkey's face puckered up in one corner and kept time with the toe of a cracked patent-leather shoe. Bud Korpenning sat on the rail watching him, his back to the river. The breeze made the hair stir round the tight line of his cap and dried the sweat on his temples. His feet were blistered, he was leadentired, but when the ferry moved out of the slip, bucking the little slapping scalloped waves of the river he felt something warm and tingling shoot suddenly through all his veins. "Say, friend, how fur is it into the city from where this ferry lands?"

he asked a young man in a straw hat wearing a blue and white striped necktie who stood beside him.

The young man's glance moved up from Bud's road-swelled shoes to the red wrist that stuck out from the frayed sleeves of his coat, past the skinny turkey's throat and slid up cockily into the intent eyes under the broken-visored cap.

"That depends where you want to get to."

"How do I get to Broadway? . . . I want to get to the center of things."

"Walk east a block and turn down Broadway and you'll find the center of things if you walk far enough."

"Thank you sir. I'll do that."

The violinist was going through the crowd with his hat held out, the wind ruffling the wisps of gray hair on his shabby bald head. Bud found the face tilted up at him, the crushed eyes like two black pins looking into his. "Nothin," he said gruffly and turned away to look at the expanse of river bright as knifeblades. The plank walls of the slip closed in, cracked as the ferry lurched against them; there was rattling of chains, and Bud was pushed forward among the crowd through the ferryhouse. He walked between two coal wagons and out over a dusty expanse of street towards yellow streetcars. A trembling took hold of his knees. He thrust his hands deep in his pockets.

EAT on a lunchwagon halfway down the block. He slid stiffly onto a revolving stool and looked for a long while at the pricelist.

"Fried eggs and a cup o coffee."

"Want 'em turned over?" asked the redhaired man behind the counter who was wiping off his beefy freckled forearms with his apron. Bud Korpenning sat up with a start.

"What?"

"The eggs? Want em turned over or sunny side up?"

"Oh sure, turn 'em over." Bud slouched over the counter again with his head between his hands.

"You look all in, feller," the man said as he broke the eggs into the sizzling grease of the frying pan.

"Came down from upstate. I walked fifteen miles this mornin."

The man made a whistling sound through his eyeteeth. "Comin to the big city to look for a job, eh?"

Bud nodded. The man flopped the eggs sizzling and netted with brown out onto the plate and pushed it towards Bud with some bread and butter on the edge of it. "I'm goin to slip you a bit of advice, feller, and it won't cost you nutten. You go an git a shave and a haircut and brush the hayseeds out o yer suit a bit before you start lookin. You'll be more likely to git somethin. It's looks that count in this city."

"I kin work all right. I'm a good worker," growled Bud with his mouth full.

"I'm tellin yez, that's all," said the redhaired man and turned back to his stove.

When Ed Thatcher climbed the marble steps of the wide hospital entry he was trembling. The smell of drugs caught at his throat. A woman with a starched face was looking at him over the top of a desk. He tried to steady his voice.

"Can you tell me how Mrs. Thatcher is?"

"Yes, you can go up."

"But please, miss, is everything all right?"

"The nurse on the floor will know anything about the case. Stairs to the left, third floor, maternity ward."

Ed Thatcher held a bunch of flowers wrapped in green waxed paper. The broad stairs swayed as he stumbled up, his toes kicking against the brass rods that held the fiber matting down. The closing of a door cut off a strangled shriek. He stopped a nurse.

"I want to see Mrs. Thatcher, please."

"Go right ahead if you know where she is."

"But they've moved her."

"You'll have to ask at the desk at the end of the hall."

He gnawed his cold lips. At the end of the hall a redfaced woman looked at him, smiling.

"Everything's fine. You're the happy father of a bouncing baby girl."

"You see it's our first and Susie's so delicate," he stammered with blinking eyes.

"Oh yes, I understand, naturally you worried. . . . You can go in and talk to her when she wakes up. The baby was born two hours ago. Be sure not to tire her."

Ed Thatcher was a little man with two blond wisps of mustache and washedout gray eyes. He seized the nurse's hand and shook it showing all his uneven yellow teeth in a smile.

"You see it's our first."

"Congratulations," said the nurse.

Rows of beds under bilious gaslight, a sick smell of restlessly stirring bedclothes, faces fat, lean, yellow, white; that's her. Susie's yellow hair lay in a loose coil round her little white face that looked shriveled and twisted. He unwrapped the roses and put them on the night table. Looking out the window was like looking down into water. The trees in the square were tangled in blue cobwebs. Down the avenue lamps were coming on marking off with green shimmer brickpurple blocks of houses; chimney pots and water tanks cut sharp into a sky flushed like flesh. The blue lids slipped back off her eyes.

"That you Ed? . . . . Why Ed they are Jacks. How extravagant of you."

"I couldn't help it dearest. I knew you liked them."

A nurse was hovering near the end of the bed.

"Couldn't you let us see the baby, miss?"

The nurse nodded. She was a lanternjawed grayfaced woman with tight lips.

"I hate her," whispered Susie. "She gives me the fidgets that woman does; she's nothing but a mean old maid."

"Never mind dear, it's just for a day or two." Susie closed her eyes.

"Do you still want to call her Ellen?"

The nurse brought back a basket and set it on the bed beside Susie.

"Oh isn't she wonderful!" said Ed. "Look she's breathing. . . . And they've oiled her." He helped his wife to raise herself on her elbow; the yellow coil of her hair unrolled, fell over his hand and arm. "How can you tell them apart nurse?"

"Sometimes we cant," said the nurse, stretching her mouth in a smile. Susie was looking querulously into the minute purple face. "You're sure this is mine."

"Of course."

"But it hasnt any label on it."

"I'll label it right away."

"But mine was dark." Susie lay back on the pillow, gasping for breath.

"She has lovely little light fuzz just the color of your hair."

Susie stretched her arms out above her head and shrieked: "It's not mine. It's not mine. Take it away. . . . That woman's stolen my baby."

"Dear, for Heaven's sake! Dear, for Heaven's sake!" He tried to tuck the covers about her.

"Too bad," said the nurse, calmly, picking up the basket. "I'll have to give her a sedative."

Susie sat up stiff in bed. "Take it away," she yelled and fell back in hysterics, letting out continuous frail moaning shrieks.

"O my God!" cried Ed Thatcher, clasping his hands.

"You'd better go away for this evening, Mr. Thatcher. . . . She'll quiet down, once you've gone. . . . I'll put the roses in water."

On the last flight he caught up with a chubby man who was strolling down slowly, rubbing his hands as he went. Their eyes met.

"Everything all right, sir?" asked the chubby man.

"Oh yes, I guess so," said Thatcher faintly.

The chubby man turned on him, delight bubbling through

his thick voice. "Congradulade me, congradulade me; mein vife has giben birth to a poy."

Thatcher shook a fat little hand. "Mine's a girl," he admitted, sheepishly.

"It is fif years yet and every year a girl, and now dink of it, a poy."

"Yes," said Ed Thatcher as they stepped out on the pavement, "it's a great moment."

"Vill yous allow me sir to invite you to drink a congradulation drink mit me?"

"Why with pleasure."

The latticed halfdoors were swinging in the saloon at the corner of Third Avenue. Shuffling their feet politely they went through into the back room.

"Ach," said the German as they sat down at a scarred brown table, "family life is full of vorries."

"That it is sir; this is my first."

"Vill you haf beer?"

"All right anything suits me."

"Two pottles Culmbacher imported to drink to our little folk." The bottles popped and the sepia-tinged foam rose in the glasses. "Here's success. . . . Prosit," said the German, and raised his glass. He rubbed the foam out of his mustache and pounded on the table with a pink fist. "Vould it be indiscreet meester . . . ?"

"Thatcher's my name."

"Vould it be indiscreet, Mr. Thatcher, to inquvire vat might your profession be?"

"Accountant. I hope before long to be a certified accountant."

"I am a printer and my name is Zucher—Marcus Antonius Zucher."

"Pleased to meet you Mr. Zucher."

They shook hands across the table between the bottles.

"A certified accountant makes big money," said Mr. Zucher.

"Big money's what I'll have to have, for my little girl."

"Kids, they eat money," continued Mr. Zucher, in a deep voice.

"Wont you let me set you up to a bottle?" said Thatcher, figuring up how much he had in his pocket. Poor Susie wouldn't like me to be drinking in a saloon like this. But just this once, and I'm learning, learning about fatherhood.

"The more the merrier," said Mr. Zucher. ". . . But kids, they eat money. . . . Dont do nutten but eat and vear out clothes. Vonce I get my business on its feet. . . . Ach! Now vot mit hypothecations and the difficult borrowing of money and vot mit vages going up und these here crazy tradeunion socialists and bomsters . . . "

"Well here's how, Mr. Zucher." Mr. Zucher squeezed the foam out of his mustache with the thumb and forefinger of each hand. "It aint every day ve pring into the voirld a papy poy, Mr. Thatcher."

"Or a baby girl, Mr. Zucher."

The barkeep wiped the spillings off the table when he brought the new bottles, and stood near listening, the rag dangling from his red hands.

"And I have the hope in mein heart that ven my poy drinks to his poy, it vill be in champagne vine. Ach, that is how things go in this great city."

"I'd like my girl to be a quiet homey girl, not like these young women nowadays, all frills and furbelows and tight lacings. And I'll have retired by that time and have a little place up the Hudson, work in the garden evenings. . . . I know fellers downtown who have retired with three thousand a year. It's saving that does it."

"Aint no good in savin," said the barkeep. "I saved for ten years and the savings bank went broke and left me nutten but a bankbook for my trouble. Get a close tip and take a chance, that's the only system."

"That's nothing but gambling," snapped Thatcher.

"Well sir it's a gamblin game," said the barkeep as he walked back to the bar swinging the two empty bottles.

"A gamblin game. He aint so far out," said Mr.

Zucher, looking down into his beer with a glassy meditative eye. "A man vat is ambeetious must take chances. Ambeetions is vat I came here from Frankfort mit at the age of tvelf years, und now that I haf a son to vork for . . . Ach, his name shall be Vilhelm after the mighty Kaiser."

"My little girl's name will be Ellen after my mother." Ed Thatcher's eyes filled with tears.

Mr. Zucher got to his feet. "Vell goodpy Mr. Thatcher. Happy to have met you. I must go home to my little girls."

Thatcher shook the chubby hand again, and thinking warm soft thoughts of motherhood and fatherhood and birthday cakes and Christmas watched through a sepiatinged foamy haze Mr. Zucher waddle out through the swinging doors. After a while he stretched out his arms. Well poor little Susie wouldn't like me to be here. . . . Everything for her and the bonny wee bairn.

"Hey there yous how about settlin?" bawled the barkeep after him when he reached the door.

"Didnt the other feller pay?"

"Like hell he did."

"But he was t-t-treating me. . . . "

The barkeep laughed as he covered the money with a red lipper. "I guess that bloat believes in savin."

A small bearded bandylegged man in a derby walked up Allen Street, up the sunstriped tunnel hung with skyblue and smokedsalmon and mustardyellow quilts, littered with second hand gingerbread-colored furniture. He walked with his cold hands clasped over the tails of his frockcoat, picking his way among packing boxes and scuttling children. He kept gnawing his lips and clasping and unclasping his hands. He walked without hearing the yells of the children or the annihilating clatter of the L trains overhead or smelling the rancid sweet huddled smell of packed tenements.

At a yellowpainted drugstore at the corner of Canal, he stopped and stared abstractedly at a face on a green advertising card. It was a highbrowed cleanshaven distinguished face with arched eyebrows and a bushy neatly trimmed mustache, the face of a man who had money in the bank, poised prosperously above a crisp wing collar and an ample dark cravat. Under it in copybook writing was the signature King C. Gillette. Above his head hovered the motto NO STROPPING NO HONING. The little bearded man pushed his derby back off his sweating brow and looked for a long time into the dollarproud eyes of King C. Gillette. Then he clenched his fists, threw back his shoulders and walked into the drugstore.

His wife and daughters were out. He heated up a pitcher of water on the gasburner. Then with the scissors he found on the mantel he clipped the long brown locks of his beard. Then he started shaving very carefully with the new nickelbright safety razor. He stood trembling running his fingers down his smooth white cheeks in front of the stained mirror. He was trimming his mustache when he heard a noise behind him. He turned towards them a face smooth as the face of King C. Gillette, a face with a dollarbland smile. The two little girls' eyes were popping out of their heads. "Mommer . . . it's popper," the biggest one yelled. His wife dropped like a laundrybag into the rocker and threw the apron over her head.

"Oyoy! Oyoy!" she moaned rocking back and forth.

"Vat's a matter? Dontye like it?" He walked back and forth with the safety razor shining in his hand now and then gently fingering his smooth chin.

II. Metropolis

There were Babylon and Nineveh: they were built of brick. Athens was gold marble colums. Rome was held up on broad arches of rubble. In Constantinople the minarets flame like great candles round the Golden Horn . . . Steel, glass, tile, concrete will be the materials of the skyscrapers. Crammed on the narrow island the millionwindowed buildings will jut glittering, pyramid on pyramid like the white cloudhead above a thunderstorm.

WHEN the door of the room closed behind him, Ed Thatcher felt very lonely, full of prickly restlessness. If Susie were only here he'd tell her about the big money he was going to make and how he'd deposit ten dollars a week in the savings bank just for little Ellen; that would make five hundred and twenty dollars a year. . . . Why in ten years without the interest that'd come to more than five thousand dollars. I must compute the compound interest on five hundred and twenty dollars at four per cent. He walked excitedly about the narrow room. The gas jet purred comfortably like a cat. His eyes fell on the headline on a *Journal* that lay on the floor by the coalscuttle where he had dropped it to run for the hack to take Susie to the hospital.

MORTON SIGNS THE GREATER NEW YORK BILL
COMPLETES THE ACT MAKING NEW YORK WORLD'S SECOND METROPOLIS

Breathing deep he folded the paper and laid it on the table. The world's second metropolis. . . . And dad wanted me to stay in his ole fool store in Onteora. Might have if it hadnt been for Susie. . . . Gentlemen tonight that you do me the signal honor of offering me the junior partnership in your firm I want to present to you my little girl, my wife. I owe everything to her.

In the bow he made towards the grate his coat-tails flicked a piece of china off the console beside the bookcase. He made a little clicking noise with his tongue against his teeth as he stooped to pick it up. The head of the blue porcelain Dutch girl had broken off from her body. "And poor Susie's so fond of her knicknacks. I'd better go to bed."

He pushed up the window and leaned out. An L train was rumbling past the end of the street. A whiff of coal smoke stung his nostrils. He hung out of the window a long while looking up and down the street. The world's second metropolis. In the brick houses and the dingy lamplight and the voices of a group of boys kidding and quarreling on the steps of a house opposite, in the regular firm tread of a policeman, he felt a marching like soldiers, like a sidewheeler going up the Hudson under the Palisades, like an election parade, through long streets towards something tall white full of colonnades and stately. Metropolis.

The street was suddenly full of running. Somebody out of breath let out the word Fire.

"Where at?"

The group of boys melted off the stoop across the way. Thatcher turned back into the room. It was stifling hot. He was all tingling to be out. I ought to go to bed. Down the street he heard the splattering hoofbeats and the frenzied bell of a fire engine. Just take a look. He ran down the stairs with his hat in his hand.

"Which way is it?"

"Down on the next block."

"It's a tenement house."

It was a narrowwindowed sixstory tenement. The hook-andladder had just drawn up. Brown smoke, with here and there a little trail of sparks was pouring fast out of the lower windows. Three policemen were swinging their clubs as they packed the crowd back against the steps and railings of the houses opposite. In the empty space in the middle of the street the fire engine and the red hosewagon shone with bright brass. People watched silent staring at the upper windows where shadows moved and occasional light flickered. A thin pillar of flame began to flare above the house like a romancandle.

"The airshaft," whispered a man in Thatcher's ear. A gust of wind filled the street with smoke and a smell of burning rags. Thatcher felt suddenly sick. When the smoke cleared he saw people hanging in a kicking cluster, hanging by their hands from a windowledge. The other side firemen were helping women down a ladder. The flame in the center of the house flared brighter. Something black had dropped from a window and lay on the pavement shrieking. The policemen were shoving the crowd back to the ends of the block. New fire engines were arriving.

"Theyve got five alarms in," a man said. "What do you think of that? Everyone of 'em on the two top floors was trapped. It's an incendiary done it. Some goddam firebug."

A young man sat huddled on the curb beside the gas lamp. Thatcher found himself standing over him pushed by the crowd from behind.

"He's an Italian."

"His wife's in that buildin."

"Cops wont let him get by." "His wife's in a family way. He cant talk English to ask the cops."

The man wore blue suspenders tied up with a piece of string in back. His back was heaving and now and then he left out a string of groaning words nobody understood.

Thatcher was working his way out of the crowd. At the corner a man was looking into the fire alarm box. As Thatcher brushed past him he caught a smell of coaloil from the man's clothes. The man looked up into his face with a smile. He had tallowy sagging cheeks and bright popeyes. Thatcher's hands and feet went suddenly cold. The firebug. The papers say they hang round like that to watch it. He walked home fast, ran up the stairs, and locked the room door behind him. The room was quiet and empty. He'd forgotten that Susie wouldnt be there waiting for him. He began to undress. He couldnt forget the smell of coaloil on the man's clothes.

Mr. Perry flicked at the burdock leaves with his cane. The real-estate agent was pleading in a singsong voice:

"I dont mind telling you, Mr. Perry, it's an opportunity not to be missed. You know the old saying sir . . . opportunity knocks but once on a young man's door. In six months I can virtually guarantee that these lots will have doubled in value. Now that we are a part of New York, the second city in the world, sir, dont forget that. . . . Why the time will come, and I firmly believe that you and I will see it, when bridge after bridge spanning the East River have made Long Island and Manhattan one, when the Borough of Queens will be as much the heart and throbbing center of the great metropolis as is Astor Place today."

"I know, I know, but I'm looking for something dead safe. And besides I want to build. My wife hasnt been very well these last few years. . . . "

"But what could be safer than my proposition? Do you realize Mr. Perry, that at considerable personal loss I'm letting you in on the ground floor of one of the greatest real-estate certainties of modern times. I'm putting at your disposal not only security, but ease, comfort, luxury. We are caught up Mr. Perry on a great wave whether we will or no, a great wave of expansion and progress. A great deal is going to happen in the next few years. All these mechanical inventions—telephones, electricity, steel bridges, horseless vehicles—they are all leading somewhere. It's up to us to be on the inside, in the forefront of progress. . . . My God! I cant begin to tell you what it will mean. . . . " Poking amid the dry grass and the burdock leaves Mr. Perry had moved something with his stick. He stooped and picked up a triangular skull with a pair of spiralfluted horns. "By gad!" he said. "That must have been a fine ram."

Drowsy from the smell of lather and bayrum and singed hair that weighed down the close air of the barbershop, Bud sat nodding, his hands dangling big and red between his knees. In his eardrums he could still feel through the snipping of scissors the pounding of his feet on the hungry road down from Nyack.

"Next!"

"Whassat? . . . All right I just want a shave an a haircut."

The barber's pudgy hands moved through his hair, the scissors whirred like a hornet behind his ears. His eyes kept closing; he jerked them open fighting sleep. He could see beyond the striped sheet littered with sandy hair the bobbing hammerhead of the colored boy shining his shoes.

"Yessir" a deepvoiced man droned from the next chair, "it's time the Democratic party nominated a strong . . . "

"Want a neckshave as well?" The barber's greasyskinned moonface poked into his.

He nodded.

"Shampoo?"

"No."

When the barber threw back the chair to shave him he wanted to crane his neck like a mudturtle turned over on its back. The lather spread drowsily on his face, prickling his nose, filling up his ears. Drowning in featherbeds of lather, blue lather, black, slit by the faraway glint of the razor, glint of the grubbing hoe through blueblack lather clouds. The old man on his back in the potatofield, his beard sticking up lathery white full of blood. Full of blood his socks from those blisters on his heels. His hands gripped each other cold and horny like a dead man's hands under the sheet. Lemme git up. . . . He opened his eyes. Padded fingertips were stroking his chin. He stared up at the ceiling where four flies made figure eights round a red crêpe-paper bell. His tongue was dry leather in his mouth. The barber righted the chair again. Bud looked about blinking. "Four bits, and a nickel for the shine."

ADMITS KILLING CRIPPLED MOTHER . . .

"D'yous mind if I set here a minute an read that paper?" he hears his voice drawling in his pounding ears.

"Go right ahead."

PARKER'S FRIENDS PROTECT . . .

The black print squirms before his eyes. Russians . . . MOB STONES . . . (Special Dispatch to the *Herald*) Trenton, N. J.

Nathan Sibbetts, fourteen years old, broke down today after two weeks of steady denial of guilt and confessed to the police that he was responsible for the death of his aged and crippled mother, Hannah Sibbetts, after a quarrel in their home at Jacob's Creek, six miles above this city. Tonight he was committed to await the action of the Grand Jury.

RELIEVE PORT ARTHUR IN FACE OF ENEMY . . . Mrs. Rix Loses Husband's Ashes.

On Tuesday May 24 at about half past eight o'clock I came home after sleeping on the steam roller all night, he said, and went upstairs to sleep some more. I had only gotten to sleep when my mother came upstairs and told me to get up and if I didn't get up she would throw me downstairs. My mother grabbed hold of me to throw me downstairs. I threw her first and she fell to the bottom. I went downstairs and found that her head was twisted to one side. I then saw that she was dead and then I straightened her neck and covered her up with the cover from my bed.

Bud folds the paper carefully, lays it on the chair and leaves the barbershop. Outside the air smells of crowds, is full of noise and sunlight. No more'n a needle in a haystack . . . "An I'm twentyfive years old," he muttered aloud. Think of a kid fourteen. . . . He walks faster along roaring pavements where the sun shines through the Elevated striping the blue street with warm seething yellow stripes. No more'n a needle in a haystack.

Ed Thatcher sat hunched over the pianokeys picking out the Mosquito Parade. Sunday afternoon sunlight streamed dustily through the heavy lace curtains of the window, squirmed in the red roses of the carpet, filled the cluttered parlor with specks and splinters of light. Susie Thatcher sat limp by the window watching him out of eyes too blue for her sallow face. Between them, stepping carefully among the roses on the sunny field of the carpet, little Ellen danced. Two small hands held up the pinkfrilled dress and now and then an emphatic little voice said, "Mummy watch my expression."

"Just look at the child," said Thatcher, still playing. "She's a regular little balletdancer."

Sheets of the Sunday paper lay where they had fallen from the table; Ellen started dancing on them, tearing the sheets under her nimble tiny feet.

"Dont do that Ellen dear," whined Susie from the pink plush chair.

"But mummy I can do it while I dance."

"Dont do that mother said." Ed Thatcher had slid into the Barcarole. Ellen was dancing to it, her arms swaying to it, her feet nimbly tearing the paper.

"Ed for Heaven's sake pick the child up; she's tearing the paper."

He brought his fingers down in a lingering chord. "Deary you mustnt do that. Daddy's not finished reading it."

Ellen went right on. Thatcher swooped down on her from the pianostool and set her squirming and laughing on his knee. "Ellen you should always mind when mummy speaks to you, and dear you shouldnt be destructive. It costs money to make that paper and people worked on it and daddy went out to buy it and he hasnt finished reading it yet. Ellie understands dont she now? We need con-struction and not de-struction in this world." Then he went on with the Barcarole and Ellen went on dancing, stepping carefully among the roses on the sunny field of the carpet.

There were six men at the table in the lunch room eating fast with their hats on the backs of their heads.

"Jiminy crickets!" cried the young man at the end of the

table who was holding a newspaper in one hand and a cup of coffee in the other. "Kin you beat it?"

"Beat what?" growled a longfaced man with a toothpick in the corner of his mouth.

"Big snake appears on Fifth Avenue. . . . Ladies screamed and ran in all directions this morning at eleven thirty when a big snake crawled out of a crack in the masonry of the retaining wall of the reservoir at Fifth Avenue and Fortysecond Street and started to cross the sidewalk. . . ."

"Some fish story. . . ."

"That aint nothin," said an old man. "When I was a boy we used to go snipeshootin on Brooklyn Flats. . . ."

"Holy Moses! it's quarter of nine," muttered the young man folding his paper and hurrying out into Hudson Street that was full of men and girls walking briskly through the ruddy morning. The scrape of the shoes of hairyhoofed drayhorses and the grind of the wheels of producewagons made a deafening clatter and filled the air with sharp dust. A girl in a flowered bonnet with a big lavender bow under her pert tilted chin was waiting for him in the door of M. Sullivan & Co., Storage and Warehousing. The young man felt all fizzy inside, like a freshly uncorked bottle of pop.

"Hello Emily! . . . Say Emily I've got a raise."

"You're pretty near late, d'you know that?"

"But honest injun I've got a two-dollar raise."

She tilted her chin first to oneside and then to the other.

"I dont give a rap."

"You know what you said if I got a raise." She looked in his eyes giggling.

"An this is just the beginnin . . ."

"But what good's fifteen dollars a week?"

"Why it's sixty dollars a month, an I'm learning the import business."

"Silly boy you'll be late." She suddenly turned and ran up the littered stairs, her pleated bellshaped skirt swishing from side to side.

"God! I hate her. I hate her." Sniffing up the tears

that were hot in his eyes, he walked fast down Hudson Street to the office of Winkle & Gulick, West India Importers.

The deck beside the forward winch was warm and briny damp. They were sprawled side by side in greasy denims talking drowsily in whispers, their ears full of the seethe of broken water as the bow shoved bluntly through the long grassgray swells of the Gulf Stream.

"J'te dis mon vieux, moi j'fou l'camp à New York. . . . The minute we tie up I go ashore and I stay ashore. I'm through with this dog's life." The cabinboy had fair hair and an oval pink-and-cream face; a dead cigarette butt fell from between his lips as he spoke. "Merde!" He reached for it as it rolled down the deck. It escaped his hand and bounced into the scuppers.

"Let it go. I've got plenty," said the other boy who lay on his belly kicking a pair of dirty feet up into the hazy sunlight. "The consul will just have you shipped back."

"He wont catch me."

"And your military service?"

"To hell with it. And with France too for that matter."

"You want to make yourself an American citizen?"

"Why not? A man has a right to choose his country."

The other rubbed his nose meditatively with his fist and then let his breath out in a long whistle. "Emile you're a wise guy," he said.

"But Congo, why dont you come too? You dont want to shovel crap in a stinking ship's galley all your life."

Congo rolled himself round and sat up crosslegged, scratching his head that was thick with kinky black hair.

"Say how much does a woman cost in New York?"

"I dunno, expensive I guess. . . . I'm not going ashore to raise hell; I'm going to get a good job and work. Cant you think of nothing but women?"

"What's the use? Why not?" said Congo and settled him-

self flat on the deck again, burying his dark sootsmudged face
in his crossed arms.

"I want to get somewhere in the world, that's what I
mean. Europe's rotten and stinking. In America a fellow
can get ahead. Birth dont matter, education dont matter.
It's all getting ahead."

"And if there was a nice passionate little woman right
here now where the deck's warm, you wouldn't like to love
her up?"

"After we're rich, we'll have plenty, plenty of everything."

"And they dont have any military service?"

"Why should they? Its the coin they're after. They
dont want to fight people; they want to do business with
them."

Congo did not answer.

The cabin boy lay on his back looking at the clouds. They
floated from the west, great piled edifices with the sunlight
crashing through between, bright and white like tinfoil. He
was walking through tall white highpiled streets, stalking in
a frock coat with a tall white collar up tinfoil stairs, broad,
cleanswept, through blue portals into streaky marble halls
where money rustled and clinked on long tinfoil tables, bank-
notes, silver, gold.

"Merde v'là l'heure." The paired strokes of the bell in
the crowsnest came faintly to their ears. "But dont forget,
Congo, the first night we get ashore . . . " He made a
popping noise with his lips. "We're gone."

"I was asleep. I dreamed of a little blonde girl. I'd have
had her if you hadnt waked me." The cabinboy got to his
feet with a grunt and stood a moment looking west to
where the swells ended in a sharp wavy line against a sky
hard and abrupt as nickel. Then he pushed Congo's face
down against the deck and ran aft, the wooden clogs clattering on his bare feet as he went.

Outside, the hot June Saturday was dragging its frazzled

ends down 110th Street. Susie Thatcher lay uneasily in bed, her hands spread blue and bony on the coverlet before her. Voices came through the thin partition. A young girl was crying through her nose:

"I tell yer mommer I aint agoin back to him."

Then came expostulating an old staid Jewish woman's voice: "But Rosie, married life aint all beer and skittles. A vife must submit and vork for her husband."

"I wont. I cant help it. I wont go back to the dirty brute."

Susie sat up in bed, but she couldn't hear the next thing the old woman said.

"But I aint a Jew no more," suddenly screeched the young girl. "This aint Russia; it's little old New York. A girl's got some rights here." Then a door slammed and everything was quiet.

Susie Thatcher stirred in bed moaning fretfully. Those awful people never give me a moment's peace. From below came the jingle of a pianola playing the Merry Widow Waltz. O Lord! why dont Ed come home? It's cruel of them to leave a sick woman alone like this. Selfish. She twisted up her mouth and began to cry. Then she lay quiet again, staring at the ceiling watching the flies buzz teasingly round the electriclight fixture. A wagon clattered by down the street. She could hear children's voices screeching. A boy passed yelling an extra. Suppose there'd been a fire. That terrible Chicago theater fire. Oh I'll go mad! She tossed about in the bed, her pointed nails digging into the palms of her hands. I'll take another tablet. Maybe I can get some sleep. She raised herself on her elbow and took the last tablet out of a little tin box. The gulp of water that washed the tablet down was soothing to her throat. She closed her eyes and lay quiet.

She woke with a start. Ellen was jumping round the room, her green tam falling off the back of her head, her coppery curls wild.

"Oh mummy I want to be a little boy."

"Quieter dear. Mother's not feeling a bit well."

"I want to be a little boy."

"Why Ed what have you done to the child? She's all wrought up."

"We're just excited, Susie. We've been to the most wonderful play. You'd have loved it, it's so poetic and all that sort of thing. And Maude Adams was fine. Ellie loved every minute of it."

"It seems silly, as I said before, to take such a young child . . ."

"Oh daddy I want to be a boy."

"I like my little girl the way she is. We'll have to go again Susie and take you."

"Ed you know very well I wont be well enough." She sat bolt upright, her hair hanging a straight faded yellow down her back. "Oh, I wish I'd die . . . I wish I'd die, and not be a burden to you any more. . . . You hate me both of you. If you didnt hate me you wouldnt leave me alone like this." She choked and put her face in her hands. "Oh I wish I'd die," she sobbed through her fingers.

"Now Susie for Heaven's sakes, it's wicked to talk like that." He put his arm round her and sat on the bed beside her.

Crying quietly she dropped her head on his shoulder. Ellen stood staring at them out of round gray eyes. Then she started jumping up and down, chanting to herself, "Ellie's goin to be a boy, Ellie's goin to be a boy."

With a long slow stride, limping a little from his blistered feet, Bud walked down Broadway, past empty lots where tin cans glittered among grass and sumach bushes and ragweed, between ranks of billboards and Bull Durham signs, past shanties and abandoned squatters' shacks, past gulches heaped with wheelscarred rubbishpiles where dumpcarts were dumping ashes and clinkers, past knobs of gray outcrop where steamdrills continually tapped and nibbled, past excavations out of which wagons full of rock and clay toiled up plank roads to the street, until he was walking on new sidewalks along a row of yellow brick apartment houses, looking in the windows of grocery stores, Chinese laundries, lunchrooms, flower and vegetable shops, tailors', delicatessens. Passing under a scaffolding in front of a new building, he caught the eye of an old man who sat on the edge of the sidewalk trimming oil lamps. Bud stood beside him, hitching up his pants; cleared his throat:

"Say mister you couldnt tell a feller where a good place was to look for a job?"

"Aint no good place to look for a job, young feller. . . . There's jobs all right. . . . I'll be sixty-five years old in a month and four days an I've worked sence I was five I reckon, an I aint found a good job yet."

"Anything that's a job'll do me."

"Got a union card?"

"I aint got nothin."

"Cant git no job in the buildin trades without a union card," said the old man. He rubbed the gray bristles of his chin with the back of his hand and leaned over the lamps again. Bud stood staring into the dustreeking girder forest of the new building until he found the eyes of a man in a derby hat fixed on him through the window of the watchman's shelter. He shuffled his feet uneasily and walked on. If I could git more into the center of things. . . .

At the next corner a crowd was collecting round a highslung white automobile. Clouds of steam poured out of its rear end. A policeman was holding up a small boy by the armpits. From the car a redfaced man with white walrus whiskers was talking angrily.

"I tell you officer he threw a stone. . . . This sort of thing has got to stop. For an officer to countenance hoodlums and rowdies. . . . "

A woman with her hair done up in a tight bunch on top of her head was screaming, shaking her fist at the man in the car, "Officer he near run me down he did, he near run me down."

Bud edged up next to a young man in a butcher's apron who had a baseball cap on backwards.

"Wassa matter?"

"Hell I dunno. . . . One o them automoebile riots I guess. Aint you read the paper? I dont blame em do you? What right have those golblamed automoebiles got racin round the city knockin down wimen an children?"

"Gosh do they do that?"

"Sure they do."

"Say . . . er . . . kin you tell me about where's a good place to find out about gettin a job?" The butcherboy threw back head and laughed.

"Kerist I thought you was goin to ask for a handout. . . . I guess you aint a Newyorker. . . . I'll tell you what to do. You keep right on down Broadway till you get to City Hall. . . ."

"Is that kinder the center of things?"

"Sure it is. . . . An then you go upstairs and ask the Mayor. . . . Tell me there are some seats on the board of aldermen . . ."

"Like hell they are," growled Bud and walked away fast.

"Roll ye babies . . . roll ye lobsided sons o bitches."

"That's it talk to em Slats."

"Come seven!" Slats shot the bones out of his hand, brought the thumb along his sweaty fingers with a snap. "Aw hell."

"You're some great crapshooter I'll say, Slats."

Dirty hands added each a nickel to the pile in the center, of the circle of patched knees stuck forward. The five boys were sitting on their heels under a lamp on South Street.

"Come on girlies we're waitin for it. . . . Roll ye little bastards, goddam ye, roll."

"Cheeze it fellers! There's Big Leonard an his gang acomin down the block."

"I'd knock his block off for a . . ."

Four of them were already slouching off along the wharf, gradually scattering without looking back. The smallest boy with a chinless face shaped like a beak stayed behind quietly picking up the coins. Then he ran along the wall and vanished into the dark passageway between two houses. He flattened himself behind a chimney and waited. The confused voices of the gang broke into the passageway; then they had gone on down the street. The boy was counting the nickels in his hand. Ten. "Jez, that's fifty cents. . . . I'll tell 'em Big Leonard scooped up the dough." His pockets had no bottoms, so he tied the nickels into one of his shirt tails.

A goblet for Rhine wine hobnobbed with a champagne glass at each place along the glittering white oval table. On eight glossy white plates eight canapés of caviar were like rounds of black beads on the lettuceleaves, flanked by sections of lemon, sprinkled with a sparse chopping of onion and white of egg. "Beaucoup de soing and dont you forget it," said the old waiter puckering up his knobbly forehead. He was a short waddling man with a few black strands of hair plastered tight across a domed skull.

"Awright." Emile nodded his head gravely. His collar was too tight for him. He was shaking a last bottle of champagne into the nickelbound bucket of ice on the serving-table.

"Beaucoup de soing, sporca madonna. . . . Thisa guy trows money about lika confetti, see. . . . Gives tips, see. He's a verra rich gentleman. He dont care how much he spend." Emile patted the crease of the tablecloth to flatten it. "Fais pas, como, ça. . . . Your hand's dirty, maybe leava mark."

Resting first on one foot then on the other they stood waiting, their napkins under their arms. From the restaurant below among the buttery smells of food and the tinkle of knives and forks and plates, came the softly gyrating sound of a waltz.

When he saw the headwaiter bow outside the door Emile compressed his lips into a deferential smile. There was a longtoothed blond woman in a salmon operacloak swishing on the arm of a moonfaced man who carried his top hat ahead of him like a bumper; there was a little curlyhaired girl in blue who was showing her teeth and laughing, a stout woman in a tiara with a black velvet ribbon round her neck, a bottlenose, a long cigarcolored face . . . shirtfronts, hands straightening white ties, black gleams on top hats and patent leather shoes; there was a weazlish man with gold teeth who kept waving his arms spitting out greetings in a voice like a crow's and wore a diamond the size of a nickel in his shirtfront. The redhaired cloakroom girl was collecting the wraps. The old waiter nudged Emile. "He's de big boss," he said out of the corner of his mouth as he bowed. Emile flattened himself against the wall as they shuffled rustled into the room. A whiff of patchouli when he drew his breath made him go suddenly hot to the roots of his hair.

"But where's Fifi Waters?" shouted the man with the diamond stud.

"She said she couldnt get here for a half an hour. I guess the Johnnies wont let her get by the stage door."

"Well we cant wait for her even if it is her birthday; never waited for anyone in my life." He stood a second running a roving eye over the women round the table, then shot his cuffs out a little further from the sleeves of his swallowtail coat, and abruptly sat down. The caviar vanished in a twinkling. "And waiter what about that Rhine wine coupe?" he croaked huskily. "De suite monsieur. . . ." Emile holding his breath and sucking in his cheeks, was taking away the plates. A frost came on the goblets as the old waiter poured out the coupe from a cut glass pitcher where floated mint and ice and lemon rind and long slivvers of cucumber.

· "Aha, this'll do the trick." The man with the diamond stud raised his glass to his lips, smacked them and set it down with a slanting look at the woman next him. She was putting dabs of butter on bits of bread and popping them into her mouth, muttering all the while:

"I can only eat the merest snack, only the merest snack."

"That dont keep you from drinkin Mary does it?"

She let out a cackling laugh and tapped him on the shoulder with her closed fan. "O Lord, you're a card, you are."

"Allume moi ça, sporca madonna," hissed the old waiter in Emile's ear.

When he lit the lamps under the two chafing dishes on the serving table a smell of hot sherry and cream and lobster began to seep into the room. The air was hot, full of tinkle and perfume and smoke. After he had helped serve the lobster Newburg and refilled the glasses Emile leaned against the wall and ran his hand over his wet hair. His eyes slid along the plump shoulders of the woman in front of him and down the powdered back to where a tiny silver hook had come undone under the lace rushing. The baldheaded man next to her had his leg locked with hers. She was young, Emile's age, and kept looking up into the man's face with moist parted lips. It made Emile dizzy, but he couldn't stop looking.

"But what's happened to the fair Fifi?" creaked the man with the diamond stud through a mouthful of lobster. "I suppose that she made such a hit again this evening that our simple little party dont appeal to her."

"It's enough to turn any girl's head."

"Well she'll get the surprise of her young life if she expected us to wait. Haw, haw, haw," laughed the man with the diamond stud. "I never waited for anybody in my life and I'm not going to begin now."

Down the table the moonfaced man had pushed back his plate and was playing with the bracelet on the wrist of the woman beside him. "You're the perfect Gibson girl tonight, Olga."

"I'm sitting for my portrait now," she said holding up her goblet against the light.

"To Gibson?"

"No to a real painter."

"By Gad I'll buy it."

"Maybe you wont have a chance."

She nodded her blond pompadour at him.

"You're a wicked little tease, Olga."

She laughed keeping her lips tight over her long teeth.

A man was leaning towards the man with the diamond stud, tapping with a stubby finger on the table.

"No sir as a real estate proposition, Twentythird Street has crashed. . . . That's generally admitted. . . . But what I want to talk to you about privately sometime Mr. Godalming, is this. . . . How's all the big money in New York been made? Astor, Vanderbilt, Fish. . . . In real estate of course. Now it's up to us to get in on the next great cleanup. . . . It's almost here. . . . Buy Forty. . . ."

The man with the diamond stud raised one eyebrow and shook his head. "For one night on Beauty's lap, O put gross care away . . . or something of the sort. . . . Waiter why in holy hell are you so long with the champagne?" He got to his feet, coughed in his hand and began to sing in his croaking voice:

O would the Atlantic were all champagne
Bright billows of champagne.

Everybody clapped. The old waiter had just divided a baked Alaska and, his face like a beet, was prying out a stiff champagnecork. When the cork popped the lady in the tiara let out a yell. They toasted the man in the diamond stud.

For he's a jolly good fellow . . .

"Now what kind of a dish d'ye call this?" the man with the bottlenose leaned over and asked the girl next to him. Her black hair parted in the middle; she wore a palegreen dress with puffy sleeves. He winked slowly and then stared hard into her black eyes.

"This here's the fanciest cookin I ever put in my mouth.
. . . D'ye know young leddy, I dont come to this town
often. . . . He gulped down the rest of his glass. An
when I do I usually go away kinder disgusted. . . ." His
look bright and feverish from the champagne explored the
contours of her neck and shoulders and roamed down a bare
arm. "But this time I kinder think. . . ."

"It must be a great life prospecting," she interrupted flushing.

"It was a great life in the old days, a rough life but
a man's life. . . . I'm glad I made my pile in the old days.
. . . Wouldnt have the same luck now."

She looked up at him. "How modest you are to call
it luck."

Emile was standing outside the door of the private room.
There was nothing more to serve. The redhaired girl from
the cloakroom walked by with a big flounced cape on her
arm. He smiled, tried to catch her eye. She sniffed and
tossed her nose in the air. Wont look at me because I'm a
waiter. When I make some money I'll show 'em.

"Dis; tella Charlie two more bottle Moet and Chandon,
Gout Americain," came the old waiter's hissing voice in his
ear.

The moonfaced man was on his feet. "Ladies and Gentlemen. . . ."

"Silence in the pigsty . . ." piped up a voice.

"The big sow wants to talk," said Olga under her breath.

"Ladies and gentlemen owing to the unfortunate absence
of our star of Bethlehem and fulltime act. . . ."

"Gilly dont blaspheme," said the lady with the tiara.

"Ladies and gentlemen, unaccustomed as I am. . . ."

"Gilly you're drunk."

" . . . Whether the tide . . . I mean whether the waters
be with us or against us. . . "

Somebody yanked at his coat-tails and the moonfaced man
sat down suddenly in his chair.

"It's terrible," said the lady in the tiara addressing herself
to a man with a long face the color of tobacco who sat at the

end of the table . . . "It's terrible, Colonel, the way Gilly gets blasphemous when he's been drinking. . . "

The Colonel was meticulously rolling the tinfoil off a cigar. "Dear me, you dont say?" he drawled. Above the bristly gray mustache his face was expressionless. "There's a most dreadful story about poor old Atkins, Elliott Atkins who used to be with Mansfield. . . "

"Indeed?" said the Colonel icily as he slit the end of the cigar with a small pearlhandled penknife.

"Say Chester did you hear that Mabie Evans was making a hit?"

"Honestly Olga I dont see how she does it. She has no figure. . . "

"Well he made a speech, drunk as a lord you understand, one night when they were barnstorming in Kansas. . . "

"She cant sing. . . "

"The poor fellow never did go very strong in the bright lights. . . "

"She hasnt the slightest particle of figure. . . "

"And made a sort of Bob Ingersoll speech. . . "

"The dear old feller. . . . Ah I knew him well out in Chicago in the old days. . . "

"You dont say." The Colonel held a lighted match carefully to the end of his cigar. . .

"And there was a terrible flash of lightning and a ball of fire came in one window and went out the other."

"Was he . . . er . . . killed?" The Colonel sent a blue puff of smoke towards the ceiling.

"What, did you say Bob Ingersoll had been struck by lightning?" cried Olga shrilly. "Serve him right the horrid atheist."

"No not exactly, but it scared him into a realization of the important things of life and now he's joined the Methodist church."

"Funny how many actors get to be ministers."

"Cant get an audience any other way," creaked the man with the diamond stud.

The two waiters hovered outside the door listening to

the racket inside. "Tas de sacrés cochons . . . sporca madonna!" hissed the old waiter. Emile shrugged his shoulders. "That brunette girl make eyes at you all night. . . " He brought his face near Emile's and winked. "Sure, maybe you pick up somethin good."

"I dont want any of them or their dirty diseases either."

The old waiter slapped his thigh. "No young men nowadays. . . . When I was young man I take heap o chances."

"They dont even look at you. . . " said Emile through clenched teeth. "An animated dress suit that's all."

"Wait a minute, you learn by and by."

The door opened. They bowed respectfully towards the diamond stud. Somebody had drawn a pair of woman's legs on his shirtfront. There was a bright flush on each of his cheeks. The lower lid of one eye sagged, giving his weasle face a quizzical lobsided look.

"Wazzahell, Marco wazzahell?" he was muttering. "We aint got a thing to drink. . . . Bring the Atlantic Ozz-shen and two quarts."

"De suite monsieur. . . ." The old waiter bowed. "Emile tell Auguste, immediatement et bien frappé."

As Emile went down the corridor he could hear singing.

> O would the Atlantic were all champagne
> Bright bi-i-i. . . .

The moonface and the bottlenose were coming back from the lavatory reeling arm in arm among the palms in the hall.

"These damn fools make me sick."

"Yessir these aint the champagne suppers we used to have in Frisco in the ole days."

"Ah those were great days those."

"By the way," the moonfaced man steadied himself against the wall, "Holyoke ole fella, did you shee that very nobby little article on the rubber trade I got into the morning papers. . . . That'll make the investors nibble . . . like lil mishe."

"Whash you know about rubber? . . . The stuff aint no good."

"You wait an shee, Holyoke ole fella or you looshing opportunity of your life. . . . Drunk or sober I can smell money . . . on the wind."

"Why aint you got any then?" The bottlenosed man's beefred face went purple; he doubled up letting out great hoots of laughter.

"Because I always let my friends in on my tips," said the other man soberly. "Hay boy where's zis here private dinin room?"

"Par ici monsieur."

A red accordionpleated dress swirled past them, a little oval face framed by brown flat curls, pearly teeth in an openmouthed laugh.

"Fifi Waters," everyone shouted. "Why my darlin lil Fifi, come to my arms."

She was lifted onto a chair where she stood jiggling from one foot to the other, champagne dripping out of a tipped glass.

"Merry Christmas."

"Happy New Year."

"Many returns of the day. . . ."

A fair young man who had followed her in was reeling intricately round the table singing:

> O we went to the animals' fair
> And the birds and the beasts were there
> And the big baboon
> By the light of the moon
> Was combing his auburn hair.

"Hoopla," cried Fifi Waters and mussed the gray hair of the man with the diamond stud. "Hoopla." She jumped down with a kick, pranced round the room, kicking high with her skirts fluffed up round her knees.

"Oh la la ze French high kicker!"

"Look out for the Pony Ballet."

Her slender legs, shiny black silk stockings tapering to red rosetted slippers flashed in the men's faces.

"She's a mad thing," cried the lady in the tiara.

Hoopla. Holyoke was swaying in the doorway with his top hat tilted over the glowing bulb of his nose. She let out a whoop and kicked it off.

"It's a goal," everyone cried.

"For crissake you kicked me in the eye."

She stared at him a second with round eyes and then burst into tears on the broad shirtfront of the diamond stud. "I wont be insulted like that," she sobbed.

"Rub the other eye."

"Get a bandage someone."

"Goddam it she may have put his eye out."

"Call a cab there waiter."

"Where's a doctor?"

"That's hell to pay ole fella."

A handkerchief full of tears and blood pressed to his eye the bottlenosed man stumbled out. The men and women crowded through the door after him; last went the blond young man, reeling and singing:

> An the big baboon by the light of the moon
> Was combing his auburn hair.

Fifi Waters was sobbing with her head on the table.

"Dont cry Fifi," said the Colonel who was still sitting where he had sat all the evening. "Here's something I rather fancy might do you good." He pushed a glass of champagne towards her down the table.

She sniffled and began drinking it in little sips. "Hullo Roger, how's the boy?"

"The boy's quite well thank you. . . . Rather bored, dont you know? An evening with such infernal bounders. . . ."

"I'm hungry."

"There doesnt seem to be anything left to eat."

"I didnt know you'd be here or I'd have come earlier, honest."

Metropolis

"Would you indeed? . . . Now that's very nice."

The long ash dropped from the Colonel's cigar; he got to his feet. "Now Fifi, I'll call a cab and we'll go for a ride in the Park. . . . "

She drank down her champagne and nodded brightly. "Dear me it's four o'clock. . . ." "You have the proper wraps haven't you?"

She nodded again.

"Splendid Fifi . . . I say you are in form." The Colonel's cigarcolored face was unraveling in smiles. "Well, come along."

She looked about her in a dazed way. "Didnt I come with somebody?"

"Quite unnecessary!"

In the hall they came upon the fair young man quietly vomiting into a firebucket under an artificial palm.

"Oh let's leave him," she said wrinkling up her nose.

"Quite unnecessary," said the Colonel.

Emile brought their wraps. The redhaired girl had gone home.

"Look here, boy." The Colonel waved his cane. "Call me a cab please. . . . Be sure the horse is decent and the driver is sober."

"De suite monsieur."

The sky beyond roofs and chimneys was the blue of a sapphire. The Colonel took three or four deep sniffs of the dawnsmelling air and threw his cigar into the gutter. "Suppose we have a bit of breakfast at Cleremont. I haven't had anything fit to eat all night. That beastly sweet champagne, ugh!"

Fifi giggled. After the Colonel had examined the horse's fetlocks and patted his head, they climbed into the cab. The Colonel fitted in Fifi carefully under his arm and they drove off. Emile stood a second in the door of the restaurant uncrumpling a five dollar bill. He was tired and his insteps ached.

When Emile came out of the back door of the restaurant he found Congo waiting for him sitting on the doorstep.

Congo's skin had a green chilly look under the frayed turned up coatcollar.

"This is my friend," Emile said to Marco. "Came over on the same boat."

"You havent a bottle of fine under your coat have you? Sapristi I've seen some chickens not half bad come out of this place."

"But what's the matter?"

"Lost my job that's all. . . . I wont have to take any more off that guy. Come over and drink a coffee."

They ordered coffee and doughnuts in a lunchwagon on a vacant lot.

"Eh bien you like it this sacred pig of a country?" asked Marco.

"Why not? I like it anywhere. It's all the same, in France you are paid badly and live well; here you are paid well and live badly."

"Questo paese e completamente soto sopra."

"I think I'll go to sea again. . . ."

"Say why de hell doan yous guys loin English?" said the man with a cauliflower face who slapped the three mugs of coffee down on the counter.

"If we talk Engleesh," snapped Marco "maybe you no lika what we say."

"Why did they fire you?"

"Merde. I dont know. I had an argument with the old camel who runs the place. . . . He lived next door to the stables; as well as washing the carriages he made me scrub the floors in his house. . . . His wife, she had a face like this." Congo sucked in his lips and tried to look crosseyed.

Marco laughed. "Santissima Maria putana!"

"How did you talk to them?"

"They pointed to things; then I nodded my head and said Awright. I went there at eight and worked till six and they gave me every day more filthy things to do. . . . Last night they tell me to clean out the toilet in the bathroom. I shook my head. . . . That's woman's work. . . .

She got very angry and started screeching. Then I began to learn Angleesh. . . . Go awright to 'ell, I says to her. . . . Then the old man comes and chases me out into a street with a carriage whip and says he wont pay me my week. . . . While we were arguing he got a policeman, and when I try to explain to the policeman that the old man owed me ten dollars for the week, he says Beat it you lousy wop, and cracks me on the coco with his nightstick. . . . Merde alors. . . "

Marco was red in the face. "He call you lousy wop?"

Congo nodded his mouth full of doughnut.

"Notten but shanty Irish himself," muttered Marco in English. "I'm fed up with this rotten town. . . .

"It's the same all over the world, the police beating us up, rich people cheating us out of their starvation wages, and who's fault? . . . Dio cane! Your fault, my fault, Emile's fault. . . ."

"We didn't make the world. . . . They did or maybe God did."

"God's on their side, like a policeman. . . . When the day comes we'll kill God. . . . I am an anarchist."

Congo hummed "les bourgeois à la lanterne nom de dieu."

"Are you one of us?"

Congo shrugged his shoulders. "I'm not a catholic or a protestant; I haven't any money and I haven't any work. Look at that." Congo pointed with a dirty finger to a long rip on his trouserknee. "That's anarchist. . . . Hell I'm going out to Senegal and get to be a nigger."

"You look like one already," laughed Emile.

"That's why they call me Congo."

"But that's all silly," went on Emile. "People are all the same. It's only that some people get ahead and others dont. . . . That's why I came to New York."

"Dio cane I think that too twentyfive years ago. . . . When you're old like me you know better. Doesnt the shame of it get you sometimes? Here" . . . he tapped with his knuckles on his stiff shirtfront. . . "I feel it hot and like choking me here. . . . Then I say to myself Courage our day is coming, our day of blood."

"I say to myself," said Emile "When you have some money old kid."

"Listen, before I leave Torino when I go last time to see the mama I go to a meetin of comrades. . . . A fellow from Capua got up to speak . . . a very handsome man, tall and very thin. . . . He said that there would be no more force when after the revolution nobody lived off another man's work. . . . Police, governments, armies, presidents, kings . . . all that is force. Force is not real; it is illusion. The working man makes all that himself because he believes it. The day that we stop believing in money and property it will be like a dream when we wake up. We will not need bombs or barricades. . . . Religion, politics, democracy all that is to keep us asleep. . . . Everybody must go round telling people: Wake up!"

"When you go down into the street I'll be with you," said Congo.

"You know that man I tell about? . . . That man Errico Malatesta, in Italy greatest man after Garibaldi. . . . He give his whole life in jail and exile, in Egypt, in England, in South America, everywhere. . . . If I could be a man like that, I dont care what they do; they can string me up, shoot me . . . I dont care . . . I am very happy."

"But he must be crazy a feller like that," said Emile slowly. "He must be crazy."

Marco gulped down the last of his coffee. "Wait a minute. You are too young. You will understand. . . . One by one they make us understand. . . . And remember what I say. . . . Maybe I'm too old, maybe I'm dead, but it will come when the working people awake from slavery. . . . You will walk out in the street and the police will run away, you will go into a bank and there will be money poured out on the floor and you wont stoop to pick it up, no more good. . . . All over the world we are preparing. There are comrades even in China. . . . Your Commune in France was the beginning . . . socialism failed. It's for the anarchists to strike the next blow. . . . If we fail there will be others. . . ."

Congo yawned, "I am sleepy as a dog."

Outside the lemoncolored dawn was drenching the empty streets, dripping from cornices, from the rails of fire escapes, from the rims of ashcans, shattering the blocks of shadow between buildings. The streetlights were out. At a corner they looked up Broadway that was narrow and scorched as if a fire had gutted it.

"I never see the dawn," said Marco, his voice rattling in his throat, "that I dont say to myself perhaps . . . perhaps today." He cleared his throat and spat against the base of a lamppost; then he moved away from them with his waddling step, taking hard short sniffs of the cool air.

"Is that true, Congo, about shipping again?"

"Why not? Got to see the world a bit. . . "

"I'll miss you. . . . I'll have to find another room."

"You'll find another friend to bunk with."

"But if you do that you'll stay a sailor all your life."

"What does it matter? When you are rich and married I'll come and visit you."

They were walking down Sixth Avenue. An L train roared above their heads leaving a humming rattle to fade among the girders after it had passed.

"Why dont you get another job and stay on a while?"

Congo produced two bent cigarettes out of the breast pocket of his coat, handed one to Emile, struck a match on the seat of his trousers, and let the smoke out slowly through his nose. "I'm fed up with it here I tell you. . . ." He brought his flat hand up across his Adam's apple, "up to here. . . . Maybe I'll go home an visit the little girls of Bordeaux. . . . At least they are not all made of whalebone. . . . I'll engage myself as a volunteer in the navy and wear a red pompom. . . . The girls like that. That's the only life. . . . Get drunk and raise cain payday and see the extreme orient."

"And die of the syph in a hospital at thirty. . . ."

"What's it matter? . . . Your body renews itself every seven years."

The steps of their rooming house smelled of cabbage and stale beer. They stumbled up yawning.

"Waiting's a rotton tiring job. . . . Makes the soles of your feet ache. . . . Look it's going to be a fine day; I can see the sun on the watertank opposite."

Congo pulled off his shoes and socks and trousers and curled up in bed like a cat.

"Those dirty shades let in all the light," muttered Emile as he stretched himself on the outer edge of the bed. He lay tossing uneasily on the rumpled sheets. Congo's breathing beside him was low and regular. If I was only like that, thought Emile, never worrying about a thing. . . . But it's not that way you get along in the world. My God it's stupid. . . . Marco's gaga the old fool.

And he lay on his back looking up at the rusty stains on the ceiling, shuddering every time an elevated train shook the room. Sacred name of God I must save up my money. When he turned over the knob on the bedstead rattled and he remembered Marco's hissing husky voice: I never see the dawn that I dont say to myself perhaps.

"If you'll excuse me just a moment Mr. Olafson," said the houseagent. "While you and the madam are deciding about the apartment. . . " They stood side by side in the empty room, looking out the window at the slatecolored Hudson and the warships at anchor and a schooner tacking upstream.

Suddenly she turned to him with glistening eyes; "O Billy, just think of it."

He took hold of her shoulders and drew her to him slowly. "You can smell the sea, almost."

"Just think Billy that we are going to live here, on Riverside Drive. I'll have to have a day at home . . . Mrs. William C. Olafson, 218 Riverside Drive. . . . I wonder if it is all right to put the address on our visiting cards." She took his hand and led him through the empty cleanswept rooms that no one had ever lived in. He was a big shambling man with eyes of a washed out blue deepset in a white infantile head.

"It's a lot of money Bertha."

"We can afford it now, of course we can. We must live up to our income. . . . Your position demands it. . . . And think how happy we'll be."

The house agent came back down the hall rubbing his hands. "Well, well, well . . . Ah I see that we've come to a favorable decision. . . . You are very wise too, not a finer location in the city of New York and in a few months you wont be able to get anything out this way for love or money. . . ."

"Yes we'll take it from the first of the month."

"Very good. . . . You wont regret your decision, Mr. Olafson."

"I'll send you a check for the amount in the morning."

"At your own convenience. . . . And what is your present address please. . . ." The houseagent took out a notebook and moistened a stub of pencil with his tongue.

"You had better put Hotel Astor." She stepped in front of her husband.

"Our things are stored just at the moment."

Mr. Olafson turned red.

"And . . . er . . . we'd like the names of two references please in the city of New York."

"I'm with Keating and Bradley, Sanitary Engineers, 43 Park Avenue. . ."

"He's just been made assistant general manager," added Mrs. Olafson.

When they got out on the Drive walking downtown against a tussling wind she cried out: "Darling I'm so happy. . . . It's really going to be worth living now."

"But why did you tell him we lived at the Astor?"

"I couldnt tell him we lived in the Bronx could I? He'd have thought we were Jews and wouldnt have rented us the apartment."

"But you know I dont like that sort of thing."

"Well we'll just move down to the Astor for the rest of the week, if you're feeling so truthful. . . . I've never in my life stopped in a big downtown hotel."

"Oh Bertha it's the principle of the thing. . . . I don't like you to be like that."

She turned and looked at him with twitching nostrils. "You're so nambypamby, Billy. . . . I wish to heavens I'd married a man for a husband."

He took her by the arm. "Let's go up here," he said gruffly with his face turned away.

They walked up a cross street between buildinglots. At a corner the rickety half of a weatherboarded farmhouse was still standing. There was half a room with blueflowered paper eaten by brown stains on the walls, a smoked fireplace, a shattered builtin cupboard, and an iron bedstead bent double.

Plates slip endlessly through Bud's greasy fingers. Smell of swill and hot soapsuds. Twice round with the little mop, dip, rinse and pile in the rack for the longnosed Jewish boy to wipe. Knees wet from spillings, grease creeping up his forearms, elbows cramped.

"Hell this aint no job for a white man."

"I dont care so long as I eat," said the Jewish boy above the rattle of dishes and the clatter and seething of the range where three sweating cooks fried eggs and ham and hamburger steak and browned potatoes and cornedbeef hash.

"Sure I et all right," said Bud and ran his tongue round his teeth dislodging a sliver of salt meat that he mashed against his palate with his tongue. Twice round with the little mop, dip, rinse and pile in the rack for the longnosed Jewish boy to wipe. There was a lull. The Jewish boy handed Bud a cigarette. They stood leaning against the sink.

"Aint no way to make money dishwashing." The cigarette wabbled on the Jewish boy's heavy lip as he spoke.

"Aint no job for a white man nohow," said Bud. "Waitin's better, they's the tips."

A man in a brown derby came in through the swinging door from the lunchroom. He was a bigjawed man with pigeyes and a long cigar sticking straight out of the middle of his mouth. Bud caught his eye and felt the cold glint twisting his bowels.

"Whosat?" he whispered.

"Dunno. . . . Customer I guess."

"Dont he look to you like one o them detectives?"

"How de hell should I know? I aint never been in jail." The Jewish boy turned red and stuck out his jaw.

The busboy set down a new pile of dirty dishes. Twice round with the little mop, dip, rinse and pile in the rack. When the man in the brown derby passed back through the kitchen, Bud kept his eyes on his red greasy hands. What the hell even if he is a detective. . . . When Bud had finished the batch, he strolled to the door wiping his hands, took his coat and hat from the hook and slipped out the side door past the garbage cans out into the street. Fool to jump two hours pay. In an optician's window the clock was at twentyfive past two. He walked down Broadway, past Lincoln Square, across Columbus Circle, further downtown towards the center of things where it'd be more crowded.

She lay with her knees doubled up to her chin, the nightgown pulled tight under her toes.

"Now straighten out and go to sleep dear. . . . Promise mother you'll go to sleep."

"Wont daddy come and kiss me good night?"

"He will when he comes in; he's gone back down to the office and mother's going to Mrs. Spingarn's to play euchre."

"When'll daddy be home?"

"Ellie I said go to sleep. . . . I'll leave the light."

"Dont mummy, it makes shadows. . . . When'll daddy be home?"

"When he gets good and ready." She was turning down the gaslight. Shadows out of the corners joined wings and rushed together. "Good night Ellen." The streak of light of the door narrowed behind mummy, slowly narrowed to a thread up and along the top. The knob clicked; the steps went away down the hall; the front door slammed. A clock ticked somewhere in the silent room; outside the apartment, outside the house, wheels and gallumping of hoofs, trailing voices; the roar grew. It was black except for the two strings of light that made an upside down L in the corner of the door.

Ellie wanted to stretch out her feet but she was afraid to. She didnt dare take her eyes from the upside down L in the corner of the door. If she closed her eyes the light would go out. Behind the bed, out of the window-curtains, out of the closet, from under the table shadows nudged creakily towards her. She held on tight to her ankles, pressed her chin in between her knees. The pillow bulged with shadow, rummaging shadows were slipping into the bed. If she closed her eyes the light would go out.

Black spiraling roar outside was melting through the walls making the cuddled shadows throb. Her tongue clicked against her teeth like the ticking of the clock. Her arms and legs were stiff; her neck was stiff; she was going to yell. Yell above the roaring and the rattat outside, yell to make daddy hear, daddy come home. She drew in her breath and shrieked again. Make daddy come home. The roaring shadows staggered and danced, the shadows lurched round and round. Then she was crying, her eyes were full of safe warm tears, they were running over her cheeks and into her ears. She turned over and lay crying with her face in the pillow.

The gaslamps tremble a while down the purplecold streets and then go out under the lurid dawn. Gus McNiel, the sleep still gumming his eyes, walks beside his wagon swinging a wire basket of milkbottles, stopping at doors, collecting the empties, climbing chilly stairs, remembering grades A and B and pints of cream and buttermilk, while the sky behind cornices, tanks, roofpeaks, chimneys becomes rosy and yellow. Hoarfrost glistens on doorsteps and curbs. The horse with dangling head lurches jerkily from door to door. There begin to be dark footprints on the frosty pavement. A heavy brewers' dray rumbles down the street.

"Howdy Moike, a little chilled are ye?" shouts Gus McNiel at a cop threshing his arms on the corner of Eighth Avenue.

"Howdy Gus. Cows still milkin'?"

It's broad daylight when he finally slaps the reins down on the gelding's threadbare rump and starts back to the dairy, empties bouncing and jiggling in the cart behind him. At Ninth Avenue a train shoots overhead clattering downtown behind a little green engine that emits blobs of smoke white and dense as cottonwool to melt in the raw air between the stiff blackwindowed houses. The first rays of the sun pick out the gilt lettering of DANIEL McGILLYCUDDY'S WINES AND LIQUORS at the corner of Tenth Avenue. Gus McNiel's tongue is dry and the dawn has a salty taste in his mouth. A can o beer'd be the makin of a guy a cold mornin like this. He takes a turn with the reins round the whip and jumps over the wheel. His numb feet sting when they hit the pavement. Stamping to get the blood back into his toes he shoves through the swinging doors.

"Well I'll be damned if it aint the milkman bringin us a

pint o cream for our coffee." Gus spits into the newly polished cuspidor beside the bar.

"Boy, I got a thoist on me. . . ."

"Been drinkin too much milk again, Gus, I'll warrant," roars the barkeep out of a square steak face.

The saloon smells of brasspolish and fresh sawdust. Through an open window a streak of ruddy sunlight caresses the rump of a naked lady who reclines calm as a hardboiled egg on a bed of spinach in a giltframed picture behind the bar.

"Well Gus what's yer pleasure a foine cold mornin loike this?"

"I guess beer'll do, Mac."

The foam rises in the glass, trembles up, slops over. The barkeep cuts across the top with a wooden scoop, lets the foam settle a second, then puts the glass under the faintly wheezing spigot again. Gus is settling his heel comfortably against the brass rail.

"Well how's the job?"

Gus gulps the glass of beer and makes a mark on his neck with his flat hand before wiping his mouth with it. "Full up to the neck wid it. . . . I tell yer what I'm goin to do, I'm goin to go out West, take up free land in North Dakota or somewhere an raise wheat. . . . I'm pretty handy round a farm. . . . This here livin in the city's no good."

"How'll Nellie take that?"

"She wont cotton to it much at foist, loikes her comforts of home an all that she's been used to, but I think she'll loike it foine onct she's out there an all. This aint no loife for her nor me neyther."

"You're right there. This town's goin to hell. . . . Me and the misses'll sell out here some day soon I guess. If we could buy a noice genteel restaurant uptown or a roadhouse, that's what'd suit us. Got me eye on a little property out Bronxville way, within easy drivin distance." He lifts a malletshaped fist meditatively to his chin. "I'm sick o bouncin these goddam drunks every night. Whade hell did I get outen the ring for xep to stop fightin? Jus last night two guys starts asluggin an I has to mix it up with both of em to clear the place out. . . . I'm sick o fighten every drunk on Tenth Avenoo. . . . Have somethin on the house?"

"Jez I'm afraid Nellie'll smell it on me."

"Oh, niver moind that. Nellie ought to be used to a bit o drinkin. Her ole man loikes it well enough."

"But honest Mac I aint been slopped once since me weddinday."

"I dont blame ye. She's a real sweet girl Nellie is. Those little spitcurls o hers'd near drive a feller crazy."

The second beer sends a foamy acrid flush to Gus's fingertips. Laughing he slaps his thigh.

"She's a pippin, that's what she is Gus, so ladylike an all."

"Well I reckon I'll be gettin back to her."

"You lucky young divil to be goin home to bed wid your wife when we're all startin to go to work."

Gus's red face gets redder. His ears tingle. "Sometimes she's abed yet. . . . So long Mac." He stamps out into the street again.

The morning has grown bleak. Leaden clouds have settled down over the city. "Git up old skin an bones," shouts Gus jerking at the gelding's head. Eleventh Avenue is full of icy dust, of grinding rattle of wheels and scrape of hoofs on the cobblestones. Down the railroad tracks comes the clang of a locomotive bell and the clatter of shunting freightcars. Gus is in bed with his wife talking gently to her: Look here Nellie, you wouldn't moind movin West would yez? I've filed application for free farmin land in the state o North Dakota, black soil land where we can make a pile o money in wheat; some fellers git rich in foive good crops. . . . Healthier for the kids anyway. . . . "Hello Moike!" There's poor old Moike still on his beat. Cold work bein a cop. Better be a wheatfarmer an have a big farmhouse an barns an pigs an horses an cows an chickens. . . . Pretty curlyheaded Nellie feedin the chickens at the kitchen door. . . .

"Hay dere for crissake. . . ." a man is yelling at Gus from the curb. "Look out for de cars!"

A yelling mouth gaping under a visored cap, a green flag waving. "Godamighty I'm on the tracks." He yanks the horse's head round. A crash rips the wagon behind him. Cars, the gelding, a green flag, red houses whirl and crumble into blackness.

III. Dollars

*A*ll along the rails there were faces; in the port-holes there were faces. Leeward a stale smell came from the tubby steamer that rode at anchor listed a little to one side with the yellow quarantine flag drooping at the foremast.

"I'd give a million dollars," said the old man resting on his oars, "to know what they come for."

"Just for that pop," said the young man who sat in the stern. "Aint it the land of opportoonity?"

"One thing I do know," said the old man. "When I was a boy it was wild Irish came in the spring with the first run of shad. . . . Now there aint no more shad, an them folks, Lord knows where they come from."

"It's the land of opportoonity."

A LEANFACED young man with steel eyes and a thin highbridged nose sat back in a swivel chair with his feet on his new mahogany-finish desk. His skin was sallow, his lips gently pouting. He wriggled in the swivel chair watching the little scratches his shoes were making on the veneer. Damn it I dont care. Then he sat up suddenly making the swivel shriek and banged on his knee with his clenched fist. "Results," he shouted. Three months I've sat rubbing my tail on this swivel chair. . . . What's the use of going through lawschool and being admitted to the bar if you cant find anybody to practice on? He frowned at the gold lettering through the groundglass door.

NIWDLAB EGROEG
waL-tA-yenrottA

Niwdlab, Welsh. He jumped to his feet. I've read that damn sign backwards every day for three months. I'm going crazy. I'll go out and eat lunch.

He straightened his vest and brushed some flecks of dust off his shoes with a handkerchief, then, contracting his face into an expression of intense preoccupation, he hurried out of his office, trotted down the stairs and out onto Maiden Lane. In front of the chophouse he saw the headline on a pink extra; JAPS THROWN BACK FROM MUKDEN. He bought the paper and folded it under his arm as he went in through the swinging door. He took a table and pored over the bill of fare. Mustn't be extravagant now. "Waiter you can bring me a New England boiled dinner, a slice of applepie and coffee." The longnosed waiter wrote the order on his slip looking at it sideways with a careful frown. . . . That's the lunch for a lawyer without any practice. Baldwin cleared his throat and unfolded the paper. . . . Ought to liven up the Russian bonds a bit. Veterans Visit President. . . . ANOTHER ACCIDENT ON ELEVENTH AVENUE TRACKS. Milkman seriously injured. Hello, that'd make a neat little damage suit.

Augustus McNiel, 253 W. 4th Street, who drives a milkwagon for the Excelsior Dairy Co. was severely injured early this morning when a freight train backing down the New York Central tracks . . .

He ought to sue the railroad. By gum I ought to get hold of that man and make him sue the railroad. . . . Not yet recovered consciousness. . . . Maybe he's dead. Then his wife can sue them all the more. . . . I'll go to the hospital this very afternoon. . . . Get in ahead of any of these shysters. He took a determined bite of bread and chewed it vigorously. Of course not; I'll go to the house and see if there isn't a wife or mother or something: Forgive me Mrs. McNiel if I intrude upon your deep affliction, but I am engaged in an investigation at this moment. . . . Yes, retained by prominent interests. . . . He drank up the last of the coffee and paid the bill.

Repeating 253 W. 4th Street over and over he boarded an uptown car on Broadway. Walking west along 4th he skirted Washington Square. The trees spread branches of brittle purple into a dovecolored sky; the largewindowed houses opposite glowed very pink, nonchalant, prosperous. The very place for a lawyer with a large conservative practice to make his residence. We'll just see about that. He crossed Sixth Avenue and followed the street into the dingy West Side, where there was a smell of stables and the sidewalks were littered with scraps of garbage and crawling children. Imagine living down here among low Irish and foreigners, the scum of the universe. At 253 there were several unmarked bells. A woman with gingham sleeves rolled up on sausageshaped arms stuck a gray mophead out the window.

"Can you tell me if Augustus McNiel lives here?"

"Him that's up there alayin in horspital. Sure he does."

"That's it. And has he any relatives living here?"

"An what would you be wantin wid 'em?"

"It's a little matter of business."

"Go up to the top floor an you'll foind his wife there but most likely she cant see yez. . . . The poor thing's powerful wrought up about her husband, an them only eighteen months married."

The stairs were tracked with muddy footprints and sprinkled here and there with the spilling of ashcans. At the top he found a freshpainted darkgreen door and knocked.

"Who's there?" came a girl's voice that sent a little shiver through him. Must be young.

"Is Mrs. McNiel in?"

"Yes," came the lilting girl's voice again. "What is it?"

"It's a matter of business about Mr. McNiel's accident."

"About the accident is it?" The door opened in little cautious jerks. She had a sharpcut pearlywhite nose and chin and a pile of wavy redbrown hair that lay in little flat curls round her high narrow forehead. Gray eyes sharp and suspicious looked him hard in the face.

"May I speak to you a minute about Mr. McNiel's accident? There are certain legal points involved that I feel it my duty to make known to you. . . . By the way I hope he's better."

"Oh yes he's come to."

"May I come in? It's a little long to explain."

"I guess you can." Her pouting lips flattened into a wry smile. "I guess you wont eat me."

"No honestly I wont." He laughed nervously in his throat.

She led the way into the darkened sitting room. "I'm not pulling up the shades so's you wont see the pickle everythin's in."

"Allow me to introduce myself, Mrs. McNiel. . . . George Baldwin, 88 Maiden Lane. . . . You see I make a specialty of cases like this. . . . To put the whole matter in a nutshell. . . . Your husband was run down and nearly killed through the culpable or possibly criminal negligence of the employees of the New York Central Railroad. There is full and ample cause for a suit against the railroad. Now I have reason to believe that the Excelsior Dairy Company will bring suit for the losses incurred, horse and wagon etcetera. . . ."

"You mean you think Gus is more likely to get damages himself?"

"Exactly."

"How much do you think he could get?"

"Why that depends on how badly hurt he is, on the attitude of the court, and perhaps on the skill of the lawyer. . . . I think ten thousand dollars is a conservative figure."

"And you dont ask no money down?"

"The lawyer's fee is rarely paid until the case is brought to a successful termination."

"An you're a lawyer, honest? You look kinder young to be a lawyer."

The gray eyes flashed in his. They both laughed. He felt a warm inexplicable flush go through him.

"I'm a lawyer all the same. I make a specialty of cases like these. Why only last Tuesday I got six thousand dollars for a client who was kicked by a relay horse riding on the loop. . . . Just at this moment as you may know there is considerable agitation for revoking altogether the franchise of the Eleventh Avenue tracks. . . . I think this is a most favorable moment."

"Say do you always talk like that, or is it just business?"

He threw back his head and laughed.

"Poor old Gus, I always said he had a streak of luck in him."

The wail of a child crept thinly through the partition into the room.

"What's that?"

"It's only the baby. . . . The little wretch dont do nothin but squall."

"So you've got children Mrs. McNiel?" The thought chilled him somehow.

"Juss one . . . what kin ye expect?"

"Is it the Emergency Hospital?"

"Yes I reckon they'll let you see him as it's a matter of business. He's groanin somethin dreadful."

"Now if I could get a few good witnesses."

"Mike Doheny seen it all. . . . He's on the force. He's a good frien of Gus's."

"By gad we've got a case and a half. . . . Why they'll settle out of court. . . . I'll go right up to the hospital."

A fresh volley of wails came from the other room.

"Oh, that brat," she whispered, screwing up her face. "We could use the money all right Mr. Baldwin. . . ."

"Well I must go." He picked up his hat. "And I certainly will do my best in this case. May I come by and report progress to you from time to time?"

"I hope you will."

When they shook hands at the door he couldn't seem to let go her hand. She blushed.

"Well goodby and thank you very much for callin," she said stiffly.

Baldwin staggered dizzily down the stairs. His head was full of blood. The most beautiful girl I've ever seen in my life. Outside it had begun to snow. The snowflakes were cold furtive caresses to his hot cheeks.

The sky over the Park was mottled with little tiptailed clouds like a field of white chickens.

"Look Alice, lets us go down this little path."

"But Ellen, my dad told me to come straight home from school."

"Scarecat!"

"But Ellen those dreadful kidnappers. . . ."

"I told you not to call me Ellen any more."

"Well Elaine then, Elaine the lily maid of Astalot."

Ellen had on her new Black Watch plaid dress. Alice wore glasses and had legs thin as hairpins.

"Scarecat!"

"They're dreadful men sitting on that bench. Come along Elaine the fair, let's go home."

"I'm not scared of them. I could fly like Peter Pan if I wanted to."

"Why dont you do it?"

"I dont want to just now."

Alice began to whimper. "Oh Ellen I think you're mean. . . . Come along home Elaine."

"No I'm going for a walk in the Park."

Ellen started down the steps. Alice stood a minute on the top step balancing first on one foot then on the other.

"Scaredy scaredy scarecat!" yelled Ellen.

Alice ran off blubbering. "I'm goin to tell your mommer."

Ellen walked down the asphalt path among the shrubbery kicking her toes in the air.

Ellen in her new dress of Black Watch plaid mummy'd bought at Hearn's walked down the asphalt path kicking her toes in the air. There was a silver thistle brooch on the shoulder of the new dress of Black Watch plaid mummy'd bought at Hearn's. Elaine of Lammermoor was going to be married. The Betrothed. Wangnaan nainainai, went the bagpipes going through the rye. The man on the bench has a patch over his eye. A watching black patch. A black watching patch. The kidnapper of the Black Watch, among the rustling shrubs kidnappers keep their Black Watch. Ellen's toes dont kick in the air. Ellen is terribly scared of the kidnapper of the Black Watch, big smelly man of the Black Watch with a patch over his eye. She's scared to run. Her heavy feet scrape on the asphalt as she tries to run fast down the path. She's scared to turn her head. The kidnapper of the Black Watch is right behind. When I get to the lamppost I'll run as far as the nurse and the baby, when I get to the nurse and the baby I'll run as far as the big tree, when I get to the big tree. . . . Oh I'm so tired. . . . I'll run out onto Central Park West and down the street home. She was scared to turn round. She ran with a stitch in her side. She ran till her mouth tasted like pennies.

"What are you running for Ellie?" asked Gloria Drayton who was skipping rope outside the Norelands.

"Because I wanted to," panted Ellen.

Winey afterglow stained the muslin curtains and filtered into the blue gloom of the room. They stood on either side of the table. Out of a pot of narcissus still wrapped in tissue paper starshaped flowers gleamed with dim phosphorescence, giving off a damp earthsmell enmeshed in indolent prickly perfume.

"It was nice of you to bring me these Mr. Baldwin. I'll take them up to Gus at the hospital tomorrow."

"For God's sake dont call me that."

"But I dont like the name of George."

"I dont care, I like your name, Nellie."

He stood looking at her; perfumed weights coiled about his arms. His hands dangled like empty gloves. Her eyes were black, dilating, her lips pouting towards him across the flowers. She jerked her hands up to cover her face. His arm was round her little thin shoulders.

"But honest Georgy, we've got to be careful. You mustn't come here so often. I dont want all the old hens in the house to start talkin."

"Dont worry about that. . . . We mustn't worry about anything."

"I've been actin' like I was crazy this last week. . . . I've got to quit."

"You dont think I've been acting naturally, do you? I swear to God Nellie I've never done anything like this before. I'm not that kind of a person."

She showed her even teeth in a laugh. "Oh you kin never tell about men."

"But if it weren't something extraordinary and exceptional you dont think I'd be running after you this way do you? I've never been in love with anybody but you Nellie."

"That's a good one."

"But it's true. . . . I've never gone in for that sort of thing. I've worked too hard getting through lawschool and all that to have time for girls."

"Makin up for lost time I should say."

"Oh Nellie dont talk like that."

"But honestly Georgy I've got to cut this stuff out. What'll we do when Gus comes out of the hospital? An I'm neglectin the kid an everythin."

"Christ I dont care what happens. . . . Oh Nellie." He pulled her face round. They clung to each other swaying, mouths furiously mingling.

"Look out we almost had the lamp over."

"God you're wonderful, Nellie." Her head had dropped on his chest, he could feel the pungence of her tumbled hair all through him. It was dark. Snakes of light from the streetlamp wound greenly about them. Her eyes looked up into his frighteningly solemnly black.

"Look Nellie lets go in the other room," he whispered in a tiny trembling voice.

"Baby's in there."

They stood apart with cold hands looking at each other. "Come here an help me. I'll move the cradle in here. . . . Careful not to wake her or she'll bawl her head off." Her voice crackled huskily.

The baby was asleep, her little rubbery face tight closed, minute pink fists clenched on the coverlet.

"She looks happy," he said with a forced titter.

"Keep quiet cant you. . . . Here take yer shoes off. . . . There's been enough trampin o men's shoes up here. . . . Georgy I wouldn't do this, but I juss cant help. . . ."

He fumbled for her in the dark. "You darling. . . ." Clumsy he brooded over her, breathing crazily deep.

"Flatfoot you're stringin us. . . ."

"I aint, honest I'd swear by me muder's grave it's de trutt. . . . Latitude toityseven soutt by twelve west. . . . You go dere an see. . . . On dat island we made in de second officer's boat when de *Elliot P. Simkins* foundered der was four males and fortyseven females includin women an children. Waren't it me dat tole de reporter guy all about it an it came out in all de Sunday papers?"

"But Flatfoot how the hell did they ever get you away from there?"

"Dey carried me off on a stretcher or I'm a cockeyed lyer. I'll be a sonofabitch if I warnt founderin, goin down by de bows like de ole *Elliot P.*"

Heads tossed back on thick necks let out volleys of laughter, glasses were banged on the round ringmarked table, thighs resounded with slaps, elbows were poked into ribs.

"An how many guys was in de boat?"

"Six includin Mr. Dorkins de second officer."

"Seven and four makes eleven. . . . Jez. . . . Four an three-elevenths broads per capita. . . . Some island."

"When does the next ferry leave?"

"Better have another drink on that. . . . Hay Charlie fill 'em up."

Emile pulled at Congo's elbow. "Come outside a sec. J'ai que'quechose a te dire." Congo's eyes were wet, he staggered a little as he followed Emile into the outer bar. "O le p'tit mysterieux."

"Look here, I've got to go call on a lady friend."

"Oh that's what's eating you is it? I always said you was a wise guy Emile."

"Look, here's my address on a piece of paper in case you forget it: 945 West 22nd. You can come and sleep there if you're not too pickled, and dont you bring any friends or women or anything. I'm in right with the landlady and I dont want to spoil it. . . . Tu comprends."

"But I wanted you to come on a swell party. . . . Faut faire un peu la noce, nom de dieu! . . ."

"I got to work in the morning."

"But I got eight months' pay in my pocket. . . .

"Anyway come round tomorrow at about six. I'll wait for you."

"Tu m'emmerdes tu sais avec tes manières;" Congo aimed a jet of saliva at the spittoon in the corner of the bar and turned back frowning into the inside room.

"Hay dere sit down Congo; Barney's goin to sing de Bastard King of England."

Emile jumped on a streetcar and rode uptown. At Eighteenth Street he got off and walked west to Eighth Avenue. Two doors from the corner was a small store. Over one window was CONFISERIE, over the other DELICATESSEN. In the middle of the glass door white enamel letters read Emile Rigaud, High Class Table Dainties. Emile went in. The bell jangled on the door. A dark stout woman with black hairs over the corners of her mouth was drowsing behind the counter. Emile took off his hat. "Bonsoir Madame Rigaud." She looked up with a start, then showed two dimples in a profound smile.

"Tieng c'est comma ça qu'ong oublie ses ami-es," she said in a booming Bordelais voice. "Here's a week that I say to myself, Monsieur Loustec is forgetting his friends."

"I never have any time any more."

"Lots of work, lots of money, heing?" When she laughed her shoulders shook and the big breasts under the tight blue bodice.

Emile screwed up one eye. "Might be worse. . . . But I'm sick of waiting. . . . It's so tiring; nobody regards a waiter."

"You are a man of ambition, Monsieur Loustec."

"Que voulez vous?" He blushed, and said timidly "My name's Emile."

Mme. Rigaud rolled her eyes towards the ceiling. "That was my dead husband's name. I'm used to that name." She sighed heavily.

"And how's business?"

"Comma ci comma ça. . . . Ham's gone up again."

"It's the Chicago ring's doing that. . . . A corner in pork, that's the way to make money."

Emile found Mme. Rigaud's bulgy black eyes probing his. "I enjoyed your singing so last time. . . . I've thought of it often. . . . Music does one good dont it?" Mme. Rigaud's dimples stretched and stretched as she smiled. "My poor husband had no ear. . . . That gave me a great deal of pain."

"Couldn't you sing me something this evening?"

"If you want me to, Emile? . . . But there is nobody to wait on customers."

"I'll run in when we hear the bell, if you will permit me."

"Very well. . . . I've learned a new American song . . . C'est chic vous savez."

Mme. Rigaud locked the till with a key from the bunch that hung at her belt and went through the glass door in the back of the shop. Emile followed with his hat in his hand.

"Give me your hat Emile."

"Oh dont trouble yourself."

The room beyond was a little parlor with yellow flowered wallpaper, old salmon pink portières and, under the gasbracket from which hung a bunch of crystals, a piano with photographs on it. The pianostool creaked when Mme. Rigaud sat down. She ran her fingers over the keys. Emile sat carefully on the very edge of the chair beside the piano

with his hat on his knees and pushed his face forward so
that as she played she could see it out of the corner of her
eye tilted up towards hers. Madame Rigaud began to sing:

> Just a birrd in a geelded cage
> A beauteeful sight to see
> You'd tink se vas 'appee
> And free from all care
> Se's not zo se seems to be. . . .

The bell on the door of the shop jangled loud.
"Permettez," cried Emile running out.
"Half a pound o bolony sausage sliced," said a little girl
with pigtails. Emile passed the knife across the palm of his
hand and sliced the sausage carefully. He tiptoed back into
the parlor and put the money on the edge of the piano.
Madame Rigaud was still singing:

> Tis sad ven you tink of a vasted life
> For yout cannot mate vit age
> Beautee vas soooold
> For an old man's goooold
> Se's a birrd in a geelded cage.

Bud stood on the corner of West Broadway and Franklin
Street eating peanuts out of a bag. It was noon and his
money was all gone. The Elevated thundered overhead.
Dustmotes danced before his eyes in the girderstriped sunlight. Wondering which way to go he spelled out the names
of the streets for the third time. A black shiny cab drawn
by two black shinyrumped horses turned the corner sharp in
front of him with a rasp on the cobblestones of red shiny
wheels suddenly braked. There was a yellow leather trunk
on the seat beside the driver. In the cab a man in a brown
derby talked loud to a woman with a gray feather boa round
her neck and gray ostrich plumes in her hat. The man
jerked a revolver up to his mouth. The horses reared and

plunged in the middle of a shoving crowd. Policemen elbowing through. They had the man out on the curbstone vomiting blood, head hanging limp over his checked vest. The woman stood tall and white beside him twisting her feather boa in her hands, the gray plumes in her hat nodding in the striped sunlight under the elevated.

"His wife was taking him to Europe. . . . The *Deutschland* sailing at twelve. I'd said goodby to him forever. He was sailing on the *Deutschland* at twelve. He'd said goodby to me forever."

"Git oute de way dere;" a cop jabbed Bud in the stomach with his elbow. His knees trembled. He got to the edge of the crowd and walked away trembling. Mechanically he shelled a peanut and put it in his mouth. Better save the rest till evenin. He twisted the mouth of the bag and dropped it into his pocket.

Under the arclight that spluttered pink and green-edged violet the man in the checked suit passed two girls. The full-lipped oval face of the girl nearest to him; her eyes were like a knifethrust. He walked a few paces then turned and followed them fingering his new satin necktie. He made sure the horseshoe diamond pin was firm in its place. He passed them again. Her face was turned away. Maybe she was. . . . No he couldn't tell. Good luck he had fifty dollars on him. He sat on a bench and let them pass him. Wouldnt do to make a mistake and get arrested. They didnt notice him. He followed them down the path and out of the Park. His heart was pounding. I'd give a million dollars for . . . Pray pardon me, isn't this Miss Anderson? The girls walked fast. In the crowd crossing Columbus Circle he lost sight of them. He hurried down Broadway block after block. The full lips, the eyes like the thrust of a knife. He stared in girls' faces right and left. Where could she have gone? He hurried on down Broadway.

Ellen was sitting beside her father on a bench at the Battery. She was looking at her new brown button shoes. A glint of sunlight caught on the toes and on each of the little round buttons when she swung her feet out from under the shadow of her dress.

"Think how it'd be," Ed Thatcher was saying, "to go abroad on one of those liners. Imagine crossing the great Atlantic in seven days."

"But daddy what do people do all that time on a boat?"

"I dunno . . . I suppose they walk round the deck and play cards and read and all that sort of thing. Then they have dances."

"Dances on a boat! I should think it'd be awful tippy." Ellen giggled.

"On the big modern liners they do."

"Daddy why dont we go?"

"Maybe we will some day if I can save up the money."

"Oh daddy do hurry up an save a lot of money. Alice Vaughan's mother an father go to the White Mountains every summer, but next summer they're going abroad."

Ed Thatcher looked out across the bay that stretched in blue sparkling reaches into the brown haze towards the Narrows. The statue of Liberty stood up vague as a sleepwalker among the curling smoke of tugboats and the masts of schooners and the blunt lumbering masses of brickbarges and sandscows. Here and there the glary sun shone out white on a sail or on the superstructure of a steamer. Red ferryboats shuttled back and forth.

"Daddy why arent we rich?"

"There are lots of people poorer than us Ellie. . . . You wouldn't like your daddy any better if he were rich would you?"

"Oh yes I would daddy."

Thatcher laughed. "Well it might happen someday. . . . How would you like the firm of Edward C. Thatcher and Co., Certified Accountants?"

Ellen jumped to her feet: "Oh look at that big boat. . . . That's the boat I want to go on."

"That there's the *Harabic,*" croaked a cockney voice beside them.

"Oh is it really?" said Thatcher.

"Indeed it is, sir; as fahne a ship as syles the sea sir," explained eagerly a frayed creakyvoiced man who sat on the bench beside them. A cap with a broken patentleather visor was pulled down over a little peaked face that exuded a faded smell of whiskey. "Yes sir, the *Harabic* sir."

"Looks like a good big boat that does."

"One of the biggest afloat sir. I syled on er many's the tahme and on the *Majestic* and the *Teutonic* too sir, fahne ships both, though a bit light'eaded in a sea as you might say. I've signed as steward on the Hinman and White Star lahnes these thirty years and now in me old age they've lyed me hoff."

"Oh well, we all have hard luck sometimes."

"And some of us as it hall the tahme sir. . . . I'd be a appy man sir, if I could get back to the old country. This arent any plyce for an old man, it's for the young and strong, this is." He drew a gout-twisted hand across the bay and pointed to the statue. "Look at er, she's alookin towards Hengland she is."

"Daddy let's go away. I dont like this man," whispered Ellen tremulously in her father's ear.

"All right we'll go and take a look at the sealions. . . . Good day."

"You couldn't fahnd me the price of a cup o coffee, could you now sir? I'm fair foundered." Thatcher put a dime in the grimy knobbed hand.

"But daddy, mummy said never to let people speak to you in the street an to call a policeman if they did an to run away as fast as you could on account of those horrible kidnappers."

"No danger of their kidnapping me Ellie. That's just for little girls."

"When I grow up will I be able to talk to people on the street like that?"

"No deary you certainly will not."

"If I'd been a boy could I?"

"I guess you could."

In front of the Aquarium they stopped a minute to look down the bay. The liner with a tug puffing white smoke against either bow was abreast of them towering above the ferryboats and harborcraft. Gulls wheeled and screamed. The sun shone creamily on the upper decks and on the big yellow blackcapped funnel. From the foremast a string of little flags fluttered jauntily against the slate sky.

"And there are lots of people coming over from abroad on that boat arent there daddy?"

"Look you can see . . . the decks are black with people."

Walking across Fiftythird Street from the East River Bud Korpenning found himself standing beside a pile of coal on the sidewalk. On the other side of the pile of coal a gray-haired woman in a flounced lace shirtwaist with a big pink cameo poised on the curve of her high bosom was looking at his stubbly chin and at the wrists that hung raw below the frayed sleeves of his coat. Then he heard himself speak:

"Dont spose I could take that load of coal in back for you ma'am?" Bud shifted his weight from one foot to the other.

"That's just what you could do," the woman said in a cracked voice. "That wretched coal man left it this morning and said he'd be back to bring it in. I suppose he's drunk like the rest of them. I wonder if I can trust you in the house."

"I'm from upstate ma'am," stammered Bud.

"From where?"

"From Cooperstown."

"Hum. . . . I'm from Buffalo. This is certainly the city for everyone being from somewhere else. . . . Well you're probably a burglar's accomplice, but I cant help it I've got to have that coal in. . . . Come in my man, I'll give you a shovel and a basket and if you dont drop any in the passage or on the kitchen floor, because the scrubwoman's just left . . . naturally the coal had to come when the floor was clean. . . . I'll give you a dollar."

When he carried in the first load she was hovering in the kitchen. His caving hungersniff stomach made him totter lightheadedly, but he was happy to be working instead of dragging his feet endlessly along pavements, across streets, dodging drays and carts and streetcars.

"How is it you haven't got a regular job my man," she asked as he came back breathless with the empty basket.

"I reckon it's as I aint caught on to city ways yet. I was born an raised on a farm."

"And what did you want to come to this horrible city for?"

"Couldn't stay on the farm no more."

"It's terrible what's going to become of this country if all the fine strong young men leave the farms and come into the cities."

"Thought I could git a work as a longshoreman, ma'am, but they're layin' men off down on the wharves. Mebbe I kin go to sea as a sailor but nobody wants a green hand. . . . I aint et for two days now."

"How terrible. . . . Why you poor man couldn't you have gone to some mission or something?"

When Bud had brought the last load in he found a plate of cold stew on the corner of the kitchen table, half a loaf of stale bread and a glass of milk that was a little sour. He ate quickly barely chewing and put the last of the stale bread in his pocket.

"Well did you enjoy your little lunch?"

"Thankye ma'am." He nodded with his mouth full.

"Well you can go now and thank you very much." She put a quarter into his hand. Bud blinked at the quarter in the palm of his hand.

"But ma'am you said you'd give me a dollar."

"I never said any such thing. The idea. . . . I'll call my husband if you dont get out of here immediately. In fact I've a great mind to notify the police as it is. . . ."

Without a word Bud pocketed the quarter and shuffled out.

"Such ingratitude," he heard the woman snort as he closed the door behind him.

A cramp was tying knots in his stomach. He turned east again and walked the long blocks to the river with his fists pressed tight in under his ribs. At any moment he expected to throw up. If I lose it it wont do me no good. When he got to the end of the street he lay down on the gray rubbish slide beside the wharf. A smell of hops seeped gruelly and sweet out of the humming brewery behind him. The light of the sunset flamed in the windows of factories on the Long Island side, flashed in the portholes of tugs, lay in swaths of curling yellow and orange over the swift browngreen water, glowed on the curved sails of a schooner that was slowly bucking the tide up into Hell Gate. Inside him the pain was less. Something flamed and glowed like the sunset seeping through his body. He sat up. Thank Gawd I aint agoin to lose it.

On deck it's damp and shivery in the dawn. The ship's rail is wet when you put your hand on it. The brown harbor-water smells of washbasins, rustles gently against the steamer's sides. Sailors are taking the hatches off the hold. There's a rattle of chains and a clatter from the donkey-engine where a tall man in blue overalls stands at a lever in the middle of a cloud of steam that wraps round your face like a wet towel.

"Muddy is it really the Fourth of July?"

Mother's hand has grasped his firmly trailing him down the companionway into the dining saloon. Stewards are piling up baggage at the foot of the stairs.

"Muddy is it really the Fourth of July?"

"Yes deary I'm afraid it is. . . . A holiday is a dreadful time to arrive. Still I guess they'll all be down to meet us."

She has her blue serge on and a long trailing brown veil

and the little brown animal with red eyes and teeth that are real teeth round her neck. A smell of mothballs comes from it, of unpacking trunks, of wardrobes littered with tissue-paper. It's hot in the dining saloon, the engines sob sooth-ingly behind the bulkhead. His head nods over his cup of hot milk just colored with coffee. Three bells. His head snaps up with a start. The dishes tinkle and the coffee spills with the trembling of the ship. Then a thud and rattle of anchorchains and gradually quiet. Muddy gets up to look through the porthole.

"Why it's going to be a fine day after all. I think the sun will burn through the mist. . . . Think of it dear; home at last. This is where you were born deary."

"And it's the Fourth of July."

"Worst luck. . . . Now Jimmy you must promise me to stay on the promenade deck and be very careful. Mother has to finish packing. Promise me you wont get into any mischief."

"I promise."

He catches his toe on the brass threshold of the smoking-room door and sprawls on deck, gets up rubbing his bare knee just in time to see the sun break through chocolate clouds and swash a red stream of brightness over the putty-colored water. Billy with the freckles on his ears whose people are for Roosevelt instead of for Parker like mother is waving a silk flag the size of a handkerchief at the men on a yellow and white tugboat.

"Didjer see the sun rise?" he asks as if he owned it.

"You bet I saw it from my porthole," says Jimmy walking away after a lingering look at the silk flag. There's land close on the other side; nearest a green bank with trees and wide white grayroofed houses.

"Well young feller, how does it feel to be home?" asks the tweedy gentleman with droopy mustaches.

"Is that way New York?" Jimmy points out over the still water broadening in the sunlight.

"Yessiree-bobby, behind yonder bank of fog lies Man-hattan."

"Please sir what's that?"

"That's New York. . . . You see New York is on Manhattan Island."

"Is it really on an island?"

"Well what do you think of a boy who dont know that his own home town is on an island?"

The tweedy gentleman's gold teeth glitter as he laughs with his mouth wide open. Jimmy walks on round the deck, kicking his heels, all foamy inside; New York's on an island.

"You look right glad to get home little boy," says the Southern lady.

"Oh I am, I could fall down and kiss the ground."

"Well that's a fine patriotic sentiment. . . . I'm glad to hear you say it."

Jimmy scalds all over. Kiss the ground, kiss the ground, echoes in his head like a catcall. Round the deck.

"That with the yellow flag's the quarantine boat." A stout man with rings on his fingers—he's a Jew—is talking to the tweedy man. "Ha we're under way again. . . . That was quick, what?"

"We'll be in for breakfast, an American breakfast, a good old home breakfast."

Muddy coming down the deck, her brown veil floating. "Here's your overcoat Jimmy, you've got to carry it."

"Muddy, can I get out that flag?"

"What flag?"

"The silk American flag."

"No dear it's all put away."

"Please I'd so like to have that flag cause it's the Fourth of July an everything."

"Now dont whine Jimmy. When mother says no she means no."

Sting of tears; he swallows a lump and looks up in her eyes.

"Jimmy it's put away in the shawlstrap and mother's so tired of fussing with those wretched bags."

"But Billy Jones has one."

"Look deary you're missing things . . . There's the statue of Liberty." A tall green woman in a dressing gown standing on an island holding up her hand.

"What's that in her hand?"

"That's a light, dear . . . Liberty enlightening the world. . . . And there's Governors Island the other side. There where the trees are . . . and see, that's Brooklyn Bridge. . . . That is a fine sight. And look at all the docks . . . that's the Battery . . . and the masts and the ships . . . and there's the spire of Trinity Church and the Pulitzer building." . . . Mooing of steamboat whistles, ferries red and waddly like ducks churning up white water, a whole train of cars on a barge pushed by a tug chugging beside it that lets out cotton steampuffs all the same size. Jimmy's hands are cold and he's chugging and chugging inside.

"Dear you mustn't get too excited. Come on down and see if mother left anything in the stateroom."

Streak of water crusted with splinters, groceryboxes, orangepeel, cabbageleaves, narrowing, narrowing between the boat and the dock. A brass band shining in the sun, white caps, sweaty red faces, playing Yankee Doodle. "That's for the ambassador, you know the tall man who never left his cabin." Down the slanting gangplank, careful not to trip. *Yankee Doodle went to town.* . . . Shiny black face, white enameled eyes, white enameled teeth. "Yas ma'am, yas ma'am" . . . *Stucka feather in his hat, an called it macaroni.* . . . "We have the freedom of the port." Blue custom officer shows a bald head bowing low . . . *Tumte boomboom* BOOM BOOM BOOM . . . *cakes and sugar candy.* . . .

"Here's Aunt Emily and everybody. . . . Dear how sweet of you to come."

"My dear I've been here since six o'clock!"

"My how he's grown."

Light dresses, sparkle of brooches, faces poked into Jimmy's, smell of roses and uncle's cigar.

"Why he's quite a little man. Come here sir, let me look at you."

"Well goodby Mrs. Herf. If you ever come down our way. . . . Jimmy I didn't see you kiss the ground young man."

"Oh he's killing, he's so oldfashioned . . . such an old-fashioned child."

The cab smells musty, goes rumbling and lurching up a wide avenue swirling with dust, through brick streets sour-smelling full of grimy yelling children, and all the while the trunks creak and thump on top.

"Muddy dear, you dont think it'll break through do you?"

"No dear," she laughs tilting her head to one side. She has pink cheeks and her eyes sparkle under the brown veil.

"Oh muddy." He stands up and kisses her on the chin. "What lots of people muddy."

"That's on account of the Fourth of July."

"What's that man doing?"

"He's been drinking dear I'm afraid."

From a little stand draped with flags a man with white whiskers with little red garters on his shirtsleeves is making a speech. "That's a Fourth of July orator. . . . He's reading the Declaration of Independence."

"Why?"

"Because it's the Fourth of July."

Crang! . . . that's a cannon-cracker. "That wretched boy might have frightened the horse. . . . The Fourth of July dear is the day the Declaration of Independence was signed in 1776 in the War of the Revolution. My great grandfather Harland was killed in that war."

A funny little train with a green engine clatters overhead.

"That's the Elevated . . . and look this is Twentythird Street . . . and the Flatiron Building."

The cab turns sharp into a square glowering with sunlight, smelling of asphalt and crowds and draws up before a tall door where colored men in brass buttons run forward.

"And here we are at the Fifth Avenue Hotel."

Icecream at Uncle Jeff's, cold sweet peachy taste thick against the roof of the mouth. Funny after you've left the ship you can still feel the motion. Blue chunks of dusk melting into the squarecut uptown streets. Rockets spurting bright in the blue dusk, colored balls falling, Bengal fire, Uncle Jeff tacking pinwheels on the tree outside the apartmenthouse door, lighting them with his cigar. Roman candles you have to hold. "Be sure and turn your face away, kiddo." Hot thud and splutter in your hands, eggshaped balls soaring, red, yellow, green, smell of powder and singed paper. Down the fizzing glowing street a bell clangs, clangs nearer, clangs faster. Hoofs of lashed horses striking sparks, a fire engine roars by, round the corner red and smoking and brassy. "Must be on Broadway." After it the hookandladder and the firechief's highpacing horses. Then the tinkletinkle of an ambulance. "Somebody got his."

The box is empty, gritty powder and sawdust get under your nails when you feel along it, it's empty, no there are still some little wooden fire engines on wheels. Really truly fire engines. "We must set these off Uncle Jeff. Oh these are the best of all Uncle Jeff." They have squibs in them and go sizzling off fast over the smooth asphalt of the street, pushed by sparkling plumed fiery tails, leaving smoke behind some real fire engines.

Tucked into bed in a tall unfriendly room, with hot eyes and aching legs. "Growing pains darling," muddy said when she tucked him in, leaning over him in a glimmering silk dress with drooping sleeves.

"Muddy what's that little black patch on your face?"

"That," she laughed and her necklace made a tiny tinkling, "is to make mother look prettier."

He lay there hemmed by tall nudging wardrobes and dressers. From outside came the sound of wheels and shouting, and once in a while a band of music in the distance. His legs ached as if they'd fall off, and when he closed his eyes he was speeding through flaring blackness on a red fire engine that shot fire and sparks and colored balls out of its sizzling tail.

The July sun pricked out the holes in the worn shades on the office windows. Gus McNiel sat in the morris-chair with his crutches between his knees. His face was white and puffy from months in hospital. Nellie in a straw hat with red poppies rocked herself to and fro in the swivel chair at the desk.

"Better come an set by me Nellie. That lawyer might not like it if he found yez at his desk."

She wrinkled up her nose and got to her feet. "Gus I declare you're scared to death."

"You'd be scared too if you'd had what I'd had wid de railroad doctor pokin me and alookin at me loike I was a jailbird and the Jew doctor the lawyer got tellin me as I was totally in-cap-aciated. Gorry I'm all in. I think he was lyin though."

"Gus you do as I tell ye. Keep yer mouth shut an let the other guys do the talkin'."

"Sure I wont let a peep outa me."

Nellie stood behind his chair and began stroking the crisp hair back from his forehead.

"It'll be great to be home again, Nellie, wid your cookin an all." He put an arm round her waist and drew her to him.

"Juss think, maybe I wont have to do any."

"I don't think I'd loike that so well. . . . Gosh if we dont git that money I dunno how we'll make out."

"Oh pop'll help us like he's been doin."

"Hope to the Lord I aint goin to be sick all me loife."

George Baldwin came in slamming the glass door behind him. He stood looking at the man and his wife a second with his hands in his pockets. Then he said quietly smiling:

"Well it's done people. As soon as the waiver of any further claims is signed the railroad's attorneys will hand me a check for twelve thousand five hundred. That's what we finally compromised on."

"Twelve thousand iron men," gasped Gus. "Twelve thousand five hundred. Say wait a second. . . . Hold me crutches while I go out an git run over again. . . . Wait till

I tell McGillycuddy about it. The ole divil'll be throwin hisself in front of a market train. . . . Well Mr. Baldwin sir," Gus propped himself onto his feet. . . . "you're a great man. . . . Aint he Nellie?"

"To be sure he is."

Baldwin tried to keep from looking her in the eye. Spurts of jangling agitation were going through him, making his legs feel weak and trembly.

"I'll tell yez what let's do," said Gus. "Sposin we all take a horsecab up to ole McGillycuddy's an have somethin to wet our whistles in the private bar. . . . My treat. I need a bit of a drink to cheer me up. Come on Nellie."

"I wish I could," said Baldwin, "but I'm afraid I cant. I'm pretty busy these days. But just give me your signature before you go and I'll have the check for you tomorrow. . . . Sign here . . . and here."

McNiel had stumped over to the desk and was leaning over the papers. Baldwin felt that Nellie was trying to make a sign to him. He kept his eyes down. After they had left he noticed her purse, a little leather purse with pansies burned on the back, on the corner of the desk. There was a tap on the glass door. He opened.

"Why wouldn't you look at me?" she said breathlessly low.

"How could I with him here." He held the purse out to her.

She put her arms round his neck and kissed him hard on the mouth. "What are we goin to do? Shall I come in this afternoon? Gus'll be liquorin up to get himself sick again now he's out of the hospital."

"No I cant Nellie. . . . Business . . . business. . . . I'm busy every minute."

"Oh yes you are. . . . All right have it your own way." She slammed the door.

Baldwin sat at his desk biting his knuckles without seeing the pile of papers he was staring at. "I've got to cut it out," he said aloud and got to his feet. He paced back and forth across the narrow office looking at the shelves of lawbooks and the Gibson girl calendar over the telephone and the dusty square of sunlight by the window. He looked at his watch. Lunchtime. He drew the palm of a hand over his forehead and went to the telephone.

"Rector 1237. . . . Mr. Sandbourne there? . . . Say Phil suppose I come by for you for lunch? Do you want to go out right now? . . . Sure. . . . Say Phil I clinched it, I got the milkman his damages. I'm pleased as the dickens. I'll set you up to a regular lunch on the strength of it. . . So long. . . ."

He came away from the telephone smiling, took his hat off its hook, fitted it carefully on his head in front of the little mirror over the hatrack, and hurried down the stairs.

On the last flight he met Mr. Emery of Emery & Emery who had their offices on the first floor.

"Well Mr. Baldwin how's things?" Mr. Emery of Emery & Emery was a flatfaced man with gray hair and eyebrows and a protruding wedgeshaped jaw. "Pretty well sir, pretty well."

"They tell me you are doing mighty well. . . . Something about the New York Central Railroad."

"Oh Simsbury and I settled it out of court."

"Humph," said Mr. Emery of Emery & Emery.

As they were about to part in the street Mr. Emery said suddenly "Would you care to dine with me and my wife some time?"

"Why . . . er . . . I'd be delighted."

"I like to see something of the younger fellows in the profession you understand. . . . Well I'll drop you a line. . . . Some evening next week. It would give us a chance to have a chat."

Baldwin shook a blueveined hand in a shinystarched cuff and went off down Maiden Lane hustling with a springy step through the noon crowd. On Pearl Street he climbed a steep flight of black stairs that smelt of roasting coffee and knocked on a groundglass door.

"Come in," shouted a bass voice. A swarthy man lanky in his shirtsleeves strode forward to meet him. "Hello

George, thought you were never comin'. I'm hongry as hell."

"Phil I'm going to set you up to the best lunch you ever ate in your life."

"Well I'm juss waitin' to be set."

Phil Sandbourne put on his coat, knocked the ashes out of his pipe on the corner of a draftingtable, and shouted into a dark inner office, "Goin out to eat, Mr. Specker."

"All right go ahead," replied a goaty quavering from the inner office.

"How's the old man?" asked Baldwin as they went out the door.

"Ole Specker? Bout on his last legs . . . but he's been thataway for years poa ole soul. Honest George I'd feel mighty mean if anythin happened to poa ole Specker. . . . He's the only honest man in the city of New York, an he's got a head on his shoulders too."

"He's never made anything much by it," said Baldwin.

"He may yet. . . . He may yet. . . . Man you ought to see his plans for allsteel buildins. He's got an idea the skyscraper of the future'll be built of steel and glass. We've been experimenting with vitrous tile recently. . . . cristamighty some of his plans would knock yer eye out. . . . He's got a great sayin about some Roman emperor who found Rome of brick and left it of marble. Well he says he's found New York of brick an that he's goin to leave it of steel . . . steel an glass. I'll have to show you his project for a rebuilt city. It's some pipedream."

They settled on a cushioned bench in the corner of the restaurant that smelled of steak and the grill. Sandbourne stretched his legs out under the table.

"Wow this is luxury," he said.

"Phil let's have a cocktail," said Baldwin from behind the bill of fare. "I tell you Phil, it's the first five years that's the hardest."

"You needn't worry George, you're the hustlin kind. . . . I'm the ole stick in the mud "

"I don't see why, you can always get a job as a drafts-man."

"That's a fine future I muss say, to spend ma life with the corner of a draftintable stuck in ma bally. . . . Christamighty man!"

"Well Specker and Sandbourne may be a famous firm yet."

"People'll be goin round in flyin machines by that time an you and me'll be laid out with our toes to the daisies."

"Here's luck anyway."

"Here's lead in yer pencil, George."

They drank down the Martinis and started eating their oysters.

"I wonder if it's true that oysters turn to leather in your stomach when you drink alcohol with em."

"Search me. . . . Say by the way Phil how are you getting on with that little stenographer you were taking out?"

"Man the food an drink an theaters I've wasted on that lil girl. . . . She's got me run to a standstill. . . . Honest she has. You're a sensible feller, George, to keep away from the women."

"Maybe," said Baldwin slowly and spat an olive stone into his clenched fist.

The first thing they heard was the quavering whistle that came from a little wagon at the curb opposite the entrance to the ferry. A small boy broke away from the group of immigrants that lingered in the ferryhouse and ran over to the little wagon.

"Sure it's like a steam engine an its fulla monkeynuts," he yelled running back.

"Padraic you stay here."

"And this here's the L station, South Ferry," went on Tim Halloran who had come down to meet them. "Up thataway's Battery Park an Bowling Green an Wall Street an th' financial district. . . . Come along Padraic your Uncle Timothy's goin to take ye on th' Ninth Avenoo L."

There were only three people left at the ferrylanding, an old woman with a blue handkerchief on her head and a young woman with a magenta shawl, standing at either end of a big corded trunk studded with brass tacks; and an old man with a greenish stub of a beard and a face lined and twisted like the root of a dead oak. The old woman was whimpering with wet eyes: "Dove andiamo Madonna mia, Madonna mia?" The young woman was unfolding a letter blinking at the ornate writing. Suddenly she went over to the old man, "Non posso leggere," holding out the letter to him. He wrung his hands, letting his head roll back and forth, saying over and over again something she couldn't understand. She shrugged her shoulders and smiled and went back to the trunk. A Sicilian with sideburns was talking to the old woman. He grabbed the trunk by its cord and pulled it over to a spring wagon with a white horse that stood across the street. The two women followed the trunk. The Sicilian held out his hand to the young woman. The old woman still muttering and whimpering hoisted herself painfully onto the back of the wagon. When the Sicilian leaned over to read the letter he nudged the young woman with his shoulder. She stiffened. "Awright," he said. Then as he shook the reins on the horse's back he turned back towards the old woman and shouted, "Cinque le due. . . . Awright."

IV. Tracks

The rumpetybump rumpetybump spaced out, slackened; bumpers banged all down the train. The man dropped off the rods. He couldnt move for stiffness. It was pitchblack. Very slowly he crawled out, hoisted himself to his knees, to his feet until he leaned panting against the freightcar. His body was not his own; his muscles were smashed wood, his bones were twisted rods. A lantern burst his eyes.

"Get outa here quick yous. Company detectives is beatin through de yards."

"Say feller, is this New York?"

"You're goddam right it is. Juss foller my lantern; you kin git out along de waterfront."

His feet could barely stumble through the long gleaming v's and crisscrossed lines of tracks, he tripped and fell over a bundle of signal rods. At last he was sitting on the edge of a wharf with his head in his hands. The water made a soothing noise against the piles like the lapping of a dog. He took a newspaper out of his pocket and unwrapped a hunk of bread and a slice of gristly meat. He ate them dry, chewing and chewing before he could get any moisture in his mouth. Then he got unsteadily to his feet, brushed the crumbs off his knees, and looked about him. Southward beyond the tracks the murky sky was drenched with orange glow.

"The Gay White Way," he said aloud in a croaking voice. "The Gay White Way."

THROUGH the rainstriped window Jimmy Herf was watching the umbrellas bob in the slowly swirling traffic that flowed up Broadway. There was a knock at the door; "Come in," said Jimmy and turned back to the window when he saw that the waiter wasn't Pat. The waiter switched on the light. Jimmy saw him reflected in the windowpane, a lean spikyhaired man holding aloft in one hand the dinnertray on which the silver covers were grouped like domes. Breathing hard the waiter advanced into the room dragging a folding stand after him with his free hand. He jerked open the stand, set the tray on it and laid a cloth on the round table. A greasy pantry smell came from him. Jimmy waited till he'd gone to turn round. Then he walked about the table tipping up the silver covers; soup with little green things in it, roast lamb, mashed potatoes, mashed turnips, spinach, no desert either.

"Muddy." "Yes deary," the voice wailed frailly through the folding doors.

"Dinner's ready mother dear."

"You begin darling boy, I'll be right in. . . ."

"But I dont want to begin without you mother."

He walked round the table straightening knives and forks. He put a napkin over his arm. The head waiter at Delmonico's was arranging the table for Graustark and the Blind King of Bohemia and Prince Henry the Navigator and . . .

"Mother who d'you want to be Mary Queen of Scots or Lady Jane Grey?"

"But they both had their heads chopped off honey. . . . I dont want to have my head chopped off." Mother had on her salmoncolored teagown. When she opened the folding doors a wilted smell of cologne and medicines seeped out of the bedroom, trailed after her long lacefringed sleeves. She had put a little too much powder on her face, but her hair, her lovely brown hair was done beautifully. They sat down opposite one another; she set a plate of soup in front of him, lifting it between two long blueveined hands.

He ate the soup that was watery and not hot enough. "Oh I forgot the croûtons, honey."

"Muddy . . . mother why arent you eating your soup?"

"I dont seem to like it much this evening. I couldn't

think what to order tonight my head ached so. It doesn't matter."

"Would you rather be Cleopatra? She had a wonderful appetite and ate everything that was put before her like a good little girl."

"Even pearls. . . . She put a pearl in a glass of vinegar and drank it down. . . ." Her voice trembled. She stretched out her hand to him across the table; he patted her hand manfully and smiled. "Only you and me Jimmy boy. . . . Honey you'll always love your mother wont you?"

"What's the matter muddy dear?"

"Oh nothing; I feel strange this evening. . . . Oh I'm so tired of never really feeling well."

"But after you've had your operation. . . ."

"Oh yes after I've had my operation. . . . Deary there's a paper of fresh butter on the windowledge in the bathroom. . . . I'll put some on these turnips if you fetch it for me. . . . I'm afraid I'll have to complain about the food again. This lamb's not all it should be; I hope it wont make us sick."

Jimmy ran through the folding doors and his mother's room into the little passage that smelled of mothballs and silky bits of clothing littered on a chair; the red rubber tubing of a douche swung in his face as he opened the bathroom door; the whiff of medicines made his ribs contract with misery. He pushed up the window at the end of the tub. The ledge was gritty and feathery specks of soot covered the plate turned up over the butter. He stood a moment staring down the airshaft, breathing through his mouth to keep from smelling the coalgas that rose from the furnaces. Below him a maid in a white cap leaned out of a window and talked to one of the furnacemen who stood looking up at her with his bare grimy arms crossed over his chest. Jimmy strained his ears to hear what they were saying; to be dirty and handle coal all day and have grease in your hair and up to your armpits.

"Jimmee!"

"Coming mother." Blushing he slammed down the window and walked back to the sittingroom, slowly so that the red would have time to fade out of his face.

"Dreaming again, Jimmy. My little dreamer."

He put the butter beside his mother's plate and sat down.

"Hurry up and eat your lamb while it's hot. Why dont you try a little French mustard on it? It'll make it taste better."

The mustard burnt his tongue, brought tears to his eyes.

"Is it too hot?" mother asked laughing. "You must learn to like hot things. . . . He always liked hot things."

"Who mother?"

"Someone I loved very much."

They were silent. He could hear himself chewing. A few rattling sounds of cabs and trolleycars squirmed in brokenly through the closed windows. The steampipes knocked and hissed. Down the airshaft the furnaceman with grease up to his armpits was spitting words out of his wabbly mouth up at the maid in the starched cap—dirty words. Mustard's the color of . . .

"A penny for your thoughts."

"I wasn't thinking of anything."

"We mustn't have any secrets from each other dear. Remember you're the only comfort your mother has in the world."

"I wonder what it'd be like to be a seal, a little harbor seal."

"Very chilly I should think."

"But you wouldn't feel it. . . . Seals are protected by a layer of blubber so that they're always warm even sitting on an iceberg. But it would be such fun to swim around in the sea whenever you wanted to. They travel thousands of miles without stopping."

"But mother's traveled thousands of miles without stopping and so have you."

"When?"

"Going abroad and coming back." She was laughing at him with bright eyes.

"Oh but that's in a boat."

"And when we used to go cruising on the *Mary Stuart*."

"Oh tell me about that muddy."

There was a knock. "Come." The spikyhaired waiter put his head in the door.

"Can I clear mum?"

"Yes and bring me some fruit salad and see that the fruit is fresh cut. . . . Things are wretched this evening."

Puffing, the waiter was piling dishes on the tray. "I'm sorry mum," he puffed.

"All right, I know it's not your fault waiter. . . . What'll you have Jimmy?"

"May I have a meringue glacé muddy?"

"All right if you'll be very good."

"Yea," Jimmy let out a yell.

"Darling you mustn't shout like that at table."

"But we dont mind when there are just the two of us. . . . Hooray meringue glacé."

"James a gentleman always behaves the same way whether he's in his own home or in the wilds of Africa."

"Gee I wish we were in the wilds of Africa."

"I'd be terrified, dear."

"I'd shout like that and scare away all the lions and tigers. . . . Yes I would."

The waiter came back with two plates on the tray. "I'm sorry mum but meringue glacé's all out. . . . I brought the young gentleman chocolate icecream instead."

"Oh mother."

"Never mind dear. . . . It would have been too rich anyway. . . . You eat that and I'll let you run out after dinner and buy some candy."

"Oh goody."

"But dont eat the icecream too fast or you'll have collywobbles."

"I'm all through."

"You bolted it you little wretch. . . . Put on your rubbers honey."

"But it's not raining at all."

"Do as mother wants you dear. . . . And please dont

be long. I put you on your honor to come right back. Mother's not a bit well tonight and she gets so nervous when you're out in the street. There are such terrible dangers. . . ."

He sat down to pull on his rubbers. While he was snapping them tight over his heels she came to him with a dollar bill. She put her arm with its long silky sleeve round his shoulder. "Oh my darling."

She was crying.

"Mother you mustnt." He squeezed her hard; he could feel the ribs of her corset against his arms. "I'll be back in a minute, in the teenciest weenciest minute."

On the stairs where a brass rod held the dull crimson carpet in place on each step, Jimmy pulled off his rubbers and stuffed them into the pockets of his raincoat. With his head in the air he hurried through the web of prying glances of the bellhops on the bench beside the desk. "Goin fer a walk?" the youngest lighthaired bellhop asked him. Jimmy nodded wisely, slipped past the staring buttons of the doorman and out onto Broadway full of clangor and footsteps and faces putting on shadowmasks when they slid out of the splotches of light from stores and arclamps. He walked fast uptown past the Ansonia. In the doorway lounged a blackbrowed man with a cigar in his mouth, maybe a kidnapper. But nice people live in the Ansonia like where we live. Next a telegraph office, drygoods stores, a dyers and cleaners, a Chinese laundry sending out a scorched mysterious steamy smell. He walks faster, the chinks are terrible kidnappers. Footpads. A man with a can of coaloil brushes past him, a greasy sleeve brushes against his shoulder, smells of sweat and coaloil; suppose he's a firebug. The thought of firebug gives him gooseflesh. Fire. Fire.

Huyler's; there's a comfortable fudgy odor mixed with the smell of nickel and wellwiped marble outside the door, and the smell of cooking chocolate curls warmly from the gratings under the windows. Black and orange crêpepaper favors for Hallowe'en. He is just going in when he thinks of the Mirror place two blocks further up, those little silver steamengines and automobiles they give you with your change. I'll hurry; on rollerskates it'd take less time, you could escape from bandits, thugs, holdupmen, on rollerskates, shooting over your shoulder with a long automatic, bing . . . one of em down! that's the worst of em, bing . . . there's another; the rollerskates are magic rollerskates, whee . . . up the brick walls of the houses, over the roofs, vaulting chimneys, up the Flatiron Building, scooting across the cables of Brooklyn Bridge.

Mirror candies; this time he goes in without hesitating. He stands at the counter a while before anyone comes to wait on him. "Please a pound of sixty cents a pound mixed chocolate creams," he rattled off. She is a blond lady, a little crosseyed, and looks at him spitefully without answering. "Please I'm in a hurry if you dont mind."

"All right, everybody in their turn," she snaps. He stands blinking at her with flaming cheeks. She pushes him a box all wrapped up with a check on it "Pay at the desk." I'm not going to cry. The lady at the desk is small and greyhaired. She takes his dollar through a little door like the little doors little animals go in and out of in the Small Mammal House. The cash register makes a cheerful tinkle, glad to get the money. A quarter, a dime, a nickel and a little cup, is that forty cents? But only a little cup instead of a steamengine or an automobile. He picks up the money and leaves the little cup and hurries out with the box under his arm. Mother'll say I've been too long. He walks home looking straight ahead of him, smarting from the meanness of the blond lady.

"Ha . . . been out abuyin candy," said the lighthaired bellhop. "I'll give you some if you come up later," whispered Jimmy as he passed. The brass rods rang when he kicked them running up the stairs. Outside the chocolate-colored door that had 503 on it in white enameled letters he remembered his rubbers. He set the candy on the floor and pulled them on over his damp shoes. Lucky Muddy wasn't waiting for him with the door open. Maybe she'd seen him coming from the window.

"Mother." She wasn't in the sittingroom. He was terrified. She'd gone out, she'd gone away. "Mother!"

"Come here dear," came her voice weakly from the bedroom.

He pulled off his hat and raincoat and rushed in. "Mother what's the matter?"

"Nothing honey. . . . I've a headache that's all, a terrible headache. . . . Put some cologne on a handkerchief and put it on my head nicely, and dont please dear get it in my eye the way you did last time."

She lay on the bed in a skyblue wadded wrapper. Her face was purplish pale. The silky salmoncolored teagown hung limp over a chair; on the floor lay her corsets in a tangle of pink strings. Jimmy put the wet handkerchief carefully on her forehead. The cologne reeked strong, prickling his nostrils as he leaned over her.

"That's so good," came her voice feebly. "Dear call up Aunt Emily, Riverside 2466, and ask her if she can come round this evening. I want to talk to her. . . . Oh my head's bursting."

His heart thumping terribly and tears blearing his eyes he went to the telephone. Aunt Emily's voice came unexpectedly soon.

"Aunt Emily mother's kinder sick. . . . She wants you to come around. . . . She's coming right away mother dear," he shouted, "isn't that fine? She's coming right around." He tiptoed back into his mother's room, picked up the corset and the teagown and hung them in the wardrobe.

"Deary" came her frail voice "take the hairpins out of my hair, they hurt my head. . . . Oh honeyboy I feel as if my head would burst. . . ." He felt gently through her brown hair that was silkier than the teagown and pulled out the hairpins.

"Ou dont, you are hurting me."

"Mother I didn't mean to."

Aunt Emily, thin in a blue mackintosh thrown over her evening dress, hurried into the room, her thin mouth in a pucker of sympathy. She saw her sister lying twisted with pain on the bed and the skinny whitefaced boy in short pants standing beside her with his hands full of hairpins.

"What is it Lil?" she asked quietly.

"My dear something terrible's the matter with me," came Lily Herf's voice in a gasping hiss.

"James," said Aunt Emily harshly, "you must run off to bed. . . . Mother needs perfect quiet."

"Good night muddy dear," he said.

Aunt Emily patted him on the back. "Dont worry James I'll attend to everything." She went to the telephone and began calling a number in a low precise voice.

The box of candy was on the parlor table; Jimmy felt guilty when he put it under his arm. As he passed the bookcase he snatched out a volume of the American Cyclopædia and tucked it under the other arm. His aunt did not notice when he went out the door. The dungeon gates opened. Outside was an Arab stallion and two trusty retainers waiting to speed him across the border to freedom. Three doors down was his room. It was stuffed with silent chunky darkness. The light switched on obediently lighting up the cabin of the schooner *Mary Stuart*. All right Captain weigh anchor and set your course for the Windward Isles and dont let me be disturbed before dawn; I have important papers to peruse. He tore off his clothes and knelt beside the bed in his pyjamas. Nowilaymedowntosleep Ipraythelordmysoultokeep Ifishoulddiebeforeiwake Ipraythe lordmysoultotake.

Then he opened the box of candy and set the pillows together at the end of the bed under the light. His teeth broke through the chocolate into a squashysweet filling. Let's see . . .

A the first of the vowels, the first letter in all written alphabets except the Amharic or Abyssinian, of which it is the thirteenth, and the Runic of which it is the tenth. . . .

Darn it that's a hairy one. . . .

AA, Aachen (see Aix-la-Chapelle).

Aardvark . . .

Gee he's funny looking . . .

(orycteropus capensis), a plantigrade animal of the class mammalia, order edentata, peculiar to Africa.

Abd,

Abd-el-halim, an Egyptian prince, son of Mehmet Ali and a white slave woman. . . .

His cheeks burned as he read:

The Queen of the White Slaves.

Abdomen (lat. of undetermined etymology) . . . the lower part of the body included between the level of the diaphragm and that of the pelvis. . . .

Abelard . . . The relation of master and pupil was not long preserved. A warmer sentiment than esteem filled their hearts and the unlimited opportunities of intercourse which were afforded them by the canon who confided in Abelard's age (he was now almost forty), and in his public character, were fatal to the peace of both. The condition of Heloise was on the point of betraying their intimacy. . . . Fulbert now abandoned himself to a transport of savage vindictiveness . . . burst into Abelard's chamber with a band of ruffians and gratified his revenge by inflicting on him an atrocious mutilation. . . .

Abelites . . . denounced sexual intercourse as service of Satan.

Abimelech I, son of Gideon by a Sheshemite concubine, who made himself king after murdering all his seventy brethren except Jotham, and was killed while besieging the tower of Thebez . . .

Abortion . . .

No; his hands were icy and he felt a little sick from stuffing down so many chocolates.

Abracadabra.

Abydos . . .

He got up to drink a glass of water before Abyssinia with engravings of desert mountains and the burning of Magdala by the British.

His eyes smarted. He was stiff and sleepy. He looked at his Ingersoll. Eleven o'clock. Terror gripped him suddenly. If mother was dead . . . ? He pressed his face into the pillow. She stood over him in her white ballgown that had lace crisply on it and a train sweeping behind on satin rustling ruffles and her hand softly fragrant gently stroked his cheek. A rush of sobs choked him. He tossed on the bed with his face shoved hard into the knotty pillow. For a long time he couldn't stop crying.

He woke up to find the light burning dizzily and the room stuffy and hot. The book was on the floor and the candy squashed under him oozing stickily from its box. The watch had stopped at 1.45. He opened the window, put the chocolates in the bureau drawer and was about to snap off the light when he remembered. Shivering with terror he put on his bathrobe and slippers and tiptoed down the darkened hall. He listened outside the door. People were talking low. He knocked faintly and turned the knob. A hand pulled the door open hard and Jimmy was blinking in the face of a tall cleanshaven man with gold eyeglasses. The folding doors were closed; in front of them stood a starched nurse.

"James dear, go back to bed and dont worry," said Aunt Emily in a tired whisper. "Mother's very ill and must be absolutely quiet, but there's no more danger."

"Not for the present at least, Mrs. Merivale," said the doctor breathing on his eyeglasses.

"The little dear," came the nurse's voice low and purry and reassuring, "he's been sitting up worrying all night and he never bothered us once."

"I'll go back and tuck you into bed," said Aunt Emily. "My James always likes that."

"May I see mother, just a peek so's I'll know she's all right." Jimmy looked up timidly at the big face with the eyeglasses.

The doctor nodded. "Well I must go. . . . I shall drop by at four or five to see how things go. . . . Goodnight Mrs. Merivale. Goodnight Miss Billings. Goodnight son. . . ."

"This way. . . ." The trained nurse put her hand on Jimmy's shoulder. He wriggled out from under and walked behind her.

There was a light on in the corner of mother's room shaded by a towel pinned round it. From the bed came the rasp of breathing he did not recognize. Her crumpled face was towards him, the closed eyelids violet, the mouth screwed to one side. For a half a minute he stared at her. "All right I'll go back to bed now," he whispered to the nurse. His blood pounded deafeningly. Without looking at his aunt or at the nurse he walked stiffly to the outer door. His aunt said something. He ran down the corridor to his own room, slammed the door and bolted it. He stood stiff and cold in the center of the room with his fists clenched. "I hate them. I hate them," he shouted aloud. Then gulping a dry sob he turned out the light and slipped into bed between the shiverycold sheets.

"With all the business you have, madame," Emile was saying in a singsong voice, "I should think you'd need some-one to help you with the store."

"I know that . . . I'm killing myself with work; I know that," sighed Madame Rigaud from her stool at the cash-desk. Emile was silent a long time staring at the cross section of a Westphalia ham that lay on a marble slab beside his elbow. Then he said timidly: "A woman like you, a beautiful woman like you, Madame Rigaud, is never without friends."

"Ah ça. . . . I have lived too much in my time. . . . I have no more confidence. . . . Men are a set of brutes, and women, Oh I dont get on with women a bit!"

"History and literature . . ." began Emile.

The bell on the top of the door jangled. A man and a woman stamped into the shop. She had yellow hair and a hat like a flowerbed.

"Now Billy dont be extravagant," she was saying.

"But Norah we got have sumpen te eat. . . . An I'll be all jake by Saturday."

"Nutten'll be jake till you stop playin the ponies."

"Aw go long wud yer. . . . Let's have some liverwurst. . . . My that cold breast of turkey looks good. . . ."

"Piggywiggy," cooed the yellowhaired girl.

"Lay off me will ye, I'm doing this."

"Yes sir ze breast of turkee is veree goud. . . . We ave ole cheekens too, steel 'ot. . . . Emile mong ami cherchez moi uns de ces petits poulets dans la cuisin-e." Madame Rigaud spoke like an oracle without moving from her stool by the cashdesk. The man was fanning himself with a thickbrimmed straw hat that had a checked band.

"Varm tonight," said Madame Rigaud.

"It sure is. . . . Norah we ought to have gone down to the Island instead of bummin round this town."

"Billy you know why we couldn't go perfectly well."

"Don't rub it in. Aint I tellin ye it'll be all jake by Saturday."

"History and literature," continued Emile when the customers had gone off with the chicken, leaving Madame Rigaud a silver half dollar to lock up in the till . . . "history and literature teach us that there are friendships, that there sometimes comes love that is worthy of confidence. . . ."

"History and literature!" Madame Rigaud growled with internal laughter. "A lot of good that'll do us."

"But dont you ever feel lonely in a big foreign city like this . . . ? Everything is so hard. Women look in your pocket not in your heart. . . . I cant stand it any more."

Madame Rigaud's broad shoulders and her big breasts shook with laughter. Her corsets creaked when she lifted herself still laughing off the stool. "Emile, you're a goodlooking fellow and steady and you'll get on in the world. . . . But I'll never put myself in a man's power again. . . . I've suffered too much. . . . Not if you came to me with five thousand dollars."

"You're a very cruel woman."

Madame Rigaud laughed again. "Come along now, you can help me close up."

Sunday weighed silent and sunny over downtown. Baldwin sat at his desk in his shirtsleeves reading a calfbound lawbook. Now and then he wrote down a note on a scratchpad in a wide regular hand. The phone rang loud in the hot stillness. He finished the paragraph he was reading and strode over to answer it.

"Yes I'm here alone, come on over if you want to." He

put down the receiver. "God damn it," he muttered through clenched teeth.

Nellie came in without knocking, found him pacing back and forth in front of the window.

"Hello Nellie," he said without looking up; she stood still staring at him.

"Look here Georgy this cant go on."

"Why cant it?"

"I'm sick of always pretendin an deceivin."

"Nobody's found out anything, have they?"

"Oh of course not."

She went up to him and straightened his necktie. He kissed her gently on the mouth. She wore a frilled muslin dress of a reddish lilac color and had a blue sunshade in her hand.

"How's things Georgy?"

"Wonderful. D'you know, you people have brought me luck? I've got several good cases on hand now and I've made some very valuable connections."

"Little luck it's brought me. I haven't dared go to confession yet. The priest'll be thinkin I've turned heathen."

"How's Gus?"

"Oh full of his plans. . . . Might think he'd earned the money, he's gettin that cocky about it."

"Look Nellie how would it be if you left Gus and came and lived with me? You could get a divorce and we could get married. . . . Everything would be all right then."

"Like fun it would. . . . You dont mean it anyhow."

"But it's been worth it Nellie, honestly it has." He put his arms round her and kissed her hard still lips. She pushed him away.

"Anyways I aint comin here again. . . . Oh I was so happy comin up the stairs thinkin about seein you. . . . You're paid an the business is all finished."

He noticed that the little curls round her forehead were loose. A wisp of hair hung over one eyebrow.

"Nellie we mustn't part bitterly like this."

"Why not will ye tell me?"

"Because we've both loved one another."

"I'm not goin to cry." She patted her nose with a little rolledup handkerchief. "Georgy I'm goin to hate ye. . . . Goodby." The door snapped sharply to behind her.

Baldwin sat at his desk and chewed the end of a pencil. A faint pungence of her hair lingered in his nostrils. His throat was stiff and lumpy. He coughed. The pencil fell out of his mouth. He wiped the saliva off with his handkerchief and settled himself in his chair. From bleary the crowded paragraphs of the lawbook became clear. He tore the written sheet off the scratchpad and clipped it to the top of a pile of documents. On the new sheet he began: Decision of the Supreme Court of the State of New York. . . . Suddenly he sat up straight in his chair, and started biting the end of his pencil again. From outside came the endless sultry whistle of a peanut wagon. "Oh well, that's that," he said aloud. He went on writing in a wide regular hand: Case of Patterson vs. The State of New York. . . . Decision of the Supreme . . .

Bud sat by a window in the Seamen's Union reading slowly and carefully through a newspaper. Next him two men with freshly shaved rawsteak cheeks cramped into white collars and blue serge storesuits were ponderously playing chess. One of them smoked a pipe that made a little clucking noise when he drew on it. Outside rain beat incessantly on a wide glimmering square.

Banzai, live a thousand years, cried the little gray men of the fourth platoon of Japanese sappers as they advanced to repair the bridge over the Yalu River . . . Special correspondent of the New York Herald . . .

"Checkmate," said the man with the pipe. "Damn it all let's go have a drink. This is no night to be sitting here sober."

"I promised the ole woman . . ."

"None o that crap Jess, I know your kinda promises."
A big crimson hand thickly furred with yellow hairs brushed
the chessmen into their box. "Tell the ole woman you had
to have a nip to keep the weather out."

"That's no lie neither."

Bud watched their shadows hunched into the rain pass
the window.

"What you name?"

Bud turned sharp from the window startled by a shrill
squeaky voice in his ear. He was looking into the fireblue
eyes of a little yellow man who had a face like a toad, large
mouth, protruding eyes and thick closecropped black hair.

Bud's jaw set. "My name's Smith, what about it?"

The little man held out a square callouspalmed hand.
"Plis to meet yez. Me Matty."

Bud took the hand in spite of himself. It squeezed his
until he winced. "Matty what?" he asked. "Me juss
Matty . . . Laplander Matty . . . Come have drink."

"I'm flat," said Bud. "Aint got a red cent."

"On me. Me too much money, take some. . . ." Matty
shoved a hand into either pocket of his baggy checked suit
and punched Bud in the chest with two fistfuls of greenbacks.

"Aw keep yer money . . . I'll take a drink with yous
though."

By the time they got to the saloon on the corner of Pearl
Street Bud's elbows and knees were soaked and a trickle
of cold rain was running down his neck. When they went
up to the bar Laplander Matty put down a five dollar bill.

"Me treat everybody; very happy yet tonight."

Bud was tackling the free lunch. "Hadn't et in a dawg's
age," he explained when he went back to the bar to take
his drink. The whisky burnt his throat all the way down,
dried wet clothes and made him feel the way he used to feel
when he was a kid and got off to go to a baseball game
Saturday afternoon.

"Put it there Lap," he shouted slapping the little man's
broad back. "You an me's friends from now on."

"Hey landlubber, tomorrow me an you ship togezzer. What say?"

"Sure we will."

"Now we go up Bowery Street look at broads. Me pay."

"Aint a Bowery broad would go wid yer, ye little Yap," shouted a tall drunken man with drooping black mustaches who had lurched in between them as they swayed in the swinging doors.

"Zey vont, vont zey?" said the Lap hauling off. One of his hammershaped fists shot in a sudden uppercut under the man's jaw. The man rose off his feet and soared obliquely in through the swinging doors that closed on him. A shout went up from inside the saloon.

"I'll be a sonofabitch, Lappy, I'll be a sonofabitch," roared Bud and slapped him on the back again.

Arm in arm they careened up Pearl Street under the drenching rain. Bars yawned bright to them at the corners of rainseething streets. Yellow light off mirrors and brass rails and gilt frames round pictures of pink naked women was looped and slopped into whiskyglasses guzzled fiery with tipped back head, oozed bright through the blood, popped bubbly out of ears and eyes, dripped spluttering off fingertips. The raindark houses heaved on either side, streetlamps swayed like lanterns carried in a parade, until Bud was in a back room full of nudging faces with a woman on his knees. Laplander Matty stood with his arms round two girls' necks, yanked his shirt open to show a naked man and a naked woman tattooed in red and green on his chest, hugging, stiffly coiled in a seaserpent and when he puffed out his chest and wiggled the skin with his fingers the tatooed man and woman wiggled and all the nudging faces laughed.

Phineas P. Blackhead pushed up the wide office window. He stood looking out over the harbor of slate and mica in the uneven roar of traffic, voices, racket of building that soared from the downtown streets bellying and curling like smoke in the stiff wind shoving down the Hudson out of the northwest.

"Hay Schmidt, bring me my field glasses," he called over his shoulder. "Look . . ." He was focusing the glasses on a thickwaisted white steamer with a sooty yellow stack that was abreast of Governors Island. "Isn't that the *Anonda* coming in now?"

Schmidt was a fat man who had shrunk. The skin hung in loose haggard wrinkles on his face. He took one look through the glasses. "Sure it is." He pushed down the window; the roar receded tapering hollowly like the sound of a sea shell.

"Jiminy they were quick about it. . . . They'll be docked in half an hour. . . . You beat it along over and get hold of Inspector Mulligan. He's all fixed. . . . Dont take your eyes off him. Old Matanzas is out on the warpath trying to get an injunction against us. If every spoonful of manganese isnt off by tomorrow night I'll cut your commission in half. . . . Do you get that?"

Schmidt's loose jowls shook when he laughed. "No danger sir. . . . You ought to know me by this time."

"Of course I do. . . . You're a good feller Schmidt. I was just joking."

Phineas P. Blackhead was a lanky man with silver hair and a red hawkface; he slipped back into the mahogany armchair at his desk and rang an electric bell. "All right Charlie, show em in." he growled at the towheaded officeboy who appeared in the door. He rose stiffly from his desk and held out a hand. "How do you do Mr. Storrow . . . How do you do Mr. Gold. . . . Make yourselves comfortable. . . . That's it. . . . Now look here, about this strike. The attitude of the railroad and docking interests that I represent is one of frankness and honesty, you know that. . . . I have confidence, I can say I have the completest confidence, that we can settle this matter amicably and agreeably. . . . Of course you must meet me halfway. . . . We have I know the same interests at heart, the interests of this great city, of this great seaport. . . ." Mr. Gold moved his hat to the back of his head and cleared his throat with a loud barking noise. "Gentlemen, one of two roads lies before us . . ."

In the sunlight on the windowledge a fly sat scrubbing his wings with his hinder legs. He cleaned himself all over, twisting and untwisting his forelegs like a person soaping his hands, stroking the top of his lobed head carefully; brushing his hair. Jimmy's hand hovered over the fly and slapped down. The fly buzzed tinglingly in his palm. He groped for it with two fingers, held it slowly squeezing it into mashed gray jelly between finger and thumb. He wiped it off under the windowledge. A hot sick feeling went through him. Poor old fly, after washing himself so carefully, too. He stood a long time looking down the airshaft through the dusty pane where the sun gave a tiny glitter to the dust. Now and then a man in shirtsleeves crossed the court below with a tray of dishes. Orders shouted and the clatter of dishwashing came up faintly from the kitchens.

He stared through the tiny glitter of the dust on the windowpane. Mother's had a stroke and next week I'll go back to school.

"Say Herfy have you learned to fight yet?"

"Herfy an the Kid are goin to fight for the flyweight championship before lights."

"But I dont want to."

"Kid wants to. . . . Here he comes. Make a ring there you ginks."

"I dont want to, please."

"You've damn well got to, we'll beat hell outa both of ye if you dont."

"Say Freddy that's a nickel fine from you for swearing."

"Jez I forgot."

"There you go again. . . . Paste him in the slats."

"Go it Herfy, I'm bettin on yer."

"That's it sock him."

The Kid's white screwedup face bouncing in front of him like a balloon; his fist gets Jimmy in the mouth; a salty taste of blood from the cut lip. Jimmy strikes out, gets him down on the bed, pokes his knee in his belly. They pull him off and throw him back against the wall.

"Go it Kid."

"Go it Herfy."

There's a smell of blood in his nose and lungs; his breath rasps. A foot shoots out and trips him up.

"That's enough, Herfy's licked."

"Girlboy . . . Girlboy."

"But hell Freddy he had the Kid down."

"Shut up, don't make such a racket. . . . Old Hoppy'll be coming up."

"Just a little friendly bout, wasn't it Herfy?"

"Get outa my room, all of you, all of you," Jimmy screeches, tear-blinded, striking out with both arms.

"Crybaby . . . crybaby."

He slams the door behind them, pushes the desk against it and crawls trembling into bed. He turns over on his face and lies squirming with shame, biting the pillow.

Jimmy stared through the tiny glitter of the dust on the windowpane.

DARLING

Your poor mother was very unhappy when she finally put you on the train and went back to her big empty rooms at the hotel. Dear, I am very lonely without you. Do you know what I did? I got out all your toy soldiers, the ones that used to be in the taking of Port Arthur, and set them all out in battalions on the library shelf. Wasn't that silly? Never mind dear, Christmas'll soon come round and I'll have my boy again. . . .

A crumpled face on a pillow; mother's had a stroke and next week I'll go back to school. Darkgrained skin growing flabby under her eyes, gray creeping up her brown hair. Mother never laughs. The stroke.

He turned back suddenly into the room, threw himself on the bed with a thin leather book in his hand. The surf thundered loud on the barrier reef. He didn't need to read. Jack was swimming fast through the calm blue waters of the lagoon, stood in the sun on the yellow beach shaking the briny drops off him, opened his nostrils wide to the smell of breadfruit roasting beside his solitary campfire. Birds of bright plumage shrieked and tittered from the tall ferny tops of the coconut palms. The room was drowsy hot. Jimmy fell asleep. There was a strawberry lemon smell, a smell of pineapples on the deck and mother was there in a white suit and a dark man in a yachtingcap, and the sunlight rippled on the milkytall sails. Mother's soft laugh rises into a shriek O-o-o-ohee. A fly the size of a ferryboat walks towards them across the water, reaching out jagged crabclaws. "Yump Yimmy, yump; you can do it in two yumps," the dark man yells in his ear. "But please I dont want to . . . I dont want to," Jimmy whines. The dark man's beating him, yump yump yump. . . . "Yes one moment. Who is it?"

Aunt Emily was at the door. "Why do you keep your door locked Jimmy. . . . I never allow James to lock his door."

"I like it better that way, Aunt Emily."

"Imagine a boy asleep this time of the afternoon."

"I was reading *The Coral Island* and I fell asleep." Jimmy was blushing.

"All right. Come along. Miss Billings said not to stop by mother's room. She's asleep."

They were in the narrow elevator that smelled of castor oil; the colored boy grinned at Jimmy.

"What did the doctor say Aunt Emily?"

"Everything's going as well as could be expected. . . . But you mustn't worry about that. This evening you must have a real good time with your little cousins. . . . You dont see enough children of your own age Jimmy."

They were walking towards the river leaning into a gritty wind that swirled up the street cast out of iron under a dark silvershot sky.

"I guess you'll be glad to get back to school, James."

"Yes Aunt Emily."

"A boy's school days are the happiest time in his life. You must be sure to write your mother once a week at least James. . . . You are all she has now. . . . Miss Billings and I will keep you informed."

"Yes Aunt Emily."

"And James I want you to know my James better. He's the same age you are, only perhaps a little more developed and all that, and you ought to be good friends. . . . I wish Lily had sent you to Hotchkiss too."

"Yes Aunt Emily."

There were pillars of pink marble in the lower hall of Aunt Emily's apartmenthouse and the elevatorboy wore a chocolate livery with brass buttons and the elevator was square and decorated with mirrors. Aunt Emily stopped before a wide red mahogany door on the seventh floor and fumbled in her purse for her key. At the end of the hall was a leaded window through which you could see the Hudson and steamboats and tall trees of smoke rising against the yellow sunset from the yards along the river. When Aunt Emily got the door open they heard the piano. "That's Maisie doing her practicing." In the room where the piano was the rug was thick and mossy, the wallpaper was yellow with silveryshiny roses between the cream woodwork and the gold frames of oilpaintings of woods and people in a gondola and a fat cardinal drinking. Maisie tossed the pigtails off her shoulders as she jumped off the pianostool. She had a round creamy face and a slight pugnose. The metronome went on ticking.

"Hello James," she said after she had tilted her mouth up to her mother's to be kissed. "I'm awfully sorry poor Aunt Lily's so sick."

"Arent you going to kiss your cousin, James?" said Aunt Emily.

Jimmy shambled up to Maisie and pushed his face against hers.

"That's a funny kind of a kiss," said Maisie.

"Well you two children can keep each other company till

dinner." Aunt Emily rustled through the blue velvet curtains into the next room.

"We wont be able to go on calling you James." After she had stopped the metronome, Maisie stood staring with serious brown eyes at her cousin. "There cant be two Jameses can there?"

"Mother calls me Jimmy."

"Jimmy's a kinder common name, but I guess it'll have to do till we can think of a better one. . . . How many jacks can you pick up?"

"What are jacks?"

"Gracious dont you know what jackstones are? Wait till James comes back, wont he laugh!"

"I know Jack roses. Mother used to like them better'n any other kind."

"American Beauties are the only roses I like," announced Maisie flopping into a Morris chair. Jimmy stood on one leg kicking his heel with the toes of the other foot.

"Where's James?"

"He'll be home soon. . . . He's having his riding lesson."

The twilight became leadensilent between them. From the trainyards came the scream of a locomotivewhistle and the clank of couplings on shunted freight cars. Jimmy ran to the window.

"Say Maisie, do you like engines?" he asked.

"I think they are horrid. Daddy says we're going to move on account of the noise and smoke."

Through the gloom Jimmy could make out the beveled smooth bulk of a big locomotive. The smoke rolled out of the stack in huge bronze and lilac coils. Down the track a red light snapped green. The bell started to ring slowly, lazily. Forced draft snorting loud the train clankingly moved, gathered speed, slid into dusk swinging a red taillight.

"Gee I wish we lived here," said Jimmy. "I've got two hundred and seventytwo pictures of locomotives, I'll show em to you sometime if you like. I collect em."

"What a funny thing to collect. . . . Look Jimmy you pull the shade down and I'll light the light."

When Maisie pushed the switch they saw James Merivale standing in the door. He had light wiry hair and a freckled face with a pugnose like Maisie's. He had on riding breeches and black leather gaiters and was flicking a long peeled stick about.

"Hullo Jimmy," he said. "Welcome to our city."

"Say James," cried Maisie, "Jimmy doesn't know what jackstones are."

Aunt Emily appeared through the blue velvet curtains. She wore a highnecked green silk blouse with lace on it. Her white hair rose in a smooth curve from her forehead. "It's time you children were washing up," she said, "dinner's in five minutes. . . . James take your cousin back to your room and hurry up and take off those ridingclothes."

Everybody was already seated when Jimmy followed his cousin into the diningroom. Knives and forks tinkled discreetly in the light of six candles in red and silver shades. At the end of the table sat Aunt Emily, next to her a rednecked man with no back to his head, and at the other end Uncle Jeff with a pearl pin in his checked necktie filled a broad armchair. The colored maid hovered about the fringe of light passing toasted crackers. Jimmy ate his soup stiffly, afraid of making a noise. Uncle Jeff was talking in a booming voice between spoonfuls of soup.

"No I tell you, Wilkinson, New York is no longer what it used to be when Emily and I first moved up here about the time the Ark landed. . . . City's overrun with kikes and low Irish, that's what's the matter with it. . . . In ten years a Christian wont be able to make a living. . . . I tell you the Catholics and the Jews are going to run us out of our own country, that's what they are going to do."

"It's the New Jerusalem," put in Aunt Emily laughing.

"It's no laughing matter; when a man's worked hard all his life to build up a business and that sort of thing he dont want to be run out by a lot of damn foreigners, does he Wilkinson?"

"Jeff you are getting all excited. You know it gives you indigestion. . . ."

"I'll keep cool, mother."

"The trouble with the people of this country is this, Mr. Merivale" . . . Mr. Wilkinson frowned ponderously. "The people of this country are too tolerant. There's no other country in the world where they'd allow it. . . . After all we built up this country and then we allow a lot of foreigners, the scum of Europe, the offscourings of Polish ghettos to come and run it for us."

"The fact of the matter is that an honest man wont soil his hands with politics, and he's given no inducement to take public office."

"That's true, a live man, nowadays, wants more money, needs more money than he can make honestly in public life. . . . Naturally the best men turn to other channels."

"And add to that the ignorance of these dirty kikes and shanty Irish that we make voters before they can even talk English . . ." began Uncle Jeff.

The maid set a highpiled dish of fried chicken edged by corn fritters before Aunt Emily. Talk lapsed while everyone was helped. "Oh I forgot to tell you Jeff," said Aunt Emily, "we're to go up to Scarsdale Sunday."

"Oh mother I hate going out Sundays."

"He's a perfect baby about staying home."

"But Sunday's the only day I get at home."

"Well it was this way: I was having tea with the Harland girls at Maillard's and who should sit down at the next table but Mrs. Burkhart . . . "

"Is that Mrs. John B. Burkhart? Isnt he one of the vice-presidents of the National City Bank?"

"John's a fine feller and a coming man downtown."

"Well as I was saying dear, Mrs. Burkhart said we just had to come up and spend Sunday with them and I just couldn't refuse."

"My father," continued Mr. Wilkinson, "used to be old Johannes Burkhart's physician. The old man was a cranky old bird, he'd made his pile in the fur trade way back in

Colonel Astor's day. He had the gout and used to swear
something terrible. . . . I remember seeing him once, a redfaced old man with long white hair and a silk skullcap over
his baldspot. He had a parrot named Tobias and people
going along the street never knew whether it was Tobias
or Judge Burkhart cussing."

"Ah well, times have changed," said Aunt Emily.

Jimmy sat in his chair with pins and needles in his legs.
Mother's had a stroke and next week I'll go back to school.
Friday, Saturday, Sunday, Monday. . . . He and Skinny
coming back from playing with the hoptoads down by the
pond, in their blue suits because it was Sunday afternoon.
Smokebushes were in bloom behind the barn. A lot of
fellows teasing little Harris, calling him Iky because he
was supposed to be a Jew. His voice rose in a singsong
whine; "Cut it fellers, cant you fellers. I've got my best
suit on fellers."

"Oy Oy Meester Solomon Levy with his best Yiddisher
garments all marked down," piped jeering voices. "Did you
buy it in a five and ten Iky?"

"I bet he got it at a firesale."

"If he got it at a firesale we ought to turn the hose on
him."

"Let's turn the hose on Solomon Levy."

"Oh stop it fellers."

"Shut up; dont yell so loud."

"They're juss kiddin, they wont hurt him," whispered
Skinny.

Iky was carried kicking and bawling down towards the
pond, his white tearwet face upside down. "He's not a Jew
at all," said Skinny. "But I'll tell you who is a Jew, that
big bully Fat Swanson."

"Howjer know?"

"His roommate told me."

"Gee whiz they're going to do it."

They ran in all directions. Little Harris with his hair
full of mud was crawling up the bank, water running out
of his coatsleeves.

There was hot chocolate sauce with the icecream. "An Irishman and a Scotchman were walking down the street and the Irishman said to the Scotchman; Sandy let's have a drink. . . ." A prolonged ringing at the front door bell was making them inattentive to Uncle Jeff's story. The colored maid flurried back into the diningroom and began whispering in Aunt Emily's ear. ". . . And the Scotchman said, Mike . . . Why what's the matter?"

"It's Mr. Joe sir."

"The hell it is."

"Well maybe he's all right," said Aunt Emily hastily.

"A bit whipsey, ma'am."

"Sarah why the dickens did you let him in?"

"I didnt let him, he juss came."

Uncle Jeff pushed his plate away and slapped down his napkin. "Oh hell . . . I'll go talk to him."

"Try and make him go . . ." Aunt Emily had begun; she stopped with her mouth partly open. A head was stuck through the curtains that hung in the wide doorway to the livingroom. It had a birdlike face, with a thin drooping nose, topped by a mass of straight black hair like an Indian's. One of the redrimmed eyes winked quietly.

"Hullo everybody! . . . How's every lil thing? Mind if I butt in?" His voice perked hoarsely as a tall skinny body followed the head through the curtains. Aunt Emily's mouth arranged itself in a frosty smile. "Why Emily you must . . . er . . . excuse me; I felt an evening . . . er . . . round the family hearth . . . er . . . would be . . . er . . . er . . . beneficial. You understand, the refining influence of the home." He stood jiggling his head behind Uncle Jeff's chair. "Well Jefferson ole boy, how's the market?" He brought a hand down on Uncle Jeff's shoulder.

"Oh all right. Want to sit down?" he growled.

"They tell me . . . if you'll take a tip from an old timer . . . er . . . a retired broker . . . broker and broker every day . . . ha-ha. . . . But they tell me that Interborough Rapid Transit's worth trying a snifter of. . . . Doan look at me crosseyed like that Emily. I'm going right away. . . .

Why howdedo Mr. Wilkinson. . . . Kids are looking well.
Well I'll be if that isn't Lily Herf's lil boy. . . . Jimmy you
dont remember your . . . er . . . cousin, Joe Harland do
you? Nobody remembers Joe Harland. . . . Except you
Emily and you wish you could forget him . . . ha-ha. . . .
How's your mother Jimmy?"

"A little better thank you," Jimmy forced the words out
through a tight throat.

"Well when you go home you give her my love . . . she'll
understand. Lily and I have always been good friends even
if I am the family skeleton. . . . They dont like me, they
wish I'd go away. . . . I'll tell you what boy, Lily's the
best of the lot. Isn't she Emily, isn't she the best of the
lot of us?"

Aunt Emily cleared her throat. "Sure she is, the best
looking, the cleverest, the realest. . . . Jimmy your mother's
an emperess. . . . Aways been too fine for all this. By
gorry I'd like to drink her health."

"Joe you might moderate your voice a little;" Aunt Emily
clicked out the words like a typewriter.

"Aw you all think I'm drunk. . . . Remember this Jimmy"
. . . he leaned across the table, stroked Jimmy's face with
his grainy whisky breath . . . "these things aren't always a
man's fault . . . circumstances . . . er . . . circumstances."
He upset a glass staggering to his feet. "If Emily insists
on looking at me crosseyed I'm goin out. . . . But remember
give Lily Herf Joe Harland's love even if he has gone to
the demnition bowbows." He lurched out through the curtains again.

"Jeff I know he'll upset the Sèvres vase. . . . See that
he gets out all right and get him a cab." James and Maisie
burst into shrill giggles from behind their napkins. Uncle
Jeff was purple.

"I'll be damned to hell if I put him in a cab. He's not
my cousin. . . . He ought to be locked up. And next time
you see him you can tell him this from me, Emily: if he
ever comes here in that disgusting condition again I'll throw
him out."

"Jefferson dear, it's no use getting angry. . . . There's no harm done. He's gone."

"No harm done! Think of our children. Suppose there'd been a stranger here instead of Wilkinson. What would he have thought of our home?"

"Dont worry about that," croaked Mr. Wilkinson, "accidents will happen in the best regulated families."

"Poor Joe's such a sweet boy when he's himself," said Aunt Emily. "And think that it looked for a while years ago as if Harland held the whole Curb Market in the palm of his hand. The papers called him the King of the Curb, dont you remember?" "That was before the Lottie Smithers affair. . . ."

"Well suppose you children go and play in the other room while we have our coffee," chirped Aunt Emily. "Yes, they ought to have gone long ago."

"Can you play Five Hundred, Jimmy?" asked Maisie.

"No I cant."

"What do you think of that James, he cant play jacks and he cant play Five Hundred."

"Well they're both girl's games," said James loftily. "I wouldn't play em either xept on account of you."

"Oh wouldn't you, Mr. Smarty."

"Let's play animal grabs."

"But there aren't enough of us for that. It's no fun without a crowd."

"An last time you got the giggles so bad mother made us stop."

"Mother made us stop because you kicked little Billy Schmutz in the funnybone an made him cry."

"Spose we go down an look at the trains," put in Jimmy.

"We're not allowed to go down stairs after dark," said Maisie severely.

"I'll tell you what lets play stock exchange. . . . I've got a million dollars in bonds to sell and Maisie can be the bulls an Jimmy can be the bears."

"All right, what do we do?"

"Oh juss run round an yell mostly. . . . I'm selling short."

"All right Mr. Broker I'll buy em all at five cents each."

"No you cant say that. . . . You say ninetysix and a half or something like that."

"I'll give you five million for them," cried Maisie waving the blotter of the writing desk.

"But you fool, they're only worth one million," shouted Jimmy.

Maisie stood still in her tracks. "Jimmy what did you say then?" Jimmy felt shame flame up through him; he looked at his stubby shoes. "I said, you fool."

"Haven't you ever been to Sunday school? Don't you know that God says in the Bible that if you call anybody Thou fool you'll be in danger of hellfire?"

Jimmy didn't dare raise his eyes.

"Well I'm not going to play any more," said Maisie drawing herself up. Jimmy somehow found himself out in the hall. He grabbed his hat and ran out the door and down the six flights of white stone stairs past the brass buttons and chocolate livery of the elevator boy, out through the hall that had pink marble pillars in to Seventysecond Street. It was dark and blowy, full of ponderous advancing shadows and chasing footsteps. At last he was climbing the familiar crimson stairs of the hotel. He hurried past his mother's door. They'd ask him why he had come home so soon. He burst into his own room, shot the bolt, doublelocked the door and stood leaning against it panting.

"Well are you married yet?" was the first thing Congo asked when Emile opened the door to him. Emile was in his undershirt. The shoebox-shaped room was stuffy, lit and heated by a gas crown with a tin cap on it.

"Where are you in from this time?"

"Bizerta and Trondjeb. . . . I'm an able seaman."

"That's a rotten job, going to sea. . . . I've saved two hundred dollars. I'm working at Delmonico's."

They sat down side by side on the unmade bed. Congo

produced a package of gold tipped Egyptian Deities. "Four
months' pay"; he slapped his thigh. "Seen May Sweitzer?"
Emile shook his head. "I'll have to find the little son of a
gun. . . . In those goddam Scandinavian ports they come out
in boats, big fat blond women in bumboats. . . . "

They were silent. The gas hummed. Congo let his breath
out in a whistle. "Whee . . . C'est chic ça, Delmonico . . .
Why havent you married her?"

"She likes to have me hang around. . . . I'd run the store
better than she does."

"You're too easy; got to use rough stuff with women to get
anything outa them. . . . Make her jealous."

"She's got me going."

"Want to see some postalcards?" Congo pulled a package,
wrapped in newspaper out of his pocket. "Look these are
Naples; everybody there wants to come to New York. . . .
That's an Arab dancing girl. Nom d'une vache they got slippery bellybuttons. . . ."

"Say, I know what I'll do," cried Emile suddenly dropping
the cards on the bed. "I'll make her jealous. . . ."

"Who?"

"Ernestine . . . Madame Rigaud. . . . "

"Sure walk up an down Eighth Avenue with a girl a couple
of times an I bet she'll fall like a ton of bricks."

The alarmclock went off on the chair beside the bed.
Emile jumped up to stop it and began splashing water on his
face in the washbasin.

"Merde I got to go to work."

"I'll go over to Hell's Kitchen an see if I can find May."

"Don't be a fool an spend all your money," said Emile who
stood at the cracked mirror with his face screwed up, fasten-
ing the buttons in the front of a clean boiled shirt.

"It's a sure thing I'm tellin yer," said the man again and
again, bringing his face close to Ed Thatcher's face and
rapping the desk with his flat hand.

"Maybe it is Viler but I seen so many of em go under, honest I dont see how I can risk it."

"Man I've hocked the misses's silver teaset and my diamond ring an the baby's mug. . . . It's a sure sure thing. . . . I wouldn't let you in on it, xept you an me's been pretty good friends an I owe you money an everythin. . . . You'll make twentyfive percent on your money by tomorrow noon. . . . Then if you want to hold you can on a gamble, but if you sell three quarters and hold the rest two or three days on a chance you're safe as . . . as the Rock of Gibraltar."

"I know Viler, it certainly sounds good. . . ."

"Hell man you dont want to be in this damned office all your life, do you? Think of your little girl."

"I am, that's the trouble."

"But Ed, Gibbons and Swandike had started buying already at three cents when the market closed this evening. . . . Klein got wise an'll be right there with bells on first thing in the morning. The market'll go crazy on it. . . . "

"Unless the fellers doin the dirty work change their minds. I know that stuff through and through, Viler. . . . Sounds like a topnotch proposition. . . . But I've examined the books of too many bankrupts."

Viler got to his feet and threw his cigar into the cuspidor. "Well do as you like, damn it all. . . . I guess you must like commuting from Hackensack an working twelve hours a day. . . . "

"I believe in workin my way up, that's all."

"What's the use of a few thousands salted away when you're old and cant get any satisfaction? Man I'm goin in with both feet."

"Go to it Viler. . . . You tellem," muttered Thatcher as the other man stamped out slamming the office door.

The big office with its series of yellow desks and hooded typewriters was dark except for the tent of light in which Thatcher sat at a desk piled with ledgers. The three windows at the end were not curtained. Through them he could see the steep bulk of buildings scaled with lights and a plankshaped bit of inky sky. He was copying memoranda on a long sheet of legal cap.

FanTan Import and Export Company (statement of assets and liabilities up to and including February 29) . . . Branches New York, Shanghai, Hongkong and Straights Settlements. . . .

Balance carried over $345,789.84
Real Estate   500,087.12
Profit and Loss   399,765.90

"A bunch of goddam crooks," growled Thatcher out loud. "Not an item on the whole thing that aint faked. I dont believe they've got any branches in Hongkong or anywhere. . . . "

He leaned back in his chair and stared out of the window. The buildings were going dark. He could just make out a star in the patch of sky. Ought to go out an eat, bum for the digestion to eat irregularly like I do. Suppose I'd taken a plunge on Viler's red hot tip. Ellen, how do you like these American Beauty roses? They have stems eight feet long, and I want you to look over the itinerary of the trip abroad I've mapped out to finish your education. Yes it will be a shame to leave our fine new apartment looking out over Central Park. . . . And downtown; The Fiduciary Accounting Institute, Edward C. Thatcher, President. . . . Blobs of steam were drifting up across the patch of sky, hiding the star. Take a plunge, take a plunge . . . they're all crooks and gamblers anyway . . . take a plunge and come up with your hands full, pockets full, bankaccount full, vaults full of money. If I only dared take the risk. Fool to waste your time fuming about it. Get back to the FanTan Import. Steam faintly ruddy with light reflected from the streets swarmed swiftly up across the patch of sky, twisting scattering.

Goods on hand in U. S. bonded warehouses . . . $325,666.00

Take a plunge and come up with three hundred and

twentyfive thousand, six hundred and sixtysix dollars. Dollars swarming up like steam, twisting scattering against the stars. Millionaire Thatcher leaned out of the window of the bright patchouliscented room to look at the dark-jutting city steaming with laughter, voices, tinkling and lights; behind him orchestras played among the azaleas, private wires click click clickclicked dollars from Singapore, Valparaiso, Mukden, Hongkong, Chicago. Susie leaned over him in a dress made of orchids, breathed in his ear.

Ed Thatcher got to his feet with clenched fists sniveling; You poor fool whats the use now she's gone. I'd better go eat or Ellen'll scold me.

V. Steamroller

Dusk gently smooths crispangled streets. Dark presses tight the steaming asphalt city, crushes the fretwork of windows and lettered signs and chimneys and watertanks and ventilators and fire-escapes and moldings and patterns and corrugations and eyes and hands and neckties into blue chunks, into black enormous blocks. Under the rolling heavier heavier pressure windows blurt light. Night crushes bright milk out of arclights, squeezes the sullen blocks until they drip red, yellow, green into streets resounding with feet. All the asphalt oozes light. Light spurts from lettering on roofs, mills dizzily among wheels, stains rolling tons of sky.

A STEAMROLLER was clattering back and forth over the freshly tarred metaling of the road at the cemetery gate. A smell of scorched grease and steam and hot paint came from it. Jimmy Herf picked his way along the edge of the road; the stones were sharp against his feet through the worn soles of his shoes. He brushed past swarthy-necked workmen and walked on over the new road with a whiff of garlic and sweat from them in his nostrils. After a hundred yards he stopped over the gray suburban road, laced tight on both sides with telegraph poles and wires, over the gray paperbox houses and the gray jagged lots of monumentmakers, the sky was the color of a robin's egg. Little worms of May were writhing in his blood. He yanked off his black necktie and put it in his pocket. A tune was grinding crazily through his head:

I'm so tired of vi-olets
Take them all away.

There is one glory of the sun and another glory of the moon and another glory of the stars: for one star differeth from another star in glory. So also is the resurrection of the dead. . . . He walked on fast splashing through puddles full of sky, trying to shake the droning welloiled words out of his ears, to get the feeling of black crêpe off his fingers, to forget the smell of lilies.

> I'm so tired of vi-olets
> Take them all away.

He walked faster. The road climbed a hill. There was a bright runnel of water in the ditch, flowing through patches of grass and dandelions. There were fewer houses; on the sides of barns peeling letters spelled out LYDIA PINK-HAM'S VEGETABLE COMPOUND, BUDWEISER, RED HEN, BARKING DOG. . . . And muddy had had a stroke and now she was buried. He couldn't think how she used to look; she was dead that was all. From a fencepost came the moist whistling of a songsparrow. The minute rusty bird flew ahead, perched on a telegraph wire and sang, and flew ahead to the rim of an abandoned boiler and sang, and flew ahead and sang. The sky was getting a darker blue, filling with flaked motherofpearl clouds. For a last moment he felt the rustle of silk beside him, felt a hand in a trailing lacefrilled sleeve close gently over his hand. Lying in his crib with his feet pulled up cold under the menace of the shaggy crouching shadows; and the shadows scuttled melting into corners when she leaned over him with curls round her forehead, in silkpuffed sleeves, with a tiny black patch at the corner of the mouth that kissed his mouth. He walked faster. The blood flowed full and hot in his veins. The flaked clouds were melting into rosecolored foam. He could hear his steps on the worn macadam. At a crossroad the sun glinted on the sticky pointed buds of a beechsapling. Opposite a sign read YONKERS. In the middle of the road teetered a dented tomatocan. Kicking it hard in front of him he walked on. One glory of the sun and another glory of the moon and another glory of the stars. . . . He walked on.

"Hullo Emile!" Emile nodded without turning his head. The girl ran after him and grabbed his coatsleeve. "That's the way you treat your old friends is it? Now that you're keepin company with that delicatessen queen . . ."

Emile yanked his hand away. "I am in a 'urree zat's all."

"How'd ye like it if I went an told her how you an me framed it up to stand in front of the window on Eighth Avenue huggin an kissin juss to make her fall for yez."

"Zat was Congo's idea."

"Well didn't it woik?"

"Sure."

"Well aint there sumpen due me?"

"May you're a veree nice leetle girl. Next week my night off is Wednesday. . . . I'll come by an take you to a show. . . . 'Ow's 'ustlin?"

"Worse'n hell. . . . I'm tryin out for a dancin job up at the Campus. . . . That's where you meet guys wid jack. . . . No more of dese sailor boys and shorefront stiffs. . . . I'm gettin respectable."

"May 'ave you 'eard from Congo?"

"Got a postalcard from some goddam place I couldn't read the name of. . . . Aint it funny when you write for money an all ye git 's a postal ca-ard. . . . That's the kid gits me for the askin any night. . . . An he's the only one, savvy, Frogslegs?"

"Goodby May." He suddenly pushed the straw bonnet trimmed with forgetmenots back on her head and kissed her.

"Hey quit dat Frogslegs . . . Eighth Avenue aint no place to kiss a girl," she whined pushing a yellow curl back under her hat. "I could git you run in an I've half a mind to."

Emile walked off.

A fire engine, a hosewagon, and a hookandladder passed him, shattering the street with clattering roar. Three blocks down smoke and an occasional gasp of flame came from the roof of a house. A crowd was jammed up against the policelines. Beyond backs and serried hats Emile caught a glimpse of firemen on the roof of the next house and of three silently glittering streams of water playing into the upper windows. Must be right opposite the delicatessen. He was making his way through the jam on the sidewalk when the crowd suddenly opened. Two policemen were dragging out a negro whose arms snapped back and forth like broken cables. A third cop came behind cracking the negro first on one side of the head, then on the other with his billy.

"It's a shine 'at set the fire."

"They caught the firebug."

" 'At's 'e incendiary."

"God he's a meanlookin smoke."

The crowd closed in. Emile was standing beside Madame Rigaud in front of the door of her store.

"Cheri que ça me fait une emotiong. . . . J'ai horriblemong peu du feu."

Emile was standing a little behind her. He let one arm crawl slowly round her waist and patted her arm with his other hand, "Everyting awright. Look no more fire, only smoke. . . . But you are insured, aint you?"

"Oh yes for fifteen tousand." He squeezed her hand and then took his arms away. "Viens ma petite on va rentrer."

Once inside the shop he took both her plump hands. "Ernestine when we get married?"

"Next month."

"I no wait zat long, imposseeble. . . . Why not next Wednesday? Then I can help you make inventory of stock. . . . I tink maybe we can sell this place and move uptown, make bigger money."

She patted him on the cheek. "P'tit ambitieux," she said through her hollow inside laugh that made her shoulders and her big bust shake.

They had to change at Manhattan Transfer. The thumb of Ellen's new kid glove had split and she kept rubbing it nervously with her forefinger. John wore a belted raincoat and a pinkishgray felt hat. When he turned to her and smiled she couldn't help pulling her eyes away and staring out at the long rain that shimmered over the tracks.

"Here we are Elaine dear. Oh prince's daughter, you see we get the train that comes from the Penn station. . . . It's funny this waiting in the wilds of New Jersey this way." They got into the parlorcar. John made a little clucking sound in his mouth at the raindrops that made dark dimes on his pale hat. "Well we're off, little girl. . . . Behold thou art fair my love, thou art fair, thou hast dove's eyes within thy locks."

Ellen's new tailored suit was tight at the elbows. She wanted to feel very gay and listen to his purring whisper in her ears, but something had set her face in a tight frown; she could only look out at the brown marshes and the million black windows of factories and the puddly streets of towns and a rusty steamboat in a canal and barns and Bull Durham signs and roundfaced Spearmint gnomes all barred and crisscrossed with bright flaws of rain. The jeweled stripes on the window ran straight down when the train stopped and got more and more oblique as it speeded up. The wheels rumbled in her head, saying Man-hattan Tran-sfer. Man-hattan Tran-sfer. Anyway it was a long time before Atlantic City. By the time we get to Atlantic City . . . *Oh it rained forty days* . . . I'll be feeling gay. . . . *And it rained forty nights.* . . . I've got to be feeling gay.

"Elaine Thatcher Oglethorpe, that's a very fine name, isn't it, darling? Oh stay me with flagons, comfort me with apples for I am sick of love. . . ."

It was so comfortable in the empty parlorcar in the green velvet chair with John leaning towards her reciting nonsense with the brown marshlands slipping by behind the rainstriped window and a smell like clams seeping into the car. She looked into his face and laughed. A blush ran all over his face to the roots of his redblond hair. He put his hand in its yellow glove over her hand in its white glove "You're my wife now Elaine."

"You're my husband now John." And laughing they looked at each other in the coziness of the empty parlorcar.

White letters, ATLANTIC CITY, spelled doom over the rainpitted water.

Rain lashed down the glaring boardwalk and crashed in gusts against the window like water thrown out of a bucket. Beyond the rain she could hear the intermittent rumble of the surf along the beach between the illuminated piers. She lay on her back staring at the ceiling. Beside her in the big bed John lay asleep breathing quietly like a child with a pillow doubled up under his head. She was icy cold. She slid out of bed very carefully not to wake him, and stood looking out the window down the very long V of lights of the boardwalk. She pushed up the window. The rain lashed in her face spitefully stinging her flesh, wetting her nightdress. She pushed her forehead against the frame. Oh I want to die. I want to die. All the tight coldness of her body was clenching in her stomach. Oh I'm going to be sick. She went into the bathroom and closed the door. When she had vomited she felt better. Then she climbed into bed again careful not to touch John. If she touched him she would die. She lay on her back with her hands tight against her sides and her feet together. The parlor-car rumbled cozily in her head; she fell asleep.

Wind rattling the windowframes wakened her. John was far away, the other side of the big bed. With the wind and the rain streaming in the window it was as if the room and the big bed and everything were moving, running forward like an airship over the sea. *Oh it rained forty days....* Through a crack in the cold stiffness the little tune trickled warm as blood. . . . *And it rained forty nights.* Gingerly she drew a hand over her husband's hair. He screwed his face up in his sleep and whined "Dont" in a littleboy's voice that made her giggle. She lay giggling on the far edge of the bed, giggling desperately as she used to with girls at school. And the rain lashed through the window and the song grew louder until it was a brass band in her ears:

Oh it rained forty days
And it rained forty nights
And it didn't stop till Christmas
And the only man that survived the flood
Was longlegged Jack of the Isthmus.

Jimmy Herf sits opposite Uncle Jeff. Each has before
him on a blue plate a chop, a baked potato, a little mound
of peas and a sprig of parsely.

"Well look about you Jimmy," says Uncle Jeff. Bright
topstory light brims the walnutpaneled diningroom, glints
twistedly on silver knives and forks, gold teeth, watch-chains,
scarfpins, is swallowed up in the darkness of broadcloth
and tweed, shines roundly on polished plates and bald heads
and covers of dishes. "Well what do you think of it?" asks
Uncle Jeff burying his thumbs in the pockets of his fuzzy
buff vest.

"It's a fine club all right," says Jimmy.

"The wealthiest and the most successful men in the
country eat lunch up here. Look at the round table in the
corner. That's the Gausenheimers' table. Just to the left."
. . . Uncle Jeff leans forward lowering his voice, "the
man with the powerful jaw is J. Wilder Laporte." Jimmy
cuts into his muttonchop without answering. "Well Jimmy,
you probably know why I brought you down here . . . I
want to talk to you. Now that your poor mother has . . .
has been taken, Emily and I are your guardians in the eyes
of the law and the executors of poor Lily's will. . . . I want
to explain to you just how things stand." Jimmy puts down
his knife and fork and sits staring at his uncle, clutching the
arms of his chair with cold hands, watching the jowl move
blue and heavy above the ruby stickpin in the wide satin
cravat. "You are sixteen now aren't you Jimmy?"

"Yes sir."

"Well it's this way. . . . When your mother's estate is
all settled up you'll find yourself in the possession of approximately fiftyfive hundred dollars. Luckily you are a bright

fellow and will be ready for college early. Now, properly husbanded that sum ought to see you through Columbia, since you insist on going to Columbia. . . . I myself, and I'm sure your Aunt Emily feels the same way about it, would much rather see you go to Yale or Princeton. . . . You are a very lucky fellow in my estimation. At your age I was sweeping out an office in Fredericksburg and earning fifteen dollars a month. Now what I wanted to say was this . . . I have not noticed that you felt sufficient responsibility about moneymatters . . . er . . . sufficient enthusiasm about earning your living, making good in a man's world. Look around you. . . . Thrift and enthusiasm has made these men what they are. It's made me, put me in the position to offer you the comfortable home, the cultured surroundings that I do offer you. . . . I realize that your education has been a little peculiar, that poor Lily did not have quite the same ideas that we have on many subjects, but the really formative period of your life is beginning. Now's the time to take a brace and lay the foundations of your future career. . . . What I advise is that you follow James's example and work your way up through the firm. . . . From now on you are both sons of mine. . . . It will mean hard work but it'll eventually offer a very substantial opening. And dont forget this, if a man's a success in New York, he's a success!" Jimmy sits watching his uncle's broad serious mouth forming words, without tasting the juicy mutton of the chop he is eating. "Well what are you going to make of yourself?" Uncle Jeff leaned towards him across the table with bulging gray eyes.

Jimmy chokes on a piece of bread, blushes, at last stammers weakly, "Whatever you say Uncle Jeff."

"Does that mean you'll go to work for a month this summer in my office? Get a taste of how it feels to make a living, like a man in a man's world, get an idea of how the business is run?" Jimmy nods his head. "Well I think you've come to a very sensible decision," booms Uncle Jeff leaning back in his chair so that the light strikes across the wave of his steelgray hair. "By the way what'll you have for dessert? . . . Years from now Jimmy, when you are a successful man with a business of your own we'll remember this talk. It's the beginning of your career."

The hatcheck girl smiles from under the disdainful pile of her billowy blond hair when she hands Jimmy his hat that looks squashed flat and soiled and limp among the big-bellied derbies and the fedoras and the majestic panamas hanging on the pegs. His stomach turns a somersault with the drop of the elevator. He steps out into the crowded marble hall. For a moment not knowing which way to go, he stands back against the wall with his hands in his pockets, watching people elbow their way through the perpetually revolving doors; softcheeked girls chewing gum, hatchetfaced girls with bangs, creamfaced boys his own age, young toughs with their hats on one side, sweatyfaced messengers, crisscross glances, sauntering hips, red jowls masticating cigars, sallow concave faces, flat bodies of young men and women, paunched bodies of elderly men, all elbowing, shoving, shuffling, fed in two endless tapes through the revolving doors out into Broadway, in off Broadway. Jimmy fed in a tape in and out the revolving doors, noon and night and morning, the revolving doors grinding out his years like sausage meat. All of a sudden his muscles stiffen. Uncle Jeff and his office can go plumb to hell. The words are so loud inside him he glances to one side and the other to see if anyone heard him say them.

They can all go plumb to hell. He squares his shoulders and shoves his way to the revolving doors. His heel comes down on a foot. "For crissake look where yer steppin." He's out in the street. A swirling wind down Broadway blows grit in his mouth and eyes. He walks down towards the Battery with the wind in his back. In Trinity Churchyard stenographers and officeboys are eating sandwiches among the tombs. Outlandish people cluster outside steamship lines; towhaired Norwegians, broadfaced Swedes, Polacks, swarthy stumps of men that smell of garlic from the Mediterranean, mountainous Slavs, three Chinamen, a bunch of Lascars. On the little triangle in front of the

Customhouse, Jim Herf turns and stares long up the deep gash of Broadway, facing the wind squarely. Uncle Jeff and his office can go plumb to hell.

Bud sat on the edge of his cot and stretched out his arms and yawned. From all round through a smell of sweat and sour breath and wet clothes came snores, the sound of men stirring in their sleep, creaking of bedsprings. Far away through the murk burned a single electric light. Bud closed his eyes and let his head fall over on his shoulder. O God I want to go to sleep. Sweet Jesus I want to go to sleep. He pressed his knees together against his clasped hands to keep them from trembling. Our father which art in Heaven I want to go to sleep.

"Wassa matter pardner cant ye sleep?" came a quiet whisper from the next cot.

"Hell, no." "Me neither."

Bud looked at the big head of curly hair held up on an elbow turned towards him.

"This is a hell of a lousy stinking flop," went on the voice evenly. "I'll tell the world . . . Forty cents too! They can take their Hotel Plaza an . . . "

"Been long in the city?"

"Ten years come August."

"Great snakes!"

A voice rasped down the line of cots, "Cut de comedy yous guys, what do you tink dis is, a Jewish picnic?"

Bud lowered his voice: "Funny, it's years I been thinkin an wantin to come to the city. . . . I was born an raised on a farm upstate."

"Why dont ye go back?"

"I cant go back." Bud was cold; he wanted to stop trembling. He pulled the blanket up to his chin and rolled over facing the man who was talking. "Every spring I says to myself I'll hit the road again, go out an plant myself among the weeds an the grass an the cows comin home milkin time, but I dont; I juss kinder hangs on."

"What d'ye do all this time in the city?"

"I dunno. . . . I used to set in Union Square most of the time, then I set in Madison Square. I been up in Hoboken an Joisey and Flatbush an now I'm a Bowery bum."

"God I swear I'm goin to git outa here tomorrow. I git sceered here. Too many bulls an detectives in this town."

"You could make a livin in handouts. . . . But take it from me kid you go back to the farm an the ole folks while the goin's good."

Bud jumped out of bed and yanked roughly at the man's shoulder. "Come over here to the light, I want to show ye sumpen." Bud's own voice crinkled queerly in his ears. He strode along the snoring lane of cots. The bum, a shambling man with curly weatherbleached hair and beard and eyes as if hammered into his head, climbed fully dressed out from the blankets and followed him. Under the light Bud unbuttoned the front of his unionsuit and pulled it off his knottymuscled gaunt arms and shoulders. "Look at my back."

"Christ Jesus," whispered the man running a grimy hand with long yellow nails over the mass of white and red deepgouged scars. "I aint never seen nothin like it."

"That's what the ole man done to me. For twelve years he licked me when he had a mind to. Used to strip me and take a piece of light chain to my back. They said he was my dad but I know he aint. I run away when I was thirteen. That was when he ketched me an began to lick me. I'm twentyfive now."

They went back without speaking to their cots and lay down.

Bud lay staring at the ceiling with the blanket up to his eyes. When he looked down towards the door at the end of the room, he saw standing there a man in a derby hat with a cigar in his mouth. He crushed his lower lip between his teeth to keep from crying out. When he looked again the man was gone. "Say are you awake yet?" he whispered.

The bum grunted. "I was goin to tell yer. I mashed his head in with the grubbinhoe, mashed it in like when you kick a rotten punkin. I told him to lay offn me an he wouldn't. . . . He was a hard godfearin man an he wanted you to be sceered of him. We was grubbin the sumach outa the old pasture to plant pertoters there. . . . I let him lay till night with his head mashed in like a rotten punkin. A bit of scrub along the fence hid him from the road. Then I buried him an went up to the house an made me a pot of coffee. He hadn't never let me drink no coffee. Before light I got up an walked down the road. I was tellin myself in a big city it'd be like lookin for a needle in a haystack to find yer. I knowed where the ole man kep his money; he had a roll as big as your head but I was sceered to take more'en ten dollars. . . . You awake yet?"

The bum grunted. "When I was a kid I kep company with ole man Sackett's girl. Her and me used to keep company in the ole icehouse down in Sackett's woods an we used to talk about how we'd come to New York City an git rich and now I'm here I cant git work an I cant git over bein sceered. There's detectives follow me all round, men in derbyhats with badges under their coats. Last night I wanted to go with a hooker an she saw it in my eyes an throwed me out. . . . She could see it in my eyes." He was sitting on the edge of the cot, leaning over, talking into the other man's face in a hissing whisper. The bum suddenly grabbed him by the wrists.

"Look here kid, you're goin blooy if you keep up like this. . . . Got any mazuma?" Bud nodded. "You better give it to me to keep. I'm an old timer an I'll git yez outa this. You put yer clothes on a take a walk round the block to a hash joint an eat up strong. How much you got?"

"Change from a dollar."

"You give me a quarter an eat all the stuff you kin git offn the rest." Bud pulled on his trousers and handed the man a quarter. "Then you come back here an you'll sleep good an tomorrer me'n you'll go upstate an git that roll of bills. Did ye say it was as big as yer head? Then we'll beat it where they cant ketch us. We'll split fifty fifty. Are you on?"

Bud shook his hand with a wooden jerk, then with the laces flickering round his shoes he shuffled to the door and down the spitmarked stairs.

The rain had stopped, a cool wind that smelled of woods and grass was ruffling the puddles in the cleanwashed streets. In the lunchroom in Chatham Square three men sat asleep with their hats over their eyes. The man behind the counter was reading a pink sportingsheet. Bud waited long for his order. He felt cool, unthinking, happy. When it came he ate the browned corned beef hash, deliberately enjoying every mouthful, mashing the crisp bits of potato against his teeth with his tongue, between sips of heavily sugared coffee. After polishing the plate with a crust of bread he took a toothpick and went out.

Picking his teeth he walked through the grimydark entrance to Brooklyn Bridge. A man in a derby hat was smoking a cigar in the middle of the broad tunnel. Bud brushed past him walking with a tough swagger. I dont care about him; let him follow me. The arching footwalk was empty except for a single policeman who stood yawning, looking up at the sky. It was like walking among the stars. Below in either direction streets tapered into dotted lines of lights between square blackwindowed buildings. The river glimmered underneath like the Milky Way above. Silently smoothly the bunch of lights of a tug slipped through the moist darkness. A car whirred across the bridge making the girders rattle and the spiderwork of cables thrum like a shaken banjo.

When he got to the tangle of girders of the elevated railroads of the Brooklyn side, he turned back along the southern driveway. Dont matter where I go, cant go nowhere now. An edge of the blue night had started to glow behind him the way iron starts to glow in a forge. Beyond black chimneys and lines of roofs faint rosy contours of the downtown buildings were brightening. All the darkness was growing pearly, warming. They're all of em detectives chasin me,

all of em, men in derbies, bums on the Bowery, old women
in kitchens, barkeeps, streetcar conductors, bulls, hookers,
sailors, longshoremen, stiffs in employment agencies. . . .
He thought I'd tell him where the ole man's roll was, the
lousy bum. . . . One on him. One on all them goddam
detectives. The river was smooth, sleek as a bluesteel gun-
barrel. Dont matter where I go; cant go nowhere now.
The shadows between the wharves and the buildings were
powdery like washingblue. Masts fringed the river; smoke,
purple chocolatecolor fleshpink climbed into light. Cant go
nowhere now.

In a swallowtail suit with a gold watchchain and a red seal
ring riding to his wedding beside Maria Sackett, riding in a
carriage to City Hall with four white horses to be made an
alderman by the mayor; and the light grows behind them
brighter brighter, riding in satins and silks to his wedding,
riding in pinkplush in a white carriage with Maria Sackett
by his side through rows of men waving cigars, bowing,
doffing brown derbies, Alderman Bud riding in a carriage
full of diamonds with his milliondollar bride. . . . Bud is
sitting on the rail of the bridge. The sun has risen behind
Brooklyn. The windows of Manhattan have caught fire.
He jerks himself forward, slips, dangles by a hand with the
sun in his eyes. The yell strangles in his throat as he drops.

Captain McAvoy of the tugboat *Prudence* stood in the
pilothouse with one hand on the wheel. In the other he held
a piece of biscuit he had just dipped into a cup of coffee that
stood on the shelf beside the binnacle. He was a wellset
man with bushy eyebrows and a bushy black mustache waxed
at the tips. He was about to put the piece of coffeesoaked
biscuit into his mouth when something black dropped and
hit the water with a thudding splash a few yards off the bow.
At the same moment a man leaning out of the engineroom
door shouted, "A guy juss jumped offn de bridge."

"God damn it to hell," said Captain McAvoy dropping his
piece of biscuit and spinning the wheel. The strong ebbtide
whisked the boat round like a straw. Three bells jangled in

the engineroom. A negro ran forward to the bow with a boathook.

"Give a hand there Red," shouted Captain McAvoy.

After a tussle they landed a long black limp thing on the deck. One bell. Two bells, Captain McAvoy frowning and haggard spun the tug's nose into the current again.

"Any life in him Red?" he asked hoarsely. The negro's face was green, his teeth were chattering.

"Naw sir," said the redhaired man slowly. "His neck's broke clear off."

Captain McAvoy sucked a good half of his mustache into his mouth. "God damn it to hell," he groaned. "A pretty thing to happen on a man's wedding day."

Second Section

I. Great Lady on a White Horse

Morning clatters with the first L train down Allen Street. Daylight rattles through the windows, shaking the old brick houses, splatters the girders of the L structure with bright confetti.

The cats are leaving the garbage cans, the chinches are going back into the walls, leaving sweaty limbs, leaving the grimetender necks of little children asleep. Men and women stir under blankets and bedquilts on mattresses in the corners of rooms, clots of kids begin to untangle to scream and kick.

At the corner of Riverton the old man with the hempen beard who sleeps where nobody knows is putting out his picklestand. Tubs of gherkins, pimentos, melonrind, piccalilli give out twining vines and cold tendrils of dank pepperyfragrance that grow like a marshgarden out of the musky bedsmells and the rancid clangor of the cobbled awakening street.

The old man with the hempen beard who sleeps where nobody knows sits in the midst of it like Jonah under his gourd.

JIMMY HERF walked up four creaky flights and knocked at a white door fingermarked above the knob where the name *Sunderland* appeared in old English characters on a card neatly held in place by brass thumbtacks. He waited a long while beside a milkbottle, two creambottles, and a copy of the Sunday *Times*. There was a rustle behind the door and the creak of a step, then no more sound. He pushed a white button in the doorjamb.

"An he said, Margie I've got a crush on you so bad, an she said, Come in outa the rain, you're all wet. . . ." Voices coming down the stairs, a man's feet in button shoes, a girl's feet in sandals, pink silk legs; the girl in a fluffy dress

and a Spring Maid hat; the young man had white edging
on his vest and a green, blue, and purple striped necktie.

"But you're not that kind of a girl."

"How do you know what kind of a girl I am?"

The voices trailed out down the stairs.

Jimmy Herf gave the bell another jab.

"Who is it?" came a lisping female voice through a crack
in the door.

"I want to see Miss Prynne please."

Glimpse of a blue kimono held up to the chin of a fluffy
face. "Oh I don't know if she's up yet."

"She said she would be."

"Look will you please wait a second to let me make my getaway," she tittered behind the door. "And then come in.
Excuse us but Mrs. Sunderland thought you were the rent
collector. They sometimes come on Sunday just to fool
you." A smile coyly bridged the crack in the door.

"Shall I bring in the milk?"

"Oh do and sit down in the hall and I'll call Ruth." The
hall was very dark; smelled of sleep and toothpaste and
massagecream; across one corner a cot still bore the im-
print of a body on its rumpled sheets. Straw hats, silk
eveningwraps, and a couple of men's dress overcoats hung
in a jostling tangle from the staghorns of the hatrack.
Jimmy picked a corsetcover off a rockingchair and sat down.
Women's voices, a subdued rustling of people dressing,
Sunday newspaper noises seeped out through the partitions
of the different rooms.

The bathroom door opened; a stream of sunlight reflected
out of a pierglass cut the murky hall in half, out of it came a
head of hair like copper wire, bluedark eyes in a brittle-
white eggshaped face. Then the hair was brown down the
hall above a slim back in a tangerine-colored slip, nonchalant
pink heels standing up out of the bathslippers at every step.

"Ou-ou, Jimmee. . ." Ruth was yodling at him from behind her door. "But you mustn't look at me or at my
room." A head in curlpapers stuck out like a turtle's.

"Hullo Ruth."

"You can come in if you promise not to look. . . . I'm a sight and my room's a pigeon. . . . I've just got to do my hair. Then I'll be ready." The little gray room was stuffed with clothes and photographs of stage people. Jimmy stood with his back to the door, some sort of silky stuff that dangled from the hook tickling his ears.

"Well how's the cub reporter?"

"I'm on Hell's Kitchen. . . . It's swell. Got a job yet Ruth?"

"Um-um. . . . A couple of things may materialize during the week. But they wont. Oh Jimmy I'm getting desperate." She shook her hair loose of the crimpers and combed out the new mousybrown waves. She had a pale startled face with a big mouth and blue underlids. "This morning I knew I ought to be up and ready, but I just couldn't. It's so discouraging to get up when you haven't got a job. . . . Sometimes I think I'll go to bed and just stay there till the end of the world."

"Poor old Ruth."

She threw a powderpuff at him that covered his necktie and the lapels of his blue serge suit with powder. "Dont you poor old me you little rat."

"That's a nice thing to do after all the trouble I took to make myself look respectable. . . . Darn your hide Ruth. And the smell of the carbona not off me yet."

Ruth threw back her head with a shrieking laugh. "Oh you're so comical Jimmy. Try the whisk-broom."

Blushing he blew down his chin at his tie. "Who's the funnylooking girl opened the halldoor?"

"Shush you can hear everything through the partition. . . . That's Cassie," she whispered giggling. "Cassah-ndrah Wilkins . . . used to be with the Morgan Dancers. But we oughtnt to laugh at her, she's very nice. I'm very fond of her." She let out a whoop of laughter. "You nut Jimmy." She got to her feet and punched him in the muscle of the arm. "You always make me act like I was crazy."

"God did that. . . . No but look, I'm awfully hungry. I walked up."

"What time is it?"

"It's after one."

"Oh Jimmy I dont know what to do about time. . . . Like this hat? . . . Oh I forgot to tell you. I went to see Al Harrison yesterday. It was simply dreadful. . . . If I hadnt got to the phone in time and threatened to call the police. . . ."

"Look at that funny woman opposite. She's got a face exactly like a llama."

"It's on account of her I have to keep my shades drawn all the time . . ."

"Why?"

"Oh you're much too young to know. You'd be shocked Jimmy." Ruth was leaning close to the mirror running a stick of rouge between her lips.

"So many things shock me, I dont see that it matters much. . . . But come along let's get out of here. The sun's shining outside and people are coming out of church and going home to overeat and read at their Sunday papers among the rubberplants . . ."

"Oh Jimmy you're a shriek . . . Just one minute. Look out you're hooked onto my best shimmy."

A girl with short black hair in a yellow jumper was folding the sheets off the cot in the hall. For a second under the ambercolored powder and the rouge Jimmy did not recognize the face he had seen through the crack in the door.

"Hello Cassie, this is . . . Beg pardon, Miss Wilkins this is Mr. Herf. You tell him about the lady across the airshaft, you know Sappo the Monk."

Cassandra Wilkins lisped and pouted. "Isn't she dweadful Mr. Herf. . . . She says the dweadfullest things."

"She merely does it to annoy."

"Oh Mr. Herf I'm so pleased to meet you at last, Ruth does nothing but talk about you. . . . Oh I'm afwaid I was indiscweet to say that. . . . I'm dweadfully indiscweet."

The door across the hall opened and Jimmy found himself looking in the white face of a crookednosed man whose red hair rode in two unequal mounds on either side of a straight part.   He wore a green satin bathrobe and red morocco slippers.

"What heow Cassahndrah?" he said in a careful Oxford drawl.   "What prophecies today?"

"Nothing except a wire from Mrs. Fitzsimmons Green. She wants me to go to see her at Scarsdale tomorrow to talk about the Gweenery Theater. . . . Excuse me this is Mr. Herf, Mr. Oglethorpe."   The redhaired man raised one eyebrow and lowered the other and put a limp hand in Jimmy's.

"Herf, Herf. . . . Let me see, it's not a Georgiah Herf? In Atlahnta there's an old family of Herfs. . . ."

"No I dont think so."

"Too bad.   Once upon a time Josiah Herf and I were boon companions.   Today he is the president of the First National Bank and leading citizen of Scranton Pennsylvahnia and I . . . a mere mountebank, a thing of rags and patches." When he shrugged his shoulders the bathrobe fell away exposing a flat smooth hairless chest.

"You see Mr. Oglethorpe and I are going to do the Song of Songs.   He weads it and I interpwet it in dancing. You must come up and see us wehearse sometime."

"Thy navel is like a round goblet which wanteth not liquor, thy belly is like a heap of wheat set about with lilies . . ."

"Oh dont begin now."   She tittered and pressed her legs together.

"Jojo close that door," came a quiet deep girl's voice from inside the room.

"Oh poo-er deah Elaine, she wants to sleep. . . . So glahd to have met you, Mr. Herf."

"Jojo!"

"Yes my deah. . . ."

Through the leaden drowse that cramped him the girl's voice set Jimmy tingling.   He stood beside Cassie constrainedly without speaking in the dingydark hall. A smell of coffee and singeing toast seeped in from somewhere. Ruth came up behind them.

"All right Jimmy I'm ready. . . . I wonder if I've forgotten anything."

"I dont care whether you have or not, I'm starving." Jimmy took hold of her shoulders and pushed her gently towards the door. "It's two o'clock."

"Well goodby Cassie dear, I'll call you up at about six."

"All wight Wuthy . . . So pleased to have met you Mr. Herf." The door closed on Cassie's tittering lisp.

"Wow, Ruth that place gives me the infernal jimjams."

"Now Jimmy dont get peevish because you need food."

"But tell me Ruth, what the hell is Mr. Oglethorpe? He beats anything I ever saw."

"Oh did the Ogle come out of his lair?" Ruth let out a whoop of laughter. They came out into grimy sunlight. "Did he tell you he was of the main brawnch, dontcher know, of the Oglethorpes of Georgiah?"

"Is that lovely girl with copper hair his wife?"

"Elaine Oglethorpe has reddish hair. She's not so darn lovely either. . . . She's just a kid and she's upstage as the deuce already. All because she made a kind of a hit in Peach Blossoms. You know one of these tiny exquisite bits everybody makes such a fuss over. She can act all right."

"It's a shame she's got that for a husband."

"Ogle's done everything in the world for her. If it hadnt been for him she'd still be in the chorus . . ."

"Beauty and the beast."

"You'd better look out if he sets his lamps on you Jimmy."

"Why?"

"Strange fish, Jimmy, strange fish."

An Elevated train shattered the barred sunlight overhead. He could see Ruth's mouth forming words.

"Look," he shouted above the diminishing clatter. "Let's go have brunch at the Campus and then go for a walk on the Palisades."

"You nut Jimmy what's brunch?"

"You'll eat breakfast and I'll eat lunch."

"It'll be a scream." Whooping with laughter she put her arm in his. Her silvernet bag knocked against his elbow as they walked.

"And what about Cassie, the mysterious Cassandra?"

"You mustn't laugh at her, she's a peach. . . . If only she wouldn't keep that horrid little white poodle. She keeps it in her room and it never gets any exercise and it smells something terrible. She has that little room next to mine. . . . Then she's got a steady . . ." Ruth giggled. "He's worse than the poodle. They're engaged and he borrows all her money away from her. For Heaven's sake dont tell anybody."

"I dont know anybody to tell."

"Then there's Mrs. Sunderland . . ."

"Oh yes I got a glimpse of her going into the bathroom— an old lady in a wadded dressing gown with a pink boudoir cap on."

"Jimmy you shock me. . . . She keeps losing her false teeth," began Ruth; an L train drowned out the rest. The restaurant door closing behind them choked off the roar of wheels on rails.

An orchestra was playing *When It's Appleblossom Time in Normandee*. The place was full of smokewrithing slants of sunlight, paper festoons, signs announcing LOBSTERS ARRIVE DAILY, EAT CLAMS NOW, TRY OUR DELICIOUS FRENCH STYLE STEAMED MUSSELS (Recommended by the Department of Agriculture). They sat down under a redlettered placard BEEFSTEAK PARTIES UPSTAIRS and Ruth made a pass at him with a breadstick. "Jimmy do you think it'd be immoral to eat scallops for breakfast? But first I've got to have coffee coffee coffee . . ."

"I'm going to eat a small steak and onions."

"Not if you're intending to spend the afternoon with me, Mr. Herf."

"Oh all right. Ruth I lay my onions at your feet."

"That doesn't mean I'm going to let you kiss me."

"What . . . on the Palisades?"　Ruth's giggle broke into
a whoop of laughter.　Jimmy blushed crimson.　"I never
axed you maam, he say-ed."

Sunlight dripped in her face through the little holes in
the brim of her straw hat.　She was walking with brisk
steps too short on account of her narrow skirt; through the
thin china silk the sunlight tingled like a hand stroking her
back.　In the heavy heat streets, stores, people in Sunday
clothes, strawhats, sunshades, surfacecars, taxis, broke and
crinkled brightly about her grazing her with sharp cutting
glints as if she were walking through piles of metalshavings.
She was groping continually through a tangle of gritty saw-
edged brittle noise.

At Lincoln Square a girl rode slowly through the traffic
on a white horse; chestnut hair hung down in even faky
waves over the horse's chalky rump and over the giltedged
saddlecloth where in green letters pointed with crimson, read
DANDERINE.　She had on a green Dolly Varden hat with
a crimson plume; one hand in a white gauntlet nonchalantly
jiggled at the reins, in the other wabbled a goldknobbed riding crop.

Ellen watched her pass; then she followed a smudge of
green through a cross-street to the Park.　A smell of
trampled sunsinged grass came from boys playing baseball.
All the shady benches were full of people.　When she
crossed the curving automobile road her sharp French heels
sank into the asphalt.　Two sailors were sprawling on a
bench in the sun; one of them popped his lips as she passed,
she could feel their seagreedy eyes cling stickily to her neck,
her thighs, her ankles.　She tried to keep her hips from
swaying so much as she walked.　The leaves were shriveled
on the saplings along the path.　South and east sunnyfaced
buildings hemmed in the Park, to the west they were violet
with shadow.　Everything was itching sweaty dusty con-
strained by policemen and Sunday clothes.　Why hadn't

she taken the L? She was looking in the black eyes of a young man in a straw hat who was drawing up a red Stutz roadster to the curb. His eyes twinkled in hers, he jerked back his head smiling an upsidedown smile, pursing his lips so that they seemed to brush her cheek. He pulled the lever of the brake and opened the door with the other hand. She snapped her eyes away and walked on with her chin up. Two pigeons with metalgreen necks and feet of coral waddled out of her way. An old man was coaxing a squirrel to fish for peanuts in a paper bag.

All in green on a white stallion rode the Lady of the Lost Battalion. . . . Green, green, danderine . . . Godiva in the haughty mantle of her hair. . . .

General Sherman in gold interrupted her. She stopped a second to look at the Plaza that gleamed white as mother-ofpearl. . . . Yes this is Elaine Oglethorpe's apartment. . . . She climbed up onto a Washington Square bus. Sunday afternoon Fifth Avenue filed by rosily dustily jerkily. On the shady side there was an occasional man in a top hat and frock coat. Sunshades, summer dresses, straw hats were bright in the sun that glinted in squares on the upper windows of houses, lay in bright slivers on the hard paint of limousines and taxicabs. It smelled of gasoline and asphalt, of spearmint and talcumpowder and perfume from the couples that jiggled closer and closer together on the seats of the bus. In an occasional storewindow, paintings, maroon draperies, varnished antique chairs behind plate glass. The St. Regis. Sherry's. The man beside her wore spats and lemon gloves, a floorwalker probably. As they passed St. Patrick's she caught a whiff of incense through the tall doors open into gloom. Delmonico's. In front of her the young man's arm was stealing round the narrow gray flannel back of the girl beside him.

"Jez ole Joe had rotten luck, he had to marry her. He's only nineteen."

"I suppose you would think it was hard luck."

"Myrtle I didn't mean us."

"I bet you did. An anyways have you ever seen the girl?"

"I bet it aint his."

"What?"

"The kid."

"Billy how dreadfully you do talk."

Fortysecond Street. Union League Club. "It was a most amusing gathering . . . most amusing. . . . Everybody was there. For once the speeches were delightful, made me think of old times," croaked a cultivated voice behind her ear. The Waldorf. "Aint them flags swell Billy. . . . That funny one is cause the Siamese ambassador is staying there. I read about it in the paper this morning."

When thou and I my love shall come to part, Then shall I press an ineffable last kiss Upon your lips and go . . . heart, start, who art . . . Bliss, this, miss . . . When thou . . . When you and I my love . . .

Eighth Street. She got down from the bus and went into the basement of the Brevoort. George sat waiting with his back to the door snapping and unsnapping the lock of his briefcase. "Well Elaine it's about time you turned up. . . . There aren't many people I'd sit waiting three quarters of an hour for."

"George you mustn't scold me; I've been having the time of my life. I haven't had such a good time in years. I've had the whole day all to myself and I walked all the way down from 105th Street to Fiftyninth through the Park. It was full of the most comical people."

"You must be tired." His lean face where the bright eyes were caught in a web of fine wrinkles kept pressing forward into hers like the prow of a steamship.

"I suppose you've been at the office all day George."

"Yes I've been digging out some cases. I cant rely on anyone else to do even routine work thoroughly, so I have to do it myself."

"Do you know I had it all decided you'd say that."

"What?"

"About waiting three quarters of an hour."

"Oh you know altogether too much Elaine. . . . Have some pastries with your tea?"

"Oh but I dont know anything about anything, that's the trouble. . . . I think I'll take lemon please."

Glasses clinked about them; through blue cigarettesmoke faces hats beards wagged, repeated greenish in the mirrors,

"But my de-e-ar it's always the same old complex. It may be true of men but it says nothing in regard to women," droned a woman's voice from the next table. . . . "Your feminism rises into an insuperable barrier," trailed a man's husky meticulous tones. "What if I am an egoist? God knows I've suffered for it." "Fire that purifies, Charley. . . ." George was speaking, trying to catch her eye. "How's the famous Jojo?"

"Oh let's not talk about him."

"The less said about him the better eh?"

"Now George I wont have you sneer at Jojo, for better or worse he is my husband, till divorce do us part. . . . No I wont have you laugh. You're too crude and simple to understand him anyway. Jojo's a very complicated rather tragic person."

"For God's sake don't let's talk about husbands and wives. The important thing, little Elaine, is that you and I are sitting here together without anyone to bother us. . . . Look when are we going to see each other again, really see each other, really. . . ."

"We're not going to be too real about this, are we George?" She laughed softly into her cup.

"Oh but I have so many things to say to you. I want to ask you so many things."

She looked at him laughing, balancing a small cherry tartlet that had one bite out of it between a pink squaretipped finger and thumb. "Is that the way you act when you've got some miserable sinner on the witnessbox? I thought it was more like: Where were you on the night of February thirtyfirst?"

"But I'm dead serious, that's what you cant understand, or wont."

A young man stood at the table, swaying a little, looking down at them. "Hello Stan, where the dickens did you come from?" Baldwin looked up at him without smiling. "Look Mr. Baldwin I know it's awful rude, but may I sit down at your table a second. There's somebody looking for me who I just cant meet. O God that mirror! Still they'd never look for me if they saw you."

"Miss Oglethorpe this is Stanwood Emery, the son of the senior partner in our firm."

"Oh it's so wonderful to meet you Miss Oglethorpe. I saw you last night, but you didn't see me."

"Did you go to the show?"

"I almost jumped over the foots I thought you were so wonderful."

He had a ruddy brown skin, anxious eyes rather near the bridge of a sharp fragillycut nose, a big mouth never still, wavy brown hair that stood straight up. Ellen looked from one to the other inwardly giggling. They were all three stiffening in their chairs.

"I saw the danderine lady this afternoon," she said. "She impressed me enormously. Just my idea of a great lady on a white horse."

"With rings on her finger and bells on her toes, And she shall make mischief wherever she goes." Stan rattled it off quickly under his breath.

"Music, isnt it?" put in Ellen laughing. "I always say mischief."

"Well how's college?" asked Baldwin in a dry uncordial voice.

"I guess it's still there," said Stan blushing. "I wish they'd burn it down before I got back." He got to his feet. "You must excuse me Mr. Baldwin. . . . My intrusion was infernally rude." As he turned leaning towards Ellen she smelled his grainy whiskey breath. "Please forgive it, Miss Oglethorpe."

She found herself holding out her hand; a dry skinny hand squeezed it hard. He strode out with swinging steps bumping into a waiter as he went.

"I cant make out that infernal young puppy," burst out Baldwin. "Poor old Emery's heartbroken about it. He's darn clever and has a lot of personality and all that sort of thing, but all he does is drink and raise Cain. . . . I guess all he needs is to go to work and get a sense of values. Too much money's what's the matter with most of those college-boys. . . . Oh but Elaine thank God we're alone again. I have worked continuously all my life ever since I was fourteen. The time has come when I want to lay aside all that for a while. I want to live and travel and think and be happy. I cant stand the pace of downtown the way I used to. I want to learn to play, to ease off the tension. . . . That's where you come in."

"But I don't want to be the nigger on anybody's safety-valve." She laughed and let the lashes fall over her eyes.

"Let's go out to the country somewhere this evening. I've been stifling in the office all day. I hate Sunday anyway."

"But my rehearsal."

"You could be sick. I'll phone for a car."

"Golly there's Jojo. . . . Hello Jojo"; she waved her gloves above her head.

John Oglethorpe, his face powdered, his mouth arranged in a careful smile above his standup collar, advanced between the crowded tables, holding out his hand tightly squeezed into buff gloves with black stripes. "Heow deo you deo, my deah, this is indeed a surprise and a pleajah."

"You know each other, don't you? This is Mr. Baldwin."

"Forgive me if I intrude . . . er . . . upon a tête à tête."

"Nothing of the sort, sit down and we'll all have a high-ball. . . . I was just dying to see you really Jojo. . . . By the way if you havent anything else to do this evening you might slip in down front for a few minutes. I want to know what you think about my reading of the part. . . . "

"Certainly my deah, nothing could give me more pleajah."

His whole body tense George Baldwin leaned back with his hand clasped behind the back of his chair. "Waiter . . ." He broke his words off sharp like metal breaking. "Three Scotch highballs at once please."

Oglethorpe rested his chin on the silver ball of his cane. "Confidence, Mr. Baldwin," he began, "confidence between husband and wife is a very beautiful thing. Space and time have no effect on it. Were one of us to go to China for a thousand years it would not change our affection one tittle."

"You see George, what's the matter with Jojo is that he read too much Shakespeare in his youth. . . . But I've got to go or Merton will be bawling me out again. . . . Talk about industrial slavery. Jojo tell him about Equity."

Baldwin got to his feet. There was a slight flush on his cheekbones. "Wont you let me take you up to the theater," he said through clenched teeth.

"I never let anyone take me anywhere . . . And Jojo you must stay sober to see me act."

Fifth Avenue was pink and white under pink and white clouds in a fluttering wind that was fresh after the cloying talk and choke of tobaccosmoke and cocktails. She waved the taxistarter off merrily and smiled at him. Then she found a pair of anxious eyes looking into hers seriously out of a higharched brown face.

"I waited round to see you come out. Cant I take you somewhere? I've got my Ford round the corner. . . . Please."

"But I'm just going up to the theater. I've got a rehearsal."

"All right do let me take you there."

She began putting a glove on thoughtfully. "All right, but it's an awful imposition on you."

"That's fine. It's right round here. . . . It was awfully rude of me to butt in that way, wasn't it? But that's another story. . . . Anyway I've met you. The Ford's name is Dingo, but that's another story too. . . . "

"Still it's nice to meet somebody humanly young. There's nobody humanly young round New York."

His face was scarlet when he leaned to crank the car. "Oh I'm too damn young."

The motor sputtered, started with a roar. He jumped round and cut off the gas with a long hand. "We'll probably get arrested; my muffler's loose and liable to drop off."

At Thirtyfourth Street they passed a girl riding slowly

through the traffic on a white horse; chestnut hair hung down in even faky waves over the horse's chalky rump and over the giltedged saddlecloth where in green letters pointed with crimson read DANDERINE.

"Rings on her fingers," chanted Stan pressing his buzzer, "And bells on her toes, And she shall cure dandruff wherever it grows."

II. Longlegged Jack of the Isthmus

Noon on Union Square. Selling out. Must vacate. WE HAVE MADE A TERRIBLE MISTAKE. Kneeling on the dusty asphalt little boys shine shoes lowshoes tans buttonshoes oxfords. The sun shines like a dandelion on the toe of each new-shined shoe. Right this way buddy, mister miss maam at the back of the store our new line of fancy tweeds highest value lowest price ... Gents, misses, ladies, cutrate ... WE HAVE MADE A TERRIBLE MISTAKE. Must vacate.

Noon sunlight spirals dimly into the chopsuey joint. Muted music spirals Hindustan. He eats fooyong, she eats chowmein. They dance with their mouths full, slim blue jumper squeezed to black slick suit, peroxide curls against black slick hair.

Down Fourteenth Street, Glory Glory comes the Army, striding lasses, Glory Glory four abreast, the rotund shining, navy blue, Salvation Army band.

Highest value, lowest price. Must vacate. WE HAVE MADE A TERRIBLE MISTAKE. Must vacate.

From Liverpool, British steamer Raleigh, Captain Kettlewell; 933 bales, 881 boxes, 10 baskets, 8 packages fabrics: 57 boxes, 89 bales, 18 baskets cotton thread: 156 bales felt: 4 bales asbestos: 100 sacks spools. . . .

JOE HARLAND stopped typing and looked up at the ceiling. The tips of his fingers were sore. The office smelled stalely of paste and manifests and men in shirtsleeves. Through the open window he could see a piece of the dun wall of an airshaft and a man with a green eyeshade staring vacantly out of a window. The towheaded officeboy set a note on the corner of his desk: Mr. Pollock will see

you at 5 :10.   A hard lump caught in his throat ; he's going to
fire me.   His fingers started tapping again :

From Glasgow, Dutch steamer Delft, Captain Tromp; 200 bales,
123 boxes, 14 kegs. . . .

Joe Harland roamed about the Battery till he found an
empty seat on a bench, then he let himself flop into it.   The
sun was drowning in tumultuous saffron steam behind Jersey.
Well that's over.   He sat a long while staring at the sunset
like at a picture in a dentist's waiting room.   Great whorls of
smoke from a passing tug curled up black and scarlet against
it.   He sat staring at the sunset, waiting.   That's eighteen
dollars and fifty cents I had before, less six dollars for the
room, one dollar and eighty-four cents for laundry, and four
dollars and fifty cents I owe Charley, makes seven dollars and
eighty-four cents, eleven dollars and eighty four cents, twelve
dollars and thirty-four cents from eighteen dollars and fifty
cents leaves me six dollars and sixteen cents, three days to
find another job if I go without drinks.   O God wont my
luck ever turn; used to have good enough luck in the old
days.   His knees were trembling, there was a sick burning in
the pit of his stomach.

A fine mess you've made of your life Joseph Harland.
Forty-five and no friends and not a cent to bless yourself
with.

The sail of a catboat was a crimson triangle when it luffed
a few feet from the concrete walk.   A young man and a
young girl ducked together as the slender boom swung
across.   They both were bronzed with the sun and had
yellow weather bleached hair.   Joe Harland gnawed his lip
to keep back the tears as the catboat shrank into the ruddy
murk of the bay.   By God I need a drink.

"Aint it a croime?   Aint it a croime?"   The man in the seat
to the left of him began to say over and over again.   Joe
Harland turned his head; the man had a red puckered face
and silver hair.   He held the dramatic section of the paper
taut between two grimy flippers.   "Them young actresses all
dressed naked like that. . . . "Why cant they let you alone."

"Dont you like to see their pictures in the papers?"

"Why cant they let you alone I say. . . . If you aint got no work and you aint got no money, what's the good of em I say?"

"Well lots of people like to see their pictures in the paper. Used to myself in the old days."

"Used to be work in the old days. . . . You aint got no job now?" he growled savagely. Joe Harland shook his head. "Well what the hell? They ought to leave you alone oughtn't they? Wont be no jobs till snow shoveling begins."

"What'll you do till then?"

The old man didnt answer. He bent over the paper again screwing up his eyes and muttering. "All dressed naked, it's a croime I'm tellin yez."

Joe Harland got to his feet and walked away.

It was almost dark; his knees were stiff from sitting still so long. As he walked wearily he could feel his potbelly cramped by his tight belt. Poor old warhorse you need a couple of drinks to think about things. A mottled beery smell came out through swinging doors. Inside the barkeep's face was like a russet apple on a snug mahogany shelf.

"Gimme a shot of rye." The whiskey stung his throat hot and fragrant. Makes a man of me that does. Without drinking the chaser he walked over to the free lunch and ate a ham sandwich and an olive. "Let's have another rye Charley. That's the stuff to make a man of you. I been laying off it too much, that's what's the matter with me. You wouldnt think it to look at me now, would you friend, but they used to call me the Wizard of Wall Street which is only another illustration of the peculiar predominance of luck in human affairs. . . . Yes sir with pleasure. Well, here's health and long life and to hell with the jinx. . . . Hah makes a man of you . . . Well I suppose there's not one of you gentlemen here who hasnt at some time or other taken a plunger, and how many of you hasnt come back sadder and wiser. Another illustration of the peculiar predominance of luck in human affairs. But not so with me; gentlemen for ten years I played the market, for ten years I didn't

have a ticker ribbon out of my hand day or night, and in ten
years I only took a cropper three times, till the last time.
Gentlemen I'm going to tell you a secret. I'm going to tell
you a very important secret. . . . Charley give these very
good friends of mine another round, my treat, and have a
nip yourself. . . . My, that tickles her in the right place. . . .
Gentlemen just another illustration of the peculiar predominance of luck in human affairs. Gentlemen the secret of my
luck . . . this is exact I assure you; you can verify it yourselves in newspaper articles, magazines, speeches, lectures
delivered in those days; a man, and a dirty blackguard he
turned out to be eventually, even wrote a detective story
about me called the Secret of Success, which you can find in
the New York Public Library if you care to look the matter
up. . . . The secret of my success was . . . and when you
hear it you'll laugh among yourselves and say Joe Harland's
drunk, Joe Harland's an old fool. . . . Yes you will. . . .
For ten years I'm telling you I traded on margins, I bought
outright, I covered on stocks I'd never even heard the name
of and every time I cleaned up. I piled up money. I had
four banks in the palm of my hand. I began eating my way
into sugar and gutta percha, but in that I was before my
time. . . . But you're getting nervous to know my secret,
you think you could use it. . . . Well you couldnt. . . . It
was a blue silk crocheted necktie that my mother made for me
when I was a little boy. . . . Dont you laugh, God damn you.
. . . No I'm not starting anything. Just another illustration of the peculiar predominance of luck. The day I chipped
in with another fellow to spread a thousand dollars over some
Louisville and Nashville on margin I wore that necktie.
Soared twentyfive points in twentyfive minutes. That was
the beginning. Then gradually I began to notice that the
times I didnt wear that necktie were the times I lost money.
It got so old and ragged I tried carrying it in my pocket.
Didnt do any good. I had to wear it, do you understand?
. . . The rest is the old old story gentlemen. . . . There
was a girl, God damn her and I loved her. I wanted to show
her that there was nothing in the world I wouldnt do for her

so I gave it to her. I pretended it was a joke and laughed it
off, ha ha ha. She said, Why it's no good, it's all worn out,
and she threw it in the fire. . . . Only another illustration.
. . . Friend you wouldn't set me up to another drink would
you? I find myself unexpectedly out of funds this afternoon. . . . I thank you sir. . . . Ah that puts ginger in you
again."

In the crammed subway car the messenger boy was pressed
up against the back of a tall blond woman who smelled of
Mary Garden. Elbows, packages, shoulders, buttocks,
jiggled closer with every lurch of the screeching express. His
sweaty Western Union cap was knocked onto the side of his
head. If I could have a dame like dat, a dame like dat'd be
wort havin de train stalled, de lights go out, de train wrecked.
I could have her if I had de noive an de jack. As the train
slowed up she fell against him, he closed his eyes, didnt
breathe, his nose was mashed against her neck. The train
stopped. He was carried in a rush of people out the door.
Dizzy he staggered up into the air and the blinking blocks
of lights. Upper Broadway was full of people. Sailors
lounged in twos and threes at the corner of Ninetysixth. He
ate a ham and a leberwurst sandwich in a delicatessen store.
The woman behind the counter had buttercolored hair like the
girl in the subway but she was fatter and older. Still chewing the crust of the last sandwich he went up in the elevator
to the Japanese Garden. He sat thinking a while with the
flicker of the screen in his eyes. Jeze dey'll tink it funny to
see a messengerboy up here in dis suit. I better get de hell
outa here. I'll go deliver my telegrams.
He tightened his belt as he walked down the stairs. Then
he slouched up Broadway to 105th Street and east towards
Columbus Avenue, noting doors, fire escapes, windows, cornices, carefully as he went. Dis is de joint. The only lights
were on the second floor. He rang the second floor bell.
The doorcatch clicked. He ran up the stairs. A woman

with weedy hair and a face red from leaning over the stove poked her head out.

"Telegram for Santiono."

"No such name here."

"Sorry maam I musta rung de wrong bell."

Door slammed in his nose. His sallow sagging face tightened up all of a sudden. He ran lightly on tiptoe up the stairs to the top landing then up the little ladder to a trapdoor. The bolt ground as he slid it back. He caught in his breath. Once on the cindergritty roof he let the trapdoor back softly into place. Chimneys stood up in alert ranks all about him, black against the glare from the streets. Crouching he stepped gingerly to the rear edge of the house, let himself down from the gutter to the fire escape. His foot grazed a flowerpot as he landed. Everything dark. Crawled through a window into a stuffy womansmelling room, slid a hand under the pillow of an unmade bed, along a bureau, spilled some facepowder, in tiny jerks pulled open the drawer, a watch, ran a pin into his finger, a brooch, something that crinkled in the back corner; bills, a roll of bills. Getaway, no chances tonight. Down the fire escape to the next floor. No light. Another window open. Takin candy from a baby. Same room, smelling of dogs and incense, some kind of dope. He could see himself faintly, fumbling, in the glass of the bureau, put his hand into a pot of cold cream, wiped it off on his pants. Hell. Something fluffysoft shot with a yell from under his feet. He stood trembling in the middle of the narrow room. The little dog was yapping loud in a corner.

The room swung into light. A girl stood in the open door, pointing a revolver at him. There was a man behind her.

"What are you doing? Why it's a Western Union boy. . . ." The light was a coppery tangle about her hair, picked out her body under the red silk kimono. The young man was wiry and brown in his unbuttoned shirt. "Well what are you doing in that room?"

"Please maam it was hunger brought me to it, hunger an my poor ole muder starvin "

"Isnt that wonderful Stan? He's a burglar." She brandished the revolver. "Come on out in the hall."

"Yes miss anythin you say miss, but dont give me up to de bulls. Tink o de ole muder starvin her heart out."

"All right but if you took anything you must give it back."

"Honest I didn't have a chanct."

Stan flopped into a chair laughing and laughing. "Ellie you take the cake. . . . Wouldnt a thought you could do it."

"Well didnt I play this scene in stock all last summer? . . . Give up your gun."

"No miss I wouldn't carry no gun."

"Well I dont believe you but I guess I'll let you go."

"Gawd bless you miss."

"But you must make some money as a messengerboy."

"I was fired last week miss, it's only hunger made me take to it."

Stan got to his feet. "Let's give him a dollar an tell him to get the hell out of here."

When he was outside the door she held out the dollarbill to him.

"Jez you're white," he said choking. He grabbed the hand with the bill in it and kissed it; leaning over her hand kissing it wetly he caught a glimpse of her body under the arm in the drooping red silk sleeve. As he walked, still trembling, down the stairs, he looked back and saw the man and the girl standing side by side with their arms around each other watching him. His eyes were full of tears. He stuffed the dollarbill into his pocket.

Kid if you keep on bein a softie about women you're goin to find yourself in dat lil summer hotel up de river. . . . Pretty soft though. Whistling under his breath he walked to the L and took an uptown train. Now and then he put his hand over his back pocket to feel the roll of bills. He ran up to the third floor of an apartmenthouse that smelled of fried fish and coal gas, and rang three times at a grimy glass door. After a pause he knocked softly.

"Zat you Moike?" came faintly the whine of a woman's voice.

"No it's Nicky Schatz."

A sharpfaced woman with henna hair opened the door. She had on a fur coat over frilly lace underclothes.

"Howsa boy?"

"Jeze a swell dame caught me when I was tidying up a little job and whatjer tink she done?" He followed the woman, talking excitedly, into a dining room with peeling walls. On the table were used glasses and a bottle of Green River whiskey. "She gave me a dollar an tole me to be a good little boy."

"The hell she did?"

"Here's a watch."

"It's an Ingersoll, I dont call 'at a watch."

"Well set yer lamps on dis." He pulled out the roll of bills. "Aint dat a wad o lettuce? . . . Got in himmel, dey's tousands."

"Lemme see." She grabbed the bills out of his hand, her eyes popping. "Hay ye're cookoo kid." She threw the roll on the floor and wrung her hands with a swaying Jewish gesture. "Oyoy it's stage money. It's stage money ye simple saphead, you goddam . . ."

Giggling they sat side by side on the edge of the bed. Through the stuffy smell of the room full of little silky bits of clothing falling off chairs a fading freshness came from a bunch of yellow roses on the bureau. Their arms tightened round each other's shoulders; suddenly he wrenched himself away and leaned over her to kiss her mouth. "Some burglar," he said breathlessly.

"Stan . . ."

"Ellie."

"I thought it might be Jojo;" she managed to force a whisper through a tight throat. "It'll be just like him to come sneaking around."

"Ellie I don't understand how you can live with him among all these people. You're so lovely. I just dont see you in all this."

"It was easy enough before I met you. . . . And honestly Jojo's all right. He's just a peculiar very unhappy person."

"But you're out of another world old kid. . . . You ought to live on top of the Woolworth Building in an apartment made of cutglass and cherry blossoms."

"Stan your back's brown all the way down."

"That's swimming."

"So soon?"

"I guess most of it's left over from last summer."

"You're the fortunate youth all right. I never learned how to swim properly."

"I'll teach you. . . . Look next Sunday bright and early we'll hop into Dingo and go down to Long Beach. Way down at the end there's never anybody. . . . You dont even have to wear a bathingsuit."

"I like the way you're so lean and hard Stan. . . . Jojo's white and flabby almost like a woman."

"For crissake don't talk about him now."

Stan stood with his legs apart buttoning his shirt. "Look Ellie let's beat it out an have a drink. . . . God I'd hate to run into somebody now an have to talk lies to 'em. . . . I bet I'd crown 'em with a chair."

"We've got time. Nobody ever comes home here before twelve. . . . I'm just here myself because I've got a sick headache."

"Ellie, d'you like your sick headache?"

"I'm crazy about it Stan."

"I guess that Western Union burglar knew that. . . . Gosh. . . . Burglary, adultery, sneaking down fireescapes, cattreading along gutters. Judas it's a great life."

Ellen gripped his hand hard as they came down the stairs stepping together. In front of the letterboxes in the shabby hallway he grabbed her suddenly by the shoulders and pressed her head back and kissed her. Hardly breathing they floated down the street toward Broadway. He had his hand under her arm, she squeezed it tight against her ribs with her elbow. Aloof, as if looking through thick glass into an aquarium, she watched faces, fruit in storewindows, cans of vegetables, jars of olives, redhotpokerplants in a florist's, newspapers, electric signs drifting by. When they passed cross-streets a puff of air came in her face off the river. Sudden jetbright glances of eyes under straw hats, attitudes of chins, thin lips, pouting lips, Cupid's bows, hungry shadow under cheekbones, faces of girls and young men nuzzled fluttering against her like moths as she walked with her stride even to his through the tingling yellow night.

Somewhere they sat down at a table. An orchestra throbbed. "No Stan I cant drink anything. . . . You go ahead."

"But Ellie, arent you feeling swell like I am?"

"Sweller. . . . I just couldnt stand feeling any better. . . . I couldnt keep my mind on a glass long enough to drink it." She winced under the brightness of his eyes.

Stan was bubbling drunk. "I wish earth had thy body as fruit to eat," he kept repeating. Ellen was all the time twisting about bits of rubbery cold Welsh rabbit with her fork. She had started to drop with a lurching drop like a rollercoaster's into shuddering pits of misery. In a square place in the middle of the floor four couples were dancing the tango. She got to her feet.

"Stan I'm going home. I've got to get up early and rehearse all day. Call me up at twelve at the theater."

He nodded and poured himself another highball. She stood behind his chair a second looking down at his long head of close ruffled hair. He was spouting verses softly to himself. "Saw the white implacable Aphrodite, damn fine. Saw the hair unbound and the feet unsandaled, Jiminy. . . . Shine as fire of sunset on western waters. Saw the reluctant . . . goddam fine sapphics."

Once out on Broadway again she felt very merry. She stood in the middle of the street waiting for the uptown car. An occasional taxi whizzed by her. From the river on the warm wind came the long moan of a steamboat whistle. In the pit inside her thousands of gnomes were building tall brittle glittering towers. The car swooped ringing along the rails, stopped. As she climbed in she remembered swooningly the smell of Stan's body sweating in her arms. She let herself drop into a seat, biting her lips to keep from crying out. God it's terrible to be in love. Opposite two men with chinless bluefish faces were talking hilariously, slapping fat knees.

"I'll tell yer Jim it's Irene Castle that makes the hit wid me. . . . To see her dance the onestep juss makes me hear angels hummin."

"Naw she's too skinny."

"But she's made the biggest hit ever been made on Broadway."

Ellen got off the car and walked east along the desolate empty pavements of 105th Street. A fetor of mattresses and sleep seeped out from the blocks of narrow-windowed houses. Along the gutters garbagecans stank sourly. In the shadow of a doorway a man and girl swayed tightly clamped in each other's arms. Saying good night. Ellen smiled happily. Greatest hit on Broadway. The words were an elevator carrying her up dizzily, up into some stately height where electric light signs crackled scarlet and gold and green, where were bright roofgardens that smelled of orchids, and the slow throb of a tango danced in a goldgreen dress with Stan while handclapping of millions beat in gusts like a hailstorm about them. Greatest hit on Broadway.

She was walking up the scaling white stairs. Before the door marked Sunderland a feeling of sick disgust suddenly choked her. She stood a long time her heart pounding with the key poised before the lock. Then with a jerk she pushed the key in the lock and opened the door.

"Strange fish, Jimmy, strange fish." Herf and Ruth Prynne sat giggling over plates of paté in the innermost corner of a clattery lowceilinged restaurant. "All the ham actors in the world seem to eat here."

"All the ham actors in the world live up at Mrs. Sunderland's."

"What's the latest news from the Balkans?"

"Balkans is right. . . ."

Beyond Ruth's black straw hat with red poppies round the crown Jimmy looked at the packed tables where faces decomposed into a graygreen blur. Two sallow hawkfaced waiters elbowed their way through the seesawing chatter of talk. Ruth was looking at him with dilated laughing eyes while she bit at a stalk of celery.

"Whee I feel so drunk," she was spluttering. "It went straight to my head. . . . Isnt it terrible?"

"Well what were these shocking goingson at 105th Street?"

"O you missed it. It was a shriek. . . . Everybody was out in the hall, Mrs. Sunderland with her hair in curlpapers, and Cassie was crying and Tony Hunter was standing in his door in pink pyjamas. . . ."

"Who's he?"

"Just a juvenile. . . . But Jimmy I must have told you about Tony Hunter. Peculiar poissons Jimmy, peculiar poissons."

Jimmy felt himself blushing, he bent over his plate. "Oh is that's what's his trouble?" he said stiffly.

"Now you're shocked, Jimmy; admit that you're shocked."

"No I'm not; go ahead, spill the dirt."

"Oh Jimmy you're such a shriek. . . . Well Cassie was sobbing and the little dog was barking, and the invisible Costello was yelling Police and fainting into the arms of an unknown man in a dress suit. And Jojo was brandishing a revolver, a little nickel one, may have been a waterpistol for all I know. . . . The only person who looked in their right senses was Elaine Olgethorpe. . . . You know the titianhaired vision that so impressed your infant mind."

"Honestly Ruth my infant mind wasnt as impressed as all that."

"Well at last the Ogle got tired of his big scene and cried out in ringing tones, Disarm me or I shall kill this woman. And Tony Hunter grabbed the pistol and took it into his room. Then Elaine Oglethorpe made a little bow as if she were taking a curtaincall, said Well goodnight everybody, and ducked into her room cool as a cucumber. . . . Can you picture it?" Ruth suddenly lowered her voice, "But everybody in the restaurant is listening to us. . . . And really I think its very disgusting. But the worst is yet to come. After the Ogle had banged on the door a couple of times and not gotten any answer he went up to Tony and rolling his eyes like Forbes Robertson in Hamlet put his arm round him and said Tony can a broken man crave asylum in your room for the night. . . . Honestly I was just so shocked."

"Is Oglethorpe that way too?"

Ruth nodded several times.

"Then why did she marry him?"

"Why that girl'd marry a trolleycar if she thought she could get anything by it."

"Ruth honestly I think you've got the whole thing sized up wrong."

"Jimmy you're too innocent to live. But let me finish the tragic tale. . . . After those two had disappeared and locked the door behind them the most awful powwow you've ever imagined went on in the hall. Of course Cassie had been having hysterics all along just to add to the excitement. When I came back from getting her some sweet spirits of ammonia in the bathroom I found the court in session. It was a shriek. Miss Costello wanted the Oglethorpes thrown out at dawn and said she'd leave if they didn't and Mrs. Sunderland kept moaning that in thirty years of theatrical experience she'd never seen a scene like that, and the man in the dress suit who was Benjamin Arden . . . you know he played a character part in Honeysuckle Jim . . . said he thought people like Tony Hunter ought to be in jail. When I went to bed it was still going on. Do you wonder that I slept late after all that and kept you waiting, poor child, an hour in the Times Drug Store?"

Joe Harland stood in his hall bedroom with his hands in his pockets staring at the picture of The Stag at Bay that hung crooked in the middle of the verdegris wall that hemmed in the shaky iron bed. His clawcold fingers moved restlessly in the bottoms of his trousers pockets. He was talking aloud in a low even voice: "Oh, it's all luck you know, but that's the last time I try the Merivales. Emily'd have given it to me if it hadn't been for that damned old tightwad. Got a soft spot in her heart Emily has. But none of em seem to realize that these things aren't always a man's own fault. It's luck that's all it is, and Lord knows they used to eat out of my hand in the old days." His rising voice grated on his ears. He pressed his lips together. You're getting batty old man. He stepped back and forth in the narrow space between the bed and the wall. Three steps. Three steps. He went to the washstand and drank out of the pitcher. The water tasted of rank wood and sloppails. He spat the last mouthful back. I need a good tenderloin steak not water. He pounded his clenched fists together. I got to do something. I got to do something.

He put on his overcoat to hide the rip in the seat of his trousers. The frayed sleeves tickled his wrists. The dark stairs creaked. He was so weak he kept grabbing the rail for fear of falling. The old woman pounced out of a door on him in the lower hall. The rat had squirmed sideways on her head as if trying to escape from under the thin gray pompadour.

"Meester Harland how about you pay me tree veeks rent?

"I'm just on my way out to cash a check now, Mrs. Budkowitz. You've been so kind about this little matter. . . . And perhaps it will interest you to know that I have the promise, no I may say the certainty of a very good position beginning Monday."

"I vait tree veeks . . . I not vait any more."

"But my dear lady I assure you upon my honor as a gentleman. . . ."

Mrs. Budkowitz began to jerk her shoulders about. Her voice rose thin and wailing like the sound of a peanut wagon. "You pay me tat fifteen dollar or I rent te room to somebody else."

"I'll pay you this very evening."

"Vat time?"

"Six o'clock."

"Allright. Plis you give me key."

"But I cant do that. Suppose I was late?"

"Tat's vy I vant te key. I'm trough vit vaiting."

"All right take the key. . . . . I hope you understand that after this insulting behavior it will be impossible for me to remain longer under your roof."

Mrs. Budkowitz laughed hoarsely. "Allright ven you pay me fifteen dollar you can take avay your grip." He put the two keys tied together with string into her gray hand and slammed the door and strode down the street.

At the corner of Third Avenue he stopped and stood shivering in the hot afternoon sunlight, sweat running down behind his ears. He was too weak to swear. Jagged oblongs of harsh sound broke one after another over his head as an elevated past over. Trucks grated by along the avenue raising a dust that smelled of gasoline and trampled horsedung. The dead air stank of stores and lunchrooms. He began walking slowly uptown towards Fourteenth Street. At a corner a crinkly warm smell of cigars stopped him like a hand on his shoulder. He stood a while looking in the little shop watching the slim stained fingers of the cigarroller shuffle the brittle outside leaves of tobacco. Remembering Romeo and Juliet Arguelles Morales he sniffed deeply. The slick tearing of tinfoil, the careful slipping off of the band, the tiny ivory penknife for the end that slit delicately as flesh, the smell of the wax match, the long inhaling of bitter crinkled deep sweet smoke. And now sir about this little matter of the new Northern Pacific bond issue. . . . He clenched his fists in the clammy pockets of his raincoat. Take my key would she the old harridan? I'll show her, damn it. Joe Harland may be down and out but he's got his pride yet.

He walked west along Fourteenth and without stopping to think and lose his nerve went down into a small basement stationery store, strode through unsteadily to the back, and stood swaying in the doorway of a little office where sat at a rolltop desk a blueeyed baldheaded fat man.

"Hello Felsius," croaked Harland.

The fat man got to his feet bewildered. "God it aint Mr. Harland is it?"

"Joe Harland himself Felsius . . . er somewhat the worse for wear." A titter died in his throat.

"Well I'll be . . . Sit right down Mr. Harland."

"Thank you Felsius. . . . Felsius I'm down and out."

"It must be five years since I've seen you Mr. Harland."

"A rotten five years it's been for me. . . . I suppose its all luck. My luck wont ever change on this earth again. Remember when I'd come in from romping with the bulls and raise hell round the office? A pretty good bonus I gave the office force that Christmas."

"Indeed it was Mr. Harland."

"Must be a dull life storekeeping after the Street."

"More to my taste Mr. Harland, nobody to boss me here."

"And how's the wife and kids?"

"Fine, fine; the oldest boy's just out of highschool."

"That the one you named for me?"

Felsius nodded. His fingers fat as sausages were tapping uneasily on the edge of the desk.

"I remember I thought I'd do something for that kid someday. It's a funny world." Harland laughed feebly. He felt a shuddery blackness stealing up behind his head. He clenched his hands round his knee and contracted the muscles of his arms. "You see Felsius, it's this way. . . . I find myself for the moment in a rather embarrassing situation

financially. . . . You know how those things are." Felsius
was staring straight ahead of him into the desk. Beads of
sweat were starting out of his bald head. "We all have our
spell of bad luck dont we? I want to float a very small loan
for a few days, just a few dollars, say twentyfive until certain combinations. . . ."

"Mr. Harland I cant do it." Felsius got to his feet. "I'm
sorry but principles is principles. . . . I've never borrowed
or lent a cent in my life. I'm sure you understand that.
. . ."

"All right, dont say any more." Harland got meekly to
his feet. "Let me have a quarter. . . . I'm not so young as
I was and I haven't eaten for two days," he mumbled, looking down at his cracked shoes. He put out his hand to
steady himself by the desk.

Felsius moved back against the wall as if to ward off a
blow. He held out a fiftycent piece on thick trembling
fingers. Harland took it, turned without a word and stumbled out through the shop. Felsius pulled a violet bordered
handkerchief out of his pocket, mopped his brow and turned
to his letters again.

We take the liberty of calling the trade's attention to four new
superfine Mullen products that we feel the greatest confidence in
recommending to our customers as a fresh and absolutely unparalleled
departure in the papermanufacturer's art . . .

They came out of the movie blinking into bright pools of
electric glare. Cassie watched him stand with his feet apart
and eyes absorbed lighting a cigar. McAvoy was a stocky
man with a beefy neck; he wore a single-button coat, a
checked vest and a dogshead pin in his brocade necktie.

"That was a rotton show or I'm a Dutchman," he was
growling.

"But I loved the twavel pictures, Morris, those Swiss
peasants dancing; I felt I was wight there."

"Damn hot in there. . . . I'd like a drink."

"Now Morris you promised," she whined.

"Oh I just meant sodawater, dont get nervous."   "Oh that'd be lovely. I'd just love a soda."

"Then we'll go for a walk in the Park."

She let the lashes fall over her eyes "Allwight Morris," she whispered without looking at him. She put her hand a little tremulously through his arm.

"If only I wasn't so goddam broke."

"I dont care Morris."

"I do by God."

At Columbus Circle they went into a drugstore. Girls in green, violet, pink summer dresses, young men in straw hats were three deep along the sodafountain. She stood back and admiringly watched him shove his way through. A man was leaning across the table behind her talking to a girl; their faces were hidden by their hatbrims.

"You juss tie that bull outside, I said to him, then I resigned."

"You mean you were fired."

"No honest I resigned before he had a chance. . . . He's a stinker d'you know it? I wont take no more of his lip. When I was walkin outa the office he called after me. . . . Young man lemme tell ye sumpen. You wont never make good till you learn who's boss around this town, till you learn that it aint you."

Morris was holding out a vanilla icecream soda to her. "Dreamin' again Cassie; anybody'd think you was a snow-bird." Smiling brighteyed, she took the soda; he was drinking coca-cola. "Thank you," she said. She sucked with pouting lips at a spoonful of icecream. "Ou Morris it's delicious."

The path between round splashes of arclights ducked into darkness. Through slant lights and nudging shadows came a smell of dusty leaves and trampled grass and occasionally a rift of cool fragrance from damp earth under shrubberies.

"Oh I love it in the Park," chanted Cassie. She stifled a belch. "D'you know Morris I oughtnt to have eaten that ice-cweam. It always gives me gas."

Morris said nothing. He put his arm round her and held her tight to him so that his thigh rubbed against hers as they walked. "Well Pierpont Morgan is dead. . . . I wish he'd left me a couple of million."

"Oh Morris wouldn't it be wonderful? Where'd we live? On Central Park South." They stood looking back at the glow of electric signs that came from Columbus Circle. To the left they could see curtained lights in the windows of a whitefaced apartmenthouse. He looked stealthily to the right and left and then kissed her. She twisted her mouth out from under his.

"Dont. . . . Somebody might see us," she whispered breathless. Inside something like a dynamo was whirring, whirring. "Morris I've been saving it up to tell you. I think Goldweiser's going to give me a specialty bit in his next show. He's stagemanager of the second woad company and he's got a lot of pull up at the office. He saw me dance yesterday."

"What did he say?"

"He said he'd fix it up for me to see the big boss Monday. . . . Oh but Morris it's not the sort of thing I want to do, it's so vulgar and howid. . . . I want to do such beautiful things. I feel I've got it in me, something without a name fluttering inside, a bird of beautiful plumage in a howid iron cage."

"That's the trouble with you, you'll never make good, you're too upstage." She looked up at him with streaming eyes that glistened in the white powdery light of an arclamp.

"Oh don't cry for God's sake. I didnt mean anythin."

"I'm not upstage with you Morris, am I?" She sniffed and wiped her eyes.

"You are kinda, that's what makes me sore. I like my little girl to pet me an love me up a little. Hell Cassie life aint all beer an sourkraut." As they walked tightly pressed one to another they felt rock under their feet. They were on a little hill of granite outcrop with shrubbery all round. The lights from the buildings that hemmed in the end of the

Park shone in their faces. They stood apart holding each other's hands.

"Take that redhaired girl up at 105th Street. . . . I bet she wouldnt be upstage when she was alone with a feller."

"She's a dweadful woman, she dont care what kind of a wep she has. . . . Oh I think you're howid." She began to cry again.

He pulled her to him roughly, pressed her to him hard with his spread hands on her back. She felt her legs tremble and go weak. She was falling through colored shafts of faintness. His mouth wouldnt let her catch her breath.

"Look out," he whispered pulling himself away from her. They walked on unsteadily down the path through the shrubbery. "I guess it aint."

"What Morris?"

"A cop. God it's hell not havin anywhere to go. Cant we go to your room?"

"But Morris they'll all see us."

"Who cares? They all do it in that house."

"Oh I hate you when you talk that way. . . . Weal love is all pure and lovely. . . . Morris you don't love me."

"Quit pickin on me cant you Cassie for a minute. . . ? Goddam it's hell to be broke."

They sat down on a bench in the light. Behind them automobiles slithered with a constant hissing scuttle in two streams along the roadway. She put her hand on his knee and he covered it with his big stubby hand.

"Morris I feel that we are going to be very happy from now on, I feel it. You're going to get a fine job, I'm sure you are."

"I aint so sure. . . . I'm not so young as I was Cassie. I aint got any time to lose."

"Why you're terribly young, you're only thirtyfive Morris. . . . And I think that something wonderful is going to happen. I'm going to get a chance to dance."

"Why you ought to make more than that redhaired girl."

"Elaine Oglethorpe. . . . She doesnt make so much. But

I'm different from her. I dont care about money; I want
to live for my dancing."

"I want money. Once you got money you can do what
you like."

"But Morris dont you believe that you can do anything
if you just want to hard enough? I believe that." He edged
his free arm round her waist. Gradually she let her head
fall on his shoulder. "Oh I dont care," she whispered with
dry lips. Behind them limousines, roadsters, touringcars,
sedans, slithered along the roadway with snaky glint of lights
running in two smooth continuous streams.

The brown serge smelled of mothballs as she folded it.
She stooped to lay it in the trunk; a layer of tissuepaper
below rustled when she smoothed the wrinkles with her hand.
The first violet morning light outside the window was making the electriclight bulb grow red like a sleepless eye. Ellen
straightened herself suddenly and stood stiff with her arms
at her sides, her face flushed pink. "It's just too low," she
said. She spread a towel over the dresses and piled brushes,
a handmirror, slippers, chemises, boxes of powder in pellmell
on top of them. Then she slammed down the lid of the
trunk, locked it and put the key in her flat alligatorskin
purse. She stood looking dazedly about the room sucking a
broken fingernail. Yellow sunlight was obliquely drenching
the chimneypots and cornices of the houses across the street.
She found herself staring at the white E.T.O. at the end of
her trunk. "It's all too terribly disgustingly low," she said
again. Then she grabbed a nailfile off the bureau and
scratched out the O. "Whee," she whispered and snapped
her fingers. After she had put on a little bucketshaped black
hat and a veil, so that people wouldn't see she'd been crying,
she piled a lot of books, *Youth's Encounter, Thus Spoke
Zarathustra, The Golden Ass, Imaginary Conversations,
Aphrodite, Chansons de Bilitis* and the *Oxford Book of
French Verse* in a silk shawl and tied them together.

There was a faint tapping at the door. "Who's that," she whispered.

"It just me," came a tearful voice.

Ellen unlocked the door. "Why Cassie what's the matter?" Cassie rubbed her wet face in the hollow of Ellen's neck. "Oh Cassie you're gumming my veil. . . . What on earth's the matter?"

"I've been up all night thinking how unhappy you must be."

"But Cassie I've never been happier in my life."

"Aren't men dweadful?"

"No. . . . They are much nicer than women anyway."

"Elaine I've got to tell you something. I know you dont care anything about me but I'm going to tell you all the same."

"Of course I care about you Cassie. . . . Dont be silly. But I'm busy now. . . . Why dont you go back to bed and tell me later?"

"I've got to tell you now." Ellen sat down on her trunk resignedly. "Elaine I've bwoken it off with Morris. . . . Isn't it tewible?" Cassie wiped her eyes on the sleeve of her lavender dressinggown and sat down beside Ellen on the trunk.

"Look dear," said Ellen gently. "Suppose you wait just a second, I'm going to telephone for a taxi. I want to make a getaway before Jojo's up. I'm sick of big scenes." The hall smelled stuffily of sleep and massagecream. Ellen talked very low into the receiver. The gruff man's voice at the garage growled pleasantly in her ears. "Sure right away miss." She tiptoed springily back into the room and closed the door.

"I thought he loved me, honestly I did Elaine. Oh men are so dweadful. Morris was angwy because I wouldn't live with him. I think it would be wicked. I'd work my fingers to the bone for him, he knows that. Havent I been doing it two years? He said he couldnt go on unless he had me weally, you know what he meant, and I said our love was so beautiful it could go on for years and years. I could love him for a lifetime without even kissing him. Dont you think love should be pure? And then he made fun of my dancing and said I was Chalif's mistwess and just kidding him along and we quaweled dweadfully and he called me dweadful names and went away and said he'd never come back."

"Dont worry about that Cassie, he'll come back all right."

"No but you're so material, Elaine. I mean spiwitually our union is bwoken forever. Cant you see there was this beautiful divine spiwitual thing between us and it's bwoken." She began to sob again with her face pressed into Ellen's shoulder.

"But Cassie I dont see what fun you get out of it all?"

"Oh you dont understand. You're too young. I was like you at first except that I wasnt mawied and didnt wun awound with men. But now I want spiwitual beauty. I want to get it through my dancing and my life, I want beauty everywhere and I thought Morris wanted it."

"But Morris evidently did."

"Oh Elaine you're howid, and I love you so much."

Ellen got to her feet. "I'm going to run downstairs so that the taximan wont ring the bell."

"But you cant go like this."

"You just watch me." Ellen gathered up the bundle of books in one hand and in the other carried the black leather dressingcase. "Look Cassie will you be a dear and show him the trunk when he comes up to get it. . . . And one other thing, when Stan Emery calls up tell him to call me at the Brevoort or at the Lafayette. Thank goodness I didnt deposit my money last week. . . . And Cassie if you find any little odds and ends of mine around you just keep em. . . . Goodby." She lifted her veil and kissed Cassie quickly on the cheeks.

"Oh how can you be so bwave as to go away all alone like this. . . . You'll let Wuth and me come down to see you wont you? We're so fond of you. Oh Elaine you're going to have a wonderful career, I know you are."

"And promise not to tell Jojo where I am. . . . He'll

find out soon enough anyway. . . . I'll call him up in a week."

She found the taxidriver in the hall looking at the names above the pushbuttons. He went up to fetch her trunk. She settled herself happily on the dusty buff seat of the taxi, taking deep breaths of the riversmelling morning air. The taxidriver smiled roundly at her when he had let the trunk slide off his back onto the dashboard.

"Pretty heavy, miss."

"It's a shame you had to carry it all alone."

"Oh I kin carry heavier'n 'at."

"I want to go to the Hotel Brevoort, Fifth Avenue at about Eighth Street."

When he leaned to crank the car the man pushed his hat back on his head letting ruddy curly hair out over his eyes. "All right I'll take you anywhere you like," he said as he hopped into his seat in the jiggling car. When they turned down into the very empty sunlight of Broadway a feeling of happiness began to sizzle and soar like rockets inside her. The air beat fresh, thrilling in her face. The taxidriver talked back at her through the open window.

"I thought yous was catchin a train to go away somewhere, miss."

"Well I am going away somewhere."

"It'd be a foine day to be goin away somewhere."

"I'm going away from my husband." The words popped out of her mouth before she could stop them.

"Did he trow you out?"

"No I cant say he did that," she said laughing.

"My wife trun me out tree weeks ago."

"How was that?"

"Locked de door when I came home one night an wouldnt let me in. She'd had the lock changed when I was out workin."

"That's a funny thing to do."

"She says I git slopped too often. I aint goin back to her an I aint goin to support her no more. . . . She can put me in jail if she likes. I'm troo. I'm gettin an apartment on

Twentysecond Avenoo wid another feller an we're goin to
git a pianer an live quiet an lay offen the skoits."

"Matrimony isnt much is it?"

"You said it. What leads up to it's all right, but gettin
married is loike de mornin after."

Fifth Avenue was white and empty and swept by a sparkling wind. The trees in Madison Square were unexpectedly
bright green like ferns in a dun room. At the Brevoort a
sleepy French nightporter carried her baggage. In the
low whitepainted room the sunlight drowsed on a faded
crimson armchair. Ellen ran about the room like a small
child kicking her heels and clapping her hands. With pursed
lips and tilted head she arranged her toilet things on the
bureau. Then she hung her yellow nightgown on a chair
and undressed, caught sight of herself in the mirror, stood
naked looking at herself with her hands on her tiny firm
appleshaped breasts.

She pulled on her nightgown and went to the phone.
"Please send up a pot of chocolate and rolls to 108 . . . as
soon as you can please." Then she got into bed. She lay
laughing with her legs stretched wide in the cool slippery
sheets.

Hairpins were sticking into her head. She sat up and
pulled them all out and shook the heavy coil of her hair
down about her shoulders. She drew her knees up to her
chin and sat thinking. From the street she could hear the
occasional rumble of a truck. In the kitchens below her room
a sound of clattering had begun. From all around came a
growing rumble of traffic beginning. She felt hungry and
alone. The bed was a raft on which she was marooned
alone, always alone, afloat on a growling ocean. A shudder
went down her spine. She drew her knees up closer to her
chin.

III. Nine Days' Wonder

*The sun's moved to Jersey, the sun's behind Ho-
boken.*

*Covers are clicking on typewriters, rolltop desks
are closing; elevators go up empty, come down
jammed. It's ebbtide in the downtown district,
flood in Flatbush, Woodlawn, Dyckman Street,
Sheepshead Bay, New Lots Avenue, Canarsie.*

*Pink sheets, green sheets, gray sheets, FULL
MARKET REPORTS, FINALS ON HAVRE
DE GRACE. Print squirms among the shop-
worn officeworn sagging faces, sore fingertips,
aching insteps, strongarm men cram into subway
expresses. SENATORS 8, GIANTS 2, DIVA
RECOVERS PEARLS, $800,000 ROBBERY.*

*It's ebbtide on Wall Street, floodtide in the
Bronx.*

The sun's gone down in Jersey.

"**G**ODAMIGHTY," shouted Phil Sandbourne and
pounded with his fist on the desk, "I don't think
so. . . . A man's morals arent anybody's business.
It's his work that counts."

"Well?"

"Well I think Stanford White has done more for the city
of New York that any other man living. Nobody knew there
was such a thing as architecture before he came. . . . And
to have this Thaw shoot him down in cold blood and then
get away with it. . . . By gad if the people of this town had
the spirit of guineapigs they'd——"

"Phil you're getting all excited over nothing." The other
man took his cigar out of his mouth and leaned back in his
swivel chair and yawned.

"Oh hell I want a vacation. Golly it'll be good to get
out in those old Maine woods again."

"What with Jew lawyers and Irish judges . . . " spluttered Phil.

"Aw pull the chain, old man."

"A fine specimen of a public-spirited citizen you are Hartly."

Hartly laughed and rubbed the palm of his hand over his bald head. "Oh that stuff's all right in winter, but I cant go it in summer. . . . Hell all I live for is three weeks' vacation anyway. What do I care if all the architects in New York get bumped off as long as it dont raise the price of commutation to New Rochelle. . . . Let's go eat." As they went down in the elevator Phil went on talking: "The only other man I ever knew who was really a born in the bone architect was ole Specker, the feller I worked for when I first came north, a fine old Dane he was too. Poor devil died o cancer two years ago. Man, he was an architect. I got a set of plans and specifications home for what he called a communal building. . . . Seventyfive stories high stepped back in terraces with a sort of hanging garden on every floor, hotels, theaters, Turkish baths, swimming pools, department stores, heating plant, refrigerating and market space all in the same buildin."

"Did he eat coke?"

"No siree he didnt."

They were walking east along Thirtyfourth Street, sparse of people in the sultry midday. "Gad," burst out Phil Sandbourne, suddenly. "The girls in this town get prettier every year. Like these new fashions, do you?"

"Sure. All I wish is that I was gettin younger every year instead of older."

"Yes about all us old fellers can do is watch em go past."

"That's fortunate for us or we'd have our wives out after us with bloodhounds. . . . Man when I think of those mighthavebeens!"

As they crossed Fifth Avenue Phil caught sight of a girl in a taxicab. From under the black brim of a little hat with a red cockade in it two gray eyes flash green black into his. He swallowed his breath. The traffic roars dwindled into distance. She shant take her eyes away. Two steps and open the door and sit beside her, beside her slenderness perched like a bird on the seat. Driver drive to beat hell. Her lips are pouting towards him, her eyes flutter gray caught birds. "Hay look out. . ." A pouncing iron rumble crashes down on him from behind. Fifth Avenue spins in red blue purple spirals. O Kerist. "That's all right, let me be. I'll get up myself in a minute." "Move along there. Git back there." Braying voices, blue pillars of policemen. His back, his legs are all warm gummy with blood. Fifth Avenue throbs with loudening pain. A little bell jingle-jangling nearer. As they lift hi minto the ambulance Fifth Avenue shrieks to throttling agony and bursts. He cranes his neck to see her, weakly, like a terrapin on its back; didnt my eyes snap steel traps on her? He finds himself whimpering. She might have stayed to see if I was killed. The jinglejangling bell dwindles fainter, fainter into the night.

The burglaralarm across the street had rung on steadily. Jimmy's sleep had been strung on it in hard knobs like beads on a string. Knocking woke him. He sat up in bed with a lurch and found Stan Emery, his face gray with dust, his hands in the pockets of a red leather coat, standing at the foot of the bed. He was laughing swaying back and forth on the balls of his feet.

"Gosh what time is it?" Jimmy sat up in bed digging his knuckles into his eyes. He yawned and looked about with bitter dislike, at the wallpaper the dead green of Poland Water bottles, at the split green shade that let in a long trickle of sunlight, at the marble fireplace blocked up by an enameled tin plate painted with scaly roses, at the frayed blue bathrobe on the foot of the bed, at the mashed cigarette-butts in the mauve glass ashtray.

Stan's face was red and brown and laughing under the chalky mask of dust. "Eleven thirty," he was saying.

"Let's see that's six hours and a half. I guess that'll do. But Stan what the hell are you doing here?"

"You havent got a little nip of liquor anywhere have you Herf? Dingo and I are extraordinarily thirsty. We came all the way from Boston and only stopped once for gas and water. I havent been to bed for two days. I want to see if I can last out the week."

"Kerist I wish I could last out the week in bed."

"What you need's a job on a newspaper to keep you busy Herfy."

"What's going to happen to you Stan . . ." Jimmy twisted himself round so that he was sitting on the edge of the bed " . . . is that you're going to wake up one morning and find yourself on a marble slab at the morgue."

The bathroom smelled of other people's toothpaste and of chloride disinfectant. The bathmat was wet and Jimmy folded it into a small square before he stepped gingerly out of his slippers. The cold water set the blood jolting through him. He ducked his head under and jumped out and stood shaking himself like a dog, the water streaming into his eyes and ears. Then he put on his bathrobe and lathered his face.

> Flow river flow
> Down to the sea,

he hummed off key as he scraped his chin with the safety-razor. Mr. Grover I'm afraid I'm going to have to give up the job after next week. Yes I'm going abroad; I'm going to do foreign correspondent work for the A. P. To Mexico for the U. P. To Jericho more likely, Halifax Correspondent of the Mudturtle Gazette. *It was Christmas in the harem and the eunuchs all were there.*

> . . . from the banks of the Seine
> To the banks of the Saskatchewan.

He doused his face with listerine, bundled his toilet things into his wet towel and smarting ran back up a flight of greencarpeted cabbagy stairs and down the hall to his bed-room. Halfway he passed the landlady dumpy in a mob cap who stopped her carpet sweeper to give an icy look at his skinny bare legs under the blue bathrobe.

"Good morning Mrs. Maginnis."

"It's goin to be powerful hot today, Mr. Herf."

"I guess it is all right."

Stan was lying on the bed reading *La Revolte des Anges*. "Darn it, I wish I knew some languages the way you do Herfy."

"Oh I dont know any French any more. I forget em so much quicker than I learn em."

"By the way I'm fired from college."

"How's that?"

"Dean told me he thought it advisable I shouldnt come back next year . . . felt that there were other fields of activity where my activities could be more actively active. You know the crap."

"That's a darn shame."

"No it isnt; I'm tickled to death. I asked him why he hadnt fired me before if he felt that way. Father'll be sore as a crab . . . but I've got enough cash on me not to go home for a week. I dont give a damn anyway. Honest havent you got any liquor?"

"Now Stan how's a poor wageslave like myself going to have a cellar on thirty dollars a week?"

"This is a pretty lousy room. . . . You ought to have been born a capitalist like me."

"Room's not so bad. . . . What drives me crazy is that paranoiac alarm across the street that rings all night."

"That's a burglar alarm isn't it?"

"There cant be any burglars because the place is vacant. The wires must get crossed or something. I dont know when it stopped but it certainly drove me wild when I went to bed this morning."

"Now James Herf you dont mean me to infer that you come home sober every night?"

"A man'd have to be deaf not to hear that damn thing, drunk or sober."

"Well in my capacity of bloated bondholder I want you to come out and eat lunch. Do you realize that you've been playing round with your toilet for exactly one hour by the clock?"

They went down the stairs that smelled of shavingsoap and then of brasspolish and then of bacon and then of singed hair and then of garbage and coalgas.

"You're damn lucky Herfy, never to have gone to college."

"Didnt I graduate from Columbia you big cheese, that's more than you could do?"

The sunlight swooped tingling in Jimmy's face when he opened the door.

"That doesnt count."

"God I like sun," cried Jimmy, I wish it'd been real Colombia. . . . "

"Do you mean Hail Columbia?"

"No I mean Bogota and the Orinoco and all that sort of thing."

"I knew a darn good feller went down to Bogota. Had to drink himself to death to escape dying of elephantiasis."

"I'd be willing to risk elephantiasis and bubonic plague and spotted fever to get out of this hole."

"City of orgies walks and joys . . ."

"Orgies nutten, as we say at a hun'an toitytoird street. . . . Do you realize that I've lived all my life in this goddam town except four years when I was little and that I was born here and that I'm likely to die here? . . . I've a great mind to join the navy and see the world."

"How do you like Dingo in her new coat of paint?"

"Pretty nifty, looks like a regular Mercedes under the dust."

"I wanted to paint her red like a fire engine, but the garageman finally persuaded me to paint her blue like a cop. . . . Do you mind going to Mouquin's and having an absinthe cocktail."

"Absinthe for breakfast. . . . Good Lord."

They drove west along Twenty-third Street that shone with sheets of reflected light off windows, oblong glints off delivery wagons, figureeight-shaped flash of nickel fittings.

"How's Ruth, Jimmy?"

"She's all right. She hasnt got a job yet."

"Look there's a Daimlier."

Jimmy grunted vaguely. As they turned up Sixth Avenue a policeman stopped them.

"Your cut out," he yelled.

"I'm on my way to the garage to get it fixed. Muffler's coming off."

"Better had. . . . Get a ticket another time."

"Gee you get away with murder Stan . . . in everything," said Jimmy. "I never can get away with a thing even if I am three years older than you."

"It's a gift."

The restaurant smelled merrily of fried potatoes and cocktails and cigars and cocktails. It was hot and full of talking and sweaty faces.

"But Stan dont roll your eyes romantically when you ask about Ruth and me. . . . We're just very good friends."

"Honestly I didnt mean anything, but I'm sorry to hear it all the same. I think it's terrible."

"Ruth doesn't care about anything but her acting. She's so crazy to succeed, she cuts out everything else."

"Why the hell does everybody want to succeed? I'd like to meet somebody who wanted to fail. That's the only sublime thing."

"It's all right if you have a comfortable income."

"That's all bunk. . . . Golly this is some cocktail. Herfy I think you're the only sensible person in this town. You have no ambitions."

"How do you know I havent?"

"But what can you do with success when you get it? You cant eat it or drink it. Of course I understand that people who havent enough money to feed their faces and all that should scurry round and get it. But success . . ."

"The trouble with me is I cant decide what I want most, so my motion is circular, helpless and confoundedly discouraging."

"Oh but God decided that for you. You know all the time, but you wont admit it to yourself."

"I imagine what I want most is to get out of this town, preferably first setting off a bomb under the Times Building."

"Well why don't you do it? It's just one foot after another."

"But you have to know which direction to step."

"That's the last thing that's of any importance."

"Then there's money."

"Why money's the easiest thing in the world to get."

"For the eldest son of Emery and Emery."

"Now Herf it's not fair to cast my father's iniquities in my face. You know I hate that stuff as much as you do."

"I'm not blaming you Stan; you're a damn lucky kid, that's all. Of course I'm lucky too, a hell of a lot luckier than most. My mother's leftover money supported me until I was twentytwo and I still have a few hundreds stowed away for that famous rainy day, and my uncle, curse his soul, gets me new jobs when I get fired."

"Baa baa black sheep."

"I guess I'm really afraid of my uncles and aunts. . . . You ought to see my cousin James Merivale. Has done everything he was told all his life and flourished like a green bay tree. . . . The perfect wise virgin."

"Ah guess youse one o dem dere foolish virgins."

"Stan you're feeling your liquor, you're beginning to talk niggertalk."

"Baa baa." Stan put down his napkin and leaned back laughing in his throat.

The smell of absinthe sicklytingling grew up like the magician's rosebush out of Jimmy's glass. He sipped it wrinkling his nose. "As a moralist I protest," he said. "Whee it's amazing."

"What I need is a whiskey and soda to settle those cocktails."

"I'll watch you. I'm a working man. I must be able to tell between the news that's fit and the news that's not fit. . . . God I dont want to start talking about that. It's all so criminally silly. . . . I'll say that this cocktail sure does knock you for a loop."

"You neednt think you're going to do anything else but drink this afternoon. There's somebody I want to introduce you to."

"And I was going to sit down righteously and write an article."

"What's that?"

"Oh a dodaddle called Confessions of a Cub Reporter."

"Look is this Thursday?"

"Yare."

"Then I know where she'll be."

"I'm going to light out of it all," said Jimmy somberly, "and go to Mexico and make my fortune. . . . I'm losing all the best part of my life rotting in New York."

"How'll you make your fortune?"

"Oil, gold, highway robbery, anything so long as it's not newspaper work."

"Baa baa black sheep baa baa."

"You quit baaing at me."

"Let's get the hell out of here and take Dingo to have her muffler fastened."

Jimmy stood waiting in the door of the reeking garage. The dusty afternoon sunlight squirmed in bright worms of heat on his face and hands. Brownstone, redbrick, asphalt flickering with red and green letters of signs, with bits of paper in the gutter rotated in a slow haze about him. Two carwashers talking behind him:

"Yep I was making good money until I went after that lousy broad."

"I'll say she's a goodlooker, Charley. I should worry. . . . Dont make no difference after the first week."

Stan came up behind him and ran him along the street by the shoulders. "Car wont be fixed until five o'clock. Let's taxi. . . . Hotel Lafayette," he shouted at the driver and slapped Jimmy on the knee. "Well Herfy old fossil, you know what the Governor of North Carolina said to the Governor of South Carolina."

"No."

"It's a long time between drinks."

"Baa, baa," Stan was bleating under his breath as they stormed into the café. "Ellie here are the black sheep," he shouted laughing. His face froze suddenly stiff. Opposite Ellen at the table sat her husband, one eyebrow lifted very high and the other almost merging with the eyelashes. A teapot sat impudently between them.

"Hello Stan, sit down," she said quietly. Then she continued smiling into Oglethorpe's face. "Isnt that wonderful Jojo?"

"Ellie this is Mr. Herf," said Stan gruffly.

"Oh I'm so glad to meet you. I used to hear about you up at Mrs. Sunderland's."

They were silent. Oglethorpe was tapping on the table with his spoon. "Why heow deo you deo Mr. Herf," he said with sudden unction. "Dont you remember how we met?"

"By the way how's everything up there Jojo?"

"Just topping thanks. Cassahndrah's beau has left her and there's been the most appalling scandal about that Costello creature. It seems that she came home foxed the other night, to the ears my deah, and tried to take the taxi driver into her room with her, and the poor boy protesting all the time that all he wanted was his fare. . . . It was appalling."

Stan got stiffly to his feet and walked out.

The three of them sat without speaking. Jimmy tried to keep from fidgeting in his chair. He was about to get up, when something velvetsoft in her eyes stopped him.

"Has Ruth got a job yet, Mr. Herf?" she asked.

"No she hasnt."

"It's the rottenest luck."

"Oh it's a darn shame. I know she can act. The trouble

is she has too much sense of humor to play up to managers and people."

"Oh the stage is a nasty dirty game, isn't it Jojo?"

"The nawstiest, my deah."

Jimmy couldn't keep his eyes off her; her small squarely shaped hands, her neck molded with a gold sheen between the great coil of coppery hair and the bright blue dress.

"Well my deah . . ." Oglethorpe got to his feet.

"Jojo I'm going to sit here a little longer."

Jimmy was staring at the thin triangles of patent leather that stuck out from Oglethorpe's pink buff spats. Cant be feet in them. He stood up suddenly.

"Now Mr. Herf couldnt you keep me company for fifteen minutes? I've got to leave here at six and I forgot to bring a book and I cant walk in these shoes."

Jimmy blushed and sat down again stammering: "Why of course I'd be delighted. . . . Suppose we drink something."

"I'll finish my tea, but why dont you have a gin fizz? I love to see people drink gin fizzes. It makes me feel that I'm in the tropics sitting in a jujube grove waiting for the riverboat to take us up some ridiculous melodramatic river all set about with fevertrees."

"Waiter I want a gin fizz please."

Joe Harland had slumped down in his chair until his head rested on his arms. Between his grimestiff hands his eyes followed uneasily the lines in the marbletop table. The gutted lunchroom was silent under the sparse glower of two bulbs hanging over the counter where remained a few pies under a bellglass, and a man in a white coat nodding on a tall stool. Now and then the eyes in his gray doughy face flicked open and he grunted and looked about. At the last table over were the hunched shoulders of men asleep, faces crumpled like old newspapers pillowed on arms. Joe Harland sat up straight and yawned. A woman blobby under a raincoat with a face red and purplish streaked like rancid meat was asking for a cup of coffee at the counter. Carrying the mug carefully between her two hands she brought it over to the table and sat down opposite him. Joe Harland let his head down onto his arms again.

"Hay yous how about a little soivice?" The woman's voice shrilled in Harland's ears like the screech of chalk on a blackboard.

"Well what d'ye want?" snarled the man behind the counter. The woman started sobbing. "He asts me what I want. . . . I aint used to bein talked to brutal."

"Well if there's anythin you want you kin juss come an git it. . . . Soivice at this toime o night!"

Harland could smell her whiskey breath as she sobbed. He raised his head and stared at her. She twisted her flabby mouth into a smile and bobbed her head towards him.

"Mister I aint accustomed to bein treated brutal. If my husband was aloive he wouldn't have the noive. Who's the loikes o him to say what toime o night a lady ought to have soivice, the little shriveled up shrimp." She threw back her head and laughed so that her hat fell off backwards. "That's what he is, a little shriveled up shrimp, insultin a lady with his toime o night."

Some strands of gray hair with traces of henna at the tips had fallen down about her face. The man in the white coat walked over to the table.

"Look here Mother McCree I'll trow ye out o here if you raise any more distoirbance. . . . What do you want?"

"A nickel's woirt o doughnuts," she sniveled with a side-long leer at Harland.

Joe Harland shoved his face into the hollow of his arm again and tried to go to sleep. He heard the plate set down followed by her toothless nibbling and an occasional sucking noise when she drank the coffee. A new customer had come in and was talking across the counter in a low growling voice.

"Mister, mister aint it terrible to want a drink?" He raised his head again and found her eyes the blurred blue of watered milk looking into his. "What ye goin to do now darlin?"

"God knows."

"Virgin an Saints it'd be noice to have a bed an a pretty lace shimmy and a noice feller loike you darlin . . . mister."

"Is that all?"

"Oh mister if my poor husband was aloive, he wouldn't let em treat me loike they do. I lost my husband on the *General Slocum* might ha been yesterday."

"He's not so unlucky."

"But he doid in his sin without a priest, darlin. It's terrible to die in yer sin . . ."

"Oh hell I want to sleep."

Her voice went on in a faint monotonous screech setting his teeth on edge. "The Saints has been agin me ever since I lost my husband on the *General Slocum*. I aint been an honest woman." . . . She began to sob again. "The Virgin and Saints an Martyrs is agin me, everybody's agin me. . . . Oh wont somebody treat me noice."

"I want to sleep. . . . Cant you shut up?"

She stooped and fumbled for her hat on the floor. She sat sobbing rubbing her swollen redgrimed knuckles into her eyes.

"Oh mister dont ye want to treat me noice?"

Joe Harland got to his feet breathing hard. "Goddam you cant you shut up?" His voice broke into a whine. "Isnt there anywhere you can get a little peace? There's nowhere you can get any peace." He pulled his cap over his eyes, shoved his hands down into his pockets and shambled out of the lunchroom. Over Chatham Square the sky was brightening redviolet through the latticework of elevated tracks. The lights were two rows of bright brass knobs up the empty Bowery.

A policeman passed swinging his nightstick. Joe Harland felt the policeman's eyes on him. He tried to walk fast and briskly as if he were going somewhere on business.

"Well Miss Oglethorpe how do you like it?"

"Like what?"

"Oh you know . . . being a nine days' wonder."

"Why I don't know at all Mr. Goldweiser."

"Women know everything but they wont let on."

Ellen sits in a gown of nilegreen silk in a springy armchair at the end of a long room jingling with talk and twinkle of chandeliers and jewelry, dotted with the bright moving black of evening clothes and silveredged colors cf women's dresses. The curve of Harry Goldweiser's nose merges directly into the curve of his bald forehead, his big rump bulges over the edges of a triangular gilt stool, his small brown eyes measure her face like antennæ as he talks to her. A woman nearby smells of sandalwood. A woman with orange lips and a chalk face under an orange turban passes talking to a man with a pointed beard. A hawkbeaked woman with crimson hair puts her hand on a man's shoulder from behind. "Why how do you do, Miss Cruikshank; it's surprising isn't it how everybody in the world is always at the same place at the same time." Ellen sits in the armchair drowsily listening, coolness of powder on her face and arms, fatness of rouge on her lips, her body just bathed fresh as a violet under the silk dress, under the silk underclothes; she sits dreamily, drowsily listening. A sudden twinge of men's voices knotting about her. She sits up cold white out of reach like a lighthouse. Men's hands crawl like bugs on the unbreakable glass. Men's looks blunder and flutter against it helpless as moths. But in deep pitblackness inside something clangs like a fire engine.

George Baldwin stood beside the breakfast table with a copy of the New York *Times* folded in his hand. "Now Cecily," he was saying "we must be sensible about these things."

"Cant you see that I'm trying to be sensible?" she said in

a jerking snivelly voice. He stood looking at her without sitting down rolling a corner of the paper between his finger and thumb. Mrs. Baldwin was a tall woman with a mass of carefully curled chestnut hair piled on top of her head. She sat before the silver coffeeservice fingering the sugarbowl with mushroomwhite fingers that had very sharp pink nails.

"George I cant stand it any more that's all." She pressed her quaking lips hard together.

"But my dear you exaggerate. . . ."

"How exaggerate? . . . It means our life has been a pack of lies."

"But Cecily we're fond of each other."

"You married me for my social position, you know it. . . . I was fool enough to fall in love with you. All right, it's over."

"It's not true. I really loved you. Dont you remember how terrible you thought it was you couldnt really love me?"

"You brute to refer to that. . . . Oh it's horrible!"

The maid came in from the pantry with bacon and eggs on a tray. They sat silent looking at each other. The maid swished out of the room and closed the door. Mrs. Baldwin put her forehead down on the edge of the table and began to cry. Baldwin sat staring at the headlines in the paper. ASSASSINATION OF ARCHDUKE WILL HAVE GRAVE CONSEQUENCES. AUSTRIAN ARMY MOBILIZED. He went over and put his hand on her crisp hair.

"Poor old Cecily," he said.

"Dont touch me."

She ran out of the room with her handkerchief to her face. He sat down, helped himself to bacon and eggs and toast and began to eat; everything tasted like paper. He stopped eating to scribble a note on a scratchpad he kept in his breast pocket behind his handkerchief: See Collins vs. Arbuthnot, N.Y.S.C. Appel. Div.

The sound of a step in the hall outside caught his ear, the click of a latch. The elevator had just gone down. He ran four flights down the steps. Through the glass and wrought-iron doors of the vestibule downstairs he caught sight of her on the curb, standing tall and stiff, pulling on her gloves. He rushed out and took her by the hand just as a taxi drove up. Sweat beaded on his forehead and was prickly under his collar. He could see himself standing there with the napkin ridiculous in his hand and the colored doorman grinning and saying, "Good mornin, Mr. Baldwin, looks like it going to be a fine day." Gripping her hand tight, he said in a low voice through his teeth:

"Cecily there's something I want to talk to you about. Wont you wait a minute and we'll go downtown together? . . . Wait about five minutes please," he said to the taxi-driver. We'll be right down." Squeezing her wrist hard he walked back with her to the elevator. When they stood in the hall of their own apartment, she suddenly looked him straight in the face with dry blazing eyes.

"Come in here Cecily" he said gently. He closed their bedroom door and locked it. "Now lets talk this over quietly. Sit down dear." He put a chair behind her. She sat down suddenly stiffly like a marionette.

"Now look here Cecily you have no right to talk the way you do about my friends. Mrs. Oglethorpe is a friend of mine. We occasionally take tea together in some perfectly public place and that's all. I would invite her up here but I've been afraid you would be rude to her. . . . You cant go on giving away to your insane jealousy like this. I allow you complete liberty and trust you absolutely. I think I have the right to expect the same confidence from you. . . . Cecily do be my sensible little girl again. You've been lis-tening to what a lot of old hags fabricate out of whole cloth maliciously to make you miserable."

"She's not the only one."

"Cecily I admit frankly there were times soon after we were married . . . when . . . But that's all over years ago. . . . And who's fault was it? . . . Oh Cecily a woman like you cant understand the physical urgences of a man like me."

"Havent I done my best?"

"My dear these things arent anybody's fault. . . . I dont blame you. . . . If you'd really loved me then . . ."

"What do you think I stay in this hell for except for you? Oh you're such a brute." She sat dryeyed staring at her feet in their gray buckskin slippers, twisting and untwisting in her fingers the wet string of her handkerchief.

"Look here Cecily a divorce would be very harmful to my situation downtown just at the moment, but if you really dont want to go on living with me I'll see what I can arrange. . . . But in any event you must have more confidence in me. You know I'm fond of you. And for God's sake dont go to see anybody about it without consulting me. You dont want a scandal and headlines in the papers, do you?"

"All right . . . leave me alone. . . . I dont care about anything."

"All right. . . . I'm pretty late. I'll go on downtown in that taxi. You don't want to come shopping or anything?"

She shook her head. He kissed her on the forehead, took his straw hat and stick in the hall and hurried out.

"Oh I'm the most miserable woman," she groaned and got to her feet. Her head ached as if it were bound with hot wire. She went to the window and leaned out into the sunlight. Across Park Avenue the flameblue sky was barred with the red girder cage of a new building. Steam riveters rattled incessantly; now and then a donkeyengine whistled and there was a jingle of chains and a fresh girder soared crosswise in the air. Men in blue overalls moved about the scaffolding. Beyond to the northwest a shining head of clouds soared blooming compactly like a cauliflower. Oh if it would only rain. As the thought came to her there was a low growl of thunder above the din of building and of traffic. Oh if it would only rain.

Ellen had just hung a chintz curtain in the window to hide with its blotchy pattern of red and purple flowers the vista of desert backyards and brick flanks of downtown houses. In the middle of the bare room was a boxcouch cumbered with teacups, a copper chafingdish and percolator; the yellow hardwood floor was littered with snippings of chintz and curtainpins; books, dresses, bedlinen cascaded from a trunk in the corner; from a new mop in the fireplace exuded a smell of cedar oil. Ellen was leaning against the wall in a daffodilcolored kimono looking happily about the big shoebox-shaped room when the buzzer startled her. She pushed a rope of hair up off her forehead and pressed the button that worked the latch. There was a little knock on the door. A woman was standing in the dark of the hall.

"Why Cassie I couldn't make out who you were. Come in. . . . What's the matter?"

"You are sure I'm not intwuding?"

"Of course not." Ellen leaned to give her a little pecking kiss. Cassandra Wilkins was very pale and there was a nervous quiver about her eyelids. "You can give me some advice. I'm just getting my curtains up. . . . Look do you think that purple goes all right with the gray wall? It looks kind of funny to me."

"I think it's beautiful. What a beautiful woom. How happy you're going to be here."

"Put that chafingdish down on the floor and sit down. I'll make some tea. There's a kind of bathroom kitchenette in the alcove there."

"You're sure it wouldn't be too much twouble?"

"Of course not. . . .But Cassie what's the matter?"

"Oh everything. . . . I came down to tell you but I cant. I cant ever tell anybody."

"I'm so excited about this apartment. Imagine Cassie it's the first place of my own I ever had in my life. Daddy wants me to live with him in Passaic, but I just felt I couldn't."

"And what does Mr. Oglethorpe . . . ? Oh but that's

impertinent of me. . . . Do forgive me Elaine. I'm almost cwazy. I don't know what I'm saying."

"Oh Jojo's a dear. He's even going to let me divorce him if I want to. . . . Would you if you were me?" Without waiting for an answer she disappeared between the folding doors. Cassie remained hunched up on the edge of the couch.

Ellen came back with a blue teapot in one hand and a pan of steaming water in the other. "Do you mind not having lemon or cream? There's some sugar on the mantelpiece. These cups are clean because I just washed them. Dont you think they are pretty? Oh you cant imagine how wonderful and domestic it makes you feel to have a place all to yourself. I hate living in a hotel. Honestly this place makes me just so domestic . . . Of course the ridiculous thing is that I'll probably have to give it up or sublet as soon as I've got it decently fixed up. Show's going on the road in three weeks. I want to get out of it but Harry Goldweiser wont let me." Cassie was taking little sips of tea out of her spoon. She began to cry softly. "Why Cassie buck up, what's the matter?"

"Oh, you're so lucky in everything Elaine and I'm so miserable."

"Why I always thought it was my jinx that got the beauty-prize, but what is the matter?"

Cassie put down her cup and pushed her two clenched hands into her neck. "It's just this," she said in a strangled voice. . . . "I think I'm going to have a baby." She put her head down on her knees and sobbed.

"Are you sure? Everybody's always having scares."

"I wanted our love to be always pure and beautiful, but he said he'd never see me again if I didn't . . . and I hate him." She shook the words out one by one between tearing sobs.

"Why don't you get married?"

"I cant. I wont. It would interfere."

"How long since you knew?"

"Oh it must have been ten days ago easily. I know it's that

. . . I dont want to have anything but my dancing." She stopped sobbing and began taking little sips of tea again.

Ellen walked back and forth in front of the fireplace. "Look here Cassie there's no use getting all wrought up over things, is there? I know a woman who'll help you. . . . Do pull yourself together please."

"Oh I couldn't, I couldn't." . . . The saucer slid off her knees and broke in two on the floor. "Tell me Elaine have you ever been through this? . . . Oh I'm so sowy. I'll buy you another saucer Elaine." She got totteringly to her feet and put the cup and spoon on the mantelpiece.

"Oh of course I have. When we were first married I had a terrible time. . . ."

"Oh Elaine isn't it hideous all this? Life would be so beautiful and free and natural without it. . . . I can feel the howor of it cweeping up on me, killing me."

"Things are rather like that," said Ellen gruffly.

Cassie was crying again. "Men are so bwutal and selfish."

"Have another cup of tea, Cassie."

"Oh I couldn't. My dear I feel a deadly nausea. . . . Oh I think I'm going to be sick."

"The bathroom is right through the folding doors and to the left."

Ellen walked up and down the room with clenched teeth. I hate women. I hate women.

After a while Cassie came back into the room, her face greenish white, dabbing her forehead with a washrag.

"Here lie down here you poor kid," said Ellen clearing a space on the couch. ". . . Now you'll feel much better."

"Oh will you ever forgive me for causing all this twouble?"

"Just lie still a minute and forget everything."

"Oh if I could only relax."

Ellen's hands were cold. She went to the window and looked out. A little boy in a cowboy suit was running about the yard waving an end of clothesline. He tripped and fell. Ellen could see his face puckered with tears as he got to his feet again. In the yard beyond a stumpy woman with black hair was hanging out clothes. Sparrows were chirping and fighting on the fence.

"Elaine dear could you let me have a little powder? I've lost my vanity case."

She turned back into the room. "I think. . . . Yes there's some on the mantelpiece. . . . Do you feel better now Cassie?"

"Oh yes," said Cassie in a trembly voice. "And have you got a lipstick?"

"I'm awfully sorry. . . . I've never worn any street makeup. I'll have to soon enough if I keep on acting." She went into the alcove to take off her kimono, slipped on a plain green dress, coiled up her hair and pushed a small black hat down over it. "Let's run along Cassie. I want to have something to eat at six. . . . I hate bolting my dinner five minutes before a performance."

"Oh I'm so tewified. . . . Pwomise you wont leave me alone."

"Oh she wouldnt do anything today. . . . She'll just look you over and maybe give you something to take. . . . Let's see, have I got my key?"

"We'll have to take a taxi. And my dear I've only got six dollars in the world."

"I'll make daddy give me a hundred dollars to buy furniture. That'll be all right."

"Elaine you're the most angelic cweature in the world. . . . You deserve every bit of your success."

At the corner of Sixth Avenue they got into a taxi.

Cassie's teeth were chattering. "Please let's go another time. I'm too fwightened to go now."

"My dear child it's the only thing to do."

Joe Harland, puffing on his pipe, pulled to and bolted the wide quaking board gates. A last splash of garnet-colored sunlight was fading on the tall housewall across the excavation. Blue arms of cranes stood out dark against it.

Harland's pipe had gone out, he stood puffing at it with his back to the gate looking at the files of empty wheelbarrows, the piles of picks and shovels, the little shed for the donkey-engine and the steam drills that sat perched on a split rock like a mountaineer's shack. It seemed to him peaceful in spite of the rasp of traffic from the street that seeped through the hoarding. He went into the leanto by the gate where the telephone was, sat down in the chair, knocked out, filled and lit his pipe and spread the newspaper out on his knees.' CONTRACTORS PLAN LOCKOUT TO ANSWER BUILDERS' STRIKE. He yawned and threw back his head. The light was too blue-dim to read. He sat a long time staring at the stub scarred toes of his boots. His mind was a fuzzy comfortable blank. Suddenly he saw himself in a dress-suit wearing a top hat with an orchid in his buttonhole. The Wizard of Wall Street looked at the lined red face and the gray hair under the mangy cap and the big hands with their grimy swollen knuckles and faded with a snicker. He remembered faintly the smell of a Corona-Corona as he reached into the pocket of the peajacket for a can of Prince Albert to refill his pipe. "What dif does it make I'd like to know?" he said aloud. When he lit a match the night went suddenly inky all round. He blew out the match. His pipe was a tiny genial red volcano that made a discreet cluck each time he pulled on it. He smoked very slowly inhaling deep. The tall buildings all round were haloed with ruddy glare from streets and electriclight signs. Looking straight up through glimmering veils of reflected light he could see the blueblack sky and stars. The tobacco was sweet. He was very happy.

A glowing cigarend crossed the door of the shack. Harland grabbed his lantern and went out. He held the lantern up in the face of a blond young man with a thick nose and lips and a cigar in the side of his mouth.

"How did you get in here?"

"Side door was open."

"The hell it was? Who are you looking for?"

"You the night watchman round here?" Harland nodded.

"Glad to meet yez. . . . Have a cigar. I jus wanted to have a little talk wid ye, see? . . . I'm organizer for Local 47, see? Let's see your card."

"I'm not a union man."

"Well ye're goin to be aint ye. . . . Us guys of the buildin trades have got to stick together. We're tryin to get every bloke from night watchmen to inspectors lined up to make a solid front against this here lockout sitooation."

Harland lit his cigar. "Look here, bo, you're wasting your breath on me. They'll always need a watchman, strike or no strike. . . . I'm an old man and I havent got much fight left in me. This is the first decent job I've had in five years and they'll have to shoot me to get it away from me. . . . All that stuff's for kids like you. I'm out of it. You sure are wasting your breath if you're going round trying to organize night watchmen."

"Say you don't talk like you'd always been in this kind o woik."

"Well maybe I aint."

The young man took off his hat and rubbed his hand over his forehead and up across his dense cropped hair. "Hell it's warm work arguin. . . . Swell night though aint it?"

"Oh the night's all right," said Harland.

"Say my name's O'Keefe, Joe O'Keefe. . . . Gee I bet you could tell a guy a lot o things." He held out his hand.

"My name's Joe too . . . Harland. . . . Twenty years ago that name meant something to people."

"Twenty years from now . . ."

"Say you're a funny fellow for a walking delegate. . . . You take an old man's advice before I run you off the lot, and quit it. . . . It's no game for a likely young feller who wants to make his way in the world."

"Times are changin you know. . . . There's big fellers back o this here strike, see? I was talkin over the sitooation with Assemblyman McNiel jus this afternoon in his office."

"But I'm telling you straight if there's one thing that'll queer you in this town it's this labor stuff. . . . You'll remember someday that an old drunken bum told you that and it'll be too late."

"Oh it was drink was it? That's one thing I'm not afraid of. I don't touch the stuff, except beer to be sociable."

"Look here bo the company detective'll be makin his rounds soon. You'd better be making tracks."

"I ain't ascared of any goddam company detective. . . . Well so long I'll come in to see you again someday."

"Close that door behind you."

Joe Harland drew a little water from a tin container, settled himself in his chair and stretched his arms out and yawned. Eleven o'clock. They would just be getting out of the theaters, men in eveningclothes, girls in lowneck dresses; men were going home to their wives and mistresses; the city was going to bed. Taxis honked and rasped outside the hoarding, the sky shimmered with gold powder from electric signs. He dropped the butt of the cigar and crushed it on the floor with his heel. He shuddered and got to his feet, then paced slowly round the edge of the buildinglot swinging his lantern.

The light from the street yellowed faintly a big sign on which was a picture of a skyscraper, white with black windows against blue sky and white clouds. Segal and Haynes will erect on this site a modern uptodate Twentyfour Story Office Building open for occupancy January 1915 renting space still available inquire. . . .

Jimmy Herf sat reading on a green couch under a bulb that lit up a corner of a wide bare room. He had come to the death of Olivier in *Jean Christophe* and read with tightening gullet. In his memory lingered the sound of the Rhine swirling, restlessly gnawing the foot of the garden of the house where Jean Christophe was born. Europe was a green park in his mind full of music and red flags and mobs marching. Occasionally the sound of a steamboat whistle from the river settled breathless snowysoft into the room. From the street came a rattle of taxis and the whining sound of streetcars.

There was a knock at the door. Jimmy got up, his eyes blurred and hot from reading.

"Hello Stan, where the devil did you come from?"

"Herfy I'm tight as a drum."

"That's no novelty."

"I was just giving you the weather report."

"Well perhaps you can tell me why in this country nobody ever does anything. Nobody ever writes any music or starts any revolutions or falls in love. All anybody ever does is to get drunk and tell smutty stories. I think it's disgusting. . . ."

" 'Ear, 'ear. . . . But speak for yourself. I'm going to stop drinking. . . . No good drinking, liquor just gets monotonous. . . . Say, got a bathtub?"

"Of course there's a bathtub. Whose apartment do you think this is, mine?"

"Well whose is it Herfy?"

"It belongs to Lester. I'm just caretaker while he's abroad, the lucky dog." Stan started peeling off his clothes letting them drop in a pile about his feet. "Gee I'd like to go swimming. . . . Why the hell do people live in cities?"

"Why do I go on dragging out a miserable existence in this crazy epileptic town . . . that's what I want to know."

"Lead on Horatius, to the baawth slave," bellowed Stan who stood on top of his pile of clothes, brown with tight rounded muscles, swaying a little from his drunkenness.

"It's right through that door." Jimmy pulled a towel out of the steamertrunk in the corner of the room, threw it after him and went back to reading.

Stan tumbled back into the room, dripping, talking through the towel. "What do you think, I forgot to take my hat off. And look Herfy, there's something I want you to do for me. Do you mind?"

"Of course not. What is it?"

"Will you let me use your back room tonight, this room?"

"Sure you can."

"I mean with somebody."

"Go as far as you like. You can bring the entire Winter Garden Chorus in here and nobody will see them. And there's an emergency exit down the fire escape into the alley. I'll go to bed and close my door so you can have this room and the bath all to yourselves."

"It's a rotten imposition but somebody's husband is on the rampage and we have to be very careful."

"Dont worry about the morning. I'll sneak out early and you can have the place to yourselves."

"Well I'm off so long."

Jimmy gathered up his book and went into his bedroom and undressed. His watch said fifteen past twelve. The night was sultry. When he had turned out the light he sat a long while on the edge of the bed. The faraway sounds of sirens from the river gave him gooseflesh. From the street he heard footsteps, the sound of men and women's voices, low youthful laughs of people going home two by two. A phonograph was playing *Secondhand Rose*. He lay on his back on top of the sheet. There came on the air through the window a sourness of garbage, a smell of burnt gasoline and traffic and dusty pavements, a huddled stuffiness of pigeonhole rooms where men and women's bodies writhed alone tortured by the night and the young summer. He lay with seared eyeballs staring at the ceiling, his body glowed in a brittle shivering agony like redhot metal.

A woman's voice whispering eagerly woke him; someone was pushing open the door. "I wont see him. I wont see him. Jimmy for Heaven's sake you go talk to him. I wont see him." Elaine Oglethorpe draped in a sheet walked into the room.

Jimmy tumbled out of bed. "What on earth?"

"Isn't there a closet or something in here. . . . I will not talk to Jojo when he's in that condition."

Jimmy straightened his pyjamas. "There's a closet at the head of the bed."

"Of course. . . . Now Jimmy do be an angel, talk to him and make him go away."

Jimmy walked dazedly into the outside room. "Slut, slut," was yelling a voice from the window. The lights were on. Stan, draped like an Indian in a gray and pink-striped blanket was squatting in the middle of the two couches made up together into a vast bed. He was staring impassively at John Oglethorpe who leaned in through the upper part of the window screaming and waving his arms and scolding like a Punch and Judy show. His hair was in a tangle over his eyes, in one hand he waved a stick, in the other a creamandcoffeecolored felt hat. "Slut come here. . . . Flagrante delictu that's what it is. . . . Flagrante delictu. It was not for nothing that inspiration led me up Lester Jones's fire escape." He stopped and stared a minute at Jimmy with wide drunken eyes. "So here's the cub reporter, the yellow journalist is it, looking as if butter wouldnt melt in his mouth is it? Do you know what my opinion of you is, would you like to know what my opinion of you is? Oh I've heard about you from Ruth and all that. I know you think you're one of the dynamiters and aloof from all that. . . . How do you like being a paid prostitute of the public press? How d'you like your yellow ticket? The brass check, that's the kind of thing. . . . You think that as an actor, an artiste, I dont know about those things. I've heard from Ruth your opinion of actors and all that."

"Why Mr. Oglethorpe I am sure you are mistaken."

"I read and keep silent. I am one of the silent watchers. I know that every sentence, every word, every picayune punctuation that appears in the public press is perused and revised and deleted in the interests of advertisers and bondholders. The fountain of national life is poisoned at the source."

"Yea, you tell em," suddenly shouted Stan from the bed. He got to his feet clapping his hands. "I should prefer to be the meanest stagehand. I should prefer to be the old and feeble charwoman who scrubs off the stage . . . than to sit on velvet in the office of the editor of the greatest daily in the city. Acting is a profession honorable, decent, humble, gentlemanly." The oration ended abruptly.

"Well I dont see what you expect me to do about it," said Jimmy crossing his arms.

"And now it's starting to rain," went on Oglethorpe in a squeaky whining voice.

"You'd better go home," said Jimmy.

"I shall go I shall go where there are no sluts . . . no male and female sluts. . . . I shall go into the great night."

"Do you think he can get home all right Stan?"

Stan had sat down on the edge of the bed shaking with laughter. He shrugged his shoulders.

"My blood will be on your head Elaine forever. . . . Forever, do you hear me? . . . into the night where people dont sit laughing and sneering. Dont you think I dont see you. . . . If the worst happens it will not be my fault."

"Go-od night," shouted Stan. In a last spasm of laughing he fell off the edge of the bed and rolled on the floor. Jimmy went to the window and looked down the fire escape into the alley. Oglethorpe had gone. It was raining hard. A smell of wet bricks rose from the housewalls.

"Well if this isnt the darnedest fool business?" He walked back into his room without looking at Stan. In the door Ellen brushed silkily past him.

"I'm terribly sorry Jimmy . . ." she began.

He closed the door sharply in her face and locked it. "The goddam fools they act like crazy people," he said through his teeth. "What the hell do they think this is?"

His hands were cold and trembling. He pulled a blanket up over him. He lay listening to the steady beat of the rain and the hissing spatter of a gutter. Now and then a puff of wind blew a faint cool spray in his face. There still lingered in the room a frail cedarwood gruff smell of her heavycoiled hair, a silkiness of her body where she had crouched wrapped in the sheet hiding.

Ed Thatcher sat in his bay window among the Sunday papers. His hair was grizzled and there were deep folds in his cheeks. The upper buttons of his pongee trousers were undone to ease his sudden little potbelly. He sat in the open window looking out over the blistering asphalt at the endless stream of automobiles that whirred in either direction past the yellowbrick row of stores and the redbrick station under the eaves of which on a black ground gold letters glinted feebly in the sun: PASSAIC. Apartments round about emitted a querulous Sunday grinding of phonographs playing *It's a Bear*. The Sextette from *Lucia*, selections from *The Quaker Girl*. On his knees lay the theatrical section of the New York *Times*. He looked out with bleared eyes into the quivering heat feeling his ribs tighten with a breathless ache. He had just read a paragraph in a marked copy of *Town Topics*.

Malicious tongues are set wagging by the undeniable fact that young Stanwood Emery's car is seen standing every night outside the Knickerbocker Theatre and never does it leave they say, without a certain charming young actress whose career is fast approaching stellar magnitude. This same young gentleman, whose father is the head of one of the city's most respected lawfirms, who recently left Harvard under slightly unfortunate circumstances, has been astonishing the natives for some time with his exploits which we are sure are merely the result of the ebullience of boyish spirits. A word to the wise.

The bell rang three times. Ed Thatcher dropped his papers and hurried quaking to the door. "Ellie you're so late. I was afraid you weren't coming."

"Daddy dont I always come when I say I will?"

"Of course you do deary."

"How are you getting on? How's everything at the office?"

"Mr. Elbert's on his vacation. . . . I guess I'll go when he comes back. I wish you'd come down to Spring Lake with me for a few days. It'd do you good."

"But daddy I cant." . . . She pulled off her hat and

dropped it on the davenport. "Look I brought you some roses, daddy."

"Think of it; they're red roses like your mother used to like. That was very thoughtful of you I must say. . . . But I dont like going all alone on my vacation."

"Oh you'll meet lots of cronies daddy, sure you will."

"Why couldnt you come just for a week?"

"In the first place I've got to look for a job . . . show's going on the road and I'm not going just at present. Harry Goldweiser's awfully sore about it." Thatcher sat down in the bay window again and began piling up the Sunday papers on a chair. "Why daddy what on earth are you doing with that copy of *Town Topics?*"

"Oh nothing. I'd never read it; I just bought it to see what it was like." He flushed and compressed his lips as he shoved it in among the *Times*.

"It's just a blackmail sheet." Ellen was walking about the room. She had put the roses in a vase. A spiced coolness was spreading from them through the dustheavy air. "Daddy, there's something I want to tell you about . . . Jojo and I are going to get divorced." Ed Thatcher sat with his hands on his knees nodding with tight lips, saying nothing. His face was gray and dark, almost the speckled gray of his pongee suit. "It's nothing to take on about. We've just decided we cant get along together. It's all going through quietly in the most approved style . . . George Baldwin, who's a friend of mine, is going to run it through."

"He with Emery and Emery?"

"Yes."

"Hum."

They were silent. Ellen leaned over to breathe deep of the roses. She watched a little green measuring worm cross a bronzed leaf.

"Honestly I'm terribly fond of Jojo, but it drives me wild to live with him. . . . I owe him a whole lot, I know that."

"I wish you'd never set eyes on him."

Thatcher cleared his throat and turned his face away

from her to look out the window at the two endless bands of automobiles that passed along the road in front of the station. Dust rose from them and angular glitter of glass enamel and nickel. Tires made a swish on the oily macadam. Ellen dropped onto the davenport and let her eyes wander among the faded red roses of the carpet.

The bell rang. "I'll go daddy. . . . How do you do Mrs. Culveteer?"

A redfaced broad woman in a black and white chiffon dress came into the room puffing. "Oh you must forgive my butting in, I'm just dropping by for a second. . . . How are you Mr. Thatcher? . . . You know my dear your poor father has really been very poorly."

"Nonsense; all I had was a little backache."

"Lumbago my dear."

"Why daddy you ought to have let me know."

"The sermon today was most inspiring, Mr. Thatcher. . . . Mr. Lourton was at his very best."

"I guess I ought to rout out and go to church now and then, but you see I like to lay round the house Sundays."

"Of course Mr. Thatcher it's the only day you have. My husband was just like that. . . . But I think it's different with Mr. Lourton than with most clergymen. He has such an uptodate commonsense view of things. It's really more like attending an intensely interesting lecture than going to church. . . . You understand what I mean."

"I'll tell you what I'll do Mrs. Culveteer, next Sunday if it's not too hot I'll go. . . . I guess I'm getting too set in my ways."

"Oh a little change does us all good. . . . Mrs. Oglethorpe you have no idea how closely we follow your career, in the Sunday papers and all. . . . I think it's simply wonderful. . . . As I was telling Mr. Thatcher only yesterday it must take a lot of strength of character and deep Christian living to withstand the temptations of stage life nowadays. It's inspiring to think of a young girl and wife coming so sweet and unspoiled through all that."

Ellen kept looking at the floor so as not to catch her

father's eye. He was tapping with two fingers on the arm of his morrischair. Mrs. Culveteer beamed from the middle of the davenport. She got to her feet. "Well I just must run along. We have a green girl in the kitchen and I'm sure dinner's all ruined. . . . Wont you drop in this afternoon . . . ? quite informally. I made some cookies and we'll have some gingerale out just in case somebody turns up."

"I'm sure we'd be delighted Mrs. Culveteer," said Thatcher getting stiffly to his feet. Mrs. Culveteer in her bunchy dress waddled out the door.

"Well Ellie suppose we go eat. . . . She's a very nice kindhearted woman. She's always bringing me pots of jam and marmalade. She lives upstairs with her sister's family. She's the widow of a traveling man."

"That was quite a line about the temptations of stage life," said Ellen with a little laugh in her throat. "Come along or the place'll be crowded. Avoid the rush is my motto."

Said Thatcher in a peevish crackling voice, "Let's not dawdle around."

Ellen spread out her sunshade as they stepped out of the door flanked on either side by bells and letterboxes. A blast of gray heat beat in their faces. They passed the stationery store, the red A. and P., the corner drugstore from which a stale coolness of sodawater and icecream freezers drifted out under the green awning, crossed the street, where their feet sank into the sticky melting asphalt, and stopped at the Sagamore Cafeteria. It was twelve exactly by the clock in the window that had round its face in old English lettering, TIME TO EAT. Under it was a large rusty fern and a card announcing Chicken Dinner $1.25. Ellen lingered in the doorway looking up the quivering street. "Look daddy we'll probably have a thunderstorm." A cumulus soared in unbelievable snowy contours in the slate sky. "Isnt that a fine cloud? Wouldnt it be fine if we had a riproaring thunderstorm?"

Ed Thatcher looked up, shook his head and went in through the swinging screen door. Ellen followed him. Inside it smelled of varnish and waitresses. They sat down at a table near the door under a droning electric fan.

"How do you do Mr. Thatcher? How you been all the week sir? How do you do miss?" The bonyfaced peroxidehaired waitress hung over them amicably. What'll it be today sir, roast Long Island duckling or roast Philadelphia milkfed capon?"

IV. Fire Engine

Such afternoons the buses are crowded into line like elephants in a circusparade. Morningside Heights to Washington Square, Penn Station to Grant's Tomb. Parlorsnakes and flappers joggle hugging downtown uptown, hug joggling gray square after gray square, until they see the new moon giggling over Weehawken and feel the gusty wind of a dead Sunday blowing dust in their faces, dust of a typsy twilight.

THEY are walking up the Mall in Central Park.
"Looks like he had a boil on his neck," says Ellen in front of the statue of Burns.

"Ah," whispers Harry Goldweiser with a fat-throated sigh, "but he was a great poet."

She is walking in her wide hat in her pale loose dress that the wind now and then presses against her legs and arms, silkily, swishily walking in the middle of great rosy and purple and pistachiogreen bubbles of twilight that swell out of the grass and trees and ponds, bulge against the tall houses sharp gray as dead teeth round the southern end of the park, melt into the indigo zenith. When he talks, forming sentences roundly with his thick lips, continually measuring her face with his brown eyes, she feels his words press against her body, nudge in the hollows where her dress clings; she can hardly breathe for fear of listening to him.

"The Zinnia Girl's going to be an absolute knockout, Elaine, I'm telling you and that part's just written for you. I'd enjoy working with you again, honest. . . . You're so different, that's what it is about you. All these girls round New York here are just the same, they're monotonous. Of course you could sing swell if you wanted to. . . . I've been crazy as a loon since I met you, and that's a good six months now. I sit down to eat and the food dont have any taste. . . . You cant understand how lonely a man gets when year after year he's had to crush his feelings down into himself. When I was a young fellow I was different, but what are you to do? I had to make money and make my way in the world. And so I've gone on year after year. For the first time I'm glad I did it, that I shoved ahead and made big money, because now I can offer it all to you. Understand what I mean? . . . All those ideels and beautiful things pushed down into myself when I was making my way in a man's world were like planting seed and you're their flower."

Now and then as they walk the back of his hand brushes against hers; she clenches her fist sullenly drawing it away from the hot determined pudginess of his hand.

The Mall is full of couples, families waiting for the music to begin. It smells of children and dress-shields and talcum powder. A balloonman passes them trailing red and yellow and pink balloons like a great inverted bunch of grapes behind him. "Oh buy me a balloon." The words are out of her mouth before she can stop them.

"Hay you gimme one of each color. . . . And how about one of those gold ones? No keep the change."

Ellen put the strings of the balloons into the dirtsticky hands of three little monkeyfaced girls in red tams. Each balloon caught a crescent of violet glare from the arclight.

"Aw you like children, Elaine, dont you? I like a woman to like children."

Ellen sits numb at a table on the terrace of the Casino. A hot gust of foodsmell and the rhythm of a band playing *He's a Ragpicker* swirls chokingly about her; now and then she butters a scrap of roll and puts it in her mouth. She feels very helpless, caught like a fly in his sticky trickling sentences.

"There's nobody else in New York could have got me to walk that far, I'll tell you that. . . . I walked too much in the old days, do you understand, used to sell papers when I was a kid and run errands for Schwartz's Toystore . . . on my feet all day except when I was in nightschool. I thought I was going to be a lawyer, all us East Side fellers thought we were goin to be lawyers. Then I worked as an usher one summer at the Irving Place and got the theater bug. . . . Not such a bad hunch it turned out to be, but it's too uncertain. Now I dont care any more, only want to cover my losses. That's the trouble with me. I'm thirtyfive an I dont care any more. Ten years ago I was still only a kind of clerk in old man Erlanger's office, and now there's lots of em whose shoes I used to shine in the old days'd be real glad of the opportunity to sweep my floors on West Forty-eighth. . . . Tonight I can take you anywhere in New York, I dont care how expensive or how chic it is . . . an in the old days us kids used to think it was paradise if we had five plunks to take a couple of girls down to the Island. . . . I bet all that was different with you Elaine. . . . But what I want to do is get that old feelin back, understand? . . . Where shall we go?"

"Why dont we go down to Coney Island then? I've never been?

"It's a pretty rough crowd . . . still we can just ride round. Let's do it. I'll go phone for the car."

Ellen sits alone looking down into her coffeecup. She puts a lump of sugar on her spoon, dips it in the coffee and pops it into her mouth where she crunches it slowly, rubbing the grains of sugar against the roof of her mouth with her tongue. The orchestra is playing a tango.

The sun streaming into the office under the drawn shades cut a bright slanting layer like watered silk through the cigarsmoke.

"Mighty easy," George Baldwin was saying dragging out the words. "Gus we got to go mighty easy on this." Gus McNiel bullnecked redfaced with a heavy watchchain in his vest sat in the armchair nodding silently, pulling on his cigar. "As things are now no court would sustain such an injunction . . . an injunction that seems to me a pure piece of party politics on Judge Connor's part, but there are certain elements. . . ."

"You said it. . . . Look here George I'm goin to leave this whole blame thing to you. You pulled me through the East New York dockin space mess and I guess you can pull me through this."

"But Gus your position in this whole affair has been entirely within the bounds of legality. If it werent I certainly should not be able to take the case, not even for an old friend like you."

"You know me George. . . . I never went back on a guy yet and I dont expect to have anybody go back on me." Gus got heavily to his feet and began to limp about the office leaning on a goldknobbed cane. "Connor's a son of a bitch . . . an honest, you wouldn't believe it but he was a decent guy before he went up to Albany."

"My position will be that your attitude in this whole matter has been willfully misconstrued. Connor has been using his position on the bench to further a political end."

"God I wish we could get him. Jez I thought he was one of the boys; he was until he went up an got mixed up with all those lousy upstate Republicans. Albany's been the ruination of many a good man."

Baldwin got up from the flat mahogany table where he sat between tall sheaves of foolscap and put his hand on Gus's shoulder. "Dont you lose any sleep over it. . . ."

"I'd feel all right if it wasn't for those Interborough bonds."

"What bonds? Who's seen any bonds? . . . Let's get this young fellow in here . . . Joe . . . And one more thing Gus, for heaven's sakes keep your mouth shut. . . . If any reporters or anybody comes round to see you tell 'em about your trip to Bermuda. . . . We can get publicity enough when we need it. Just at present we want to keep the papers out of it or you'll have all the reformers on your heels."

"Well aint they friends of yours? You can fix it up with em."

"Gus I'm a lawyer and not a politician. . . . I dont meddle in those things at all. They dont interest me."

Baldwin brought the flat of his hand down on a pushbell. An ivoryskinned young woman with heavy sullen eyes and jetty hair came into the room.

"How do you do Mr. McNeil."

"My but you're looking well Miss Levitsky."

"Emily tell em to send that young fellow that's waiting for Mr. McNiel in."

Joe O'Keefe came in dragging his feet a little, with his straw hat in his hand. "Howde do sir."

"Look here Joe, what does McCarthy say?"

"Contractors and Builders Association's goin to declare a lockout from Monday on."

"And how's the union?"

"We got a full treasury. We're goin to fight."

Baldwin sat down on the edge of the desk. "I wish I knew what Mayor Mitchel's attitude was on all this."

"That reform gang's just treadin water like they always do," said Gus savagely biting the end off a cigar. "When's this decision going to be made public?"

"Saturday."

"Well keep in touch with us."

"All right gentlemen. And please dont call me on the phone. It dont look exactly right. You see it aint my office."

"Might be wiretappin goin on too. Those fellers wont stop at nothin. Well see ye later Joey."

Joe nodded and walked out. Baldwin turned frowning to Gus.

"Gus I dont know what I'm goin to do with you if you dont keep out of all this labor stuff. A born politician like you ought to have better sense. You just cant get away with it."

"But we got the whole damn town lined up."

"I know a whole lot of the town that isnt lined up. But thank Heavens that's not my business. This bond stuff is all right, but if you get into a mess with this strike business

I couldn't handle your case. The firm wouldnt stand for it," he whispered fiercely. Then he said aloud in his usual voice, "Well how's the wife, Gus?"

Outside in the shiny marble hall, Joe O'Keefe was whistling *Sweet Rosy O'Grady* waiting for the elevator. Imagine a guy havin a knockout like that for a secretary. He stopped whistling and let the breath out silently through pursed lips. In the elevator he greeted a walleyed man in a check suit. "Hullo Buck."

"Been on your vacation yet?"

Joe stood with his feet apart and his hands in his pockets. He shook his head. "I get off Saturday."

"I guess I'll take in a couple o days at Atlantic City myself."

"How do you do it?"

"Oh the kid's clever."

Coming out of the building O'Keefe had to make his way through people crowding into the portal. A slate sky sagging between the tall buildings was spatting the pavements with fiftycent pieces. Men were running to cover with their straw hats under their coats. Two girls had made hoods of newspaper over their summer bonnets. He snatched blue of their eyes, a glint of lips and teeth as he passed. He walked fast to the corner and caught an uptown car on the run. The rain advanced down the street in a solid sheet glimmering, swishing, beating newspapers flat, prancing in silver nipples along the asphalt, striping windows, putting shine on the paint of streetcars and taxicabs. Above Fourteenth there was no rain, the air was sultry.

"A funny thing weather," said an old man next to him. O'Keefe grunted. "When I was a boy onct I saw it rain on one side of the street an a house was struck by lightnin an on our side not a drop fell though the old man wanted it bad for some tomatoplants he'd just set out."

Crossing Twentythird O'Keefe caught sight of the tower of Madison Square Garden. He jumped off the car; the momentum carried him in little running steps to the curb. Turning his coatcollar down again he started across the square. On the end of a bench under a tree drowsed Joe Harland. O'Keefe plunked down in the seat beside him.

"Hello Joe. Have a cigar."

"Hello Joe. I'm glad to see you my boy. Thanks. It's many a day since I've smoked one of these things. . . . What are you up to? Aint this kind of out of your beat?"

"I felt kinder blue so I thought I'd buy me a ticket to the fight Saturday."

"What's the matter?"

"Hell I dunno. . . . Things dont seem to go right. Here I've got myself all in deep in this political game and there dont seem to be no future in it. God I wish I was educated like you."

"A lot of good it's done me."

"I wouldn't say that. . . . If I could ever git on the track you were on I bet ye I wouldn't lose out."

"You cant tell Joe, funny things get into a man."

"There's women and that sort of stuff."

"No I dont mean that. . . . You get kinder disgusted."

"But hell I dont see how a guy with enough jack can git disgusted."

"Then maybe it was booze, I dont know."

They sat silent a minute. The afternoon was flushing with sunset. The cigarsmoke was blue and crinkly about their heads.

"Look at the swell dame. . . . Look at the way she walks. Aint she a peacherino? That's the way I like 'em, all slick an frilly with their lips made up. . . . Takes jack to go round with dames like that."

"They're no different from anybody else, Joe."

"The hell you say."

"Say Joe you havent got an extra dollar on you?"

"Maybe I have."

"My stomach's a little out of order. . . . I'd like to take a little something to steady it, and I'm flat till I get paid Saturday . . . er . . . you understand . . . you're sure you dont mind? Give me your address and I'll send it to you first thing Monday morning."

"Hell dont worry about it, I'll see yez around somewheres."

"Thank you Joe. And for God's sake dont buy any more
Blue Peter Mines on a margin without asking me about it.
I may be a back number but I can still tell a goldbrick with
my eyes closed."

"Well I got my money back."

"It took the devil's own luck to do it."

"Jez it strikes me funny me loanin a dollar to the guy
who owned half the Street."

"Oh I never had as much as they said I did."

"This is a funny place. . . ."

"Where?"

"Oh I dunno, I guess everywhere. . . . Well so long Joe,
I guess I'll go along an buy that ticket. . . . Jez it's goin to
be a swell fight."

Joe Harland watched the young man's short jerky stride
as he went off down the path with his straw hat on the side
of his head. Then he got to his feet and walked east along
Twentythird Street. The pavements and housewalls still
gave off heat although the sun had set. He stopped outside
a corner saloon and examined carefully a group of stuffed
ermines, gray with dust, that occupied the center of the
window. Through the swinging doors a sound of quiet
voices and a malty coolness seeped into the street. He
suddenly flushed and bit his upper lip and after a furtive
glance up and down the street went in through the swinging
doors and shambled up to the brassy bottleglittering bar.

After the rain outdoors the plastery backstage smell was
pungent in their nostrils. Ellen hung the wet raincoat on
the back of the door and put her umbrella in a corner of the
dressing room where a little puddle began to spread from it.
"And all I could think of," she was saying in a low voice to
Stan who followed her staggering, "was a funny song somebody'd told me when I was a little girl about: And the only

man who survived the flood was longlegged Jack of the Isthmus."

"God I dont see why people have children. It's an admission of defeat. Procreation is the admission of an incomplete organism. Procreation is an admission of defeat."

"Stan for Heaven's sake dont shout, you'll shock the stagehands. . . . I oughtnt to have let you come. You know the way people gossip round a theater."

"I'll be quiet just like a lil mouse. . . . Just let me wait till Milly comes to dress you. Seeing you dress is my only remaining pleasure . . . I admit that as an organism I'm incomplete."

"You wont be an organism of any kind if you dont sober up."

"I'm going to drink . . . I'm going to drink till when I cut myself whiskey runs out. What's the good of blood when you can have whiskey?"

"Oh Stan."

"The only thing an incomplete organism can do is drink. . . . You complete beautiful organisms dont need to drink. . . . I'm going to lie down and go byby."

"Dont Stan for Heaven's sake. If you go and pass out here I'll never forgive you."

There was a soft doubleknock at the door. "Come in Milly." Milly was a small wrinklefaced woman with black eyes. A touch of negro blood made her purplegray lips thick, gave a lividness to her verywhite skin.

"It's eight fifteen dear," she said as she bustled in. She gave a quick look at Stan and turned to Ellen with a little wry frown.

"Stan you've got to go away. . . . I'll meet you at the Beaux Arts or anywhere you like afterwards."

"I want to go byby."

Sitting in front of the mirror at her dressingtable Ellen was wiping cold cream off her face with quick dabs of a little towel. From her makeup box a smell of greasepaint and cocoabutter melted fatly through the room.

"I dont know what to do with him tonight," she whispered

to Milly as she slipped off her dress. Oh I wish he would
stop drinking."

"I'd put him in the shower and turn cold water on him
deary."

"How's the house tonight Milly?"

"Pretty thin Miss Elaine."

"I guess it's the bad weather . . . I'm going to be
terrible."

"Dont let him get you worked up deary. Men aint
worth it."

"I want to go byby." Stan was swaying and frowning in
the center of the room. "Miss Elaine I'll put him in the
bathroom; nobody'll notice him there."

"That's it, let him go to sleep in the bathtub."

"Ellie I'll go byby in the bathtub."

The two women pushed him into the bathroom. He
flopped limply into the tub, and lay there asleep with his
feet in the air and his head on the faucets. Milly was
making little rapid clucking noises with her tongue.

"He's like a sleepy baby when he's like this," whispered
Ellen softly. She stuck the folded bathmat under his head
and brushed the sweaty hair off his forehead. He was
hardly breathing. She leaned and kissed his eyelids very
softly.

"Miss Elaine you must hurry . . . curtain's ringing up."

"Look quick am I all right?"

"Pretty as a picture. . . . Lord love you dear."

Ellen ran down the stairs and round to the wings, stood
there, panting with terror as if she had just missed being
run over by an automobile grabbed the musicroll she had to
go on with from the property man, got her cue and walked
on into the glare.

"How do you do it Elaine?" Harry Goldweiser was saying,
shaking his calf's head from the chair behind her. She could
see him in the mirror as she took her makeup off. A taller
man with gray eyes and eyebrows stood beside him. "You
remember when they first cast you for the part I said to Mr.
Fallik, Sol she cant do it, didnt I Sol?"

"Sure you did Harry."

"I thought that no girl so young and beautiful could put, you know . . . put the passion and terror into it, do you understand? . . . Sol and I were out front for that scene in the last act."

"Wonderful, wonderful," groaned Mr. Fallik. "Tell us how you do it Elaine."

The makeup came off black and pink on the cloth. Milly moved discreetly about the background hanging up dresses.

"Do you know who it was who coached me up on that scene? John Oglethorpe. It's amazing the ideas he has about acting."

"Yes it's a shame he's so lazy. . . . He'd be a very valuable actor."

"It's not exactly laziness . . ." Ellen shook down her hair and twisted it in a coil in her two hands. She saw Harry Goldweiser nudge Mr. Fallik.

"Beautiful isn't it?"

"How's Red Red Rose going?"

"Oh dont ask me Elaine. Played exclusively to the ushers last week, do you understand? I dont see why it dont go, it's catchy. . . . Mae Merrill has a pretty figure. Oh, the show business has all gone to hell."

Ellen put the last bronze pin in the copper coil of her hair. She tossed her chin up. "I'd like to try something like that."

"But one thing at a time my dear young lady; we've just barely got you started as an emotional actress."

"I hate it; it's all false. Sometimes I want to run down to the foots and tell the audience, go home you damn fools. This is a rotten show and a lot of fake acting and you ought to know it. In a musical show you could be sincere."

"Didnt I tell ye she was nuts Sol? Didnt I tell ye she was nuts?"

"I'll use some of that little speech in my publicity next week. . . . I can work it in fine."

"You cant have her crabbin the show."

"No but I can work it in in that column about aspirations

of celebrities. . . . You know, this guy is President of the Zozodont Company and would rather have been a fireman and another would rather have been a keeper at the Zoo. . . . Great human interest stuff."

"You can tell them Mr. Fallik that I think the woman's place is in the home . . . for the feebleminded."

"Ha ha ha," laughed Harry Goldweiser showing the gold teeth in the sides of his mouth. "But I know you could dance and sing with the best of em, Elaine."

"Wasnt I in the chorus for two years before I married Oglethorpe?"

"You must have started in the cradle," said Mr. Fallik leering under his gray lashes.

"Well I must ask you gentlemen to get out of here a minute while I change. I'm all wringing wet every night after that last act."

"We got to get along anyway . . . do you understand? . . . Mind if I use your bathroom a sec?"

Milly stood in front of the bathroom door. Ellen caught the jetty glance of her eyes far apart in her blank white face. "I'm afraid you cant Harry, it's out of order."

"I'll go over to Charley's. . . . I'll tell Thompson to have a plumber come and look at it. . . . Well good night kid. Be good."

"Good night Miss Oglethorpe," said Mr. Fallik creakily, "and if you cant be good be careful." Milly closed the door after them.

"Whee, that's a relief," cried Ellen and stretched out her arms.

"I tell you I was scared deary. . . . Dont you ever let any feller like that come to the theater with ye. I've seen many a good trouper ruined by things like that. I'm tellin ye because I'm fond of you Miss Elaine, an I'm old an I know about the showbusiness."

"Of course you are Milly, and you're quite right too . . . Lets see if we can wake him up."

"My God Milly, look at that."

Stan was lying as they had left him in the bathtub full of

water. The tail of his coat and one hand were floating on top of the water. "Get up out of there Stan you idiot. . . . He might catch his death. You fool, you fool." Ellen took him by the hair and shook his head from side to side.

"Ooch that hurts," he moaned in a sleepy child's voice.

"Get up out of there Stan. . . . You're soaked."

He threw back his head and his eyes snapped open. "Why so I am." He raised himself with his hands on the sides of the tub and stood swaying, dripping into the water that was yellow from his clothes and shoes, braying his loud laugh. Ellen leaned against the bathroom door laughing with her eyes full of tears.

"You cant get mad at him Milly, that's what makes him so exasperating. Oh what are we going to do?"

"Lucky he wasnt drownded. . . . Give me your papers and pocketbook sir. I'll try and dry em with a towel," said Milly.

"But you cant go past the doorman like that . . . even if we wring you out. . . . Stan you've got to take off all your clothes and put on a dress of mine. Then you can wear my rain cape and we can whisk into a taxicab and take you home. . . . What do you think Milly?"

Milly was rolling her eyes and shaking her head as she wrung out Stan's coat. In the washbasin she had piled the soppy remains of a pocketbook, a pad, pencils, a jacknife, two rolls of film, a flask.

"I wanted a bath anyway," said Stan.

"Oh I could beat you. Well you're sober at least."

"Sober as a penguin."

"Well you've got to dress up in my clothes that's all. . . ."

"I cant wear girl's clothes."

"You've got to. . . . You havent even got a raincoat to cover that mess. If you dont I'll lock you up in the bathroom and leave you."

"All right Ellie. . . . Honest I'm terribly sorry."

Milly was wrapping the clothes in newspaper after wringing them out in the bathtub. Stan looked at himself in the mirror. "Gosh I'm an indecent sight in this dress. . . . Ish gebibble."

"I've never seen anything so disgusting looking. . . . No you look very sweet, a little tough perhaps. . . . Now for God's sake keep your face towards me when you go past old Barney."

"My shoes are all squudgy."

"It cant be helped. . . . Thank Heaven I had this cape here. . . . Milly you're an angel to clear up all this mess."

"Good night deary, and remember what I said. . . . I'm tellin ye that's all. . . ."

"Stan take little steps and if we meet anybody go right on and jump in a taxi. . . . You can get away with anything if you do it quick enough." Ellen's hands were trembling as they came down the steps. She tucked one in under Stan's elbow and began talking in a low chatty voice. . . . "You see dear, daddy came round to see the show two or three nights ago and he was shocked to death. He said he thought a girl demeaned herself showing her feelings like that before a lot of people. . . . Isn't it killing? . . . Still he was impressed by the writeups the *Herald* and *World* gave me Sunday. . . . Goodnight Barney, nasty night. . . . My God. . . . Here's a taxi, get in. Where are you going?" Out of the dark of the taxi, out of his long face muffled in the blue hood, his eyes were so bright black they frightened her like coming suddenly on a deep pit in the dark.

"All right we'll go to my house. Might as well be hanged for a sheep. . . . Driver please go to Bank Street. The taxi started. They were jolting through the crisscross planes of red light, green light, yellow light beaded with lettering of Broadway. Suddenly Stan leaned over her and kissed her hard very quickly on the mouth.

"Stan you've got to stop drinking. It's getting beyond a joke."

"Why shouldn't things get beyond a joke? You're getting beyond a joke and I dont complain."

"But darling you'll kill yourself."

"Well?"

"Oh I dont understand you Stan."

"I dont understand you Ellie, but I love you very . . . exordinately much." There was a broken tremor in his very low voice that stunned her with happiness.

Ellen paid the taxi. Siren throbbing in an upward shriek that burst and trailed in a dull wail down the street, a fire engine went by red and gleaming, then a hookandladder with bell clanging.

"Let's go to the fire Ellie."

"With you in those clothes. . . . We'll do no such thing."

He followed her silent into the house and up the stairs. Her long room was cool and fresh smelling.

"Ellie you're not sore at me?"

"Of course not idiot child."

She undid the sodden bundle of his clothes and took them into the kitchenette to dry beside the gas stove. The sound of the phonograph playing *He's a devil in his own home town* called her back. Stan had taken off the dress. He was dancing round with a chair for a partner, her blue padded dressingown flying out from his thin hairy legs.

"Oh Stan you precious idiot."

He put down the chair and came towards her brown and male and lean in the silly dressingown. The phonograph came to the end of the tune and the record went on rasping round and round.

V. Went to the Animals' Fair

Red light. Bell.
A block deep four ranks of cars wait at the grade crossing, fenders in taillights, mudguards scraping mudguards, motors purring hot, exhausts reeking, cars from Babylon and Jamaica, cars from Montauk, Port Jefferson, Patchogue, limousines from Long Beach, Far Rockaway, roadsters from Great Neck . . . cars full of asters and wet bathingsuits, sunsinged necks, mouths sticky from sodas and hotdawgs . . . cars dusted with pollen of ragweed and goldenrod.

Green light. Motors race, gears screech into first. The cars space out, flow in a long ribbon along the ghostly cement road, between blackwindowed blocks of concrete factories, between bright slabbed colors of signboards towards the glow over the city that stands up incredibly into the night sky like the glow of a great lit tent, like the yellow tall bulk of a tentshow.

SARAJEVO, the word stuck in her throat when she tried to say it. . . .

"It's terrible to think of, terrible," George Baldwin was groaning. "The Street'll go plumb to hell. . . . They'll close the Stock Exchange, only thing to do."

"And I've never been to Europe either. . . . A war must be an extraordinary thing to see." Ellen in her blue velvet dress with a buff cloak over it leaned back against the cushions of the taxi that whirred smoothly under them. "I always think of history as lithographs in a schoolbook, generals making proclamations, little tiny figures running across fields with their arms spread out, facsimiles of signatures." Cones of light cutting into cones of light along the hot humming roadside, headlights splashing trees, houses, billboards, telegraph poles with broad brushes of whitewash.

The taxi made a half turn and stopped in front of a roadhouse that oozed pink light and ragtime through every chink.

"Big crowd tonight," said the taximan to Baldwin when he paid him.

"I wonder why," asked Ellen.

"De Canarsie moider has sumpen to do wid it I guess."

"What's that?"

"Sumpen terrible. I seen it."

"You saw the murder?"

"I didn't see him do it. I seen de bodies laid out stiff before dey took em to de morgue. Us kids used to call de guy Santa Claus cause he had white whiskers. . . . Knowed him since I was a little feller." The cars behind were honking and rasping their klaxons. "I better git a move on. . . . Good night lady."

The red hallway smelt of lobster and steamed clams and cocktails.

"Why hello Gus! . . . Elaine let me introduce Mr. and Mrs. McNiel. . . . This is Miss Oglethorpe." Ellen shook the big hand of a rednecked snubnosed man and the small precisely gloved hand of his wife. "Gus I'll see you before we go. . . ."

Ellen was following the headwaiter's swallowtails along the edge of the dancefloor. They sat at a table beside the wall. The music was playing *Everybody's Doing It.* Baldwin hummed it as he hung over her a second arranging the wrap on the back of her chair.

"Elaine you are the loveliest person . . ." he began as he sat down opposite her. "It seems so horrible. I dont see how it's possible."

"What?"

"This war. I cant think of anything else."

"I can . . ." She kept her eyes on the menu. "Did you notice those two people I introduced to you?"

"Yes. Is that the McNiel whose name is in the paper all the time? Some row about a builders' strike and the Interborough bond issue."

"It's all politics. I bet he's glad of the war, poor old Gus.

It'll do one thing, it'll keep that row off the front page. . . .
I'll tell you about him in a minute. . . . I dont suppose you
like steamed clams do you? They are very good here."

"George I adore steamed clams."

"Then we'll have a regular old fashioned Long Island
shore dinner. What do you think of that?" Laying her
gloves away on the edge of the table her hand brushed against
the vase of rusty red and yellow roses. A shower of faded
petals fluttered onto her hand, her gloves, the table. She
shook them off her hands.

"And do have him take these wretched roses away George.
. . . I hate faded flowers."

Steam from the plated bowl of clams uncoiled in the rosy
glow from the lampshade. Baldwin watched her fingers,
pink and limber, pulling the clams by their long necks out of
their shells, dipping them in melted butter, and popping
them dripping in her mouth. She was deep in eating clams.
He sighed. "Elaine . . . I'm a very unhappy man. . . .
Seeing Gus McNiel's wife. It's the first time in years.
Think of it I was crazy in love with her and now I cant
remember what her first name was . . . Funny isn't it?
Things had been extremely slow ever since I had set up in
practice for myself. It was a rash thing to do, as I was
only two years out of lawschool and had no money to run
on. I was rash in those days. I'd decided that if I didn't
get a case that day I'd chuck everything and go back to a
clerkship. I went out for a walk to clear my head and saw
a freightcar shunting down Eleventh Avenue run into a
milkwagon. It was a horrid mess and when we'd picked
the fellow up I said to myself I'd get him his rightful
damages or bankrupt myself in the attempt. I won his case
and that brought me to the notice of various people downtown, and that started him on his career and me on mine."

"So he drove a milkwagon did he? I think milkmen are
the nicest people in the world. Mine's the cutest thing."

"Elaine you wont repeat this to anyone. . . . I feel the
completest confidence in you."

"That's very nice of you George. Isn't it amazing the

way girls are getting to look more like Mrs. Castle every day? Just look round this room."

"She was like a wild rose Elaine, fresh and pink and full of the Irish, and now she's a rather stumpy businesslike looking little woman."

"And you're as fit as you ever were. That's the way it goes."

"I wonder. . . . You dont know how empty and hollow everything was before I met you. All Cecily and I can do is make each other miserable."

"Where is she now?"

"She's up at Bar Harbor. . . . I had luck and all sorts of success when I was still a young man. . . . I'm not forty yet."

"But I should think it would be fascinating. You must enjoy the law or you wouldn't be such a success at it."

"Oh success . . . success . . . what does it mean?"

"I'd like a little of it."

"But my dear girl you have it."

"Oh not what I mean."

"But it isn't any fun any more. All I do is sit in the office and let the young fellows do the work. My future's all cut out for me. I suppose I could get solemn and pompous and practice little private vices . . . but there's more in me than that."

"Why dont you go into politics?"

"Why should I go up to Washington into that greasy backwater when I'm right on the spot where they give the orders? The terrible thing about having New York go stale on you is that there's nowhere else. It's the top of the world. All we can do is go round and round in a squirrel cage."

Ellen was watching the people in light summer clothes dancing on the waxed square of floor in the center; she caught sight of Tony Hunter's oval pink and white face at a table on the far side of the room. Oglethorpe was not with him. Stan's friend Herf sat with his back to her. She watched him laughing, his long rumpled black head poised a little askew on a scraggly neck. The other two men she didn't know.

"Who are you looking at?"

"Just some friends of Jojo's. . . . I wonder how on earth they got way out here. It's not exactly on that gang's beat."

"Always the way when I try to get away with something," said Baldwin with a wry smile.

"I should say you'd done exactly what you wanted to all your life."

"Oh Elaine if you'd only let me do what I want to now. I want you to let me make you happy. You're such a brave little girl making your way all alone the way you do. By gad you are so full of love and mystery and glitter . . . " He faltered, took a deep swallow of wine, went on with flushing face. "I feel like a schoolboy . . . I'm making a fool of myself. Elaine I'd do anything in the world for you."

"Well all I'm going to ask you to do is to send away this lobster. I dont think it's terribly good."

"The devil . . . maybe it isn't. . . . Here waiter! . . . I was so rattled I didn't know I was eating it."

"You can get me some supreme of chicken instead."

"Surely you poor child you must be starved."

". . . And a little corn on the cob. . . . I understand now why you make such a good lawyer, George. Any jury would have burst out sobbing long ago at such an impassioned plea.

"How about you Elaine?"

"George please dont ask me."

At the table where Jimmy Herf sat they were drinking whiskey and soda. A yellowskinned man with light hair and a thin nose standing out crooked between childish blue eyes was talking in a confidential singsong: "Honest I had em lashed to the mast. The police department is cookoo, absolutely cookoo treating it as a rape and suicide case. That old man and his lovely innocent daughter were murdered, foully murdered. And do you know who by . . . ?" He pointed a chubby cigarettestained finger at Tony Hunter.

"Dont give me the third degree judge I dont know anything about it" he said dropping his long lashes over his eyes.

"By the Black Hand."

"You tell em Bullock," said Jimmy Herf laughing. Bullock brought his fist down on the table so that the plates and glasses jingled. "Canarsie's full of the Black Hand, full of anarchists and kidnappers and undesirable citizens. It's our business to ferret em out and vindicate the honor of this poor old man and his beloved daughter. We are going to vindicate the honor of poor old monkeyface, what's his name?"

"Mackintosh," said Jimmy. "And the people round here used to call him Santa Claus. Of course everybody admits he's been crazy for years."

"We admit nothing but the majesty of American citizenhood. . . . But hell's bells what's the use when this goddam war takes the whole front page? I was going to have a fullpage spread and they've cut me down to half a column. Aint it the life?"

"You might work up something about how he was a lost heir to the Austrian throne and had been murdered for political reasons."

"Not such a bad idear Jimmy."

"But it's such a horrible thing," said Tony Hunter.

"You think we're a lot of callous brutes, dont you Tony?"

"No I just dont see the pleasure people get out of reading about it."

"Oh it's all in the day's work," said Jimmy. "What gives me gooseflesh is the armies mobilizing, Belgrade bombarded, Belgium invaded . . . all that stuff. I just cant imagine it. . . . They've killed Jaures." "Who's he?"

"A French Socialist."

"Those goddam French are so goddam degenerate all they

can do is fight duels and sleep with each other's wives. I
bet the Germans are in Paris in two weeks."

"It couldn't last long," said Framingham, a tall ceremoni-
ous man with a whispy blond moustache who sat beside
Hunter.

"Well I'd like to get an assignment as warcorrespondent."

"Say Jimmy do you know this French guy who's barkeep
here?"

"Congo Jake? Sure I know him."

"Is he a good guy?"

"He's swell."

"Let's go out and talk to him. He might give us some
dope about this here murder. God I'd like it if I could hitch
it on to the World Conflict."

"I have the greatest confidence," had begun Framingham,
"that the British will patch it up somehow." Jimmy followed Bullock towards the bar.

Crossing the room he caught sight of Ellen. Her hair
was very red in the glow from the lamp beside her. Baldwin was leaning towards her across the table with moist lips
and bright eyes. Jimmy felt something glittering go off in
his chest like a released spring. He turned his head away
suddenly for fear she should see him.

Bullock turned and nudged him in the ribs. "Say Jimmy
who the hell are those two guys came out with us?"

"They are friends of Ruth's. I dont know them particularly well. Framingham's an interior decorator I think."

At the bar under a picture of the Lusitania stood a dark
man in a white coat distended by a deep gorilla chest. He
was vibrating a shaker between his very hairy hands. A
waiter stood in front of the bar with a tray of cocktail
glasses. The cocktail foamed into them greenishwhite.

"Hello Congo," said Jimmy.

"Ah bonsoir monsieur 'Erf, ça biche?"

"Pretty good . . . Say Congo I want you to meet a friend
of mine. This is Grant Bullock of the *American*."

"Very please. You an Mr. 'Erf ave someting on the
'ouse sir."

The waiter raised the clinking tray of glasses to shoulder height and carried them out on the flat of his hand.

"I suppose a gin fizz'll ruin all that whiskey but I'd like one. . . . Drink something with us wont you Congo?" Bullock put a foot up on the brass rail and took a sip. "I was wondering," he said slowly, "if there was any dope going round about this murder down the road."

"Everybody ave his teyorie . . ."

Jimmy caught a faint wink from one of Congo's deepset black eyes. "Do you live out here?" he asked to keep from giggling.

"In the middle of the night I hear an automobile go by very fast wid de cutout open. I tink maybe it run into someting because it stopped very quick and come back much faster, licketysplit."

"Did you hear a shot?"

Congo shook his head mysteriously. "I ear voices, very angree voices."

"Gosh I'm going to look into this," said Bullock tossing off the end of his drink. "Let's go back to the girls."

Ellen was looking at the face wrinkled like a walnut and the dead codfish eyes of the waiter pouring coffee. Baldwin was leaning back in his chair staring at her through his eyelashes. He was talking in a low monotone:

"Cant you see that I'll go mad if I cant have you. You are the only thing in the world I ever wanted."

"George I dont want to be had by anybody. . . . Cant you understand that a woman wants some freedom? Do be a sport about it. I'll have to go home if you talk like that."

"Why have you kept me dangling then? I'm not the sort of man you can play like a trout. You know that perfectly well."

She looked straight at him with wide gray eyes; the light gave a sheen of gold to the little brown specks in the iris.

"It's not so easy never to be able to have friends." She

looked down at her fingers on the edge of the table. His eyes were on the glint of copper along her eyelashes. Suddenly he snapped the silence that was tightening between them.

"Anyway let's dance."

> J'ai fait trois fois le tour du monde
> Dans mes voyages,

hummed Congo Jake as the big shining shaker quivered between his hairy hands. The narrow greenpapered bar was swelled and warped with bubbling voices, spiral exhalations of drinks, sharp clink of ice and glasses, an occasional strain of music from the other room. Jimmy Herf stood alone in the corner sipping a gin fizz. Next him Gus McNiel was slapping Bullock on the back and roaring in his ear:

"Why if they dont close the Stock Exchange . . . godamighty . . . before the blowup comes there'll be an opportunity. . . . Well begorry dont you forget it. A panic's the time for a man with a cool head to make money."

"There have been some big failures already and this is just the first whiff. . . ."

"Opportunity knocks but once at a young man's door. . . . You listen to me when there's a big failure of one o them brokerage firms honest men can bless themselves. . . . But you're not putting everythin I'm tellin ye in the paper, are you? There's a good guy. . . . Most of you fellers go around puttin words in a man's mouth. Cant trust one of you. I'll tell you one thing though the lockout is a wonderful thing for the contractors. Wont be no housebuildin with a war on anyway." "It wont last more'n two weeks and I dont see what it has to do with us anyway."

"But conditions'll be affected all over the world. . . . Conditions. . . . Hello Joey what the hell do you want?"

"I'd like to talk to you private for a minute sir. There's some big news. . . ."

The bar emptied gradually. Jimmy Herf was still standing at the end against the wall.

"You never get drunk, Mr. 'Erf." Congo Jake sat down back of the bar to drink a cup of coffee.

"I'd rather watch the other fellows."

"Very good. No use spend a lot o money ave a eadache next day."

"That's no way for a barkeep to talk."

"I say what I tink."

"Say I've always wanted to ask you. . . . Do you mind telling me? . . . How did you get the name of Congo Jake?"

Congo laughed deep in his chest. "I dunno. . . . When I very leetle I first go to sea dey call me Congo because I have curly hair an dark like a nigger. Den when I work in America, on American ship an all zat, guy ask me How you feel Congo? and I say Jake . . . so dey call me Congo Jake."

"It's some nickname. . . . I thought you'd followed the sea."

"It's a 'ard life. . . . I tell you Mr. 'Erf, there's someting about me unlucky. When I first remember on a peniche, you know what I mean . . . in canal, a big man not my fader beat me up every day. Then I run away and work on sailboats in and out of Bordeaux, you know?"

"I was there when I was a kid I think. . . ."

"Sure. . . . You understand them things Mr. 'Erf. But a feller like you, good education, all 'at, you dont know what life is. When I was seventeen I come to New York . . . no good. I tink of notten but raising Cain. Den I shipped out again and went everywhere to hell an gone. In Shanghai I learned spik American an tend bar. I come back to Frisco an got married. Now I want to be American. But unlucky again see? Before I marry zat girl her and me lived togedder a year sweet as pie, but when we get married no good. She make fun of me and call me Frenchy because I no spik American good and den she kick no out of the house an I tell her go to hell. Funny ting a man's life."

J'ai fait trois fois le tour du monde
Dans mes voyages. . . .

he started in his growling baritone.

There was a hand on Jimmy's arm. He turned. "Why Ellie what's the matter?"

"I'm with a crazy man you've got to help me get away."

"Look this is Congo Jake. . . . You ought to know him Ellie, he's a fine man. . . . This is une tres grande artiste, Congo."

"Wont the lady have a leetle anizette?"

"Have a little drink with us. . . . It's awfully cozy in here now that everybody's gone."

"No thanks I'm going home."

"But it's just the neck of the evening."

"Well you'll have to take the consequences of my crazy man. . . . Look Herf, have you seen Stan today?"

"No I haven't."

"He didn't turn up when I expected him."

"I wish you'd keep him from drinking so much, Ellie. I'm getting worried about him."

"I'm not his keeper."

"I know, but you know what I mean."

"What does our friend here think about all this wartalk?"

"I wont go. . . . A workingman has no country. I'm going to be American citizen. . . . I was in the marine once but. . . ." He slapped his jerking bent forearm with one hand, and a deep laugh rattled in his throat. . . . "Twentee tree. Moi je suis anarchiste vous comprennez monsieur."

"But then you cant be an American citizen."

Congo shrugged his shoulders.

"Oh I love him, he's wonderful," whispered Ellen in Jimmy's ear.

"You know why they have this here war. . . . So that workingmen all over wont make big revolution. . . . Too busy fighting. So Guillaume and Viviani and l'Empereur d'Autriche and Krupp and Rothschild and Morgan they say let's have a war. . . . You know the first thing they do?

They shoot Jaures, because he socialiste. The socialists are traitors to the International but all de samee. . . . "

"But how can they make people fight if they dont want to?"

"In Europe people are slaves for thousands of years. Not like 'ere. . . . But I 've seen war. Very funny. I tended bar in Port Arthur, nutten but a kid den. It was very funny."

"Gee I wish I could get a job as warcorrespondent."

"I might go as a Red Cross nurse."

"Correspondent very good ting. . . . Always drunk in American bar very far from battlefield."

They laughed.

"But arent we rather far from the battlefield, Herf?"

"All right let's dance. You must forgive me if I dance very badly."

"I'll kick you if you do anything wrong."

His arm was like plaster when he put it round her to dance with her. High ashy walls broke and crackled within him. He was soaring like a fireballoon on the smell of her hair.

"Get up on your toes and walk in time to the music. . . . Move in straight lines that's the whole trick." Her voice cut the quick coldly like a tiny flexible sharp metalsaw. Elbows joggling, faces set, gollywog eyes, fat men and thin women, thin women and fat men rotated densely about them. He was crumbling plaster with something that rattled achingly in his chest, she was an intricate machine of sawtooth steel whitebright bluebright copperbright in his arms. When they stopped her breast and the side of her body and her thigh came against him. He was suddenly full of blood steaming with sweat like a runaway horse. A breeze through an open door hustled the tobaccosmoke and the clotted pink air of the restaurant.

"Herf I want to go down to see the murder cottage; please take me."

"As if I hadn't seen enough of X's marking the spot where the crime was committed."

In the hall George Baldwin stepped in front of them. He was pale as chalk, his black tie was crooked, the nostrils of his thin nose were dilated and marked with little veins of red.

"Hello George."

His voice croaked tartly like a klaxon. "Elaine I've been looking for you. I must speak to you. . . . Maybe you think I'm joking. I never joke."

"Herf excuse me a minute. . . . Now what is the matter George? Come back to the table."

"George I was not joking either. . . . Herf do you mind ordering me a taxi?"

Baldwin grabbed hold of her wrist. "You've been playing with me long enough, do you hear me? Some day some man's going to take a gun and shoot you. You think you can play me like all the other little sniveling fools. . . . You're no better than a common prostitute."

"Herf I told you to go get me a taxi."

Jimmy bit his lip and went out the front door.

"Elaine what are you going to do?"

"George I will not be bullied."

Something nickel flashed in Baldwin's hand. Gus McNiel stepped forward and gripped his wrist with a big red hand.

"Gimme that George. . . . For God's sake man pull yourself together." He shoved the revolver into his pocket. Baldwin tottered to the wall in front of him. The trigger finger of his right hand was bleeding.

"Here's a taxi," said Herf looking from one to another of the taut white faces.

"All right you take the girl home. . . . No harm done, just a little nervous attack, see? No cause for alarm," McNiel was shouting in the voice of a man speaking from a soapbox. The headwaiter and the coatgirl were looking at each other uneasily. "Didn't nutten happen. . . . Gentleman's a little nervous . . . overwork you understand," McNiel brought his voice down to a reassuring purr. "You just forget it."

As they were getting into the taxi Ellen suddenly said in a little child's voice: "I forgot we were going down to see the murder cottage. . . . Let's make him wait. I'd like to walk up and down in the air for a minute." There was a smell of saltmarshes. The night was marbled with clouds and moonlight. The toads in the ditches sounded like sleighbells.

"Is it far?" she asked.

"No it's right down at the corner."

Their feet crackled on gravel then ground softly on macadam. A headlight blinded them, they stopped to let the car whir by; the exhaust filled their nostrils, faded into the smell of saltmarshes again.

It was a peaked gray house with a small porch facing the road screened with broken lattice. A big locust shaded it from behind. A policeman walked to and fro in front of it whistling gently to himself. A mildewed scrap of moon came out from behind the clouds for a minute, made tinfoil of a bit of broken glass in a gaping window, picked out the little rounded leaves of the locust and rolled like a lost dime into a crack in the clouds.

Neither of them said anything. They walked back towards the roadhouse.

"Honestly Herf havent you seen Stan?"

"No I havent an idea where he could be hiding himself."

"If you see him tell him I want him to call me up at once. . . . Herf what were those women called who followed the armies in the French Revolution?"

"Let's think. Was it cantonnières?"

"Something like that . . . I'd like to do that."

An electric train whistled far to the right of them, rattled nearer and faded into whining distance.

Dripping with a tango the roadhouse melted pink like a block of icecream. Jimmy was following her into the taxicab.

"No I want to be alone, Herf."

"But I'd like very much to take you home. . . . I dont like the idea of letting you go all alone."

"Please as a friend I ask you."

They didnt shake hands. The taxi kicked dust and a rasp of burnt gasoline in his face. He stood on the steps reluctant to go back into the noise and fume.

Nellie McNiel was alone at the table. In front of her was the chair pushed back with his napkin on the back of it where her husband had sat. She was staring straight ahead of her; the dancers passed like shadows across her eyes. At the other end of the room she saw George Baldwin, pale and lean, walk slowly like a sick man to his table. He stood beside the table examining his check carefully, paid it and stood looking distractedly round the room. He was going to look at her. The waiter brought the change on a plate and bowed low. Baldwin swept the faces of the dancers with a black glance, turned his back square and walked out. Remembering the insupportable sweetness of Chinese lilies, she felt her eyes filling with tears. She took her engagement book out of her silver mesh bag and went through it hurriedly, marking carets with a silver pencil. She looked up after a little while, the tired skin of her face in a pucker of spite, and beckoned to a waiter. "Will you please tell Mr. McNiel that Mrs. McNiel wants to speak to him? He's in the bar."

"Sarajevo, Sarajevo; that's the place that set the wires on fire," Bullock was shouting at the frieze of faces and glasses along the bar.

"Say bo," said Joe O'Keefe confidentially to no one in particular, "a guy works in a telegraph office told me there'd been a big seabattle off St. John's, Newfoundland and the Britishers had sunk the German fleet of forty battleships."

"Jiminy that'd stop the war right there."

"But they aint declared war yet."

"How do you know? The cables are so choked up you cant get any news through."

"Did you see there were four more failures on Wall Street?"

"Tell me Chicago wheat pit's gone crazy."

"They ought to close all the exchanges till this blows over."

"Well maybe when the Germans have licked the pants off her England'll give Ireland her freedom."

"But they are. . . . Stock market wont be open to-morrow."

"If a man's got the capital to cover and could keep his head this here would be the time to clean up."

"Well Bullock old man I'm going home," said Jimmy. "This is my night of rest and I ought to be getting after it."

Bullock winked one eye and waved a drunken hand. The voices in Jimmy's ears were throbbing elastic roar, near, far, near, far. Dies like a dog, march on he said. He'd spent all his money but a quarter. Shot at sunrise. Declaration of war. Commencement of hostilities. And they left him alone in his glory. Leipzig, the Wilderness, Waterloo, where the embattled farmers stood and fired the shot heard round . . . Cant take a taxi, want to walk anyway. Ultimatum. Trooptrains singing to the shambles with flowers on their ears. And shame on the false Etruscan who lingers in his home when . . .

As he was walking down the gravel drive to the road an arm hooked in his.

"Do you mind if I come along? I dont want to stay here."

"Sure come ahead Tony I'm going to walk."

Herf walked with a long stride, looking straight ahead of him. Clouds had darkened the sky where remained the faintest milkiness of moonlight. To the right and left there was outside of the violetgray cones of occasional arclights black pricked by few lights, ahead the glare of streets rose in blurred cliffs yellow and ruddy.

"You dont like me do you?" said Tony Hunter breathlessly after a few minutes.

Herf slowed his pace. "Why I dont know you very well. You seem to me a very pleasant person. . . ."

"Dont lie; there's no reason why you should. . . . I think I'm going to kill myself tonight."

"Heavens! dont do that. . . . What's the matter?"

"You have no right to tell me not to kill myself. You dont know anything about me. If I was a woman you wouldnt be so indifferent."

"What's eating you anyway?"

"I'm going crazy that's all, everything's so horrible. When I first met you with Ruth one evening I thought we were going to be friends, Herf. You seemed so sympathetic and understanding. . . . I thought you were like me, but now you're getting so callous."

"I guess it's the *Times*. . . . I'll get fired soon, don't worry."

"I'm tired of being poor; I want to make a hit."

"Well you're young yet; you must be younger than I am." Tony didnt answer.

They were walking down a broad avenue between two rows of blackened frame houses. A streetcar long and yellow hissed rasping past.

"Why we must be in Flatbush."

"Herf I used to think you were like me, but now I never see you except with some woman."

"What do you mean?"

"I've never told anybody in the world. . . . By God if you tell anybody. . . . When I was a child I was horribly oversexed, when I was about ten or eleven or thirteen." He was sobbing. As they passed under an arclight, Jimmy caught the glisten of the tears on his cheeks. "I wouldn't tell you this if I wasnt drunk."

"But things like that happened to almost everybody when they were kids. . . . You oughtnt to worry about that."

"But I'm that way now, that's what's so horrible. I cant like women. I've tried and tried. . . . You see I was caught. I was so ashamed I wouldn't go to school for weeks. My mother cried and cried. I'm so ashamed. I'm so afraid people will find out about it. I'm always fighting to keep it hidden, to hide my feelings."

"But it all may be an idea. You may be able to get over it. Go to a psychoanalyist."

"I cant talk to anybody. It's just that tonight I'm drunk. I've tried to look it up in the encyclopædia. . . . It's not even in the dictionary." He stopped and leaned against a lamppost with his face in his hands. "It's not even in the dictionary."

Jimmy Herf patted him on the back. "Buck up for Heaven's sake. They're lots of people in the same boat. The stage is full of them."

"I hate them all. . . . It's not people like that I fall in love with. I hate myself. I suppose you'll hate me after tonight."

"What nonsense. It's no business of mine."

"Now you know why I want to kill myself. . . . Oh it's not fair Herf, it's not fair. . . . I've had no luck in my life. I started earning my living as soon as I got out of high-school. I used to be bellhop in summer hotels. My mother lived in Lakewood and I used to send her everything I earned. I've worked so hard to get where I am. If it were known, if there were a scandal and it all came out I'd be ruined."

"But everybody says that of all juveniles and nobody lets it worry them."

"Whenever I fail to get a part I think it's on account of that. I hate and despise all that kind of men. . . . I dont want to be a juvenile. I want to act. Oh it's hell. . . . It's hell."

"But you're rehearsing now aren't you?"

"A fool show that'll never get beyond Stamford. Now when you hear that I've done it you wont be surprised."

"Done what?"

"Killed myself."

They walked without speaking. It had started to rain. Down the street behind the low greenblack shoebox houses there was an occasional mothpink flutter of lightning. A wet dusty smell came up from the asphalt beaten by the big plunking drops.

"There ought to be a subway station near. . . . Isn't that a blue light down there? Let's hurry or we'll get soaked."

"Oh hell Tony I'd just as soon get soaked as not." Jimmy took off his felt hat and swung it in one hand. The raindrops were cool on his forehead, the smell of the rain, of roofs and mud and asphalt, took the biting taste of whiskey and cigarettes out of his mouth.

"Gosh it's horrible," he shouted suddenly.

"What?"

"All the hushdope about sex. I'd never realized it before tonight, the full extent of the agony. God you must have a rotten time. . . . We all of us have a rotten time. In your case it's just luck, hellish bad luck. Martin used to say: Everything would be so much better if suddenly a bell rang and everybody told everybody else honestly what they did about it, how they lived, how they loved. It's hiding things makes them putrefy. By God it's horrible. As if life wasn't difficult enough without that."

"Well I'm going down into this subway station."

"You'll have to wait hours for a train."

"I cant help it I'm tired and I dont want to get wet."

"Well good night."

"Good night Herf."

There was a long rolling thunderclap. It began to rain hard. Jimmy rammed his hat down on his head and yanked his coatcollar up. He wanted to run along yelling sonsobitches at the top of his lungs. Lightning flickered along the staring rows of dead windows. The rain seethed along the pavements, against storewindows, on brownstone steps. His knees were wet, a slow trickle started down his back, there were chilly cascades off his sleeves onto his wrists, his whole body itched and tingled. He walked on through Brooklyn. Obsession of all the beds in all the pigeonhole bedrooms, tangled sleepers twisted and strangled like the roots of potbound plants. Obsession of feet creaking on the stairs of lodginghouses, hands fumbling at doorknobs. Obsession of pounding temples and solitary bodies rigid on their beds.

J'ai fait trois fois le tour du monde
Vive le sang, vive le sang. . . .

Moi monsieur je suis anarchiste. . . . *And three times round went our gallant ship, and three times round went* . . . goddam it between that and money . . . *and she sank to the bottom of the sea* . . . we're in a treadmill for fair.

J'ai fait trois fois le tour du monde
Dans mes voy . . . ages.

Declaration of war . . . rumble of drums . . . beefeaters march in red after the flashing baton of a drummajor in a hat like a longhaired muff, silver knob spins flashing grump, grump, grump . . . in the face of revolution mondiale. Commencement of hostilities in a long parade through the empty rainlashed streets. Extra, extra, extra. Santa Claus shoots daughter he has tried to attack. SLAYS SELF WITH SHOTGUN . . . put the gun under his chin and pulled the trigger with his big toe. The stars look down on Fredericktown. Workers of the world, unite. Vive le sang, vive le sang.

"Golly I'm wet," Jimmy Herf said aloud. As far as he could see the street stretched empty in the rain between ranks of dead windows studded here and there with violet knobs of arclights. Desperately he walked on.

VI. Five Statutory Questions

They pair off hurriedly. Standing Up in Cab Strictly Forbidden. *The climbing chain grates, grips the cogs; jerkily the car climbs the incline out of the whirring lights, out of the smell of crowds and steamed corn and peanuts, up jerkily grating up through the tall night of September meteors.*

Sea, marshsmell, the lights of an Iron Steamboat leaving the dock. Across wide violet indigo a lighthouse blinks. Then the swoop. The sea does a flipflop, the lights soar. Her hair in his mouth, his hand in her ribs, thighs grind together.

The wind of their falling has snatched their yells, they jerk rattling upwards through the tangled girderstructure. Swoop. Soar. Bubbling lights in a sandwich of darkness and sea. Swoop. Keep Your Seats for the Next Ride.

"COME on in Joe, I'll see if the ole lady kin git us some grub."

"Very kind of you . . . er . . . I'm not . . . er . . . exactly dressed to meet a lady you see."

"Oh she wont care. She's just my mother; sit down, I'll git her."

Harland sat down on a chair beside the door in the dark kitchen and put his hands on his knees. He sat staring at his hands; they were red and dirtgrained and trembling, his tongue was like a nutmeg grater from the cheap whiskey he had been drinking the last week, his whole body felt numb and sodden and sour. He stared at his hands.

Joe O'Keefe came back into the kitchen. "She's loin down. She says there's some soup on the back of the stove. . . . Here ye are. That'll make a man of ye. . . . Joe you ought to been where I was last night. Went out to this here Seaside Inn to take a message to the chief about somebody tippin him off that they was going to close the market. . . .

237

It was the goddamnedest thing you ever saw in your life. This guy who's a wellknown lawyer down town was out in the hall bawlin out his gash about something. Jez he looked hard.   And then he had a gun out an was goin to shoot her or some goddam thing when the chief comes up cool as you make em limpin on his stick like he does and took the gun away from him an put it in his pocket before anybody'd half seen what happened. . . . This guy Baldwin's a frien o his see?   It was the goddamnedest thing I ever saw.   Then he all crumpled up like. . . ."

"I tell you kid," said Joe Harland, "it gets em all sooner or later. . . ."

"Hay there eat up strong.   You aint eaten enough."

"I cant eat very well."

"Sure you can. . . . Say Joe what's the dope about this war business?"

"I guess they are in for it this time. . . . I've known it was coming ever since the Agadir incident."

"Jez I like to see somebody wallop the pants off England after the way they wont give home rule to Ireland."

"We'd have to help em. . . . Anyway I dont see how this can last long.   The men who control international finance wont allow it.   After all it's the banker who holds the purse strings."

"We wouldn't come to the help of England, no sir, not after the way they acted in Ireland and in the Revolution and in the Civil War. . . ."

"Joey you're getting all choked up with that history you're reading up in the public library every night. . . . You follow the stock quotations and keep on your toes and dont let em fool you with all this newspaper talk about strikes and upheavals and socialism. . . . I'd like to see you make good Joey. . . . Well I guess I'd better be going."

"Naw stick around awhile, we'll open a bottle of glue." They heard a heavy stumbling in the passage outside the kitchen.

"Whossat?"

"Zat you Joe?"   A big towheaded boy with lumpy shoulders and a square red face and thickset neck lurched into the room.

"What the hell do you think this is? . . . This is my kid brother Mike."

"Well what about it?" Mike stood swaying with his chin on his chest. His shoulders bulged against the low ceiling of the kitchen.

"Aint he a whale? But for crissake Mike aint I told you not to come home when you was drinkin? . . . He's loible to tear the house down."

"I got to come home sometime aint I? Since you got to be a wardheeler Joey you been pickin on me worsen the old man. I'm glad I aint goin to stay round this goddam town long. It's enough to drive a feller cookoo. If I can get on some kind of a tub that puts to sea before the *Golden Gate* by God I'm going to do it."

"Hell I dont mind you stayin here. It's just that I dont like you raisin hell all the time, see?"

"I'm goin to do what I please, git me?"

"You get outa here, Mike. . . . Come back home when you're sober."

"I'd like to see you put me outa here, git me? I'd like to see you put me outa here."

Harland got to his feet. "Well I'm going," he said. "Got to see if I can get that job."

Mike was advancing across the kitchen with his fists clenched. Joey's jaw set; he picked up a chair.

"I'll crown you with it."

"O saints and martyrs cant a woman have no peace in her own house?" A small grayhaired woman ran screaming between them; she had lustrous black eyes set far apart in a face shrunken like a last year's apple; she beat the air with worktwisted hands. "Shut yer traps both of ye, always cursing an fightin round the house like there warnt no God. . . . Mike you go upstairs an lay down on your bed till yer sober."

"I was jus tellin him that," said Joey.

She turned on Harland, her voice like the screech of chalk

on a blackboard. "An you git along outa here. I dont allow
no drunken bums in my house. Git along outa here. I
dont care who brought you."

Harland looked at Joey with a little sour smile, shrugged
his shoulders and went out. "Charwoman," he muttered as
he stumbled with stiff aching legs along the dusty street of
darkfaced brick houses.

The sultry afternoon sun was like a blow on his back.
Voices in his ears of maids, charwomen, cooks, stenographers,
secretaries: Yes sir, Mr. Harland, Thank you sir Mr.
Harland. Oh sir thank you sir so much sir Mr. Harland
sir. . . .

Red buzzing in her eyelids the sunlight wakes her, she
sinks back into purpling cottonwool corridors of sleep, wakes
again, turns over yawning, pulls her knees up to her chin to
pull the drowsysweet cocoon tighter about her. A truck
jangles shatteringly along the street, the sun lays hot stripes
on her back. She yawns desperately and twists herself over
and lies wide awake with her hands under her head staring
at the ceiling. From far away through streets and housewalls the long moan of a steamboat whistle penetrates to her
like a blunt sprout of crabgrass nudging through gravel.
Ellen sits up shaking her head to get rid of a fly blundering
about her face. The fly flashes and vanishes in the sunlight,
but somewhere in her there lingers a droning pang, unac-
countable, something left over from last night's bitter
thoughts. But she is happy and wide awake and it's early.
She gets up and wanders round the room in her nightgown.
Where the sun hits it the hardwood floor is warm to the
soles of her feet. Sparrows chirp on the windowledge. From
upstairs comes the sound of a sewingmachine. When she
gets out of the bath her body feels smoothwhittled and tense;
she rubs herself with a towel, telling off the hours of the
long day ahead; take a walk through junky littered downtown streets to that pier on the East River where they pile

the great beams of mahogany, breakfast all alone at the Lafayette, coffee and crescent rolls and sweet butter, go shopping at Lord & Taylor's early before everything is stuffy and the salesgirls wilted, have lunch with . . . Then the pain that has been teasing all night wells up and bursts. "Stan, Stan for God's sake," she says aloud. She sits before her mirror staring in the black of her own dilating pupils.

She dresses in a hurry and goes out, walks down Fifth Avenue and east along Eighth Street without looking to the right or left. The sun already hot simmers slatily on the pavements, on plateglass, on dustmarbled enameled signs. Men's and women's faces as they pass her are rumpled and gray like pillows that have been too much slept on. After crossing Lafayette Street roaring with trucks and delivery wagons there is a taste of dust in her mouth, particles of grit crunch between her teeth. Further east she passes push-carts; men are wiping off the marble counters of softdrink stands, a grindorgan fills the street with shiny jostling coils of the *Blue Danube*, acrid pungence spreads from a pickle-stand. In Tompkins Square yelling children mill about the soggy asphalt. At her feet a squirming heap of small boys, dirty torn shirts, slobbering mouths, punching, biting, scratching; a squalid smell like moldy bread comes from them. Ellen all of a sudden feels her knees weak under her. She turns and walks back the way she came.

The sun is heavy like his arm across her back, strokes her bare forearm the way his fingers stroke her, it's his breath against her cheek.

"Nothing but the five statutory questions," said Ellen to the rawboned man with big sagging eyes like oysters into whose long shirtfront she was talking.

"And so the decree is granted?" he asked solemnly.

"Surely in an uncontested . . ."

"Well I'm very sorry to hear it as an old family friend of both parties."

"Look here Dick, honestly I'm very fond of Jojo. I owe
him a great deal. . . . He's a very fine person in many ways,
but it absolutely had to be."

"You mean there is somebody else?"

She looked up at him with bright eyes and half nodded.

"Oh but divorce is a very serious step my dear young
lady."

"Oh not so serious as all that."

They saw Harry Goldweiser coming towards them across
the big walnut paneled room. She suddenly raised her voice.
"They say that this battle of the Marne is going to end the
war."

Harry Goldweiser took her hand between his two pudgy-
palmed hands and bowed over it. "It's very charming of
you Elaine to come and keep a lot of old midsummer
bachelors from boring each other to death. Hello Snow old
man, how's things?"

"Yes how is it we have the pleasure of still finding you
here?"

"Oh various things have held me. . . . Anyway I hate
summer resorts." "Nowhere prettier than Long Beach
anyway. . . . Why Bar Harbor, I wouldnt go to Bar Harbor
if you gave me a million . . . a cool million."

Mr. Snow let out a gruff sniff. "Seems to me I've heard
you been going into the realestate game down there, Goldweiser."

"I bought myself a cottage that's all. It's amazing you
cant even buy yourself a cottage without every newsboy on
Times Square knowing about it. Let's go in and eat; my
sister'll be right here." A dumpy woman in a spangled
dress came in after they had sat down to table in the big
antlerhung diningroom; she was pigeonbreasted and had a
sallow skin.

"Oh Miss Oglethorpe I'm so glad to see you," she twittered
in a little voice like a parrakeet's. "I've often seen you
and thought you were the loveliest thing. . . . I did my best
to get Harry to bring you up to see me."

"This is my sister Rachel," said Goldweiser to Ellen without getting up. "She keeps house for me."

"I wish you'd help me, Snow, to induce Miss Oglethorpe to take that part in The Zinnia Girl. . . . Honest it was just written for you."

"But it's such a small part . . ."

"It's not a lead exactly, but from the point of view of your reputation as a versatile and exquisite artist, it's the best thing in the show."

"Will you have a little more fish, Miss Oglethorpe?" piped Miss Goldweiser.

Mr. Snow sniffed. "There's no great acting any more: Booth, Jefferson, Mansfield . . . all gone. Nowadays it's all advertising; actors and actresses are put on the market like patent medicines. Isn't it the truth Elaine? . . . Advertising, advertising."

"But that isn't what makes success. . . . If you could do it with advertising every producer in New York'd be a millionaire," burst in Goldweiser. "It's the mysterious occult force that grips the crowds on the street and makes them turn in at a particular theater that makes the receipts go up at a particular boxoffice, do you understand me? Advertising wont do it, good criticism wont do it, maybe it's genius maybe it's luck but if you can give the public what it wants at that time and at that place you have a hit. Now that's what Elaine gave us in this last show. . . . She established contact with the audience. It might have been the greatest play in the world acted by the greatest actors in the world and fallen a flat failure. . . . And I dont know how you do it, nobody dont know how you do it. . . . You go to bed one night with your house full of paper and you wake up the next morning with a howling success. The producer cant control it any more than the weather man can control the weather. Aint I tellin the truth?"

"Ah the taste of the New York public has sadly degenerated since the old days of Wallack's."

"But there have been some beautiful plays," chirped Miss Goldweiser.

The long day love was crisp in the curls . . . the dark
curls . . . broken in the dark steel light . . . hurls . . .
high O God high into the bright . . . She was cutting with
her fork in the crisp white heart of a lettuce. She was
saying words while quite other words spilled confusedly
inside her like a broken package of beads. She sat looking
at a picture of two women and two men eating at a table in
a high paneled room under a shivering crystal chandelier.
She looked up from her plate to find Miss Goldweiser's
little birdeyes kindly querulous fixed hard on her face.

"Oh yes New York is really pleasanter in midsummer
than any other time; there's less hurry and bustle."

"Oh yes that's quite true Miss Goldweiser." Ellen flashed
a sudden smile round the table. . . . All the long day love
Was crisp in the curls of his high thin brow, Flashed in his
eyes in dark steel light. . . .

In the taxi Goldweiser's broad short knees pressed against
hers; his eyes were full of furtive spiderlike industry weav-
ing a warm sweet choking net about her face and neck. Miss
Goldweiser had relapsed pudgily into the seat beside her.
Dick Snow was holding an unlighted cigar in his mouth,
rolling it with his tongue. Ellen tried to remember exactly
how Stan looked, his polevaulter's tight slenderness; she
couldn't remember his face entire, she saw his eyes, lips, an
ear.

Times Square was full of juggled colored lights, crisscrossed corrugations of glare. They went up in the elevator
at the Astor. Ellen followed Miss Goldweiser across the
roofgarden among the tables. Men and women in evening
dress, in summer muslins and light suits turned and looked
after her, like sticky tendrils of vines glances caught at her
as she passed. The orchestra was playing *In My Harem*.
They arranged themselves at a table.

"Shall we dance?" asked Goldweiser.

She smiled a wry broken smile in his face as she let him
put his arm round her back. His big ear with solemn lonely
hairs on it was on the level of her eyes.

"Elaine," he was breathing into her ear, "honest I thought

I was a wise guy." He caught his breath . . . "but I aint.
. . . You've got me goin little girl and I hate to admit it.
. . . Why cant you like me a little bit? I'd like . . . us to
get married as soon as you get your decree. . . . Wouldn't
you be kinder nice to me once in a while . . . ? I'd do
anything for you, you know that. . . . There are lots of
things in New York I could do for you. . . ." The music
stopped. They stood apart under a palm. "Elaine come over
to my office and sign that contract. I had Ferrari wait. . . .
We can be back in fifteen minutes."

"I've got to think it over . . . I never do anything without sleeping on it."

"Gosh you drive a feller wild."

Suddenly she remembered Stan's face altogether, he was
standing in front of her with a bow tie crooked in his soft
shirt, his hair rumpled, drinking again.

"Oh Ellie I'm so glad to see you. . . ."

"This is Mr. Emery, Mr. Goldweiser. . . ."

"I've been on the most exordinately spectacular trip, honestly you should have come. . . . We went to Montreal and
Quebec and came back through Niagara Falls and we never
drew a sober breath from the time we left little old New
York till they arrested us for speeding on the Boston Post
Road, did we Pearline?" Ellen was staring at a girl who
stood groggily behind Stan with a small flowered straw hat
pulled down over a pair of eyes the blue of watered milk.
"Ellie this is Pearline. . . . Isn't it a fine name? I almost
split when she told me what it was. . . . But you dont know
the joke. . . . We got so tight in Niagara Falls that when
we came to we found we were married. . . . And we have
pansies on our marriage license. . . ."

Ellen couldnt see his face. The orchestra, the jangle of
voices, the clatter of plates spouted spiraling louder and
louder about her . . .

> And the ladies of the harem
> Knew exactly how to wear 'em
> In O-riental Bagdad long ago. . . .

"Good night Stan." Her voice was gritty in her mouth, she heard the words very clearly when she spoke them.

"Oh Ellie I wish you'd come partying with us. . . ."

"Thanks . . . thanks."

She started to dance again with Harry Goldweiser. The roofgarden was spinning fast, then less fast. The noise ebbed sickeningly. "Excuse me a minute Harry," she said. "I'll come back to the table." In the ladies' room she let herself down carefully on the plush sofa. She looked at her face in the round mirror of her vanitycase. From black pinholes her pupils spread blurring till everything was black.

Jimmy Herf's legs were tired; he had been walking all afternoon. He sat down on a bench beside the Aquarium and looked out over the water. The fresh September wind gave a glint of steel to the little crisp waves of the harbor and to the slateblue smutted sky. A big white steamer with a yellow funnel was passing in front of the statue of Liberty. The smoke from the tug at the bow came out sharply scalloped like paper. In spite of the encumbering wharfhouses the end of Manhattan seemed to him like the prow of a barge pushing slowly and evenly down the harbor. Gulls wheeled and cried. He got to his feet with a jerk. "Oh hell I've got to do something."

He stood a second with tense muscles balanced on the balls of his feet. The ragged man looking at the photogravures of a Sunday paper had a face he had seen before. "Hello," he said vaguely. "I knew who you were all along," said the man without holding out his hand. "You're Lily Herf's boy . . . I thought you werent going to speak to me. . . . No reason why you should."

"Oh of course you must be Cousin Joe Harland. . . . I'm awfully glad to see you. . . . I've often wondered about you."

"Wondered what?"

"Oh I dunno . . . funny you never think of your relatives

as being people like yourself, do you?" Herf sat down in the seat again. "Will you have a cigarette. . . . It's only a Camel."

"Well I dont mind if I do. . . . What's your business Jimmy? You dont mind if I call you that do you?" Jimmy Herf lit a match; it went out, lit another and held it for Harland. "That's the first tobacco I've had in a week . . . Thank you."

Jimmy glanced at the man beside him. The long hollow of his gray cheek made a caret with the deep crease that came from the end of his mouth. "You think I'm pretty much of a wreck dont you?" spat Harland. "You're sorry you sat down aint you? You're sorry you had a mother who brought you up a gentleman instead of a cad like the rest of 'em. . . ."

"Why I've got a job as a reporter on the *Times* . . . a hellish rotten job and I'm sick of it," said Jimmy, drawling out his words.

"Dont talk like that Jimmy, you're too young. . . . You'll never get anywhere with that attitude."

"Well suppose I dont want to get anywhere."

"Poor dear Lily was so proud of you. . . . She wanted you to be a great man, she was so ambitious for you. . . . You dont want to forget your mother Jimmy. She was the only friend I had in the whole damn family."

Jimmy laughed. "I didnt say I wasnt ambitious."

"For God's sake, for your dear mother's sake be careful what you do. You're just starting out in life . . . everything'll depend on the next couple of years. Look at me."

"Well the Wizard of Wall Street made a pretty good thing of it I'll say. . . . No it's just that I dont like to take all the stuff you have to take from people in this goddam town. I'm sick of playing up to a lot of desk men I dont respect. . . . What are you doing Cousin Joe?"

"Don't ask me. . . ."

"Look, do you see that boat with the red funnels? She's French. Look, they are pulling the canvas off the gun on

her stern. . . . I want to go to the war. . . . The only
trouble is I'm very poor at wrangling things."

Harland was gnawing his upper lip; after a silence he
burst out in a hoarse broken voice. "Jimmy I'm going to
ask you to do something for Lily's sake. . . . Er . . . have
you any . . . er . . . any change with you? By a rather
unfortunate . . . coincidence I have not eaten very well for
the last two or three days. . . . I'm a little weak, do you
understand?"

"Why yes I was just going to suggest that we go have a
cup of coffee or tea or something. . . . I know a fine Syrian
restaurant on Washington street."

"Come along then," said Harland, getting up stiffly.
"You're sure you don't mind being seen with a scarecrow like
this?"

The newspaper fell out of his hand. Jimmy stooped to
pick it up. A face made out of modulated brown blurs
gave him a twinge as if something had touched a nerve in
a tooth. No it wasnt, she doesnt look like that, yes
TALENTED YOUNG ACTRESS SCORES HIT IN THE ZINNIA
GIRL. . . .

"Thanks, dont bother, I found it there," said Harland.
Jimmy dropped the paper; she fell face down.

"Pretty rotten photographs they have dont they?"

"It passes the time to look at them, I like to keep up with
what's going on in New York a little bit. . . . A cat may
look at a king you know, a cat may look at a king."

"Oh I just meant that they were badly taken."

VII. Rollercoaster

The leaden twilight weighs on the dry limbs of an old man walking towards Broadway. Round the Nedick's stand at the corner something clicks in his eyes. Broken doll in the ranks of varnished articulated dolls he plods up with drooping head into the seethe and throb into the furnace of beaded lettercut light. "I remember when it was all meadows," he grumbles to the little boy.

LOUIS EXPRESSO ASSOCIATION, the red letters on the placard jig before Stan's eyes. ANNUAL DANCE. Young men and girls going in. *Two by two the elephant And the kangaroo.* The boom and jangle of an orchestra seeping out through the swinging doors of the hall. Outside it is raining. *One more river, O there's one more river to cross.* He straightens the lapels of his coat, arranges his mouth soberly, pays two dollars and goes into a big resounding hall hung with red white and blue bunting. Reeling, so he leans for a while against the wall. *One more river . . .* The dancefloor full of jogging couples rolls like the deck of a ship. The bar is more stable. "Gus McNiel's here," everybody's saying "Good old Gus." Big hands slap broad backs, mouths roar black in red faces. Glasses rise and tip glinting, rise and tip in a dance. A husky beetfaced man with deepset eyes and curly hair limps through the bar leaning on a stick. "How's a boy Gus?"

"Yay dere's de chief."

"Good for old man McNiel come at last."

"Howde do Mr. McNiel?" The bar quiets down.

Gus McNiel waves his stick in the air. "Attaboy fellers, have a good time. . . . Burke ole man set the company up to a drink on me." "Dere's Father Mulvaney wid him too. Good for Father Mulvaney. . . . He's a prince that feller is."

For he's a jolly good fellow
That nobody can deny . . .

Broad backs deferentially hunched follow the slowly pacing group out among the dancers. *O the big baboon by the light of the moon is combing his auburn hair.* "Wont you dance, please?" The girl turns a white shoulder and walks off.

I am a bachelor and I live all alone
And I work at the weaver's trade. . . .

Stan finds himself singing at his own face in a mirror. One of his eyebrows is joining his hair, the other's an eyelash. . . . "No I'm not bejases I'm a married man. . . . Fight any man who says I'm not a married man and a citizen of City of New York, County of New York, State of New York. . . ." He's standing on a chair making a speech, banging his fist into his hand. "Friends Roooomans and countrymen, lend me five bucks. . . . We come to muzzle Cæsar not to shaaaave him. . . . According to the Constitution of the City of New York, County of New York, State of New York and duly attested and subscribed before a district attorney according to the provisions of the act of July 13th 1888. . . . To hell with the Pope."

"Hey quit dat." "Fellers lets trow dis guy out. . . . He aint one o de boys. . . . Dunno how he got in here. He's drunk as a pissant." Stan jumps with his eyes closed into a thicket of fists. He's slammed in the eye, in the jaw, shoots like out of a gun out into the drizzling cool silent street. Ha ha ha.

For I am a bachelor and I live all alone
And there's one more river to cross
One more river to Jordan
One more river to cross . . .

It was blowing cold in his face and he was sitting on the front of a ferryboat when he came to. His teeth were chattering, he was shivering . . . "I'm having DT's. Who am I? Where am I? City of New York, State of New York. . . . Stanwood Emery age twentytwo occupation student. . . . Pearline Anderson twentyone occupation actress. To hell with her. Gosh I've got fortynine dollars and eight cents and where the hell have I been? And nobody rolled me. Why I havent got the DT's at all. I feel fine, only a little delicate. All I need's a little drink, dont you? Hello, I thought there was somebody here. I guess I'd better shut up."

> Fortynine dollars ahanging on the wall
> Fortynine dollars ahanging on the wall

Across the zinc water the tall walls, the birchlike cluster of downtown buildings shimmered up the rosy morning like a sound of horns through a chocolatebrown haze. As the boat drew near the buildings densened to a granite mountain split with knifecut canyons. The ferry passed close to a tubby steamer that rode at anchor listing towards Stan so that he could see all the decks. An Ellis Island tug was alongside. A stale smell came from the decks packed with upturned faces like a load of melons. Three gulls wheeled complaining. A gull soared in a spiral, white wings caught the sun, the gull skimmed motionless in whitegold light. The rim of the sun had risen above the plumcolored band of clouds behind East New York. A million windows flashed with light. A rasp and a humming came from the city.

> The animals went in two by two
> The elephant and the kangaroo
> There's one more river to Jordan
> One more river to cross

In the whitening light tinfoil gulls wheeled above broken boxes, spoiled cabbageheads, orangerinds heaving slowly between the splintered plank walls, the green spumed under the round bow as the ferry skidding on the tide, gulped the broken water, crashed, slid, settled slowly into the slip. Handwinches whirled with jingle of chains, gates folded upward. Stan stepped across the crack, staggered up the manuresmelling wooden tunnel of the ferryhouse out into the sunny glass and benches of the Battery. He sat down on a bench, clasped his hands round his knees to keep them from shaking so. His mind went on jingling like a mechanical piano.

> With bells on her fingers and rings on her toes
> Shall ride a white lady upon a great horse
> And she shall make mischief wherever she goes . . .

There was Babylon and Nineveh, they were built of brick. Athens was goldmarble columns. Rome was held up on broad arches of rubble. In Constantinople the minarets flame like great candles round the Golden Horn. . . . O there's one more river to cross. Steel glass, tile, concrete will be the materials of the skyscrapers. Crammed on the narrow island the millionwindowed buildings will jut, glittering pyramid on pyramid, white cloudsheads piled above a thunderstorm . . .

> And it rained forty days and it rained forty nights
> And it didn't stop till Christmas
> And the only man who survived the flood
> Was longlegged Jack of the Isthmus. . . .

Kerist I wish I was a skyscraper.

The lock spun round in a circle to keep out the key. Dexterously Stan bided his time and caught it. He shot headlong through the open door and down the long hall shouting Pearline into the livingroom. It smelled funny, Pearline's smell, to hell with it. He picked up a chair; the chair wanted to fly, it swung round his head and crashed into the window, the glass shivered and tinkled. He looked out through the window. The street stood up on end. A hookandladder and a fire engine were climbing it licketysplit trailing a droning sirenshriek. *Fire fire, pour on water, Scotland's burning.* A thousand dollar fire, a hundredthousand dollar fire, a million dollar fire. Skyscrapers go up like flames, in flames, flames. He spun back into the room. The table turned a somersault. The chinacloset jumped on the table. Oak chairs climbed on top to the gas jet. *Pour on water, Scotland's burning.* Don't like the smell in this place in the City of New York, County of New York, State of New York. He lay on his back on the floor of the revolving kitchen and laughed and laughed. The only man who survived the flood rode a great lady on a white horse. Up in flames, up, up. Kerosene whispered a greasyfaced can in the corner of the kitchen. *Pour on water.* He stood swaying on the crackling upside down chairs on the upside down table. The kerosene licked him with a white cold tongue. He pitched, grabbed the gasjet, the gasjet gave way, he lay in a puddle on his back striking matches, wet wouldn't light. A match spluttered, lit; he held the flame carefully between his hands.

"Oh yes but my husband's awfully ambitious." Pearline was telling the blue gingham lady in the grocery-store. "Likes to have a good time an all that but he's much more ambitious than anybody I every knew. He's goin to get his old man to send us abroad so he can study architecture. He wants to be an architect."

"My that'll be nice for you wont it? A trip like that . . . Anything else miss?" "No I guess I didn't forget anythin. . . . If it was anybody else I'd be worryin about him. I haven't seen him for two days. Had to go and see his dad I guess."

"And you just newly wed too."

"I wouldnt be tellin ye if I thought there was anythin wrong, would I? No he's playin straight all right. . . . Well goodby Mrs. Robinson." She tucked her packages under one arm and swinging her bead bag in the free hand walked down the street. The sun was still warm although there was a tang of fall in the wind. She gave a penny to a blind man cranking the Merry Widow waltz out of a grindorgan. Still she'd better bawl him out a little when he came home, might get to doing it often. She turned into 200th Street. People were looking out of windows, there was a crowd gathering. It was a fire. She sniffed the singed air. It gave her gooseflesh; she loved seeing fires. She hurried. Why it's outside our building. Outside our apartmenthouse. Smoke dense as gunnysacks rolled out of the fifthstory window. She suddenly found herself all atremble. The colored elevatorboy ran up to her. His face was green. "Oh it's in our apartment" she shrieked, "and the furniture just came a week ago. Let me get by." The packages fell from her, a bottle of cream broke on the sidewalk. A policeman stood in her way, she threw herself at him and pounded on the broad blue chest. She couldnt stop shrieking. "That's all right little lady, that's all right," he kept booming in a deep voice. As she beat her head against it she could feel his voice rumbling in his chest. "They're bringing him down, just overcome by smoke that's all, just overcome by smoke."

"O Stanwood my husband," she shrieked. Everything was blacking out. She grabbed at two bright buttons on the policeman's coat and fainted.

VIII. One More River to Jordan

A MAN is shouting from a soapbox at Second Avenue and Houston in front of the Cosmopolitan Cafè: ". . . these fellers, men . . . wageslaves like I was . . . are sittin on your chest . . . they're takin the food outen your mouths. Where's all the pretty girls I used to see walkin up and down the bullevard? Look for em in the uptown cabarets. . . . They squeeze us dry friends . . . feller workers, slaves I'd oughter say . . . they take our work and our ideers and our women. . . . They build their Plaza Hotels and their millionaire's clubs and their million dollar theayters and their battleships and what do they leave us? . . . They leave us shopsickness an the rickets and a lot of dirty streets full of garbage cans. . . . You look pale you fellers. . . . You need blood. . . . Why dont you get some blood in your veins? . . . Back in Russia the poor people . . . not so much poorer'n we are . . . believe in wampires, things come suck your blood at night. . . . That's what Capitalism is, a wampire that sucks your blood . . . day . . . and . . . night."

It is beginning to snow. The flakes are giltedged where they pass the streetlamp. Through the plate glass the Cosmopolitan Cafè full of blue and green opal rifts of smoke looks like a muddy aquarium; faces blob whitely round the tables like illassorted fishes. Umbrellas begin to bob in clusters up the snowmottled street. The orator turns up his collar and walks briskly east along Houston, holding the muddy soapbox away from his trousers.

FACES, hats, hands, newspapers jiggled in the fetid roaring subway car like corn in a popper. The downtown express passed clattering in yellow light, window telescoping window till they overlapped like scales.

"Look George," said Sandbourne to George Baldwin who hung on a strap beside him, "you can see Fitzgerald's contraction."

"I'll be seeing the inside of an undertaking parlor if I dont get out of this subway soon."

"It does you plutocrats good now and then to see how the other half travels. . . . Maybe it'll make you induce some of your little playmates down at Tammany Hall to stop squabbling and give us wageslaves a little transportation. . . . cristamighty I could tell em a thing or two. . . . My idea's for a series of endless moving platforms under Fifth Avenue."

"Did you cook that up when you were in hospital Phil?"

"I cooked a whole lot of things up while I was in hospital."

"Look here lets get out at Grand Central and walk. I cant stand this. . . . I'm not used to it."

"Sure . . . I'll phone Elsie I'll be a little late to dinner. . . . Not often I get to see you nowadays George . . . Gee it's like the old days."

In a tangled clot of men and women, arms, legs, hats aslant on perspiring necks, they were pushed out on the platform. They walked up Lexington Avenue quiet in the claretmisted afterglow.

"But Phil how did you come to step out in front of a truck that way?"

"Honestly George I dunno. . . . The last I remember is craning my neck to look at a terribly pretty girl went by in a taxicab and there I was drinking icewater out of a teapot in the hospital."

"Shame on you Phil at your age."

"Cristamighty dont I know it? But I'm not the only one."

"It is funny the way a thing like that comes over you.
. . . Why what have you heard about me?"

"Gosh George dont get nervous, it's all right. . . . I've
seen her in The Zinnia Girl. . . . She walks away with it.
That other girl who's the star dont have a show."

"Look here Phil if you hear any rumors about Miss Oglethorpe for Heaven's sake shut them up. It's so damn silly
you cant go out to tea with a woman without everybody
starting their dirty gabble all over town. . . . By God I
will not have a scandal, I dont care what happens."

"Say hold your horses George."

"I'm in a very delicate position downtown just at the moment that's all. . . . And then Cecily and I have at last
reached a modus vivendi. . . . I wont have it disturbed."

They walked along in silence.

Sandbourne walked with his hat in his hand. His hair
was almost white but his eyebrows were still dark and bushy.
Every few steps he changed the length of his stride as if it
hurt him to walk. He cleared his throat. "George you were
asking me if I'd cooked up any schemes when I was in
hospital. . . . Do you remember years ago old man Specker
used to talk about vitreous and superenameled tile? Well
I've been workin on his formula out at Hollis. . . . A friend
of mine there has a two thousand degree oven he bakes
pottery in. I think it can be put on a commercial basis. . . .
Man it would revolutionize the whole industry. Combined
with concrete it would enormously increase the flexibility of
the materials at the architects' disposal. We could make
tile any color, size or finish. . . . Imagine this city when all
the buildins instead of bein dirty gray were ornamented
with vivid colors. Imagine bands of scarlet round the en-
tablatures of skyscrapers. Colored tile would revolutionize
the whole life of the city. . . . Instead of fallin back on the
orders or on gothic or romanesque decorations we could
evolve new designs, new colors, new forms. If there was a
little color in the town all this hardshell inhibited life'd break
down. . . . There'd be more love an less divorce. . . . "

Baldwin burst out laughing. "You tell em Phil. . . .
I'll talk to you about that sometime. You must come up
to dinner when Cecily's there and tell us about it. . . . Why
wont Parkhurst do anything?"

"I wouldnt let him in on it. He'd cotton on to the proposition and leave me out in the cold once he had the formula.
I wouldn't trust him with a rubber nickel."

"Why doesnt he take you into partnership Phil?"

"He's got me where he wants me anyway. . . . He knows
I do all the work in his goddamned office. He knows too
that I'm too cranky to make out with most people. He's a
slick article."

"Still I should think you could put it up to him."

"He's got me where he wants me and he knows it, so I
continue doin the work while he amasses the coin. . . . I
guess it's logical. If I had more money I'd just spend it.
I'm just shiftless."

"But look here man you're not so much older than I am.
. . . You've still got a career ahead of you."

"Sure nine hours a day draftin. . . . Gosh I wish you'd
go into this tile business with me."

Baldwin stopped at a corner and slapped his hand on the
briefcase he was carrying. "Now Phil you know I'd be
very glad to give you a hand in any way I could. . . . But
just at the moment my financial situation is terribly involved.
I've gotten into some rather rash entanglements and Heaven
knows how I'm going to get out of them. . . . That's why
I cant have a scandal or a divorce or anything. You dont
understand how complicatedly things interact. . . . I couldnt
take up anything new, not for a year at least. This war in
Europe has made things very unsettled downtown. Anything's liable to happen."

"All right. Good night George."

Sandbourne turned abruptly on his heel and walked down
the avenue again. He was tired and his legs ached. It was
almost dark. On the way back to the station the grimy
brick and brownstone blocks dragged past monotonously like
the days of his life.

Under the skin of her temples iron clamps tighten till her head will mash like an egg; she begins to walk with long strides up and down the room that bristles with itching stuffiness; spotty colors of pictures, carpets, chairs wrap about her like a choking hot blanket. Outside the window the backyards are striped with blue and lilac and topaz of a rainy twilight. She opens the window. No time to get tight like the twilight, Stan said. The telephone reached out shivering beady tentacles of sound. She slams the window down. O hell cant they give you any peace?

"Why Harry I didnt know you were back. . . . Oh I wonder if I can. . . . Oh yes I guess I can. Come along by after the theater. . . . Isnt that wonderful? You must tell me all about it." She no sooner puts the receiver down than the bell clutches at her again. "Hello. . . . No I dont. . . . Oh yes maybe I do. . . . When did you get back?" She laughed a tinkling telephone laugh. "But Howard I'm terribly busy. . . . Yes I am honestly. . . . Have you been to the show? Well sometime come round after a performance. . . . I'm so anxious to hear about your trip . . . you know . . . Goodby Howard."

A walk'll make me feel better. She sits at her dressingtable and shakes her hair down about her shoulders. "It's such a hellish nuisance, I'd like to cut it all off . . . spreads apace. The shadow of white Death. . . . Oughtnt to stay up so late, those dark circles under my eyes. . . . And at the door, Invisible Corruption. . . . If I could only cry; there are people who can cry their eyes out, really cry themselves blind . . . Anyway the divorce'll go through. . . .

> Far from the shore, far from the trembling throng
> Whose sails were never to the tempest given

Gosh it's six o'clock already. She starts walking up and down the room again. I am borne darkly fearfully afar. . . . The phone rings. "Hello. . . . Yes this is Miss Oglethorpe. . . . Why hello Ruth, why I haven't seen you for ages, since Mrs. Sunderland's. . . . Oh, do I'd love to see you. Come by and we'll have a bite to eat on the way to the theater. . . . It's the third floor."

She rings off and gets a raincape out of a closet. The smell of furs and mothballs and dresses clings in her nostrils. She throws up the window again and breathes deep of the wet air full of the cold rot of autumn. She hears the burring boom of a big steamer from the river. Darkly, fearfully afar from this nonsensical life, from this fuzzy idiocy and strife; a man can take a ship for his wife, but a girl. The telephone is shiveringly beadily ringing, ringing.

The buzzer burrs at the same time. Ellen presses the button to click the latch. "Hello. . . . No, I'm very sorry I'm afraid you'll have to tell me who it is. Why Larry Hopkins I thought you were in Tokyo. . . . They havent moved you again have they? Why of course we must see each other. . . . My dear it's simply horrible but I'm all dated up for two weeks. . . . Look I'm sort of crazy tonight. You call up tomorrow at twelve and I'll try to shift things around. . . . Why of course I've got to see you immediately you funny old thing." . . . Ruth Prynne and Cassandra Wilkins come in shaking the water off their umbrellas. "Well goodby Larry. . . . Why it's so so sweet of both of you. . . . Do take your things off for a second. . . . Cassie wont you have dinner with us?"

"I felt I just had to see you. . . . It's so wonderful about your wonderful success," says Cassie in a shaky voice. "And my dear I felt so terribly when I heard about Mr. Emery. I cried and cried, didnt I Ruth?"

"Oh what a beautiful apartment you have," Ruth is exclaiming at the same moment. Ellen's ears ring sickeningly. "We all have to die sometime," gruffly she blurts out.

Ruth's rubberclad foot is tapping the floor; she catches Cassie's eye and makes her stammer into silence. "Hadnt we better go along? It's getting rather late," she says.

"Excuse me a minute Ruth." Ellen runs into the bathroom and slams the door. She sits on the edge of the bathtub pounding on her knees with her clenched fists. Those women'll drive me mad. Then the tension in her snaps, she feels something draining out of her like water out of a washbasin. She quietly puts a dab of rouge on her lips.

When she goes back she says in her usual voice: "Well let's get along. . . . Got a part yet Ruth?"

"I had a chance to go out to Detroit with a stock company. I turned it down. . . . I wont go out of New York whatever happens."

"What wouldnt I give for a chance to get away from New York. . . . Honestly if I was offered a job singing in a movie in Medicine Hat I think I'd take it."

Ellen picks up her umbrella and the three women file down the stairs and out into the street. "Taxi," calls Ellen.

The passing car grinds to a stop. The red hawk face of the taxidriver craning into the light of the street lamp. "Go to Eugenie's on Fortyeighth Street," says Ellen as the others climb in. Greenish lights and darks flicker past the lightbeaded windows.

She stood with her arm in the arm of Harry Goldweiser's dinner jacket looking out over the parapet of the roofgarden. Below them the Park lay twinkling with occasional lights, streaked with nebular blur like a fallen sky. From behind them came gusts of a tango, inklings of voices, shuffle of feet on a dancefloor. Ellen felt a stiff castiron figure in her metalgreen evening dress.

"Ah but Boirnhardt, Rachel, Duse, Mrs. Siddons. . . . No Elaine I'm tellin you, d'you understand? There's no art like the stage that soars so high moldin the passions of men. . . . If I could only do what I wanted we'd be the greatest people in the world. You'd be the greatest actress. . . . I'd be the great producer, the unseen builder, d'you understand? But the public dont want art, the people of this country wont let you do anythin for em. All they want's a detective melodrama or a rotten French farce with the kick left out or a lot of pretty girls and music. Well a showman's business is to give the public what they want."

"I think that this city is full of people wanting inconceivable things. . . . Look at it."

"It's all right at night when you cant see it. There's no artistic sense, no beautiful buildins, no old-time air, that's what's the matter with it."

They stood a while without speaking. The orchestra began playing the waltz from The Lilac Domino. Suddenly Ellen turned to Goldweiser and said in a curt tone. "Can you understand a woman who wants to be a harlot, a common tart, sometimes?"

"My dear young lady what a strange thing for a sweet lovely girl to suddenly come out and say."

"I suppose you're shocked." She didnt hear his answer. She felt she was going to cry. She pressed her sharp nails into the palms of her hands, she held her breath until she had counted twenty. Then she said in a choking little girl's voice, "Harry let's go and dance a little."

The sky above the cardboard buildings is a vault of beaten lead. It would be less raw if it would snow. Ellen finds a taxi on the corner of Seventh Avenue and lets herself sink back in the seat rubbing the numb gloved fingers of one hand against the palm of the other. "West Fiftyseventh, please." Out of a sick mask of fatigue she watches fruitstores, signs, buildings being built, trucks, girls, messengerboys, policemen through the jolting window. If I have my child, Stan's child, it will grow up to jolt up Seventh Avenue under a sky of beaten lead that never snows watching fruitstores, signs, buildings being built, trucks, girls, messengerboys, policemen. . . . She presses her knees together, sits up straight on the edge of the seat with her hands clasped over her slender belly. O God the rotten joke they've played on me, taking Stan away, burning him up, leaving me nothing but this growing in me that's going to kill me. She's whimpering into her numb hands. O God why wont it snow?

As she stands on the gray pavement fumbling in her

purse for a bill, a dusteddy swirling scraps of paper along the gutter fills her mouth with grit. The elevatorman's face is round ebony with ivory inlay. "Mrs. Staunton Wells?" "Yas ma'am eighth floor."

The elevator hums as it soars. She stands looking at herself in the narrow mirror. Suddenly something recklessly gay goes through her. She rubs the dust off her face with a screwedup handkerchief, smiles at the elevatorman's smile that's wide as the full keyboard of a piano, and briskly rustles to the door of the apartment that a frilled maid opens. Inside it smells of tea and furs and flowers, women's voices chirp to the clinking of cups like birds in an aviary. Glances flicker about her head as she goes into the room.

There was wine spilled on the tablecloth and bits of tomatosauce from the spaghetti. The restaurant was a steamy place with views of the Bay of Naples painted in soupy blues and greens on the walls. Ellen sat back in her chair from the round tableful of young men, watching the smoke from her cigarette crinkle spirally round the fat Chiantibottle in front of her. In her plate a slab of tricolor icecream melted forlornly. "But good God hasnt a man some rights? No, this industrial civilization forces us to seek a complete readjustment of government and social life . . ."

"Doesnt he use long words?" Ellen whispered to Herf who sat beside her.

"He's right all the same," he growled back at her. . . . "The result has been to put more power in the hands of a few men than there has been in the history of the world since the horrible slave civilizations of Egypt and Mesopotamia. . . ."

"Hear hear."

"No but I'm serious. . . . The only way of bucking the interests is for working people, the proletariat, producers and consumers, anything you want to call them, to form unions and finally get so well organized that they can take over the whole government."

"I think you're entirely wrong, Martin, it's the interests as you call em, these horrible capitalists, that have built up this country as we have it today."

"Well look at it for God's sake. . . . That's what I'm saying. I wouldnt kennel a dog in it."

"I dont think so. I admire this country. . . . It's the only fatherland I've got. . . . And I think that all these downtrodden masses really want to be downtrodden, they're not fit for anything else. . . . If they werent they'd be flourishing businessmen . . . Those that are any good are getting to be."

"But I don't think a flourishing businessman is the highest ideal of human endeavor."

"A whole lot higher than a rotten fiddleheaded anarchist agitator. . . . Those that arent crooks are crazy."

"Look here Mead, you've just insulted something that you dont understand, that you know nothing about. . . . I cant allow you to do that. . . . You should try to understand things before you go round insulting them."

"An insult to the intelligence that's what it is all this socialistic drivel."

Ellen tapped Herf on the sleeve. "Jimmy I've got to go home. Do you want to walk a little way with me?"

"Martin, will you settle for us? We've got to go. . . . Ellie you look terribly pale."

"It's just a little hot in here. . . . Whee, what a relief. . . . I hate arguments anyway. I never can think of anything to say."

"That bunch does nothing but chew the rag night after night."

Eighth Avenue was full of fog that caught at their throats. Lights bloomed dimly through it, faces loomed, glinted in silhouette and faded like a fish in a muddy aquarium.

"Feel better Ellie?"

"Lots."

"I'm awfully glad."

"Do you know you're the only person around here who calls me Ellie. I like it. . . . Everybody tries to make me seem so grown up since I've been on the stage."

"Stan used to."

"Maybe that's why I like it," she said in a little trailing voice like a cry heard at night from far away along a beach.

Jimmy felt something clamping his throat. "Oh gosh things are rotten," he said. "God I wish I could blame it all on capitalism the way Martin does."

"It's pleasant walking like this . . . I love a fog."

They walked on without speaking. Wheels rumbled through the muffling fog underlaid with the groping distant lowing of sirens and steamboatwhistles on the river.

"But at least you have a career. . . . You like your work, you're enormously successful," said Herf at the corner of Fourteenth Street, and caught her arm as they crossed.

"Dont say that. . . . You really dont believe it. I dont kid myself as much as you think I do."

"No but it's so."

"It used to be before I met Stan, before I loved him. . . . You see I was a crazy little stagestruck kid who got launched out in a lot of things I didnt understand before I had time to learn anything about life. . . . Married at eighteen and divorced at twentytwo's a pretty good record. . . . But Stan was so wonderful. . . ."

"I know."

"Without ever saying anything he made me feel there were other things . . . unbelievable things. . . ."

"God I resent his craziness though. . . . It's such a waste."

"I cant talk about it."

"Let's not."

"Jimmy you're the only person left I can really talk to."

"Dont want to trust me. I might go berserk on you too some day."

They laughed.

"God I'm glad I'm not dead, arent you Ellie?"

"I dont know. Look here's my place. I dont want you to come up. . . . I'm going right to bed. I feel miserably. . . ." Jimmy stood with his hat off looking at her. She was fumbling in her purse for her key. "Look Jimmy I might as well tell you. . . ." She went up to him and spoke fast with her face turned away pointing at him with the latchkey that caught the light of the streetlamp. The fog was like a tent round about them. "I'm going to have a baby. . . . Stan's baby. I'm going to give up all this silly life and raise it. I dont care what happens."

"O God that's the bravest thing I ever heard of a woman doing. . . . Oh Ellie you're so wonderful. God if I could only tell you what I . . ."

"Oh no." Her voice broke and her eyes filled with tears. "I'm a silly fool, that's all." She screwed up her face like a little child and ran up the steps with the tears streaming down her face.

"Oh Ellie I want to say something to you . . ."

The door closed behind her.

Jimmy Herf stood stockstill at the foot of the brownstone steps. His temples throbbed. He wanted to break the door down after her. He dropped on his knees and kissed the step where she had stood. The fog swirled and flickered with colors in confetti about him. Then the trumpet feeling ebbed and he was falling through a black manhole. He stood stockstill. A policeman's ballbearing eyes searched his face as he passed, a stout blue column waving a nightstick. Then suddenly he clenched his fists and walked off. "O God everything is hellish," he said aloud. He wiped the grit off his lips with his coatsleeve.

She puts her hand in his to jump out of the roadster as the ferry starts, "Thanks Larry," and follows his tall ambling body out on the bow. A faint riverwind blows the dust and gasoline out of their nostrils. Through the pearly night the square frames of houses along the Drive opposite flicker like burnedout fireworks. The waves slap tinily against the shoving bow of the ferry. A hunchback with a violin is scratching Marianela.

"Nothing succeeds like success," Larry is saying in a deep droning voice.

"Oh if you knew how little I cared about anything just now you wouldnt go on teasing me with all these words. . . . You know, marriage, success, love, they're just words."

"But they mean everything in the world to me. . . . I think you'd like it in Lima Elaine. . . . I waited until you were free, didnt I? And now here I am."

"We're none of us that ever. . . . But I'm just numb." The riverwind is brackish. Along the viaduct above 125th Street cars crawl like beetles. As the ferry enters the slip they hear the squudge and rumble of wheels on asphalt.

"Well we'd better get back into the car, you wonderful creature Elaine."

"After all day it's exciting isnt it Larry, getting back into the center of things."

Beside the smudged white door are two pushbuttons marked NIGHT BELL and DAY BELL. She rings with a shaky finger. A short broad man with a face like a rat and sleek black hair brushed straight back opens. Short dollhands the color of the flesh of a mushroom hang at his sides. He hunches his shoulders in a bow.

"Are you the lady? Come in."

"Is this Dr. Abrahms?"

"Yes. . . . You are the lady my friend phoned me about. Sit down my dear lady." The office smells of something like arnica. Her heart joggles desperately between her ribs.

"You understand . . ." She hates the quaver in her voice; she's going to faint. "You understand, Dr. Abrahms that it is absolutely necessary. I am getting a divorce from my husband and have to make my own living."

"Very young, unhappily married . . . I am sorry." The doctor purrs softly as if to himself. He heaves a hissing sigh and suddenly looks in her eyes with black steel eyes like gimlets. "Do not be afraid, dear lady, it is a very simple operation. . . . Are you ready now?"

"Yes. It wont take very long will it? If I can pull myself together I have an engagement for tea at five."

"You are a brave young lady. In an hour it will be forgotten. . . . I am sorry. . . . It is very sad such a thing is necessary. . . . Dear lady you should have a home and many children and a loving husband . . . Will you go in the operating room and prepare yourself. . . . I work without an assistant."

The bright searing bud of light swells in the center of the ceiling, sprays razorsharp nickel, enamel, a dazzling sharp glass case of sharp instruments. She takes off her hat and lets herself sink shuddering sick on a little enamel chair. Then she gets stiffly to her feet and undoes the band of her skirt.

The roar of the streets breaks like surf about a shell of throbbing agony. She watches the tilt of her leather hat, the powder, the rosed cheeks, the crimson lips that are a mask on her face. All the buttons of her gloves are buttoned. She raises her hand. "Taxi!" A fire engine roars past, a hosewagon with sweatyfaced men pulling on rubber coats, a clanging hookandladder. All the feeling in her fades with the dizzy fade of the siren. A wooden Indian, painted, with a hand raised at the streetcorner.

"Taxi!"

"Yes ma'am."

"Drive to the Ritz."

Third Section

I. Rejoicing City That Dwelt Carelessly

There are flags on all the flagpoles up Fifth Avenue. In the shrill wind of history the great flags flap and tug at their lashings on the creaking goldknobbed poles up Fifth Avenue. The stars jiggle sedately against the slate sky, the red and white stripes writhe against the clouds.

In the gale of brassbands and trampling horses and rumbling clatter of cannon, shadows like the shadows of claws grasp at the taut flags, the flags are hungry tongues licking twisting curling.

Oh it's a long way to Tipperary . . . Over there! Over there!

The harbor is packed with zebrastriped skunkstriped piebald steamboats, the Narrows are choked with bullion, they're piling gold sovereigns up to the ceilings in the Subtreasury. Dollars whine on the radio, all the cables tap out dollars.

There's a long long trail awinding . . . Over there! Over there!

In the subway their eyes pop as they spell out APOCALYPSE, *typhus, cholera, shrapnel, insurrection, death in fire, death in water, death in hunger, death in mud.*

Oh it's a long way to Madymosell from Armenteers, over there! The Yanks are coming, the Yanks are coming. Down Fifth Avenue the bands blare for the Liberty Loan drive, for the Red Cross drive. Hospital ships sneak up the harbor and unload furtively at night in old docks in Jersey. Up Fifth Avenue the flags of the seventeen nations are flaring curling in the shrill hungry wind.

O the oak and the ash and the weeping willow tree
And green grows the grass in God's country.

The great flags flap and tug at their lashings on the creaking goldknobbed poles up Fifth Avenue.

CAPTAIN JAMES MERIVALE D.S.C. lay with his eyes closed while the barber's padded fingers gently stroked his chin. The lather tickled his nostrils; he could smell bay rum, hear the drone of an electric vibrator, the snipping of scissors.

"A little face massage sir, get rid of a few of those blackheads sir," burred the barber in his ear. The barber was bald and had a round blue chin.

"All right," drawled Merivale, "go as far as you like. This is the first decent shave I've had since war was declared."

"Just in from overseas, Captain?"

"Yare . . . been making the world safe for democracy."

The barber smothered his words under a hot towel. "A little lilac water Captain?"

"No dont put any of your damn lotions on me, just a little witchhazel or something antiseptic."

The blond manicure girl had faintly beaded lashes; she looked up at him bewitchingly, her rosebud lips parted. "I guess you've just landed Captain. . . . My you've got a good tan." He gave up his hand to her on the little white table. "It's a long time Captain since anybody took care of these hands."

"How can you tell?"

"Look how the cuticle's grown."

"We were too busy for anything like that. I'm a free man since eight o'clock that's all."

"Oh it must have been terr . . . ible."

"Oh it was a great little war while it lasted."

"I'll say it was . . . And now you're all through Captain?"

"Of course I keep my commission in the reserve corps."

She gave his hand a last playful tap and he got to his feet.

He put tips into the soft palm of the barber and the hard palm of the colored boy who handed him his hat, and walked slowly up the white marble steps. On the landing was a mirror. Captain James Merivale stopped to look at Captain

James Merivale. He was a tall straightfeatured young man with a slight heaviness under the chin. He wore a neat-fitting whipcord uniform picked out by the insignia of the Rainbow Division, well furnished with ribbons and service-stripes. The light of the mirror was reflected silvery on either calf of his puttees. He cleared his throat as he looked himself up and down. A young man in civilian clothes came up behind him.

"Hello James, all cleaned up?"

"You betcher. . . . Say isnt it a damn fool rule not letting us wear Sam Browne belts? Spoils the whole uniform. . . ."

"They can take all their Sam Browne's belts and hang them on the Commanding General's fanny for all I care. . . . I'm a civilian."

"You're still an officer in the reserve corps, dont forget that."

"They can take their reserve corps and shove it ten thousand miles up the creek. Let's go have a drink."

"I've got to go up and see the folks." They had come out on Fortysecond Street. "Well so long James, I'm going to get so drunk . . . Just imagine being free." "So long Jerry, dont do anything I wouldnt do."

Merivale walked west along Fortysecond. There were still flags out, drooping from windows, waggling lazily from poles in the September breeze. He looked in the shops as he walked along; flowers, women's stockings, candy, shirts and neckties, dresses, colored draperies through glinting plateglass, beyond a stream of faces, men's razorscraped faces, girls' faces with rouged lips and powdered noses. It made him feel flushed and excited. He fidgeted when he got in the subway. "Look at the stripes that one has. . . . He's a D.S.C.," he heard a girl say to another. He got out at Seventysecond and walked with his chest stuck out down the too familiar brownstone street towards the river.

"How do you do, Captain Merivale," said the elevator man

"Well, are you out James?" cried his mother running into his arms.

He nodded and kissed her. She looked pale and wilted in her black dress. Maisie, also in black, came rustling tall and rosycheeked behind her. "It's wonderful to find you both looking so well."

"Of course we are . . . as well as could be expected. My dear we've had a terrible time. . . . You're the head of the family now, James."

"Poor daddy . . . to go off like that."

"That was something you missed. . . . Thousands of people died of it in New York alone."

He hugged Maisie with one arm and his mother with the other. Nobody spoke.

"Well," said Merivale walking into the living room, "it was a great war while it lasted." His mother and sister followed on his heels. He sat down in the leather chair and stretched out his polished legs. "You dont know how wonderful it is to get home."

Mrs. Merivale drew up her chair close to his. "Now dear you just tell us all about it."

In the dark of the stoop in front of the tenement door, he reaches for her and drags her to him. "Dont Bouy, dont; dont be rough." His arms tighten like knotted cords round her back; her knees are trembling. His mouth is groping for her mouth along one cheekbone, down the side of her nose. She cant breathe with his lips probing her lips. "Oh I cant stand it." He holds her away from him. She is staggering panting against the wall held up by his big hands.

"Nutten to worry about," he whispers gently.

"I've got to go, it's late. . . . I have to get up at six."

"Well what time do you think I get up?"

"It's mommer who might catch me. . . ."

"Tell her to go to hell."

"I will some day . . . worse'n that . . . if she dont quit

pickin on me." She takes hold of his stubbly cheeks and kisses him quickly on the mouth and has broken away from him and run up the four flights of grimy stairs.

The door is still on the latch. She strips off her dancing pumps and walks carefully through the kitchenette on aching feet. From the next room comes the wheezy doublebarreled snoring of her uncle and aunt. *Somebody loves me, I wonder who. . . .* The tune is all through her body, in the throb of her feet, in the tingling place on her back where he held her tight dancing with her. Anna you've got to forget it or you wont sleep. Anna you got to forget. Dishes on the tables set for breakfast jingle tingle hideously when she bumps against it.

"That you Anna?" comes a sleepy querulous voice from her mother's bed.

"Went to get a drink o water mommer." The old woman lets the breath out in a groan through her teeth, the bedsprings creak as she turns over. Asleep all the time.

Somebody loves me, I wonder who. She slips off her party dress and gets into her nightgown. Then she tiptoes to the closet to hang up the dress and at last slides between the covers little by little so the slats wont creak. *I wonder who.* Shuffle shuffle, bright lights, pink blobbing faces, grabbing arms, tense thighs, bouncing feet. *I wonder who.* Shuffle, droning saxophone tease, shuffle in time to the drum, trombone, clarinet. Feet, thighs, cheek to cheek, *Somebody loves me. . . .* Shuffle shuffle. *I wonder who.*

The baby with tiny shut purplishpink face and fists lay asleep on the berth. Ellen was leaning over a black leather suitcase. Jimmy Herf in his shirtsleeves was looking out the porthole.

"Well there's the statue of Liberty. . . . Ellie we ought to be out on deck."

"It'll be ages before we dock. . . . Go ahead up. I'll come up with Martin in a minute."

"Oh come ahead; we'll put the baby's stuff in the bag while we're warping into the slip."

They came out on deck into a dazzling September afternoon. The water was greenindigo. A steady wind kept sweeping coils of brown smoke and blobs of whitecotton steam off the high enormous blueindigo arch of sky. Against a sootsmudged horizon, tangled with barges, steamers, chimneys of powerplants, covered wharves, bridges, lower New York was a pink and white tapering pyramid cut slenderly out of cardboard.

"Ellie we ought to have Martin out so he can see."

"And start yelling like a tugboat. . . . He's better off where he is."

They ducked under some ropes, slipped past the rattling steamwinch and out to the bow.

"God Ellie it's the greatest sight in the world. . . . I never thought I'd ever come back, did you?"

"I had every intention of coming back."

"Not like this."

"No I dont suppose I did."

"S'il vous plait madame . . ."

A sailor was motioning them back. Ellen turned her face into the wind to get the coppery whisps of hair out of her eyes. "C'est beau, n'est-ce pas?" She smiled into the wind into the sailor's red face.

"J'aime mieux le Havre . . . S'il vous plait madame."

"Well I'll go down and pack Martin up."

The hard chug, chug of the tugboat coming alongside beat Jimmy's answer out of her ears. She slipped away from him and went down to the cabin again.

They were wedged in the jam of people at the end of the gangplank.

"Look we could wait for a porter," said Ellen.

"No dear I've got them." Jimmy was sweating and staggering with a suitcase in each hand and packages under his arms. In Ellen's arms the baby was cooing stretching tiny spread hands towards the faces all round.

"D'you know it?" said Jimmy as they crossed the gangplank, "I kinder wish we were just going on board. . . . I hate getting home."

"I dont hate it. . . . There's H . . . I'll follow right along. . . . I wanted to look for Frances and Bob. Hello. . . ."   "Well I'll be . . ."   "Helena you've gained, you're looking wonderfully. Where's Jimps?"   Jimmy was rubbing his hands together, stiff and chafed from handles of the heavy suitcases.

"Hello Herf. Hello Frances. Isn't this swell?"

"Gosh I'm glad to see you. . . ."

"Jimps the thing for me to do is go right on to the Brevoort with the baby . . ."

"Isn't he sweet."

". . . Have you got five dollars?"

"I've only got a dollar in change. That hundred is in express checks."

"I've got plenty of money. Helena and I'll go to the hotel and you boys can come along with the baggage."

"Inspector is it all right if I go through with the baby? My husband will look after the trunks."

"Why surely madam, go right ahead."

"Isnt he nice? Oh Frances this is lots of fun."

"Go ahead Bob I can finish this up alone quicker. . . . You convoy the ladies to the Brevoort."

"Well we hate to leave you."

"Oh go ahead. . . . I'll be right along."

"Mr. James Herf and wife and infant . . . is that it?"

"Yes that's right."

"I'll be right with you, Mr. Herf. . . . Is all the baggage there?"

"Yes everything's there."

"Isnt he good?" clucked Frances as she and Hildebrand followed Ellen into the cab.

"Who?"

"The baby of course. . . ."

"Oh you ought to see him sometimes. . . . He seems to like traveling."

A plainclothesman opened the door of the cab and looked

in as they went out the gate. "Want to smell our breaths?" asked Hildebrand. The man had a face like a block of wood. He closed the door. "Helena doesn't know prohibition yet, does she?"

"He gave me a scare . . . Look."

"Good gracious!" From under the blanket that was wrapped round the baby she produced a brownpaper package. . . . "Two quarts of our special cognac . . . gout famille 'Erf . . . and I've got another quart in a hotwaterbottle under my waistband. . . . That's why I look as if I was going to have another baby."

The Hildebrands began hooting with laughter.

"Jimp's got a hotwaterbottle round his middle too and chartreuse in a flask on his hip. . . . We'll probably have to go and bail him out of jail."

They were still laughing so that tears were streaming down their faces when they drew up at the hotel. In the elevator the baby began to wail.

As soon as she had closed the door of the big sunny room she fished the hotwaterbottle from under her dress. "Look Bob phone down for some cracked ice and seltzer. . . . We'll all have a cognac a l'eau de selz. . . ."

"Hadn't we better wait for Jimps?"

"Oh he'll be right here. . . . We haven't anything dutiable. . . . Much too broke to have anything. . . . Frances what do you do about milk in New York?"

"How should I know, Helena?" Frances Hildebrand flushed and walked to the window.

"Oh well we'll give him his food again. . . . He's done fairly well on it on the trip." Ellen had laid the baby on the bed. He lay kicking, looking about with dark round goldstone eyes.

"Isnt he fat?"

"He's so healthy I'm sure he must be halfwitted. . . . Oh Heavens and I've got to call up my father. . . . Isnt family life just too desperately complicated?"

Ellen was setting up her little alcohol stove on the washstand. The bellboy came with glasses and a bowl of clinking ice and White Rock on a tray.

"You fix us a drink out of the hotwaterbottle. We've got to use that up or it'll eat the rubber. . . . And we'll drink to the Café d'Harcourt."

"Of course what you kids dont realize," said Hildebrand, "is that the difficulty under prohibition is keeping sober."

Ellen laughed; she stood over the little lamp that gave out a quiet domestic smell of hot nickel and burned alcohol.

George Baldwin was walking up Madison Avenue with his light overcoat on his arm. His fagged spirits were reviving in the sparkling autumn twilight of the streets. From block to block through the taxiwhirring gasoline gloaming two lawyers in black frock coats and stiff wing collars argued in his head. If you go home it will be cozy in the library. The apartment will be gloomy and quiet and you can sit in your slippers under the bust of Scipio Africanus in the leather chair and read and have dinner sent in to you. . . . Nevada would be jolly and coarse and tell you funny stories. . . . She would have all the City Hall gossip . . . good to know. . . . But you're not going to see Nevada any more . . . too dangerous; she gets you all wrought up. . . . And Cecily sitting faded and elegant and slender biting her lips and hating me, hating life. . . . Good God how am I going to get my existence straightened out? He stopped in front of a flowerstore. A moist warm honied expensive smell came from the door, densely out into the keen steelblue street. If I could at least make my financial position impregnable. . . . In the window was a minature Japanese garden with brokenback bridges and ponds where the goldfish looked big as whales. Proportion, that's it. To lay out your life like a prudent gardener, plowing and sowing. No I wont go to see Nevada tonight. I might send her some flowers though. Yellow roses, those coppery roses . . . it's Elaine who ought to wear those. Imagine her married again and with a baby. He went into the store. "What's that rose?"

"It's Gold of Ophir sir."

"All right I want two dozen sent down to the Brevoort immediately. . . . Miss Elaine . . . No Mr. and Mrs. James Herf. . . . I'll write a card."

He sat down at the desk with a pen in his hand. Incense of roses, incense out of the dark fire of her hair. . . . No nonsense for Heaven's sake . . .

DEAR ELAINE,

I hope you will allow an old friend to call on you and your husband one of these days. And please remember that I am always sincerely anxious—you know me too well to take this for an empty offer of politeness—to serve you and him in any way that could possibly contribute to your happiness. Forgive me if I subscribe myself your lifelong slave and admirer

GEORGE BALDWIN

The letter covered three of the florists' white cards. He read it over with pursed lips, carefully crossing the t's and dotting the i's. Then he paid the florist from the roll of bills he took from his back pocket and went out into the street again. It was already night, going on to seven o'clock. Still hesitating he stood at the corner watching the taxis pass, yellow, red, green, tangerinecolored.

The snubnosed transport sludges slowly through the Narrows in the rain. Sergeant-Major O'Keefe and Private 1st Class Dutch Robertson stand in the lee of the deckhouse looking at the liners at anchor in quarantine and the low wharfcluttered shores.

"Look some of em still got their warpaint—Shippin Board boats. . . . Not worth the powder to blow em up."

"The hell they aint," said Joey O'Keefe vaguely.

"Gosh little old New York's goin to look good to me. . . ."

"Me too Sarge, rain or shine I dont care."

They are passing close to a mass of steamers anchored in a block, some of them listing to one side or the other, lanky ships with short funnels, stumpy ships with tall funnels red with rust, some of them striped and splashed and dotted with puttycolor and blue and green of camouflage paint. A man in a motorboat waved his arms. The men in khaki slickers huddled on the gray dripping deck of the transport begin to sing

> Oh the infantry, the infantry,
> With the dirt behind their ears . . .

Through the brightbeaded mist behind the low buildings of Governors Island they can make out the tall pylons, the curving cables, the airy lace of Brooklyn Bridge. Robertson pulls a package out of his pocket and pitches it overboard.

"What was that?"

"Just my propho kit. . . . Wont need it no more."

"How's that?"

"Oh I'm goin to live clean an get a good job and maybe get married."

"I guess that's not such a bad idear. I'm tired o playin round myself. Jez somebody must a cleaned up good on them Shippin Board boats." "That's where the dollar a year men get theirs I guess."

"I'll tell the world they do."

Up forward they are singing

> Oh she works in a jam factoree
> And that may be all right . . .

"Jez we're goin up the East River Sarge. Where the devil do they think they're goin to land us?"

"God, I'd be willin to swim ashore myself. An just think of all the guys been here all this time cleanin up on us. . . . Ten dollars a day workin in a shipyard mind you . . ."

"Hell Sarge we got the experience."

"Experience . . ."

> Apres la guerre finee
> Back to the States for me. . . .

"I bet the skipper's been drinkin beaucoup highballs an thinks Brooklyn's Hoboken."

"Well there's Wall Street, bo."

They are passing under Brooklyn Bridge. There is a humming whine of electric trains over their heads, an occasional violet flash from the wet rails. Behind them beyond barges tugboats carferries the tall buildings, streaked white with whisps of steam and mist, tower gray into sagged clouds.

Nobody said anything while they ate the soup. Mrs. Merivale sat in black at the head of the oval table looking out through the halfdrawn portieres and the drawingroom window beyond at a column of white smoke that uncoiled in the sunlight above the trainyards, remembering her husband and how they had come years ago to look at the apartment in the unfinished house that smelled of plaster and paint. At last when she had finished her soup she roused herself and said: "Well Jimmy, are you going back to newspaper work?"

"I guess so."

"James has had three jobs offered him already. I think it's remarkable."

"I guess I'll go in with the Major though," said James Merivale to Ellen who sat next to him. "Major Goodyear you know, Cousin Helena. . . . One of the Buffalo Goodyears. He's head of the foreign exchange department of the Banker's Trust. . . . He says he can work me up quickly. We were friends overseas."

"That'll be wonderful," said Maisie in a cooing voice, "wont it Jimmy?" She sat opposite slender and rosy in her black dress.

"He's putting me up for Piping Rock," went on Merivale.

"What's that?"

"Why Jimmy you must know. . . . I'm sure Cousin Helena has been out there to tea many a time."

"You know Jimps," said Ellen with her eyes in her plate. "That's where Stan Emery's father used to go every Sunday."

"Oh did you know that unfortunate young man? That was a horrible thing," said Mrs. Merivale. "So many horrible things have been happening these years. . . . I'd almost forgotten about it."

"Yes I knew him," said Ellen.

The leg of lamb came in accompanied by fried eggplant, late corn, and sweet potatoes. "Do you know I think it is just terrible," said Mrs. Merivale when she had done carving, "the way you fellows wont tell us any of your experiences over there. . . . Lots of them must have been remarkably interesting. Jimmy I should think you'd write a book about your experiences."

"I have tried a few articles."

"When are they coming out?"

"Nobody seems to want to print them. . . . You see I differ radically in certain matters of opinion . . ."

"Mrs. Merivale it's years since I've eaten such delicious sweet potatoes. . . . These taste like yams."

"They are good. . . . It's just the way I have them cooked."

"Well it was a great war while it lasted," said Merivale.

"Where were you Armistice night, Jimmy?"

"I was in Jerusalem with the Red Cross. Isn't that absurd?"

"I was in Paris."

"So was I," said Ellen.

"And so you were over there too Helena? I'm going to call you Helena eventually, so I might as well begin now. . . . Isn't that interesting? Did you and Jimmy meet over there?"

"Oh no we were old friends. . . . But we were thrown together a lot. . . . We were in the same department of the Red Cross—the Publicity Department."

"A real war romance," chanted Mrs. Merivale. "Isn't that interesting?"

"Now fellers it's this way," shouted Joe O'Keefe, the sweat breaking out on his red face. "Are we going to put over this bonus proposition or aint we? . . . We fought for em didnt we, we cleaned up the squareheads, didnt we? And now when we come home we get the dirty end of the stick. No jobs. . . . Our girls have gone and married other fellers. . . . Treat us like a bunch o dirty bums and loafers when we ask for our just and legal and lawful compensation. . . . the bonus. Are we goin to stand for it? . . . No. Are we goin to stand for a bunch of politicians treatin us like we was goin round to the back door to ask for a handout? . . . I ask you fellers. . . ."

Feet stamped on the floor. "No." "To hell wid em," shouted voices. . . . "Now I say to hell wid de politicians. . . . We'll carry our campaign to the country . . . to the great big generous bighearted American people we fought and bled and laid down our lives for."

The long armory room roared with applause. The wounded men in the front row banged the floor with their crutches. "Joey's a good guy," said a man without arms to a man with one eye and an artificial leg who sat beside him. "He is that Buddy." While they were filing out offering each other cigarettes, a man stood in the door calling out, "Committee meeting, Committee on Bonus."

The four of them sat round a table in the room the Colonel had lent them. "Well fellers let's have a cigar." Joe hopped over to the Colonel's desk and brought out four Romeo and Juliets. "He'll never miss em."

"Some little grafter I'll say," said Sid Garnett stretching out his long legs.

"Havent got a case of Scotch in there, have you Joey?" said Bill Dougan.

"Naw I'm not drinkin myself jus for the moment."

"I know where you kin get guaranteed Haig and Haig," put in Segal cockily—"before the war stuff for six dollars a quart."

"An where are we goin to get the six dollars for crissake?"

"Now look here fellers," said Joe, sitting on the edge of the table, "let's get down to brass tacks. . . . What we've got to do is raise a fund from the gang and anywhere else we can. . . . Are we agreed about that?"

"Sure we are, you tell em," said Dougan.

"I know lot of old fellers even, thinks the boys are gettin a raw deal. . . . We'll call it the Brooklyn Bonus Agitation Committee associated with the Sheamus O'Rielly Post of the A. L. . . . No use doin anythin unless you do it up right. . . . Now are yous guys wid me or aint yer?"

"Sure we are Joey. . . . You tell em an we'll mark time."

"Well Dougan's got to be president cause he's the best lookin."

Dougan went crimson and began to stammer.

"Oh you seabeach Apollo," jeered Garnett.

"And I think I can do best as treasurer because I've had more experience."

"Cause you're the crookedest you mean," said Segal under his breath.

Joe stuck out his jaw. "Look here Segal are you wid us or aint yer? You'd better come right out wid it now if you're not."

"Sure, cut de comedy," said Dougan. "Joey's de guy to put dis ting trough an you know it. . . . Cut de comedy. . . . If you dont like it you kin git out."

Segal rubbed his thin hooked nose. "I was juss jokin gents, I didn't mean no harm."

"Look here," went on Joe angrily, "what do you think I'm givin up my time for? . . . Why I turned down fifty dollars a week only yesterday, aint that so, Sid? You seen me talkin to de guy."

"Sure I did Joey."

"Oh pipe down fellers," said Segal. "I was just stringin Joey along."

"Well I think Segal you ought to be secretary, cause you know about office work. . . ."

"Office work?"

"Sure," said Joe puffing his chest out. "We're goin to have desk space in the office of a guy I know. . . . It's all fixed. He's goin to let us have it free till we get a start. An we're goin to have office stationery. Cant get nowhere in this world without presentin things right."

"An where do I come in?" asked Sid Garnett.

"You're the committee, you big stiff."

After the meeting Joe O'Keefe walked whistling down Atlantic Avenue. It was a crisp night; he was walking on springs. There was a light in Dr. Gordon's office. He rang. A whitefaced man in a white jacket opened the door.

"Hello Doc."

"Is that you O'Keefe? Come on in my boy." Something in the doctor's voice clutched like a cold hand at his spine.

"Well did your test come out all right doc?"

"All right . . . positive all right."

"Christ."

"Dont worry too much about it, my boy, we'll fix you up in a few months."

"Months."

"Why at a conservative estimate fiftyfive percent of the people you meet on the street have a syphilitic taint."

"It's not as if I'd been a damn fool. I was careful over there."

"Inevitable in wartime. . . ."

"Now I wish I'd let loose. . . . Oh the chances I passed up."

The doctor laughed. "You probably wont even have any symptoms. . . . It's just a question of injections. I'll have you sound as a dollar in no time. . . . Do you want to take a shot now? I've got it all ready."

O'Keefe's hands went cold. "Well I guess so," he forced

a laugh. "I guess I'll be a goddam thermometer by the time you're through with me." The doctor laughed creakily. "Full up of arsenic and mercury eh. . . . That's it."

The wind was blowing up colder. His teeth were chattering. Through the rasping castiron night he walked home. Fool to pass out that way when he stuck me. He could still feel the sickening lunge of the needle. He gritted his teeth. After this I got to have some luck. . . . I got to have some luck.

Two stout men and a lean man sit at a table by a window. The light of a zinc sky catches brightedged glints off glasses, silverware, oystershells, eyes. George Baldwin has his back to the window. Gus McNiel sits on his right, and Densch on his left. When the waiter leans over to take away the empty oystershells he can see through the window, beyond the graystone parapet, the tops of a few buildings jutting like the last trees at the edge of a cliff and the tinfoil reaches of the harbor littered with ships. "I'm lecturin you this time, George. . . . Lord knows you used to lecture me enough in the old days. Honest it's rank foolishness," Gus McNiel is saying. ". . . It's rank foolishness to pass up the chance of a political career at your time of life. . . . There's no man in New York better fitted to hold office . . ."

"Looks to me as if it were your duty, Baldwin," says Densch in a deep voice, taking his tortoiseshell glasses out of a case and applying them hurriedly to his nose.

The waiter has brought a large planked steak surrounded by bulwarks of mushrooms and chopped carrots and peas and frilled browned mashed potatoes. Densch straightens his glasses and stares attentively at the planked steak.

"A very handsome dish Ben, a very handsome dish I must say. . . . It's just this Baldwin . . . as I look at it . . . the country is going through a dangerous period of reconstruction . . . the confusion attendant on the winding up of a great conflict . . . the bankruptcy of a continent . . . bolshevism and subversive doctrines rife . . . America . . ." he says, cutting with the sharp polished steel knife into the thick steak, rare and well peppered. He chews a mouthful slowly. "America," he begins again, "is in the position of taking over the receivership of the world. The great principles of democracy, of that commercial freedom upon which our whole civilization depends are more than ever at stake. Now as at no other time we need men of established ability and unblemished integrity in public office, particularly in the offices requiring expert judicial and legal knowledge."

"That's what I was tryin to tell ye the other day George."

"But that's all very well Gus, but how do you know I'd be elected. . . . After all it would mean giving up my law practice for a number of years, it would mean . . ."

"You just leave that to me. . . . George you're elected already."

"An extraordinarily good steak," says Densch, "I must say. . . . No but newspaper talk aside . . . I happen to know from a secret and reliable source that there is a subversive plot among undesirable elements in this country. . . . Good God think of the Wall Street bomb outrage. . . . I must say that the attitude of the press has been gratifying in one respect . . . in fact we're approaching a national unity undreamed of before the war."

"No but George," breaks in Gus, "put it this way. . . . The publicity value of a political career'd kinder bolster up your law practice."

"It would and it wouldn't Gus."

Densch is unrolling the tinfoil off a cigar. "At any rate it's a grand sight." He takes off his glasses and cranes his thick neck to look out into the bright expanse of harbor that stretches full of masts, smoke, blobs of steam, dark oblongs of barges, to the hazeblurred hills of Staten Island.

Bright flakes of cloud were scaling off a sky of crushing indigo over the Battery where groups of dingy darkdressed people stood round the Ellis Island landing station and the small boat dock waiting silently for something. Frayed smoke of tugs and steamers hung low and trailed along the opaque glassgreen water. A threemasted schooner was being towed down the North River. A newhoisted jib flopped awkwardly in the wind. Down the harbor loomed taller, taller a steamer head on, four red stacks packed into one, creamy superstructure gleaming. "*Mauretania* just acomin in twentyfour hours lyte," yelled the man with the telescope and fieldglasses. . . . "Tyke a look at the *Mauretania,* farstest ocean greyhound, twentyfour hours lyte." The *Mauretania* stalked like a skyscraper through the harbor shipping. A rift of sunlight sharpened the shadow under the broad bridge, along the white stripes of upper decks, glinted in the rows of portholes. The smokestacks stood apart, the hull lengthened. The black relentless hull of the *Mauretania* pushing puffing tugs ahead of it cut like a long knife into the North River.

A ferry was leaving the immigrant station, a murmur rustled through the crowd that packed the edges of the wharf. "Deportees. . . . It's the communists the Department of Justice is having deported . . . deportees . . . Reds. . . . It's the Reds they are deporting." The ferry was out of the slip. In the stern a group of men stood still tiny like tin soldiers. "They are sending the Reds back to Russia." A handkerchief waved on the ferry, a red handkerchief. People tiptoed gently to the edge of the walk, tiptoeing, quiet like in a sickroom.

Behind the backs of the men and women crowding to the edge of the water, gorillafaced chipontheshoulder policemen walked back and forth nervously swinging their billies.

"They are sending the Reds back to Russia. . . . Deportees. . . . Agitators. . . . Undesirables." . . . Gulls wheeled crying. A catsupbottle bobbed gravely in the little ground-glass waves. A sound of singing came from the ferryboat getting small, slipping away across the water.

C'est la lutte finale, groupons-nous et demain
L'Internationale sera le genre humain.

"Take a look at the deportees. . . . Take a look at the
undesirable aliens," shouted the man with the telescopes and
fieldglasses.　A girl's voice burst out suddenly, *"Arise pris-
oners of starvation,"* "Sh. . . . They could pull you for
that."

The singing trailed away across the water.　At the end
of a marbled wake the ferryboat was shrinking into haze.
International . . . shall be the human race.　The singing
died.　From up the river came the longdrawn rattling throb
of a steamer leaving dock.　Gulls wheeled above the dark
dingydressed crowd that stood silently looking down the
bay.

II. Nickelodeon

A nickel before midnight buys tomorrow . . . holdup headlines, a cup of coffee in the automat, a ride to Woodlawn, Fort Lee, Flatbush. . . . A nickel in the slot buys chewing gum. Somebody Loves Me, Baby Divine, You're in Kentucky Juss Shu' As You're Born . . . bruised notes of foxtrots go limping out of doors, blues, waltzes (We'd Danced the Whole Night Through) trail gyrating tinsel memories. . . . On Sixth Avenue on Fourteenth there are still flyspecked stereopticons where for a nickel you can peep at yellowed yesterdays. Beside the peppering shooting gallery you stoop into the flicker A HOT TIME, THE BACHELOR'S SURPRISE, THE STOLEN GARTER . . . wastebasket of tornup daydreams. . . . A nickel before midnight buys our yesterdays.

RUTH PRYNNE came out of the doctor's office pull' the fur tight round her throat. She felt faint. Taxi. As she stepped in she remembered the smell of cosmetics and toast and the littered hallway at Mrs. Sunderlands. Oh I cant go home just yet. "Driver go to the Old English Tea Room on Fortieth Street please." She opened her long green leather purse and looked in. My God, only a dollar a quarter a nickel and two pennies. She kept her eyes on the figures flickering on the taximeter. She wanted to break down and cry. . . . The way money goes. The gritty cold wind rasped at her throat when she got out. "Eighty cents miss. . . . I haven't any change miss." "All right keep the change." Heavens only thirtytwo cents. . . . Inside it was warm and smelled cozily of tea and cookies.

"Why Ruth, if it isn't Ruth. . . . Dearest come to my arms after all these years." It was Billy Waldron. He was fatter and whiter than he used to be. He gave her a stagy hug and kissed her on the forehead. "How are you? Do tell me. . . . How distinguée you look in that hat."

"I've just been having my throat X-rayed," she said with a giggle. "I feel like the wrath of God."

"What are you doing Ruth? I havent heard of you for ages."

"Put me down as a back number, hadn't you?" She caught his words up fiercely.

"After that beautiful performance you gave in The Orchard Queen. . . ."

"To tell the truth Billy I've had a terrible run of bad luck."

"Oh I know everything is dead."

"I have an appointment to see Belasco next week. . . . Something may come of that."

"Why I should say it might Ruth. . . . Are you expecting someone?"

"No. . . . Oh Billy you're still the same old tease. . . . Dont tease me this afternoon. I dont feel up to it."

"You poor dear sit down and have a cup of tea with me."

"I tell you Ruth it's a terrible year. Many a good trouper will pawn the last link of his watch chain this year. . . . I suppose you're going the rounds."

"Dont talk about it. . . . If I could only get my throat all right. . . . A thing like that wears you down."

"Remember the old days at the Somerville Stock?"

"Billy could I ever forget them? . . . Wasnt it a scream?"

"The last time I saw you Ruth was in The Butterfly on the Wheel in Seattle. I was out front. . . ."

"Why didn't you come back and see me?"

"I was still angry at you I suppose. . . . It was my lowest moment. In the valley of shadow . . . melancholia . . . neurasthenia. I was stranded penniless. . . . That night I was a little under the influence, you understand. I didn't want you to see the beast in me."

Ruth poured herself a fresh cup of tea. She suddenly felt feverishly gay. "Oh but Billy havent you forgotten all that? . . . I was a foolish little girl then. . . . I was afraid that love or marriage or anything like that would in-

terfere with my art, you understand. . . . I was so crazy to
succeed."

"Would you do the same thing again?"

"I wonder. . . ."

"How does it go? . . . *The moving finger writes and
having writ moves on . . .*"

"Something about *Nor all your tears wash out a word of
it* . . . But Billy," she threw back her head and laughed, "I
thought you were getting ready to propose to me all over
again. . . . Ou my throat."

"Ruth I wish you werent taking that X-ray treatment.
. . . I've heard it's very dangerous. Dont let me alarm you
about it my dear . . . but I have heard of cases of cancer
contracted that way."

"That's nonsense Billy. . . . That's only when X-rays are
improperly used, and it takes years of exposure. . . . No I
think this Dr. Warner's a remarkable man."

Later, sitting in the uptown express in the subway, she
still could feel his soft hand patting her gloved hand. "Goodby little girl, God bless you," he'd said huskily. He's gotten to be a ham actor if there ever was one, something was
jeering inside her all the while. "Thank heavens you will
never know." . . . Then with a sweep of his broadbrimmed
hat and a toss of his silky white hair, as if he were playing
in Monsieur Beaucaire, he had turned and walked off among
the crowd up Broadway. I may be down on my luck, but
I'm not all ham inside the way he is. . . . Cancer he said.
She looked up and down the car at the joggling faces opposite her. Of all those people one of them must have it.
Four Out of Every Five Get . . . Silly, that's not cancer. Ex-lax, Nujol, O'Sullivan's. . . . She put her
hand to her throat. Her throat was terribly swollen, her
throat throbbed feverishly. Maybe it was worse. It is
something alive that grows in flesh, eats all your life, leaves
you horrible, rotten. . . . The people opposite stared straight
ahead of them, young men and young women, middleaged
people, green faces in the dingy light, under the sourcolored
advertisements. Four Out of Every Five . . . A train-

load of jiggling corpses, nodding and swaying as the express roared shrilly towards Ninetysixth Street. At Ninetysixth she had to change for the local.

Dutch Robertson sat on a bench on Brooklyn Bridge with the collar of his army overcoat turned up, running his eye down Business Opportunities. It was a muggy fogchoked afternoon; the bridge was dripping and aloof like an arbor in a dense garden of steamboatwhistles. Two sailors passed. "Ze best joint I've been in since B. A."

Partner movie theater, busy neighborhood . . . stand investigation . . . $3,000. . . . Jez I haven't got three thousand mills. . . . Cigar stand, busy building, compelled sacrifice. . . . Attractive and completely outfitted radio and music shop . . . busy. . . . Modern mediumsized printingplant consisting of cylinders, Kelleys, Miller feeders, job presses, linotype machines and a complete bindery. . . . Kosher restaurant and delicatessen. . . . Bowling alley . . . busy. . . . Live spot large dancehall and other concessions. WE BUY FALSE TEETH, old gold, platinum, old jewelry. The hell they do. HELP WANTED MALE. That's more your speed you rummy. Addressers, first class penmen. . . . Lets me out. . . . Artist, Attendant, Auto, Bicycle and Motorcycle repair shop. . . . He took out the back of an envelope and marked down the address. Bootblacks. . . . Not yet. Boy; no I guess I aint a boy any more, Candystore, Canvassers, Carwashers, Dishwasher. EARN WHILE YOU LEARN. Mechanical dentistry is your shortest way to success. . . . No dull seasons. . . .

"Hello Dutch. . . . I thought I'd never get here." A grayfaced girl in a red hat and gray rabbit coat sat down beside him.

"Jez I'm sick o readin want ads." He stretched out his arms and yawned letting the paper slip down his legs.

"Aint you chilly, sittin out here on the bridge?"

"Maybe I am. . . . Let's go and eat." He jumped to his

feet and put his red face with its thin broken nose close to
hers and looked in her black eyes with his pale gray eyes.
He tapped her arm sharply. "Hello Francie. . . . How's
my lil girl?"

They walked back towards Manhattan, the way she had
come. Under them the river glinted through the mist. A
big steamer drifted by slowly, lights already lit; over the
edge of the walk they looked down the black smokestacks.

"Was it a boat as big as that you went overseas on
Dutch?"

"Bigger 'n that."

"Gee I'd like to go."

"I'll take you over some time and show you all them
places over there . . . I went to a lot of places that time I
went A.W.O.L."

In the L station they hesitated. "Francie got any jack
on you?"

"Sure I got a dollar. . . . I ought to keep that for tomorrer though."

"All I got's my last quarter. Let's go eat two fiftyfive
cent dinners at that chink place . . . That'll be a dollar
ten."

"I got to have a nickel to get down to the office in the
mornin."

"Oh Hell! Goddam it I wish we could have some
money."

"Got anything lined up yet?"

"Wouldn't I have told ye if I had?"

"Come ahead I've got a half a dollar saved up in my
room. I can take carfare outa that." She changed the
dollar and put two nickels into the turnstile. They sat
down in a Third Avenue train.

"Say Francie will they let us dance in a khaki shirt?"

"Why not Dutch it looks all right."

"I feel kinder fussed about it."

The jazzband in the restaurant was playing Hindustan.
It smelled of chop suey and Chinese sauce. They slipped
into a booth. Slickhaired young men and little bobhaired

girls were dancing hugged close. As they sat down they smiled into each other's eyes.

"Jez I'm hungry."

"Are you Dutch?"

He pushed forward his knees until they locked with hers. "Gee you're a good kid," he said when he had finished his soup. "Honest I'll get a job this week. And then we'll get a nice room an get married an everything."

When they got up to dance they were trembling so they could barely keep time to the music.

"Mister . . . no dance without ploper dless . . ." said a dapper Chinaman putting his hand on Dutch's arm.

"Waz he want?" he growled dancing on.

"I guess it's the shirt, Dutch."

"The hell it is."

"I'm tired. I'd rather talk than dance anyway . . ." They went back to their booth and their sliced pineapple for dessert.

Afterwards they walked east along Fourteenth. "Dutch cant we go to your room?"

"I ain't got no room. The old stiff wont let me stay and she's got all my stuff. Honest if I dont get a job this week I'm goin to a recruiting sergeant an re-enlist."

"Oh dont do that; we wouldn't ever get married then Dutch. . . . Gee though why didn't you tell me?"

"I didn't want to worry you Francie. . . . Six months out of work . . . Jez it's enough to drive a guy cookoo."

"But Dutch where can we go?"

"We might go out that wharf. . . . I know a wharf."

"It's so cold."

"I couldn't get cold when you were with me kid."

"Dont talk like that. . . . I dont like it."

They walked leaning together in the darkness up the muddy rutted riverside streets, between huge swelling gastanks, brokendown fences, long manywindowed warehouses. At a corner under a streetlamp a boy catcalled as they passed.

"I'll poke your face in you little bastard," Dutch let fly out of the corner of his mouth.

"Dont answer him," Francie whispered, "or we'll have the whole gang down on us."

They slipped through a little door in a tall fence above which crazy lumberpiles towered. They could smell the river and cedarwood and sawdust. They could hear the river lapping at the piles under their feet. Dutch drew her to him and pressed his mouth down on hers.

"Hay dere dont you know you cant come out here at night disaway?" a voice yapped at them. The watchman flashed a lantern in their eyes.

"All right keep your shirt on, we were just taking a little walk."

"Some walk."

They were dragging themselves down the street again with the black riverwind in their teeth.

"Look out." A policeman passed whistling softly to himself. They drew apart. "Oh Francie they'll be takin us to the nuthouse if we keep this up. Let's go to your room."

"Landlady'll throw me out, that's all."

"I wont make any noise. . . . You got your key aint ye? I'll sneak out before light. Goddam it they make you feel like a skunk."

"All right Dutch let's go home. . . . I dont care no more what happens."

They walked up mudtracked stairs to the top floor of the tenement.

"Take off your shoes," she hissed in his ear as she slipped the key in the lock.

"I got holes in my stockings."

"That dont matter, silly. I'll see if it's all right. My room's way back past the kitchen so if they're all in bed they cant hear us."

When she left him he could hear his heart beating. In a second she came back. He tiptoed after her down a creaky hall. A sound of snoring came through a door.

There was a smell of cabbage and sleep in the hall. Once in her room she locked the door and put a chair against it under the knob. A triangle of ashen light came in from the street. "Now for crissake keep still Dutch." One shoe still in each hand he reached for her and hugged her.

He lay beside her whispering on and on with his lips against her ear. "And Francie I'll make good, honest I will; I got to be a sergeant overseas till they busted me for goin A.W.O.L. That shows I got it in me. Onct I get a chance I'll make a whole lot of jack and you an me'll go back an see Château Teery an Paree an all that stuff; honest you'd like it Francie . . . Jez the towns are old and funny and quiet and cozylike an they have the swellest ginmills where you sit outside at little tables in the sun an watch the people pass an the food's swell too once you get to like it an they have hotels all over where we could have gone like tonight an they dont care if your married or nutten. An they have big beds all cozy made of wood and they bring ye up breakfast in bed. Jez Francie you'd like it."

They were walking to dinner through the snow. Big snowfeathers spun and spiraled about them mottling the glare of the streets with blue and pink and yellow, blotting perspectives.

"Ellie I hate to have you take that job. . . . You ought to keep on with your acting."

"But Jimps, we've got to live."

"I know . . . I know. You'd certainly didnt have your wits about you Ellie when you married me."

"Oh let's not talk about it any more."

"Do let's have a good time tonight. . . . It's the first snow."

"Is this the place?" They stood before an unlighted basement door covered by a closemeshed grating. "Let's try."

"Did the bell ring?"

"I think so."

The inner door opened and a girl in a pink apron peered out at them. "Bon soir mademoiselle."

"Ah . . . bon soir monsieur 'dame." She ushered them into a foodsmelling gaslit hall hung with overcoats and hats and mufflers. Through a curtained door the restaurant blew in their faces a hot breath of bread and cocktails and frying butter and perfumes and lipsticks and clatter and jingling talk.

"I can smell absinthe," said Ellen. "Let's get terribly tight."

"Good Lord, there's Congo. . . . Dont you remember Congo Jake at the Seaside Inn?"

He stood bulky at the end of the corridor beckoning to them. His face was very tanned and he had a glossy black mustache. "Hello Meester 'Erf. . . . Ow are you?"

"Fine as silk. Congo I want you to meet my wife."

"If you dont mind the keetchen we will 'ave a drink."

"Of course we dont. . . . It's the best place in the house. Why you're limping. . . . What did you do to your leg?"

"Foutu . . . I left it en Italie. . . . I couldnt breeng it along once they'd cut it off."

"How was that?"

"Damn fool thing on Mont Tomba. . . . My bruderinlaw e gave me a very beautiful artificial leemb. . . . Sit 'ere. Look madame now can you tell which is which?"

"No I cant," said Ellie laughing. They were at a little marble table in the corner of the crowded kitchen. A girl was dishing out at a deal table in the center. Two cooks worked over the stove. The air was rich with sizzling fatty foodsmells. Congo hobbled back to them with three glasses on a small tray. He stood over them while they drank.

"Salut," he said, raising his glass. "Absinthe cocktail, like they make it in New Orleans."

"It's a knockout." Congo took a card out of his vest pocket:

MARQUIS DES COULOMMIERS
IMPORTS

Riverside 11121

"Maybe some day you need some little ting . . . I deal in nutting but prewar imported. I am the best bootleggair in New York.

"If I ever get any money I certainly will spend it on you Congo. . . . How do you find business?"

"Veree good. . . . I tell you about it. Tonight I'm too busee. . . . Now I find you a table in the restaurant."

"Do you run this place too?"

"No this my bruderinlaw's place."

"I didnt know you had a sister."

"Neither did I."

When Congo limped away from their table silence came down between them like an asbestos curtain in a theater.

"He's a funny duck," said Jimmy forcing a laugh.

"He certainly is."

"Look Ellie let's have another cocktail."

"Allright."

"I must get hold of him and get some stories about bootleggers out of him."

When he stretched his legs out under the table he touched her feet. She drew them away. Jimmy could feel his jaws chewing, they clanked so loud under his cheeks he thought Ellie must hear them. She sat opposite him in a gray tailoredsuit, her neck curving up heartbreakingly from the ivory V left by the crisp frilled collar of her blouse, her head tilted under her tight gray hat, her lips made up; cutting up little pieces of meat and not eating them, not saying a word.

"Gosh . . . let's have another cocktail." He felt paralyzed like in a nightmare; she was a porcelaine figure under a bellglass. A current of fresh snowrinsed air from somewhere eddied all of a sudden through the blurred packed jangling glare of the restaurant, cut the reek of food and drink and tobacco. For an instant he caught the smell of her hair. The cocktails burned in him. God I dont want to pass out.

Sitting in the restaurant of the Gare de Lyon, side by side on the black leather bench. His cheek brushes hers when he reaches to put herring, butter, sardines, anchovies, sausage on her plate. They eat in a hurry, gobbling, giggling, gulp wine, start at every screech of an engine. . . .

The train pulls out of Avignon, they two awake, looking in each other's eyes in the compartment full of sleep-sodden snoring people. He lurches clambering over tangled legs, to smoke a cigarette at the end of the dim oscillating corridor. Diddledeump, going south, Diddledeump, going south, sing the wheels over the rails down the valley of the Rhone. Leaning in the window, smoking a broken cigarette, trying to smoke a crumbling cigarette, holding a finger over the torn place. Glubglub glubglub from the bushes, from the silverdripping poplars along the track.

"Ellie, Ellie there are nightingales singing along the track."

"Oh I was asleep darling." She gropes to him stumbling across the legs of sleepers. Side by side in the window in the lurching jiggling corridor.

Deedledeump, going south. Gasp of nightingales along the track among the silverdripping poplars. The insane cloudy night of moonlight smells of gardens garlic rivers freshdunged field roses. Gasp of nightingales.

Opposite him the Elliedoll was speaking. "He says the lobstersalad's all out. . . . Isnt that discouraging?"

Suddenly he had his tongue. "Gosh if that were the only thing."

"What do you mean?"

"Why did we come back to this rotten town anyway?"

"You've been burbling about how wonderful it was ever since we came back."

"I know. I guess it's sour grapes. . . . I'm going to have another cocktail. . . . Ellie for heaven's sake what's the matter with us?"

"We're going to be sick if we keep this up I tell you."

"Well let's be sick. . . . Let's be good and sick."

When they sit up in the great bed they can see across the
harbor, can see the yards of a windjammer and a white sloop
and a red and green toy tug and plainfaced houses opposite
beyond a peacock stripe of water; when they lie down they
can see gulls in the sky. At dusk dressing rockily, shakily
stumbling through the mildewed corridors of the hotel out
into streets noisy as a brass band, full of tambourine rattle,
brassy shine, crystal glitter, honk and whir of motors. . . .
Alone together in the dusk drinking sherry under a broad-
leaved plane, alone together in the juggled particolored
crowds like people invisible. And the spring night comes
up over the sea terrible out of Africa and settles about
them.

They had finished their coffee. Jimmy had drunk his very
slowly as if some agony waited for him when he finished it.

"Well I was afraid we'd find the Barneys here," said
Ellen.

"Do they know about this place?"

"You brought them here yourself Jimps. . . . And that
dreadful woman insisted on talking babies with me all the
evening. I hate talking babies."

"Gosh I wish we could go to a show."

"It would be too late anyway."

"And just spending money I havent got. . . . Lets have
a cognac to top off with. I don't care if it ruins us."

"It probably will in more ways than one."

"Well Ellie, here's to the breadwinner who's taken up
the white man's burden."

"Why Jimmy I think it'll be rather fun to have an editorial job for a while."

"I'd find it fun to have any kind of job. . . . Well I can
always stay home and mind the baby."

"Dont be so bitter Jimmy, it's just temporary."

"Life's just temporary for that matter."

The taxi drew up. Jimmy paid him with his last dollar.
Ellie had her key in the outside door. The street was a
confusion of driving absintheblurred snow. The door of
their apartment closed behind them. Chairs, tables, books,

windowcurtains crowded about them bitter with the dust
of yesterday, the day before, the day before that. Smells
of diapers and coffeepots and typewriter oil and Dutch
Cleanser oppressed them. Ellen put out the empty milkbottle
and went to bed. Jimmy kept walking nervously about the
front room. His drunkenness ebbed away leaving him icily
sober. In the empty chamber of his brain a doublefaced word
clinked like a coin: Success Failure, Success Failure.

> I'm just wild about Harree
> And Harry's just wild about me

she hums under her breath as she dances. It's a long hall
with a band at one end, lit greenishly by two clusters of
electric lights hanging among paper festoons in the center.
At the end where the door is, a varnished rail holds back
the line of men. This one Anna's dancing with is a tall
square built Swede, his big feet trail clumsily after her tiny
lightly tripping feet. The music stops. Now it's a little
blackhaired slender Jew. He tries to snuggle close.
"Quit that." She holds him away from her.
"Aw have a heart."
She doesn't answer, dances with cold precision; she's
sickeningly tired.

> Me and my boyfriend
> My boyfriend and I

An Italian breathes garlic in her face, a marine sergeant,
a Greek, a blond young kid with pink cheeks, she gives him
a smile; a drunken elderly man who tries to kiss her . . .
Charley my boy O Charley my boy . . . slickhaired, freckled
rumplehaired, pimplefaced, snubnosed, straightnosed, quick
dancers, heavy dancers. . . . *Goin souf. . . . Wid de taste
o de sugarcane right in my mouf* . . . against her back big
hands, hot hands, sweaty hands, cold hands, while her dance-

checks mount up, get to be a wad in her fist. This one's a
good waltzer, genteel-like in a black suit.

"Gee I'm tired," she whispers.

"Dancing never tires me."

"Oh it's dancin with everybody like this."

"Dont you want to come an dance with me all alone
somewhere?"

"Boyfrien's waitin for me after."

> With nothing but a photograph
> To tell my troubles to . . .
> What'll I do . . . ?

"What time's it?" she asks a broadchested wise guy.
"Time you an me was akwainted, sister. . . ." She shakes
her head. Suddenly the music bursts into Auld Lang Syne.
She breaks away from him and runs to the desk in a crowd
of girls elbowing to turn in their dancechecks. "Say Anna,"
says a broadhipped blond girl . . . "did ye see that sap was
dancin wid me? . . . He says to me the sap he says See
you later an I says to him the sap I says see yez in hell
foist . . . an then he says, Goily he says . . ."

III. Revolving Doors

Glowworm trains shuttle in the gloaming through the foggy looms of spiderweb bridges, elevators soar and drop in their shafts, harbor lights wink.

Like sap at the first frost at five o'clock men and women begin to drain gradually out of the tall buildings downtown, grayfaced throngs flood subways and tubes, vanish underground.

All night the great buildings stand quiet and empty, their million windows dark. Drooling light the ferries chew tracks across the lacquered harbor. At midnight the fourfunneled express steamers slide into the dark out of their glary berths. Bankers blearyeyed from secret conferences hear the hooting of the tugs as they are let out of side doors by lightningbug watchmen; they settle grunting into the back seats of limousines, and are whisked uptown into the Forties, clinking streets of ginwhite whiskey-yellow ciderfizzling lights.

SHE sat at the dressingtable coiling her hair. He stood over her with the lavender suspenders hanging from his dress trousers prodding the diamond studs into his shirt with stumpy fingers.

"Jake I wish we were out of it," she whined through the hairpins in her mouth.

"Out of what Rosie?"

"The Prudence Promotion Company. . . . Honest I'm worried."

"Why everything's goin swell. We've got to bluff out Nichols that's all."

"Suppose he prosecutes?"

"Oh he wont. He'd lose a lot of money by it. He'd much better come in with us. . . . I can pay him in cash in a week anyways. If we can keep him thinkin we got money

305

we'll have him eatin out of our hands. Didn't he say he'd be at the El Fey tonight?"

Rosie had just put a rhinestone comb into the coil of her black hair. She nodded and got to her feet. She was a plump broadhipped woman with big black eyes and high-arched eyebrows. She wore a corset trimmed with yellow lace and a pink silk chemise.

"Put on everythin you've got Rosie. I want yez all dressed up like a Christmas tree. We're goin to the El Fey an stare Nichols down tonight. Then tomorrer I'll go round and put the proposition up to him. . . . Lets have a little snifter anyways . . ." He went to the phone. "Send up some cracked ice and a couple of bottles of White Rock to four o four. Silverman's the name. Make it snappy."

"Jake let's make a getaway," Rosie cried suddenly. She stood in the closet door with a dress over her arm. "I cant stand all this worry. . . . It's killin me. Let's you an me beat it to Paris or Havana or somewheres and start out fresh."

"Then we would be up the creek. You can be extradited for grand larceny. Jez you wouldnt have me goin round with dark glasses and false whiskers all my life."

Rosie laughed. "No I guess you wouldnt look so good in a fake zit. . . . Oh I wish we were really married at least."

"Dont make no difference between us Rosie. Then they'd be after me for bigamy too. That'd be pretty."

Rosie shuddered at the bellboy's knock. Jake Silverman put the tray with its clinking bowl of ice on the bureau and fetched a square whiskeybottle out of the wardrobe.

"Dont pour out any for me. I havent got the heart for it."

"Kid you've got to pull yourself together. Put on the glad rags an we'll go to a show. Hell I been in lots o tighter holes than this." With his highball in his hand he went to the phone. "I want the newsstand. . . . Hello cutie. . . . Sure I'm an old friend of yours. . . . Sure you know me. . . . Look could you get me two seats for the Follies. . . . That's the idear. . . . No I cant sit back of the eighth row.

. . . That's a good little girl. . . . An you'll call me in ten
minutes will you dearie?"

"Say Jake is there really any borax in that lake?"

"Sure there is. Aint we got the affidavit of four experts?"

"Sure. I was just kinder wonderin. . . . Say Jake if this
ever gets wound up will you promise me not to go in for
any more wildcat schemes?"

"Sure; I wont need to. . . . My you're a redhot mommer
in that dress."

"Do you like it?"

"You look like Brazil . . . I dunno . . . kinder tropical."

"That's the secret of my dangerous charm."

The phone rang jingling sharp. They jumped to their
feet. She pressed the side of her hand against her lips.

"Two in the fourth row. That's fine. . . . We'll be right
down an get em . . . Jez Rosie you cant go on being
jumpy like; you're gettin me all shot too. Pull yerself together why cant you?"

"Let's go out an eat Jake. I havent had anything but
buttermilk all day. I guess I'll stop tryin to reduce. This
worryin'll make me thin enough."

"You got to quit it Rosie. . . . It's gettin my nerve."

They stopped at the flowerstall in the lobby. "I want a
gardenia" he said. He puffed his chest out and smiled his
curlylipped smile as the girl fixed it in the buttonhole of his
dinnercoat. "What'll you have dear?" he turned grandil-
oquently to Rosie. She puckered her mouth. "I dont just
know what'll go with my dress."

"While you're deciding I'll go get the theater tickets."
With his overcoat open and turned back to show the white
puffedout shirtfront and his cuffs shot out over his thick
hands he strutted over to the newsstand. Out of the corner
of her eye while the ends of the red roses were being wrapped
in silver paper Rosie could see him leaning across the
magazines talking babytalk to the blond girl. He came back
brighteyed with a roll of bills in his hand. She pinned the
roses on her fur coat, put her arm in his and together they

went through the revolving doors into the cold glistening electric night. "Taxi," he yapped.

The diningroom smelled of toast and coffee and the New York *Times*. The Merivales were breakfasting to electric light. Sleet beat against the windows. "Well Paramount's fallen off five points more," said James from behind the paper.

"Oh James I think its horrid to be such a tease," whined Maisie who was drinking her coffee in little henlike sips.

"And anyway," said Mrs. Merivale, "Jack's not with Paramount any more. He's doing publicity for the Famous Players."

"He's coming east in two weeks. He says he hopes to be here for the first of the year."

"Did you get another wire Maisie?"

Maisie nodded. "Do you know James, Jack never will write a letter. He always telegraphs," said Mrs. Merivale through the paper at her son. "He certainly keeps the house choked up with flowers," growled James from behind the paper.

"All by telegraph," said Mrs. Merivale triumphantly.

James put down his paper. "Well I hope he's as good a fellow as he seems to be."

"Oh James you're horrid about Jack. . . . I think it's mean." She got to her feet and went through the curtains into the parlor.

"Well if he's going to be my brother-in-law, I think I ought to have a say in picking him," he grumbled.

Mrs. Merivale went after her. "Come back and finish your breakfast Maisie, he's just a terrible tease."

"I wont have him talk that way about Jack."

"But Maisie I think Jack's a dear boy." She put her arm round her daughter and led her back to the table. "He's so simple and I know he has good impulses. . . . I'm sure he's going to make you very happy." Maisie sat down again pouting under the pink bow of her boudoir cap. "Mother may I have another cup of coffee?"

"Deary you know you oughtnt to drink two cups. Dr. Fernald said that was what was making you so nervous."

"Just a little bit mother very weak. I want to finish this muffin and I simply cant eat it without something to wash it down, and you know you dont want me to lose any more weight." James pushed back his chair and went out with the *Times* under his arm. "It's half past eight James," said Mrs. Merivale. "He's likely to take an hour when he gets in there with that paper."

"Well," said Maisie peevishly. "I think I'll go back to bed. I think it's silly the way we all get up to breakfast. There's something so vulgar about it mother. Nobody does it any more. At the Perkinses' it comes up to you in bed on a tray."

"But James has to be at the bank at nine."

"That's no reason why we should drag ourselves out of bed. That's how people get their faces all full of wrinkles."

"But we wouldn't see James until dinnertime, and I like to get up early. The morning's the loveliest part of the day." Maisie yawned desperately.

James appeared in the doorway to the hall running a brush round his hat.

"What did you do with the paper James?"

"Oh I left it in there."

"I'll get it, never mind. . . . My dear you've got your stickpin in crooked. I'll fix it. . . . There." Mrs. Merivale put her hands on his shoulders and looked in her son's face. He wore a dark gray suit with a faint green stripe in it, an olive green knitted necktie with a small gold nugget stickpin, olive green woolen socks with black clockmarks and dark red Oxford shoes, their laces neatly tied with doubleknots that never came undone. "James arent you carrying your cane?" He had an olive green woolen muffler round his neck and was slipping into his dark brown winter overcoat. "I notice the younger men down there dont carry

them, mother . . . People might think it was a little . . .
I dont know . . ."

"But Mr. Perkins carries a cane with a gold parrothead."

"Yes but he's one of the vicepresidents, he can do what he
likes. . . . But I've got to run." James Merivale hastily
kissed his mother and sister. He put on his gloves going
down in the elevator. Ducking his head into the sleety wind
he walked quickly east along Seventysecond. At the subway entrance he bought a *Tribune* and hustled down the
steps to the jammed soursmelling platform.

Chicago! Chicago! came in bursts out of the shut phonograph. Tony Hunter, slim in a black closecut suit, was
dancing with a girl who kept putting her mass of curly
ashblond hair on his shoulder. They were alone in the hotel
sitting room.

"Sweetness you're a lovely dancer," she cooed snuggling
closer.

"Think so Nevada?"

"Um-hum . . . Sweetness have you noticed something
about me?"

"What's that Nevada?"

"Havent you noticed something about my eyes?"

"They're the loveliest little eyes in the world."

"Yes but there's something about them."

"You mean that one of them's green and the other one
brown."

"Oh it noticed the tweet lil ting." She tilted her mouth
up at him. He kissed it. The record came to an end.
They both ran over to stop it. "That wasnt much of a kiss,
Tony," said Nevada Jones tossing her curls out of her eyes.
They put on *Shuffle Along.*

"Say Tony," she said when they had started dancing
again. "What did the psychoanalyst say when you went to
see him yesterday?"

"Oh nothing much, we just talked," said Tony with a

sigh. "He said it was all imaginary. He suggested I get to know some girls better. He's all right. He doesn't know what he's talking about though. He cant do anything."

"I bet you I could."

They stopped dancing and looked at each other with the blood burning in their faces.

"Knowing you Nevada," he said in a doleful tone "has meant more to me . . . You're so decent to me. Everybody's always been so nasty."

"Aint he solemn though?" She walked over thoughtfully and stopped the phonograph.

"Some joke on George I'll say."

"I feel horribly about it. He's been so decent. . . . And after all I could never have afforded to go to Dr. Baumgardt at all."

"It's his own fault. He's a damn fool. . . . If he thinks he can buy me with a little hotel accommodation and theater tickets he's got another think coming. But honestly Tony you must keep on with that doctor. He did wonders with Glenn Gaston. . . . He thought he was that way until he was thirtyfive years old and the latest thing I hear he's married an had a pair of twins. . . . Now give me a real kiss sweetest. Thataboy. Let's dance some more. Gee you're a beautiful dancer. Kids like you always are. I dont know why it is. . . ."

The phone cut into the room suddenly with a glittering sawtooth ring. "Hello. . . . Yes this is Miss Jones. . . . Why of course George I'm waiting for you. . . ." She put up the receiver. "Great snakes, Tony beat it. I'll call you later. Dont go down in the elevator you'll meet him coming up." Tony Hunter melted out the door. Nevada put *Baby* . . . *Babee Deevine* on the phonograph and strode nervously about the room, straightening chairs, patting her tight short curls into place.

"Oh George I thought you werent comin. . . . How do you do Mr. McNiel? I dunno why I'm all jumpy today. I thought you were never comin. Let's get some lunch up. I'm that hungry."

George Baldwin put his derby hat and stick on a table in the corner. "What'll you have Gus?" he said. "Sure I always take a lamb chop an a baked potato."

"I'm just taking crackers and milk, my stomach's a little out of order. . . . Nevada see if you cant frisk up a highball for Mr. McNiel."

"Well I could do with a highball George."

"George order me half a broiled chicken lobster and some alligator pear salad," screeched Nevada from the bathroom where she was cracking ice.

"She's the greatest girl for lobster," said Baldwin laughing as he went to the phone.

She came back from the bathroom with two highballs on a tray; she had put a scarlet and parrotgreen batik scarf round her neck. "Just you an me's drinkin Mr. McNiel. . . . George is on the water wagon. Doctor's orders."

"Nevada what do you say we go to a musical show this afternoon? There's a lot of business I want to get off my mind."

"I just love matinees. Do you mind if we take Tony Hunter. He called up he was lonesome and wanted to come round this afternoon. He's not workin this week."

"All right. . . . Nevada will you excuse us if we talk business for just a second over here by the window. We'll forget it by the time lunch comes."

"All righty I'll change my dress."

"Sit down here Gus."

They sat silent a moment looking out of the window at the red girder cage of the building under construction next door. "Well Gus," said Baldwin suddenly harshly, "I'm in the race."

"Good for you George, we need men like you."

"I'm going to run on a Reform ticket."

"The hell you are?"

"I wanted to tell you Gus rather than have you hear it by a roundabout way."

"Who's goin to elect you?"

"Oh I've got my backing. . . . I'll have a good press."

"Press hell. . . . We've got the voters. . . . But Goddam it if it hadn't been for me your name never would have come up for district attorney at all."

"I know you've always been a good friend of mine and I hope you'll continue to be."

"I never went back on a guy yet, but Jez, George, it's give and take in this world."

"Well," broke in Nevada advancing towards them with little dancesteps, wearing a flamingo pink silk dress, "havent you boys argued enough yet?"

"We're through," growled Gus. ". . . Say Miss Nevada, how did you get that name?"

"I was born in Reno. . . . My mother'd gone there to get a divorce. . . . Gosh she was sore. . . . Certainly put my foot in it that time."

Anna Cohen stands behind the counter under the sign THE BEST SANDWICH IN NEW YORK. Her feet ache in her pointed shoes with runover heels.

"Well I guess they'll begin soon or else we're in for a slack day," says the sodashaker beside her. He's a raw-faced man with a sharp adamsapple. "It allus comes all of a rush like."

"Yeh, looks like they all got the same idear at the same time." They stand looking out through the glass partition at the endless files of people jostling in and out of the subway. All at once she slips away from the counter and back into the stuffy kitchenette where a stout elderly woman is tidying up the stove. There is a mirror hanging on a nail in the corner. Anna fetches a powderbox from the pocket of her coat on the rack and starts powdering her nose. She stands a second with the tiny puff poised looking at her broad face with the bangs across the forehead and the straight black bobbed hair. A homely lookin kike, she says to herself bitterly. She is slipping back to her place at the counter when she runs into the manager, a little fat Italian with a greasy bald head. "Cant you do nutten but primp an look in de glass all day? . . . Veree good you're fired."

She stares at his face sleek like an olive. "Kin I stay out my day?" she stammers. He nods. "Getta move on; this aint no beauty parlor." She hustles back to her place at the counter. The stools are all full. Girls, officeboys, grayfaced bookkeepers. "Chicken sandwich and a cup o caufee." "Cream cheese and olive sandwich and a glass of buttermilk."

"Chocolate sundae."

"Egg sandwich, coffee and doughnuts." "Cup of boullion." "Chicken broth." "Chocolate icecream soda." People eat hurriedly without looking at each other, with their eyes on their plates, in their cups. Behind the people sitting on stools those waiting nudge nearer. Some eat standing up. Some turn their backs on the counter and eat looking out through the glass partition and the sign hcnuL eniL neerG at the jostling crowds filing in and out the subway through the drabgreen gloom.

"Well Joey tell me all about it," said Gus McNiel puffing a great cloud of smoke out of his cigar and leaning back in his swivel chair. "What are you guys up to over there in Flatbush?"

O'Keefe cleared his throat and shuffled his feet. "Well sir we got an agitation committee."

"I should say you had. . . . That aint no reason for raidin the Garment Workers' ball is it?"

"I didn't have nothin to do with that. . . . The bunch got sore at all these pacifists and reds."

"That stuff was all right a year ago, but public sentiment's changin. I tell you Joe the people of this country are pretty well fed up with war heroes."

"We got a livewire organization over there."

"I know you have Joe. I know you have. Trust you for that. . . . I'd put the soft pedal on the bonus stuff

though. . . . The State of New York's done its duty by the
ex-service man."

"That's true enough."

"A national bonus means taxes to the average business
man and nothing else. . . . Nobody wants no more taxes."

"Still I think the boys have got it comin to em."

"We've all of us got a whole lot comin to us we dont
never get. . . . For crissake dont quote me on this.
. . . Joey fetch yourself a cigar from that box over there.
Frien o mine sent em up from Havana by a naval officer."

"Thankye sir."

"Go ahead take four or five."

"Jez thank you."

"Say Joey how'll you boys line up on the mayoralty
election?"

"That depends on the general attitude towards the needs
of the ex-service man."

"Look here Joey you're a smart feller . . ."

"Oh they'll line up all right. I kin talk em around."

"How many guys have you got over there?"

"The Sheamus O'Rielly Post's got three hundred members
an new ones signin up every day. . . . We're gettin em
from all over. We're goin to have a Christmas dance an
some fights in the Armory if we can get hold of any pugs."

Gus McNiel threw back his head on his bullneck and
laughed. "Thataboy!"

"But honest the bonus is the only way we kin keep the
boys together."

"Suppose I come over and talk to em some night."

"That'd be all right, but they're dead sot against anybody
who aint got a war record."

McNiel flushed. "Come back feeling kinder smart, dont
ye, you guys from overseas?" He laughed. "That wont
last more'n a year or two. . . . I seen em come back from
the Spanish American War, remember that Joe."

An officeboy came in an laid a card on the desk. "A
lady to see you Mr. McNiel."

"All right show her in. . . . It's that old bitch from the

school board. . . . All right Joe, drop in again next week.
. . . I'll keep you in mind, you and your army."

Dougan was waiting in the outer office. He sidled up
mysteriously. "Well Joe, how's things?"

"Pretty good," said Joe puffing out his chest. "Gus tells
me Tammany'll be right behind us in our drive for the
bonus . . . planning a nation wide campaign. He gave me
some cigars a friend o his brought up by airplane from
Havana. . . . Have one?" With their cigars tilting up out
of the corners of their mouths they walked briskly cockily
across City Hall square. Opposite the old City Hall there
was a scaffolding. Joe pointed at it with his cigar. "That
there's the new statue of Civic Virtue the mayor's havin
set up."

The steam of cooking wrenched at his knotted stomach as
he passed Child's. Dawn was sifting fine gray dust over the
black ironcast city. Dutch Robertson despondently crossed
Union Square, remembering Francie's warm bed, the spicy
smell of her hair. He pushed his hands deep in his empty
pockets. Not a red, and Francie couldn't give him anything.
He walked east past the hotel on Fifteenth. A colored man
was sweeping off the steps. Dutch looked at him enviously;
he's got a job. Milkwagons jingled by. On Stuyvesant
Square a milkman brushed past him with a bottle in each
hand. Dutch stuck out his jaw and talked tough. "Give
us a swig o milk will yez?" The milkman was a frail
pinkfaced youngster. His blue eyes wilted. "Sure go round
behind the wagon, there's an open bottle under the seat.
Dont let nobody see you drink it." He drank it in deep
gulps, sweet and soothing to his parched throat. Jez I
ddin't need to talk rough like that. He waited until the
boy came back. "Thankye buddy, that was mighty white."

He walked into the chilly park and sat down on a bench.
There was hoarfrost on the asphalt. He picked up a torn

piece of pink evening newspaper. $500,000 HOLDUP. Bank
Messenger Robbed in Wall Street Rush Hour.

In the busiest part of the noon hour two men held up Adolphus
St. John, a bank messenger for the Guarantee Trust Company, and
snatched from his hands a satchel containing a half a million dollars
in bills . . .

Dutch felt his heart pounding as he read the column. He
was cold all over. He got to his feet and began thrashing
his arms about.

Congo stumped through the turnstile at the end of the L
line. Jimmy Herf followed him looking from one side to
the other. Outside it was dark, a blizzard wind whistled
about their ears. A single Ford sedan was waiting outside
the station.

"How you like, Meester 'Erf?"

"Fine Congo. Is that water?"

"That Sheepshead Bay."

They walked along the road, dodging an occasional bluesteel glint of a puddle. The arclights had a look of shrunken
grapes swaying in the wind. To the right and left were
flickering patches of houses in the distance. They stopped
at a long building propped on piles over the water. POOL;
Jimmy barely made out the letters on an unlighted window.
The door opened as they reached it. "Hello Mike," said
Congo. "This is Meester 'Erf, a frien' o mine." The door
closed behind them. Inside it was black as an oven. A
calloused hand grabbed Jimmy's hand in the dark.

"Glad to meet you," said a voice.

"Say how did you find my hand?"

"Oh I kin see in the dark." The voice laughed throatily.

By that time Congo had opened the inner door. Light
streamed through picking out billiard tables, a long bar at
the end, racks of cues. "This is Mike Cardinale," said

Congo. Jimmy found himself standing beside a tall sallow shylooking man with bunchy black hair growing low on his forehead. In the inner room were shelves full of chinaware and a round table covered by a piece of mustardcolored oilcloth. "Eh la patronne," shouted Congo. A fat Frenchwoman with red applecheeks came out through the further door; behind her came a *chiff* of sizzling butter and garlic. "This is frien o mine. . . . Now maybe we eat," shouted Congo. "She my wife," said Cardinale proudly. "Very deaf. . . . Have to talk loud." He turned and closed the door to the large hall carefully and bolted it. "No see lights from road," he said. "In summer," said Mrs. Cardinale, "sometime we give a hundred meals a day, or a hundred an fifty maybe."

"Havent you got a little peekmeup?" said Congo. He let himself down with a grunt into a chair.

Cardinale set a fat fiasco of wine on the table and some glasses. They tasted it smacking their lips. "Bettern Dago Red, eh Meester 'Erf?"

"It sure is. Tastes like real Chianti."

Mrs. Cardinale set six plates with a stained fork, knife, and spoon in each and then put a steaming tureen of soup in the middle of the table.

"Pronto pasta," she shrieked in a guineahen voice. "Thisa Anetta," said Cardinale as a pinkcheeked blackhaired girl with long lashes curving back from bright black eyes ran into the room followed by a heavily tanned young man in khaki overalls with curly sunbleached hair. They all sat down at once and began to eat the peppery thick vegetable chowder, leaning far over their plates.

When Congo had finished his soup he looked up. "Mike did you see lights?" Cardinale nodded. "Sure ting . . . be here any time." While they were eating a dish of fried eggs and garlic, frizzled veal cutlets with fried potatoes and broccoli, Herf began to hear in the distance the pop pop pop of a motorboat. Congo got up from the table with a motion to them to be quiet and looked out the window, cautiously lifting a corner of the shade. "That him," he said as he stumped back to the table. "We eat good here, eh Meester Erf?"

The young man got to his feet wiping his mouth on his forearm. "Got a nickel Congo," he said doing a double shuffle with his sneakered feet. "Here go Johnny." The girl followed him out into the dark outer room. In a moment a mechanical piano started tinkling out a waltz. Through the door Jimmy could see them dancing in and out of the oblong of light. The chugging of the motorboat drew nearer. Congo went out, then Cardinale and his wife, until Jimmy was left alone sipping a glass of wine among the debris of the dinner. He felt excited and puzzled and a little drunk. Already he began to construct the story in his mind. From the road came the grind of gears of a truck, then of another. The motorboat engine choked, backfired and stopped. There was the creak of a boat against the piles, a swash of waves and silence. The mechanical piano had stopped. Jimmy sat sipping his wine. He could smell the rankness of salt marshes seeping into the house. Under him there was a little lapping sound of the water against the piles. Another motorboat was beginning to sputter in the far distance.

"Got a nickel?" asked Congo breaking into the room suddenly. "Make music. . . . Very funny night tonight. Maybe you and Annette keep piano goin. I didnt see McGee about landin. . . . Maybe somebody come. Must be veree quick." Jimmy got to his feet and started fishing in his pockets. By the piano he found Annette. "Wont you dance?" She nodded. The piano played *Innocent Eyes*. They danced distractedly. Outside were voices and footsteps. "Please," she said all at once and they stopped dancing. The second motorboat had come very near; the motor coughed and rattled still. "Please stay here," she said and slipped away from him.

Jimmy Herf walked up and down uneasily puffing on a cigarette. He was making up the story in his mind. . . . In a lonely abandoned dancehall on Sheepshead Bay . . . lovely blooming Italian girl . . . shrill whistle in the dark

. . . I ought to get out and see what's going on. He groped for the front door. It was locked. He walked over to the piano and put another nickel in. Then he lit a fresh cigarette and started walking up and down again. Always the way . . . a parasite on the drama of life, reporter looks at everything through a peephole. Never mixes in. The piano was playing *Yes We Have No Bananas.* "Oh hell!" he kept muttering and ground his teeth and walked up and down.

Outside the tramp of steps broke into a scuffle, voices snarled. There was a splintering of wood and the crash of breaking bottles. Jimmy looked out through the window of the diningroom. He could see the shadows of men struggling and slugging on the boatlanding. He rushed into the kitchen, where he bumped into Congo sweaty and staggering into the house leaning on a heavy cane.

"Goddam . . . dey break my leg," he shouted.

"Good God." Jimmy helped him groaning into the diningroom.

"Cost me feefty dollars to have it mended last time I busted it."

"You mean your cork leg?"

"Sure what you tink?"

"Is it prohibition agents?"

"Prohibition agents nutten, goddam hijackers. . . . Go put a neeckel in the piano." *Beautiful Girl of My Dreams,* the piano responded gayly.

When Jimmy got back to him, Congo was sitting in a chair nursing his stump with his two hands. On the table lay the cork and aluminum limb splintered and dented. "Regardez moi ça . . . c'est foutu . . . completement foutu." As he spoke Cardinale came in. He had a deep gash over his eyes from which a trickle of blood ran down his cheek on his coat and shirt. His wife followed him rolling back her eyes; she had a basin and a sponge with which she kept making ineffectual dabs at his forehead. He pushed her away. "I crowned one of em good wid a piece o pipe. I think he fell in de water. God I hope he drownded." Johnny came in holding his head high. Annette had her arm round his waist. He had a black eye and one of the sleeves of his shirt hung in shreds. "Gee it was like in the movies," said Annette, giggling hysterically. "Wasnt he grand, mommer, wasn't he grand?"

"Jez it's lucky they didn't start shootin; one of em had a gun."

"Scared to I guess."

"Trucks are off."

"Just one case got busted up. . . . God there was five of them."

"Gee didnt he mix it up with em?" screamed Annette.

"Oh shut up," growled Cardinale. He had dropped into a chair and his wife was sponging off his face. "Did you get a good look at the boat?" asked Congo.

"Too goddam dark," said Johnny. "Fellers talked like they came from Joisey. . . . First ting I knowed one of em comes up to me and sez I'm a revenue officer an I pokes him one before he has time to pull a gun an overboard he goes. Jez they were yeller. That guy George on the boat near brained one of em wid an oar. Then they got back in their old teakettle an beat it."

"But how they know how we make landin?" stuttered Congo his face purple.

"Some guy blabbed maybe," said Cardinale. "If I find out who it is, by God I'll . . ." he made a popping noise with his lips.

"You see Meester 'Erf," said Congo in his suave voice again, "it was all champagne for the holidays. . . . Very valuable cargo eh?" Annette, her cheeks very red sat still looking at Johnny with parted lips and toobright eyes. Herf found himself blushing as he looked at her.

He got to his feet. "Well I must be getting back to the big city. Thank's for the feed and the melodrama, Congo."

"You find station all right?"

"Sure."

"Goodnight Meester 'Erf, maybe you buy case of champagne for Christmas, genuine Mumms."

"Too darn broke Congo."

"Then maybe you sell to your friends an I give you commission."

"All right I'll see what I can do."

"I'll phone you tomorrow to tell price."

"That's a fine idea. Good night."

Joggling home in the empty train through empty Brooklyn suburbs Jimmy tried to think of the bootlegging story he'd write for the Sunday Magazine Section. The girl's pink cheeks and toobright eyes kept intervening, blurring the orderly arrangement of his thoughts. He sank gradually into dreamier and dreamier reverie. Before the kid was born Ellie sometimes had toobright eyes like that. The time on the hill when she had suddenly wilted in his arms and been sick and he had left her among the munching, calmly staring cows on the grassy slope and gone to a shepherd's hut and brought back milk in a wooden ladle, and slowly as the mountains hunched up with evening the color had come back into her cheeks and she had looked at him that way and said with a dry little laugh: It's the little Herf inside me. God why cant I stop mooning over things that are past? And when the baby was coming and Ellie was in the American Hospital at Neuilly, ˙himself wandering distractedly through the fair, going into the Flea Circus, riding on merrygorounds and the steam swing, buying toys, candy, taking chances on dolls in a crazy blur, stumbling back to the hospital with a big plaster pig under his arm. Funny these fits of refuge in the past. Suppose she had died; I thought she would. The past would have been complete all round, framed, worn round your neck like a cameo, set up in type, molded on plates for the Magazine Section, like the first of James Herf's articles on The Bootlegging Ring. Burning slugs of thought kept dropping into place spelled out by a clanking linotype.

At midnight he was walking across Fourteenth. He didnt want to go home to bed although the rasping cold wind tore at his neck and chin with sharp ice claws. He walked west across Seventh and Eighth Avenues, found the name

Roy Sheffield beside a bell in a dimly lit hall. As soon as he pressed the bell the catch on the door began to click. He ran up the stairs. Roy had his big curly head with its glass-gray gollywog eyes stuck out the door.

"Hello Jimmy; come on in; we're all lit up like churches."

"I've just seen a fight between bootleggers and hijackers."

"Where?"

"Down at Sheepshead Bay."

"Here's Jimmy Herf, he's just been fighting prohibition agents," shouted Roy to his wife. Alice had dark chestnut dollhair and an uptilted peaches and cream dollface. She ran up to Jimmy and kissed him on the chin. "Oh Jimmy do tell us all about it. . . . We're so horribly bored."

"Hello," cried Jimmy; he had just made out Frances and Bob Hildebrand on the couch at the dim end of the room. They lifted their glasses to him. Jimmy was pushed into an armchair, had a glass of gin and ginger ale put in his hand. "Now what's all this about a fight? You'd better tell us because were certainly not going to buy the Sunday *Tribune* to find out," Bob Hildebrand said in a deep rumbling voice.

Jimmy took a long drink. "I went out with a man I know who's shiek of all the French and Italian bootleggers. He's a fine man. He's got a cork leg. He set me up to a swell feed and real Italian wine out in a deserted poolroom on the shores of Sheepshead Bay. . . ."

"By the way," asked Roy, "where's Helena."

"Dont interrupt Roy," said Alice. "This is good . . . and besides you should never ask a man where his wife is."

"Then there was a lot of flashing of signal lights and stuff and a motorboat loaded down with Mumm's extra dry champagne for Park Avenue Christmases came in and the hijackers arrived on a speedboat. . . . It probably was a hydroplane it came so fast . . ."

"My this is exciting," cooed Alice. ". . . Roy why dont you take up bootlegging?"

"Worst fight I ever saw outside of the movies, six or seven on a side all slugging each other on a little narrow landing the size of this room, people crowning each other with oars and joints of lead pipe."

"Was anybody hurt?"

"Everybody was. . . . I think two of the hijackers were drowned. At any rate they beat a retreat leaving us lapping up the spilled champagne."

"But it must have been terrible," cried the Hildebrands. "What did you do Jimmy?" asked Alice breathless.

"Oh I hopped around keeping out of harm's way. I didnt know who was on which side and it was dark and wet and confusing everywhere. . . . I finally did drag my bootlegger friend out of the fray when he got his leg broken . . . his wooden leg."

Everybody let out a shout. Roy filled Jimmy's glass up with gin again.

"Oh Jimmy," cooed Alice, "you lead the most thrilling life."

James Merivale was going over a freshly decoded cable, tapping the words with a pencil as he read them. Tasmanian Manganese Products instructs us to open credit. . . . The phone on his desk began to buzz.

"James this is your mother. Come right up; something terrible has happened."

"But I dont know if I can get away. . . ."

She had already cut off. Merivale felt himself turning pale. "Let me speak to Mr. Aspinwall please. . . . Mr. Aspinwall this is Merivale. . . . My mother's been taken suddenly ill. I'm afraid it may be a stroke. I'd like to run up there for an hour. I'll be back in time to get a cable off on that Tasmanian matter."

"All right. . . . I'm very sorry Merivale."

He grabbed his hat and coat, forgetting his muffler, and streaked out of the bank and along the street to the subway.

He burst into the apartment breathless, snapping his fingers from nervousness. Mrs. Merivale grayfaced met him in the hall.

"My dear I thought you'd been taken ill."

"It's not that . . . it's about Maisie."

"She hasnt met with an accid. . . ?"

"Come in here," interrupted Mrs. Merivale. In the parlor sat a little roundfaced woman in a round mink hat and a long mink coat. "My dear this girl says she's Mrs. Jack Cunningham and she's got a marriage certificate to prove it."

"Good Heavens, is that true?"

The girl nodded in a melancholy way.

"And the invitations are out. Since his last wire Maisie's been ordering her trousseau."

The girl unfolded a large certificate ornamented with pansies and cupids and handed it to James.

"It might be forged."

"It's not forged," said the girl sweetly.

"John C. Cunningham, 21 . . . Jessie Lincoln, 18," he read aloud. . . . "I'll smash his face for that, the blackguard. That's certainly his signature, I've seen it at the bank. . . . The blackguard."

"Now James, don't be hasty."

"I thought it would be better this way than after the ceremony," put in the girl in her little sugar voice. "I wouldnt have Jack commit bigamy for anything in the world."

"Where's Maisie?"

"The poor darling is prostrated in her room."

Merivale's face was crimson. The sweat itched under his collar. "Now dearest" Mrs. Merivale kept saying, "you must promise me not to do anything rash."

"Yes Maisie's reputation must be protected at all costs."

"My dear I think the best thing to do is to get him up here and confront him with this . . . with this . . . lady. . . . Would you agree to that Mrs. Cunningham?"

"Oh dear. . . . Yes I suppose so."

"Wait a minute," shouted Merivale and strode down the

hall to the telephone. "Rector 12305. . . . Hello. I want to speak to Mr. Jack Cunningham please. . . . Hello. Is this Mr. Cunningham's office? Mr. James Merivale speaking. . . . Out of town. . . . And when will he be back? . . . Hum." He strode back along the hall. "The damn scoundrel's out of town."

"All the years I've known him," said the little lady in the round hat, "that has always been where he was."

Outside the broad office windows the night is gray and foggy. Here and there a few lights make up dim horizontals and perpendiculars of asterisks. Phineas Blackhead sits at his desk tipping far back in the small leather armchair. In his hand protecting his fingers by a large silk handkerchief, he holds a glass of hot water and bicarbonate of soda. Densch bald and round as a billiardball sits in the deep armchair playing with his tortoiseshell spectacles. Everything is quiet except for an occasional rattling and snapping of the steampipes.

"Densch you must forgive me. . . . You know I rarely permit myself an observation concerning other people's business," Blackhead is saying slowly between sips; then suddenly he sits up in his chair. "It's a damn fool proposition, Densch, by God it is . . . by the Living Jingo it's ridiculous."

"I dont like dirtying my hands any more than you do. . . . Baldwin's a good fellow. I think we're safe in backing him a little."

"What the hell's an import and export firm got to do in politics? If any of those guys wants a handout let him come up here and get it. Our business is the price of beans . . . and its goddam low. If any of you puling lawyers could restore the balance of the exchanges I'd be willing to do anything in the world. . . . They're crooks every last goddam one of em . . . by the Living Jingo they're crooks."

His face flushes purple, he sits upright in his chair banging with his fist on the corner of the desk. "Now you're getting me all excited. . . . Bad for my stomach, bad for my heart." Phineas Blackhead belches portentously and takes a great gulp out of the glass of bicarbonate of soda. Then he leans back in his chair again letting his heavy lids half cover his eyes.

"Well old man," says Mr. Densch in a tired voice, "it may have been a bad thing to do, but I've promised to support the reform candidate. That's a purely private matter in no way involving the firm."

"Like hell it dont. . . . How about McNiel and his gang? . . . They've always treated us all right and all we've ever done for em's a couple of cases of Scotch and a few cigars now and then. . . . Now we have these reformers throw the whole city government into a turmoil. . . . By the Living Jingo . . ."

Densch gets to his feet. "My dear Blackhead I consider it my duty as a citizen to help in cleaning up the filthy conditions of bribery, corruption and intrigue that exist in the city government . . . I consider it my duty as a citizen . . ." He starts walking to the door, his round belly stuck proudly out in front of him.

"Well allow me to say Densch that I think its a damn fool proposition," Blackhead shouts after him. When his partner has gone he lies back a second with his eyes closed. His face takes on the mottled color of ashes, his big fleshy frame is shrinking like a deflating balloon. At length he gets to his feet with a groan. Then he takes his hat and coat and walks out of the office with a slow heavy step. The hall is empty and dimly lit. He has to wait a long while for the elevator. The thought of holdup men sneaking through the empty building suddenly makes him catch his breath. He is afraid to look behind him, like a child in the dark. At last the elevator shoots up.

"Wilmer," he says to the night watchman who runs it, "there ought to be more light in these halls at night. . . .

During this crime wave I should think you ought to keep the building brightly lit."

"Yassir maybe you're right sir . . . but there cant nobody get in unless I sees em first."

"You might be overpowered by a gang Wilmer."

"I'd like to see em try it."

"I guess you are right . . . mere question of nerve."

Cynthia is sitting in the Packard reading a book. "Well dear did you think I was never coming."

"I almost finished my book, dad."

"All right Butler . . . up town as fast as you can. We're late for dinner."

As the limousine whirs up Lafayette Street, Blackhead turns to his daughter. "If you ever hear a man talking about his duty as a citizen, by the Living Jingo dont trust him. . . . He's up to some kind of monkey business nine times out of ten. You dont know what a relief it is to me that you and Joe are comfortably settled in life."

"What's the matter dad? Did you have a hard day at the office?" "There are no markets, there isnt a market in the goddam world that isnt shot to blazes. . . . I tell you Cynthia it's nip and tuck. There's no telling what might happen. . . . Look, before I forget it could you be at the bank uptown at twelve tomorrow? . . . I'm sending Hudgins up with certain securities, personal you understand, I want to put in your safe deposit box."

"But it's jammed full already dad."

"That box at the Astor Trust is in your name isnt it?"

"Jointly in mine and Joe's."

"Well you take a new box at the Fifth Avenue Bank in your own name. . . . I'll have the stuff get there at noon sharp. . . . And remember what I tell you Cynthia, if you ever hear a business associate talking about civic virtue, look lively."

They are crossing Fourteenth. Father and daughter look out through the glass at the windbitten faces of people waiting to cross the street.

Jimmy Herf yawned and scraped back his chair. The nickel glints of the typewriter hurt his eyes. The tips of his fingers were sore. He pushed open the sliding doors a little and peeped into the cold bedroom. He could barely make out Ellie asleep in the bed in the alcove. At the far end of the room was the baby's crib. There was a faint milkish sour smell of babyclothes. He pushed the doors to again and began to undress. If we only had more space, he was muttering; we live cramped in our squirrelcage. . . . He pulled the dusty cashmere off the couch and yanked his pyjamas out from under the pillow. Space space cleanness quiet; the words were gesticulating in his mind as if he were addressing a vast auditorium.

He turned out the light, opened a crack of the window and dropped wooden with sleep into bed. Immediately he was writing a letter on a linotype. Now I lay me down to sleep . . . mother of the great white twilight. The arm of the linotype was a woman's hand in a long white glove. Through the clanking from behind amber foots Ellie's voice Dont, dont, dont, you're hurting me so. . . . Mr. Herf, says a man in overalls, you're hurting the machine and we wont be able to get out the bullgod edition thank dog. The linotype was a gulping mouth with nickelbright rows of teeth, gulped, crunched. He woke up sitting up in bed. He was cold, his teeth were chattering. He pulled the covers about him and settled to sleep again. The next time he woke up it was daylight. He was warm and happy. Snowflakes were dancing, hesitating, spinning, outside the tall window.

"Hello Jimps," said Ellie coming towards him with a tray.

"Why have I died and gone to heaven or something?"

"No it's Sunday morning. . . . I thought you needed a little luxury. . . . I made some corn muffins."

"Oh you're marvelous Ellie. . . . Wait a minute I must jump up and wash my teeth." He came back with his face washed, wearing his bathrobe. Her mouth winced under his kiss. "And it's only eleven o'clock. I've gained an hour on my day off. . . . Wont you have some coffee too?"

"In a minute. . . . Look here Jimps I've got something I want to talk about. Look dont you think we ought to get another place now that you're working nights again all the time?"

"You mean move?"

"No. I was thinking if you could get another room to sleep in somewhere round, then nobody'd ever disturb you in the morning."

"But Ellie we'd never see each other. . . . We hardly ever see each other as it is."

"It's terrible . . . but what can we do when our office-hours are so different?"

Martin's crying came in a gust from the other room. Jimmy sat on the edge of the bed with the empty coffeecup on his knees looking at his bare feet. "Just as you like," he said dully. An impulse to grab her hands to crush her to him until he hurt her went up through him like a rocket and died. She picked up the coffeethings and swished away. His lips knew her lips, his arms knew the twining of her arms, he knew the deep woods of her hair, he loved her. He sat for a long time looking at his feet, lanky reddish feet with swollen blue veins, shoebound toes twisted by stairs and pavements. On each little toe there was a corn. He found his eyes filling with pitying tears. The baby had stopped crying. Jimmy went into the bathroom and started the water running in the tub.

"It was that other feller you had Anna. He got you to thinkin you didnt give a damn. . . . He made you a fatalist."

"What's at?"

"Somebody who thinks there's no use strugglin, somebody who dont believe in human progress."

"Do you think Bouy was like that?"

"He was a scab anyway . . . None o these Southerners

are classconscious. . . . Didn't he make you stop payin your union dues?"

"I was sick o workin a sewin machine."

"But you could be a handworker, do fancy work and make good money. You're not one o that kind, you're one of us. . . . I'll get you back in good standin an you kin get a good job again. . . . God I'd never have let you work in a dancehall the way he did. Anna it hurt me terrible to see a Jewish girl goin round with a feller like that."

"Well he's gone an I aint got no job."

"Fellers like that are the greatest enemies of the workers. . . . They dont think of nobody but themselves."

They are walking slowly up Second Avenue through a foggy evening. He is a rustyhaired thinfaced young Jew with sunken cheeks and livid pale skin. He has the bandy legs of a garment worker. Anna's shoes are too small for her. She has deep rings under her eyes. The fog is full of strolling groups talking Yiddish, overaccented East Side English, Russian. Warm rifts of light from delicatessen stores and softdrink stands mark off the glistening pavement.

"If I didn't feel so tired all the time," mutters Anna.

"Let's stop here an have a drink. . . . You take a glass o buttermilk Anna, make ye feel good."

"I aint got the taste for it Elmer. I'll take a chocolate soda."

"That'll juss make ye feel sick, but go ahead if you wanter." She sat on the slender nickelbound stool. He stood beside her. She let herself lean back a little against him. "The trouble with the workers is" . . . He was talking in a low impersonal voice. "The trouble with the workers is we dont know nothin, we dont know how to eat, we dont know how to live, we dont know how to protect our rights. . . . Jez Anna I want to make you think of things like that. Cant you see we're in the middle of a battle just like in the war?" With the long sticky spoon Anna was fishing bits of icecream out of the thick foamy liquid in her glass.

George Baldwin looked at himself in the mirror as he washed his hands in the little washroom behind his office. His hair that still grew densely down to a point on his forehead was almost white. There was a deep line at each corner of his mouth and across his chin. Under his bright gimleteyes the skin was sagging and granulated. When he had wiped his hands slowly and meticulously he took a little box of strychnine pills from the upper pocket of his vest, swallowed one, and feeling the anticipated stimulus tingle through him went back into his office. A longnecked officeboy was fidgeting beside his desk with a card in his hand.

"A lady wants to speak to you sir."

"Has she an appointment? Ask Miss Ranke. . . . Wait a minute. Show the lady right through into this office." The card read Nellie Linihan McNiel. She was expensively dressed with a lot of lace in the opening of her big fur coat. Round her neck she had a lorgnette on an amethyst chain.

"Gus asked me to come to see you," she said as he motioned her into a chair beside the desk.

"What can I do for you?" His heart for some reason was pounding hard.

She looked at him a moment through her lorgnette. "George you stand it better than Gus does."

"What?"

"Oh all this. . . . I'm trying to get Gus to go away with me for a rest abroad . . . Marianbad or something like that . . . but he says he's in too deep to pull up his stakes."

"I guess that's true of all of us," said Baldwin with a cold smile.

They were silent a minute, then Nellie McNiel got to her feet. "Look here George, Gus is awfully cut up about this. . . . You know he likes to stand by his friends and have his friends stand by him."

"Nobody can say that I havent stood by him. . . . It's simply this, I'm not a politician, and as, probably foolishly, I've allowed myself to be nominated for office, I have to run on a nonpartisan basis."

"George that's only half the story and you know it."

"Tell him that I've always been and always shall be a good friend of his. . . . He knows that perfectly well. In this particular campaign I have pledged myself to oppose certain elements with which Gus has let himself get involved."

"You're a fine talker George Baldwin and you always were."

Baldwin flushed. They stood stiff side by side at the office door. His hand lay still on the doorknob as if paralyzed. From the outer offices came the sound of typewriters and voices. From outside came the long continuous tapping of riveters at work on a new building.

"I hope your family's all well," he said at length with an effort.

"Oh yes they are all well thanks . . . Goodby." She had gone.

Baldwin stood for a moment looking out of the window at the gray blackwindowed building opposite. Silly to let things agitate him so. Need of relaxation. He got his hat and coat from their hook behind the washroom door and went out. "Jonas," he said to a man with a round bald head shaped like a cantaloupe who sat poring over papers in the high-ceilinged library that was the central hall of the lawoffice, "bring everything up that's on my desk. . . . I'll go over it uptown tonight."

"All right sir."

When he got out on Broadway he felt like a small boy playing hooky. It was a sparkling winter afternoon with hurrying rifts of sun and cloud. He jumped into a taxi. Going uptown he lay back in the seat dozing. At Forty-second Street he woke up. Everything was a confusion of bright intersecting planes of color, faces, legs, shop windows, trolleycars, automobiles. He sat up with his gloved hands on his knees, fizzling with excitement. Outside of Nevada's apartmenthouse he paid the taxi. The driver was a negro and showed an ivory mouthful of teeth when he got a fifty-cent tip. Neither elevator was there so Baldwin ran lightly up the stairs, half wondering at himself.

He knocked on Nevada's door. No answer. He
knocked again. She opened it cautiously. He could see
her curly towhead. He brushed into the room before she
could stop him. All she had on was a kimono over a pink
chemise.

"My God," she said, "I thought you were the waiter."

He grabbed her and kissed her. "I dont know why but
I feel like a threeyear old."

"You look like you was crazy with the heat. . . . I dont
like you to come over without telephoning, you know that."

"You dont mind just this once I forgot."

Baldwin caught sight of something on the settee; he
found himself staring at a pair of darkblue trousers neatly
folded.

"I was feeling awfully fagged down at the office
Nevada. I thought I'd come up to talk to you to cheer myself up a bit."

"I was just practicing some dancing with the phonograph."

"Yes very interesting. . . ." He began to walk springily up and down. "Now look here Nevada. . . . We've got
to have a talk. I dont care who it is you've got in your bedroom." She looked suddenly in his face and sat down on
the settee beside the trousers. "In fact I've known for some
time that you and Tony Hunter were carrying on." She
compressed her lips and crossed her legs. "In fact all this
stuff and nonsense about his having to go to a psychoanalyst
at twentyfive dollars an hour amused me enormously. . . .
But just this minute I've decided I had enough. Quite
enough."

"George you're crazy," she stammered and then suddenly
she began to giggle.

"I tell you what I'll do," went on Baldwin in a clear legal
voice, "I'll send you a check for five hundred, because
you're a nice girl and I like you. The apartment's paid till
the first of the month. Does that suit you? And please
never communicate with me in any way."

She was rolling on the settee giggling helplessly beside
the neatly folded pair of darkblue trousers. Baldwin waved

his hat and gloves at her and left closing the door very gently
behind him. Good riddance, he said to himself as he closed
the door carefully behind him.

Down in the street again he began to walk briskly uptown.
He felt excited and talkative. He wondered who he could
go to see. Telling over the names of his friends made him
depressed. He began to feel lonely, deserted. He wanted
to be talking to a woman, making her sorry for the barren-
ness of his life. He went into a cigarstore and began looking through the phonebook. There was a faint flutter in
him when he found the H's. At last he found the name
Herf, Helena Oglethorpe.

Nevada Jones sat a long while on the settee giggling
hysterically. At length Tony Hunter came in in his shirt
and drawers with his bow necktie perfectly tied.

"Has he gone?"

"Gone? sure he's gone, gone for good," she shrieked. "He
saw your damn pants."

He let himself drop on a chair. "O God if I'm not the
unluckiest fellow in the world."

"Why?" she sat spluttering with laughter with the tears
running down her face.

"Nothing goes right. That means it's all off about the
matinees."

"It's back to three a day for little Nevada. . . . I dont
give a damn. . . . I never did like bein a kept woman."

"But you're not thinking of my career. . . . Women are
so selfish. If you hadn't led me on. . . . "

"Shut up you little fool. Dont you think I dont know all
about you?" She got to her feet with the kimono pulled
tight about her.

"God all I needed was a chance to show what I could do,
and now I'll never get it," Tony was groaning.

"Sure you will if you do what I tell you. I set out to
make a man of you kiddo and I'm goin to do it. . . . We'll
get up an act. Old Hirshbein'll give us a chance, he used
to be kinder smitten. . . . Come on now, I'll punch you in
the jaw if you dont. Let's start thinkin up. . . . We'll come

in with a dance number see . . . then you'll pretend to want to pick me up. . . . I'll be waitin for a streetcar . . . see . . . and you'll say Hello Girlie an I'll call Officer."

"Is that all right for length sir," asked the fitter busily making marks on the trousers with a piece of chalk.

James Merivale looked down at the fitter's little greenish wizened bald head and at the brown trousers flowing amply about his feet. "A little shorter. . . . I think it looks a little old to have trousers too long."

"Why hello Merivale I didn't know you bought your clothes at Brooks' too. Gee I'm glad to see you."

Merivale's blood stood still. He found himself looking straight in the blue alcoholic eyes of Jack Cunningham. He bit his lip and tried to stare at him coldly without speaking.

"God Almighty, do you know what we've done?" cried out Cunningham. "We've bought the same suit of clothes. . . . I tell you it's identically the same."

Merivale was looking in bewilderment from Cunningham's brown trousers to his own, the same color, the same tiny stripe of red and faint mottling of green.

"Good God man two future brothersinlaw cant wear the same suit. People'll think it's a uniform. . . . It's ridiculous."

"Well what are we going to do about it?" Merivale found himself saying in a grumbling tone.

"We have to toss up and see who gets it that's all. . . . Will you lend me a quarter please?" Cunningham turned to his salesman. "All right. . . . One toss, you yell."

"Heads," said Merivale mechanically.

"The brown suit is yours. . . . Now I've got to choose another . . . God I'm glad we met when we did. Look," he shouted out through the curtains of the booth, "why dont you have dinner with me tonight at the Salmagundi Club? . . . I'm going to be dining with the only man in the world who's crazier about hydroplanes than I am. . . . It's old man Perkins, you know him, he's one of the vicepresidents of your bank. . . . And look when you see Maisie tell her I'm coming up to see her tomorrow. An extraordinary series of events has kept me from communicating with her . . . a most unfortunate series of events that took all my time up to this moment. . . . We'll talk about it later."

Merivale cleared his throat. "Very well," he said dryly.

"All right sir," said the fitter giving Merivale a last tap on the buttocks. He went back into the booth to dress.

"All right old thing," shouted Cunningham, "I've got to go pick out another suit . . . I'll expect you at seven. I'll have a Jack Rose waiting for you."

Merivale's hands were trembling as he fastened his belt. Perkins, Jack Cunningham, the damn blackguard, hydroplanes, Jack Cunningham Salmagundi Perkins. He went to a phone booth in a corner of the store and called up his mother. "Hello Mother, I'm afraid I wont be up to dinner. . . . I'm dining with Randolph Perkins at the Salmagundi Club. . . . Yes it is very pleasant. . . . Oh well he and I have always been fairly good friends. . . . Oh yes it's essential to stand in with the men higher up. And I've seen Jack Cunningham. I put it up to him straight from the shoulder man to man and he was very much embarrassed. He promised a full explanation within twentyfour hours. . . . No I kept my temper very well. I felt I owed it to Maisie. I tell you I think the man's a blackguard but until there's proof. . . . Well good night dear, in case I'm late. Oh no please dont wait up. Tell Maisie not to worry I'll be able to give her the fullest details. Good night mother."

They sat at a small table in the back of a dimly lighted tearoom. The shade on the lamp cut off the upper parts of their faces. Ellen had on a dress of bright peacock blue and a small blue hat with a piece of green in it. Ruth Prynne's face had a sagging tired look under the street makeup.

"Elaine, you've just got to come," she was saying in a

whiny voice. "Cassie'll be there and Oglethorpe and all the old gang. . . . After all now that you're making such a success of editorial work it's no reason for completely abandoning your old friends is it? You dont know how much we talk and wonder about you."

"No but Ruth it's just that I'm getting to hate large parties. I guess I must be getting old. All right I'll come for a little while."

Ruth put down the sandwich she was nibbling at and reached for Ellen's hand and patted it. "That's the little trouper. . . . Of course I knew you were coming all along."

"But Ruth you never told me what happened to that traveling repertory company last summer. . . . "

"O my God," burst out Ruth. "That was terrible. Of course it was a scream, a perfect scream. Well the first thing that happened was that Isabel Clyde's husband Ralph Nolton who was managing the company was a dipsomaniac . . . and then the lovely Isabel wouldn't let anybody on the stage who didn't act like a dummy for fear the rubes wouldnt know who the star was. . . . Oh I cant tell about it any more. . . . It isnt funny to me any more, it's just horrible. . . . Oh Elaine I'm so discouraged. My dear I'm getting old." She suddenly burst out crying.

"Oh Ruth please dont," said Ellen in a little rasping voice. She laughed. "After all we're none of us getting any younger are we?"

"Dear you dont understand . . . You never will understand."

They sat a long while without saying anything, scraps of lowvoiced conversation came to them from other corners of the dim tearoom. The palehaired waitress brought them two orders of fruit salad.

"My it must be getting late," said Ruth eventually.

"It's only half past eight. . . . We dont want to get to this party too soon."

"By the way . . . how's Jimmy Herf. I havent seen him for ages."

"Jimps is fine. . . . He's terribly sick of newspaper work. I do wish he could get something he really enjoyed doing."

"He'll always be a restless sort of person. Oh Elaine I was so happy when I heard about your being married. . . . I acted like a damn fool. I cried and cried. . . . And now with Martin and everything you must be terribly happy."

"Oh we get along all right. . . . Martin's picking up, New York seems to agree with him. He was so quiet and fat for a long while we were terribly afraid we'd produced an imbecile. Do you know Ruth I don't think I'd ever have another baby. . . . I was so horribly afraid he'd turn out deformed or something. . . . It makes me sick to think of it."

"Oh but it must be wonderful though."

They rang a bell under a small brass placque that read: Hester Voorhees INTERPRETATION OF THE DANCE. They went up three flights of creaky freshvarnished stairs. At the door open into a room full of people they met Cassandra Wilkins in a Greek tunic with a wreath of satin rosebuds round her head and a gilt wooden panpipe in her hand.

"Oh you darlings," she cried and threw her arms round them both at once. "Hester said you wouldnt come but I just knew you would. . . . Come wight in and take off your things, we're beginning with a few classic wythms." They followed her through a long candlelit incensesmelling room full of men and women in dangly costumes.

"But my dear you didn't tell us it was going to be a costume party."

"Oh yes cant you see evewything's Gweek, absolutely Gweek, . . . Here's Hester. . . . Here they are darling. . . . Hester you know Wuth . . . and this is Elaine Oglethorpe."

"I call myself Mrs. Herf now, Cassie."

"Oh I beg your pardon, it's so hard to keep twack. . . . They're just in time. . . . Hester's going to dance an owiental dance called Wythms from the Awabian Nights. . . . Oh it's too beautiful."

When Ellen came out of the bedroom where she had left her

wraps a tall figure in Egyptian headdress with crooked rusty eyebrows accosted her. "Allow me to salute Helena Herf, distinguished editress of *Manners*, the journal that brings the Ritz to the humblest fireside . . . isnt that true?"

"Jojo you're a horrible tease. . . . I'm awfully glad to see you."

"Let's go and sit in a corner and talk, oh only woman I have ever loved. . ."

"Yes do let's . . . I dont like it here much."

"And my dear, have you heard about Tony Hunter's being straightened out by a psychoanalyst and now he's all sublimated and has gone on the vaudeville stage with a woman named California Jones."

"You'd better watch out Jojo."

They sat down on a couch in a recess between the dormer windows. Out of the corner of her eye she could see a girl dancing in green silk veils. The phonograph was playing the Cesar Frank symphony.

"We mustnt miss Cassie's daunce. The poor girl would be dreadfully offended."

"Jojo tell me about yourself, how have you been?"

He shook his head and made a broad gesture with his draped arm. "Ah let us sit upon the ground and tell sad stories of the deaths of kings."

"Oh Jojo I'm sick of this sort of thing. . . . It's all so silly and dowdy. . . . I wish I hadnt let them make me take my hat off."

"That was so that I should look upon the forbidden forests of your hair."

"Oh Jojo do be sensible."

"How's your husband, Elaine or rathah Helenah?"

"Oh he's all right."

"You dont sound terribly enthusiastic."

"Martin's fine though. He's got black hair and brown eyes and his cheeks are getting to be pink. Really he's awfully cute."

"My deah, spare me this exhibition of maternal bliss. . . . You'll be telling me next you walked in a baby parade."

She laughed. "Jojo it's lots of fun to see you again."

"I havent finished my catechism yet deah. . . . I saw you in the oval diningroom the other day with a very distinguished looking man with sharp features and gray hair."

"That must have been George Baldwin. Why you knew him in the old days."

"Of course of course. How he has changed. A much more interesting looking man than he used to be I must say. . . . A very strange place for the wife of a bolshevik pacifist and I. W. W. agitator to be seen taking lunch, I must say.

"Jimps isnt exactly that. I kind of wish he were. . . ." She wrinkled up her nose. "I'm a little fed up too with all that sort of thing."

"I suspected it my dear." Cassie was flitting selfconsciously by.

"Oh do come and help me. . . . Jojo's teasing me terribly."

"Well I'll twy to sit down just for a second, I'm going to dance next. . . . Mr. Oglethorpe's going to wead his twanslation of the songs of Bilitis for me to dance to."

Ellen looked from one to the other; Oglethorpe crooked his eyebrows and nodded.

Then Ellen sat alone for a long while looking at the dancing and the chittering crowded room through a dim haze of boredom.

The record on the phonograph was Turkish. Hester Voorhees, a skinny woman with a mop of hennaed hair cut short at the level of her ears, came out holding a pot of drawling incense out in front of her preceded by two young men who unrolled a carpet as she came. She wore silk bloomers and a clinking metal girdle and brassières. Everybody was clapping and saying, "How wonderful, how marvelous," when from another room came three tearing shrieks of a woman. Everybody jumped to his feet. A stout man in a derby hat appeared in the doorway. "All right little goils, right through into the back room. Men stay here."

"Who are you anyway?"

"Never mind who I am, you do as I say." The man's face was red as a beet under the derby hat.

"It's a detective." "It's outrageous. Let him show his badge."

"It's a holdup."

"It's a raid."

The room had filled suddenly with detectives. They stood in front of the windows. A man in a checked cap with a face knobbed like a squash stood in front of the fireplace. They were pushing the women roughly into the back room. The men were herded in a little group near the door; detectives were taking their names. Ellen still sat on the couch. " . . . complaint phoned to headquarters," she heard somebody say. Then she noticed that there was a phone on the little table beside the couch where she sat. She picked it up and whispered softly for a number.

"Hello is this the district attorney's office? . . . I want to speak to Mr. Baldwin please. . . . George. . . . It's lucky I knew where you were. Is the district attorney there? That's fine . . . no you tell him about it. There has been a horrible mistake. I'm at Hester Voorhees'; you know she has a dancing studio. She was presenting some dances to some friends and through some mistake the police are raiding the place . . ."

The man in the derby was standing over her. "All right phoning wont do no good. . . . Go 'long in the other room."

"I've got the district attorney's office on the wire. You speak to him. . . . Hello is this Mr. Winthrop? . . . Yes O . . . How do you do? Will you please speak to this man?" She handed the telephone to the detective and walked out into the center of the room. My I wish I hadnt taken my hat off, she was thinking.

From the other room came a sound of sobbing and Hester Voorhees' stagy voice shrieking, "It's a horrible mistake. . . . I wont be insulted like this."

The detective put down the telephone. He came over to Ellen. "I want to apologize miss. . . . We acted on insufficient information. I'll withdraw my men immediately."

"You'd better apologize to Mrs. Voorhees. . . . It's her studio."

"Well ladies and gents," the detective began in a loud cheerful voice, "we've made a little mistake and we're very sorry. . . . Accidents will happen . . ."

Ellen slipped into the side room to get her hat and coat. She stood some time before the mirror powdering her nose. When she went out into the studio again everybody was talking at once. Men and women stood round with sheets and bathrobes draped over their scanty dancingclothes. The detectives had melted away as suddenly as they came. Oglethorpe was talking in loud impassioned tones in the middle of a group of young men.

"The scoundrels to attack women," he was shouting, red in the face, waving his headdress in one hand. "Fortunately I was able to control myself or I might have committed an act that I should have regretted to my dying day. . . . It was only with the greatest selfcontrol. . ."

Ellen managed to slip out, ran down the stairs and out into drizzly streets. She hailed a taxi and went home. When she had got her things off she called up George Baldwin at his house. "Hello George, I'm terribly sorry I had to trouble you and Mr. Winthrop. Well if you hadnt happened to say at lunch you'd be there all the evening they probably would be just piling us out of the black maria at the Jefferson Market Court. . . . Of course it was funny. I'll tell you about it sometime, but I'm so sick of all that stuff. . . . Oh just everything like that æsthetic dancing and literature and radicalism and psychoanalysis. . . . Just an overdose I guess. . . . Yes I guess that's it George . . . I guess I'm growing up."

The night was one great chunk of black grinding cold. The smell of the presses still in his nose, the chirrup of typewriters still in his ears, Jimmy Herf stood in City Hall Square with his hands in his pockets watching ragged men with caps and earsflaps pulled down over faces and necks the color of raw steak shovel snow. Old and young their faces were the same color, their clothes were the same color. A razor wind cut his ears and made his forehead ache between the eyes.

"Hello Herf, think you'll take the job?" said a milkfaced young man who came up to him breezily and pointed to the pile of snow. "Why not, Dan. I dont know why it wouldnt be better than spending all your life rooting into other people's affairs until you're nothing but a goddam traveling dictograph."

"It'd be a fine job in summer all right. . . . Taking the West Side?"

"I'm going to walk up. . . . I've got the heebyjeebies tonight."

"Jez man you'll freeze to death."

"I dont care if I do. . . . You get so you dont have any private life, you're just an automatic writing machine."

"Well I wish I could get rid of a little of my private life. . . . Well goodnight. I hope you find some private life Jimmy."

Laughing, Jimmy Herf turned his back on the snow-shovelers and started walking up Broadway, leaning into the wind with his chin buried in his coatcollar. At Houston Street he looked at his watch. Five o'clock. Gosh he was late today. Wouldnt be a place in the world where he could get a drink. He whimpered to himself at the thought of the icy blocks he still had to walk before he could get to his room. Now and then he stopped to pat some life into his numb ears. At last he got back to his room, lit the gasstove and hung over it tingling. His room was a small square bleak room on the south side of Washington Square. Its only furnishings were a bed, a chair, a table piled with books, and the gasstove. When he had begun to be a little less cold he reached under the bed for a basketcovered bottle of rum. He put some water to heat in a tin cup on the gasstove and began drinking hot rum and water. Inside him all sorts of unnamed agonies were breaking loose. He felt like the man in the fairy story with an iron band round his heart. The iron band was breaking.

He had finished the rum. Occasionally the room would start going round him solemnly and methodically. Suddenly he said aloud: "I've got to talk to her . . . I've got to talk to her." He shoved his hat down on his head and pulled on his coat. Outside the cold was balmy. Six milkwagons in a row passed jingling.

On West Twelfth two black cats were chasing each other. Everywhere was full of their crazy yowling. He felt that something would snap in his head, that he himself would scuttle off suddenly down the frozen street eerily cater-wauling.

He stood shivering in the dark passage, ringing the bell marked Herf again and again. Then he knocked as loud as he could. Ellen came to the door in a green wrapper. "What's the matter Jimps? Havent you got a key?" Her face was soft with sleep; there was a happy cozy suave smell of sleep about her. He talked through clenched teeth breathlessly.

"Ellie I've got to talk to you."

"Are you lit, Jimps?"

"Well I know what I'm saying."

"I'm terribly sleepy."

He followed her into her bedroom. She kicked off her slippers and got back into bed, sat up looking at him with sleepweighted eyes.

"Dont talk too loud on account of Martin."

"Ellie I dont know why it's always so difficult for me to speak out about anything. . . . I always have to get drunk to speak out. . . . Look here do you like me any more?"

"You know I'm awfully fond of you and always shall be."

"I mean love, you know what I mean, whatever it is . . ." he broke in harshly.

"I guess I dont love anybody for long unless they're dead

. . . I'm a terrible sort of person. It's no use talking about it."

"I knew it. You knew I knew it. O God things are pretty rotten for me Ellie."

She sat with her knees hunched up and her hands clasped round them looking at him with wide eyes. "Are you really so crazy about me Jimps?"

"Look here lets get a divorce and be done with it."

"Dont be in such a hurry, Jimps. . . . And there's Martin. What about him?"

"I can scrape up enough money for him occasionally, poor little kid."

"I make more than you do, Jimps. . . . You shouldnt do that yet."

"I know. I know. Dont I know it?"

They sat looking at each other without speaking. Their eyes burned from looking at each other. Suddenly Jimmy wanted terribly to be asleep, not to remember anything, to let his head sink into blackness, as into his mother's lap when he was a kid.

"Well I'm going home." He gave a little dry laugh. "We didn't think it'd all go pop like this, did we?"

"Goodnight Jimps," she whined in the middle of a yawn. "But things dont end. . . . If only I weren' so terribly sleepy. . . . Will you put out the light?"

He groped his way in the dark to the door. Outside the arctic morning was growing gray with dawn. He hurried back to his room. He wanted to get into bed and be asleep before it was light.

A long low room with long tables down the middle piled with silk and crêpe fabrics, brown, salmonpink, emerald-green. A smell of snipped thread and dress materials. All down the tables bowed heads auburn, blond, black, brown of girls sewing. Errandboys pushing rolling stands of hung dresses up and down the aisles. A bell rings and the room breaks out with noise and talk shrill as a birdhouse.

Anna gets up and stretches out her arms. "My I've got a head," she says to the girl next her.

"Up last night?"

She nods.

"Ought to quit it dearie, it'll spoil your looks. A girl cant burn the candle at both ends like a feller can." The other girl is thin and blond and has a crooked nose. She puts her arm round Anna's waist. "My I wish I could put on a little of your weight."

"I wish you could," says Anna. "Dont matter what I eat it turns to fat."

"Still you aint too fat. . . . You're juss plump so's they like to squeeze ye. You try wearing boyishform like I told an you'll look fine."

"My boyfriend says he likes a girl to have shape."

On the stairs they push their way through a group of girls listening to a little girl with red hair who talks fast, opening her mouth wide and rolling her eyes. ". . . She lived just on the next block at 2230 Cameron Avenue an she'd been to the Hippodrome with some girlfriends and when they got home it was late an they let her go home alone, up Cameron Avenue, see? An the next morning when her folks began looking for her they found her behind a Spearmint sign in a back lot."

"Was she dead?"

"Sure she was. . . . A negro had done somethin terrible to her and then he'd strangled her. . . . I felt terrible. I used to go to school with her. An there aint a girl on Cameron Avenue been out after dark they're so scared."

"Sure I saw all about it in the paper last night. Imagine livin right on the next block."

"Did you see me touch that hump back?" cried Rosie as

he settled down beside her in the taxi. "In the lobby of the theater?" He pulled at the trousers that were tight over his knees. "That's goin to give us luck Jake. I never seen a hump back to fail. . . . if you touch him on the hump . . . Ou it makes me sick how fast these taxis go." They were thrown forward by the taxi's sudden stop. "My God we almost ran over a boy." Jake Silverman patted her knee. "Poor ikle kid, was it all worked up?" As they drove up to the hotel she shivered and buried her face in her coatcollar. When they went to the desk to get the key, the clerk said to Silverman, "There's a gentleman waiting to see you sir." A thickset man came up to him taking a cigar out of his mouth. "Will you step this way a minute please Mr. Silverman." Rosie thought she was going to faint. She stood perfectly still, frozen, with her cheeks deep in the fur collar of her coat.

They sat in two deep armchairs and whispered with their heads together. Step by step, she got nearer, listening. "Warrant . . . Department of Justice . . . using the mails to defraud . . ." She couldnt hear what Jake said in between. He kept nodding his head as if agreeing. Then suddenly he spoke out smoothly, smiling.

"Well I've heard your side Mr. Rogers. . . . Here's mine. If you arrest me now I shall be ruined and a great many people who have put their money in this enterprise will be ruined. . . . In a week I can liquidate the whole concern with a profit. . . . Mr. Rogers I am a man who has been deeply wronged through foolishness in misplacing confidence in others."

"I cant help that. . . . My duty is to execute the warrant. . . . I'm afraid I'll have to search your room. . . . You see we have several little items . . ." The man flicked the ash off his cigar and began to read in a monotonous voice. "Jacob Silverman, alias Edward Faversham, Simeon J. Arbuthnot, Jack Hinkley, J. J. Gold. . . . Oh we've got a pretty little list. . . . We've done some very pretty work on your case, if I do say it what shouldnt."

They got to their feet. The man with the cigar jerked his head at a lean man in a cap who sat reading a paper on the opposite side of the lobby.

Silverman walked over to the desk. "I'm called away on business," he said to the clerk. "Will you please have my bill prepared? Mrs. Silverman will keep the room for a few days."

Rosie couldnt speak. She followed the three men into the elevator. "Sorry to have to do this maam," said the lean detective pulling at the visor of his cap. Silverman opened the room door for them and closed it carefully behind him. "Thank you for your consideration, gentlemen. . . . My wife thanks you." Rosie sat in a straight chair in the corner of the room. She was biting her tongue hard, harder to try to keep her lips from twitching.

"We realize Mr. Silverman that this is not quite the ordinary criminal case."

"Wont you have a drink gentlemen?"

They shook their heads. The thickset man was lighting a fresh cigar.

"Allright Mike," he said to the lean man. "Go through the drawers and closet."

"Is that regular?"

"If this was regular we'd have the handcuffs on you and be running the lady here as an accessory."

Rosie sat with her icy hands clasped between her knees swaying her body from side to side. Her eyes were closed. While the detectives were rummaging in the closet, Silverman took the opportunity to put his hand on her shoulder. She opened her eyes. "The minute the goddam dicks take me out phone Schatz and tell him everything. Get hold of him if you have to wake up everybody in New York." He spoke low and fast, his lips barely moving.

Almost immediately he was gone, followed by the two detectives with a satchel full of letters. His kiss was still wet on her lips. She looked dazedly round the empty deathly quiet room. She noticed some writing on the lavender blotter on the desk. It was his handwriting, very scrawly: Hock everything and beat it; you are a good kid. Tears began running down her cheeks. She sat a long while with her head dropped on the desk kissing the penciled words on the blotter.

IV. Skyscraper

The young man without legs has stopped still in the middle of the south sidewalk of Fourteenth Street. He wears a blue knitted sweater and a blue stocking cap. His eyes staring up widen until they fill the paperwhite face. Drifts across the sky a dirigible, bright tinfoil cigar misted with height, gently prodding the rainwashed sky and the soft clouds. The young man without legs stops still propped on his arms in the middle of the south sidewalk of Fourteenth Street. Among striding legs, lean legs, waddling legs, legs in skirts and pants and knickerbockers, he stops perfectly still, propped on his arms, looking up at the dirigible.

JOBLESS, Jimmy Herf came out of the Pulizter Building. He stood beside a pile of pink newspapers on the curb, taking deep breaths, looking up the glistening shaft of the Woolworth. It was a sunny day, the sky was a robin's egg blue. He turned north and began to walk uptown. As he got away from it the Woolworth pulled out like a telescope. He walked north through the city of shiny windows, through the city of scrambled alphabets, through the city of gilt letter signs.

Spring rich in gluten. . . . Chockful of golden richness, delight in every bite, THE DADDY OF THEM ALL, spring rich in gluten. Nobody can buy better bread than PRINCE ALBERT. Wrought steel, monel, copper, nickel, wrought iron. *All the world loves natural beauty.* LOVE'S BARGAIN that suit at Gumpel's best value in town. Keep that schoolgirl complexion. . . . JOE KISS, starting, lightning, ignition and generators.

Everything made him bubble with repressed giggles. It was eleven o'clock. He hadnt been to bed. Life was upside down, he was a fly walking on the ceiling of a topsy-turvy city. He'd thrown up his job, he had nothing to do today, tomorrow, next day, day after. Whatever goes up comes down, but not for weeks, months. Spring rich in gluten.

He went into a lunchroom, ordered bacon and eggs, toast and coffee, sat eating them happily, tasting thoroughly every mouthful. His thoughts ran wild like a pasture full of yearling colts crazy with sundown. At the next table a voice was expounding monotonously:

"Jilted . . . and I tell you we had to do some cleaning. They were all members of your church you know. We knew the whole story. He was advised to put her away. He said, 'No I'm going to see it through'."

Herf got to his feet. He must be walking again. He went out with a taste of bacon in his teeth.

Express service meets the demands of spring. O God to meet the demands of spring. No tins, no sir, but there's rich quality in every mellow pipeful. . . . SOCONY. One taste tells more than a million words. The yellow pencil with the red band. Than a million words, than a million words. "All right hand over that million. . . . Keep him covered Ben." The Yonkers gang left him for dead on a bench in the park. They stuck him up, but all they got was a million words. . . . "But Jimps I'm so tired of book-talk and the proletariat, cant you understand?"

Chockful of golden richness, spring.

Dick Snow's mother owned a shoebox factory. She failed and he came out of school and took to standing on streetcorners. The guy in the softdrink stand put him wise. He'd made two payments on pearl earings for a blackhaired Jewish girl with a shape like a mandolin. They waited for the bankmessenger in the L station. He pitched over the turnstile and hung there. They went off with the satchel in a Ford sedan. Dick Snow stayed behind emptying his gun into the dead man. In the deathhouse he met the demands of spring by writing a poem to his mother that they published in the *Evening Graphic*.

With every deep breath Herf breathed in rumble and grind and painted phrases until he began to swell, felt himself stumbling big and vague, staggering like a pillar of smoke above the April streets, looking into the windows of machineshops, buttonfactories, tenementhouses, felt of the grime of bedlinen and the smooth whir of lathes, wrote cusswords on typewriters between the stenographer's fingers, mixed up the pricetags in departmentstores. Inside he fizzled like sodawater into sweet April syrups, strawberry, sarsaparilla, chocolate, cherry, vanilla dripping foam through the mild gasolineblue air. He dropped sickeningly fortyfour stories, crashed. And suppose I bought a gun and killed Ellie, would I meet the demands of April sitting in the deathhouse writing a poem about my mother to be published in the *Evening Graphic?*

He shrank until he was of the smallness of dust, picking his way over crags and bowlders in the roaring gutter, climbing straws, skirting motoroil lakes.

He sat in Washington Square, pink with noon, looking up Fifth Avenue through the arch. The fever had seeped out of him. He felt cool and tired. Another spring, God how many springs ago, walking from the cemetery up the blue macadam road where fieldsparrows sang and the sign said: Yonkers. In Yonkers I buried my boyhood, in Marseilles with the wind in my face I dumped my calf years into the harbor. Where in New York shall I bury my twenties? Maybe they were deported and went out to sea on the Ellis Island ferry singing the International. The growl of the International over the water, fading sighing into the mist.

DEPORTED

James Herf young newspaper man of 190 West 12th Street recently lost his twenties. Appearing before Judge Merivale they were remanded to Ellis Island for deportation as undesirable aliens. The younger four Sasha Michael Nicholas and Vladimir had been held for some time on a charge of criminal anarchy. The fifth and sixth were held on a technical charge of vagrancy. The later ones Bill Tony and Joe were held under various indictments including wifebeating, arson, assault, and prostitution. All were convicted on counts of misfeasance, malfeasance, and nonfeasance.

Oyez oyez oyez prisoner at the bar. . . . I find the evidence dubious said the judge pouring himself out a snifter. The clerk of the court who was stirring an oldfashioned cocktail became overgrown with vineleaves and the courtroom reeked with the smell of flowering grapes and the Shining Bootlegger took the bulls by the horns and led them lowing gently down the courthouse steps. "Court is adjourned by hicky," shouted the judge when he found gin in his waterbottle. The reporters discovered the mayor dressed in a leopard skin posing as Civic Virtue with his foot on the back of Princess Fifi the oriental dancer. Your correspondent was leaning out of the window of the Banker's Club in the company of his uncle, Jefferson T. Merivale, wellknown clubman of this city and two lamb chops well peppered. Meanwhile the waiters were hastily organizing an orchestra, using the potbellies of the Gausenheimers for snaredrums. The head waiter gave a truly delightful rendition of *My Old Kentucky Home*, utilizing for the first time the resonant bald heads of the seven directors of the Well Watered Gasoline Company of Delaware as a xylophone. And all the while the Shining Bootlegger in purple running drawers and a blueribbon silk hat was leading the bulls up Broadway to the number of two million, threehundred and fortytwo thousand, five hundred and one. As they reached the Spuyten Duyvil, they were incontinently drowned, rank after rank, in an attempt to swim to Yonkers.

And as I sit here, thought Jimmy Herf, print itches like a rash inside me. I sit here pockmarked with print. He got to his feet. A little yellow dog was curled up asleep under the bench. The little yellow dog looked very happy. "What I need's a good sleep," Jimmy said aloud.

"What are you goin to do with it, Dutch, are you goin to hock it?"

"Francie I wouldnt take a million dollars for that little gun."

"For Gawd's sake dont start talkin about money, now. . . . Next thing some cop'll see it on your hip and arrest you for the Sullivan law."

"The cop who's goin to arrest me's not born yet. . . . Just you forget that stuff."

Francie began to whimper. "But Dutch what are we goin to do, what are we goin to do?"

Dutch suddenly rammed the pistol into his pocket and jumped to his feet. He walked jerkily back and forth on the asphalt path. It was a foggy evening, raw; automobiles moving along the slushy road made an endless interweaving flicker of cobwebby light among the skeleton shrubberies.

"Jez you make me nervous with your whimperin an cryin. . . . Cant you shut up?" He sat down beside her sullenly again. "I thought I heard somebody movin in the bushes. . . . This goddam park's full of plainclothes men. . . . There's nowhere you can go in the whole crummy city without people watchin you."

"I wouldnt mind it if I didnt feel so rotten. I cant eat anythin without throwin up an I'm so scared all the time the other girls'll notice something."

"But I've told you I had a way o fixin everythin, aint I? I promise you I'll fix everythin fine in a couple of days. . . . We'll go away an git married. We'll go down South. . . . I bet there's lots of jobs in other places. . . . I'm gettin cold, let's get the hell outa here."

"Oh Dutch," said Francie in a tired voice as they walked down the muddyglistening asphalt path, "do you think we're ever goin to have a good time again like we used to?"

"We're S.O.L. now but that dont mean we're always goin to be. I lived through those gas attacks in the Oregon forest didnt I? I been dopin out a lot of things these last few days."

"Dutch if you go and get arrested there'll be nothin left for me to do but jump in the river."

"Didnt I tell you I wasnt goin to get arrested?"

Mrs. Cohen, a bent old woman with a face brown and blotched like a russet apple, stands beside the kitchen table with her gnarled hands folded over her belly. She sways from the hips as she scolds in an endless querulous stream of Yiddish at Anna sitting blearyeyed with sleep over a cup of coffee: "If you had been blasted in the cradle it would have been better, if you had been born dead. . . . Oy what for have I raised four children that they should all of them be no good, agitators and streetwalkers and bums . . . ? Benny in jail twice, and Sol God knows where making trouble, and Sarah accursed given up to sin kicking up her legs at Minski's, and now you, may you wither in your chair, picketing for the garment workers, walking along the street shameless with a sign on your back."

Anna dipped a piece of bread in the coffee and put it in her mouth. "Aw mommer you dont understand," she said with her mouth full.

"Understand, understand harlotry and sinfulness . . . ? Oy why dont you attend to your work and keep your mouth shut, and draw your pay quietly? You used to make good money and could have got married decent before you took to running wild in dance halls with a goy. Oy oy that I've raised daughters in my old age no decent man'd want to take to his house and marry. . . ."

Anna got to her feet shrieking "It's no business of yours. . . . I've always paid my part of the rent regular. You think a girl's worth nothin but for a slave and to grind her fingers off workin all her life. . . . I think different, do you hear? Dont you dare scold at me. . . ."

"Oy you will talk back to your old mother. If Solomon was alive he'd take a stick to you. Better to have been born dead than talk back to your mother like a goy. Get out of the house and quick before I blast you."

"All right I will." Anna ran through the narrow trunk-obstructed hallway to the bedroom and threw herself on her bed. Her cheeks were burning. She lay quiet trying to think. From the kitchen came the old woman's fierce monotonous sobbing.

Anna raised herself to a sitting posture on the bed. She caught sight in the mirror opposite of a strained teardabbled face and rumpled stringy hair. "My Gawd I'm a sight," she sighed. As she got to her feet her heel caught on the braid of her dress. The dress tore sharply. Anna sat on the edge of the bed and cried and cried. Then she sewed the rent in the dress up carefully with tiny meticulous stitches. Sewing made her feel calmer. She put on her hat, powdered her nose copiously, put a little rouge on her lips, got into her coat and went out. April was coaxing unexpected colors out of the East Side streets. Sweet voluptuous freshness came from a pushcart full of pineapples. At the corner she found Rose Segal and Lillian Diamond drinking coca-cola at the softdrink stand.

"Anna have a coke with us," they chimed.

"I will if you'll blow me. . . . I'm broke."

"Vy, didnt you get your strike pay?"

"I gave it all to the old woman. . . . Dont do no good though. She goes on scoldin all day long. She's too old."

"Did you hear how gunmen broke in and busted up Ike Goldstein's shop? Busted up everythin wid hammers an left him unconscious on top of a lot of dressgoods."

"Oh that's terrible."

"Soive him right I say."

"But they oughtnt to destroy property like that. We make our livin by it as much as he does."

"A pretty fine livin. . . . I'm near dead wid it," said Anna banging her empty glass down on the counter.

"Easy easy," said the man in the stand. "Look out for the crockery."

"But the worst thing was," went on Rose Segal, "that while they was fightin up in Goldstein's a rivet flew out the winder an fell nine stories an killed a fireman passin on a truck so's he dropped dead in the street."

"What for did they do that?"

"Some guy must have slung it at some other guy and it pitched out of the winder."

"And killed a fireman."

Anna saw Elmer coming towards them down the avenue, his thin face stuck forward, his hands hidden in the pockets of his frayed overcoat. She left the two girls and walked towards him. "Was you goin down to the house? Dont lets go, cause the old woman's scoldin somethin terrible. . . . I wish I could get her into the Daughters of Israel. I cant stand her no more."

"Then let's walk over and sit in the square," said Elmer. "Dont you feel the spring?"

She looked at him out of the corner of her eye. "Dont I? Oh Elmer I wish this strike was over. . . . It gets me crazy doin nothin all day."

"But Anna the strike is the worker's great opportunity, the worker's university. It gives you a chance to study and read and go to the Public Library."

"But you always think it'll be over in a day or two, an what's the use anyway?"

"The more educated a feller is the more use he is to his class."

They sat down on a bench with their backs to the playground. The sky overhead was glittering with motherofpearl flakes of sunset. Dirty children yelled and racketed about the asphalt paths.

"Oh," said Anna looking up at the sky, "I'd like to have a Paris evening dress an you have a dress suit and go out to dinner at a swell restaurant an go to the theater an everything."

"If we lived in a decent society we might be able to. . . . There'd be gayety for the workers then, after the revolution."

"But Elmer what's the use if we're old and scoldin like the old woman?"

"Our children will have those things."

Anna sat bolt upright on the seat. "I aint never goin to have any children," she said between her teeth, "never, never, never."

Alice touched his arm as they turned to look in the window of an Italian pastryshop. On each cake ornamented with bright analin flowers and flutings stood a sugar lamb for Easter and the resurrection banner. "Jimmy," she said turning up to him her little oval face with her lips too red like the roses on the cakes, "you've got to do something about Roy. . . . He's got to get to work. I'll go crazy if I have him sitting round the house any more reading the papers wearing that dreadful adenoid expression. . . . You know what I mean. . . . He respects you."

"But he's trying to get a job."

"He doesnt really try, you know it."

"He thinks he does. I guess he's got a funny idea about himself. . . . But I'm a fine person to talk about jobs . . ."

"Oh I know, I think it's wonderful. Everybody says you've given up newspaper work and are going to write."

Jimmy found himself looking down into her widening brown eyes, that had a glimmer at the bottom like the glimmer of water in a well. He turned his head away; there was a catch in his throat; he coughed. They walked on along the lilting brightcolored street.

At the door of the restaurant they found Roy and Martin Schiff waiting for them. They went through an outer room into a long hall crowded with tables packed between two greenish bluish paintings of the Bay of Naples. The air was heavy with a smell of parmesan cheese and cigarettesmoke and tomato sauce. Alice made a little face as she settled herself in a chair.

"Ou I want a cocktail right away quick."

"I must be kinder simpleminded," said Herf, "but these boats coquetting in front of Vesuvius always make me feel like getting a move on somewhere. . . . I think I'll be getting along out of here in a couple of weeks."

"But Jimmy where are you going?" asked Roy. "Isnt this something new?"

"Hasnt Helena got something to say about that?" put in Alice.

Herf turned red. "Why should she?" he said sharply.

"I just found there was nothing in it for me," he found himself saying a little later.

"Oh we none of us know what we want," burst out Martin. "That's why we're such a peewee generation."

"I'm beginning to learn a few of the things I dont want," said Herf quietly. "At least I'm beginning to have the nerve to admit to myself how much I dislike all the things I dont want."

"But it's wonderful," cried Alice, "throwing away a career for an ideal."

"Excuse me," said Herf pushing back his chair. In the toilet he looked himself in the eye in the wavy lookingglass.

"Dont talk," he whispered. "What you talk about you never do. . . ." His face had a drunken look. He filled the hollow of his two hands with water and washed it. At the table they cheered when he sat down

"Yea for the wanderer," said Roy.

Alice was eating cheese on long slices of pear. "I think it's thrilling," she said.

"Roy is bored," shouted Martin Schiff after a silence. His face with its big eyes and bone glasses swam through the smoke of the restaurant like a fish in a murky aquarium.

"I was just thinking of all the places I had to go to look for a job tomorrow."

"You want a job?" Martin went on melodramatically. "You want to sell your soul to the highest bidder?"

"Jez if that's all you had to sell. . . ." moaned Roy.

"It's my morning sleep that worries me. . . . Still it is lousy putting over your personality and all that stuff. It's not your ability to do the work it's your personality."

"Prostitutes are the only honest . . ."

"But good Lord a prostitute sells her personality."

"She only rents it."

"But Roy is bored. . . . You are all bored. . . . I'm boring you all."

"We're having the time of our lives," insisted Alice. "Now Martin we wouldn't be sitting here if we were bored, would we? . . . I wish Jimmy would tell us where he expected to go on his mysterious travels."

"No, you are saying to yourselves what a bore he is, what use is he to society? He has no money, he has no pretty wife, no good conversation, no tips on the stockmarket. He's a useless fardel on society. . . . The artist is a fardel."

"That's not so Martin. . . . You're talking through your hat."

Martin waved an arm across the table. Two wineglasses upset. A scaredlooking waiter laid a napkin over the red streams. Without noticing, Martin went on, "It's all pretense. . . . When you talk you talk with the little lying tips of your tongues. You dont dare lay bare your real souls. . . . But now you must listen to me for the last time. . . . For the last time I say. . . . Come here waiter you too, lean over and look into the black pit of the soul of man. And Herf is bored. You are all bored, bored flies buzzing on the windowpane. You think the windowpane is the room. You dont know what there is deep black inside. . . . I am very drunk. Waiter another bottle."

"Say hold your horses Martin. . . . I dont know if we can pay the bill as it is. . . . We dont need any more."

"Waiter another bottle of wine and four grappas."

"Well it looks as if we were in for a rough night," groaned Roy.

"If there is need my body can pay. . . . Alice take off your mask. . . . You are a beautiful little child behind your mask. . . . Come with me to the edge of the pit. . . . O I am too drunk to tell you what I feel." He brushed off his tortoiseshell glasses and crumpled them in his hand, the lenses shot glittering across the floor. The gaping waiter ducked among the tables after them.

For a moment Martin sat blinking. The rest of them looked at each other. Then he shot to his feet. "I see your little smirking supercil-superciliosity. No wonder we can no longer have decent dinners, decent conversations. . . . I must prove my atavistic sincerity, prove. . . ." He started pulling at his necktie.

"Say Martin old man, pipe down," Roy was reiterating.

"Nobody shall stop me. . . . I must run into the sincerity of black. . . . I must run to the end of the black wharf on the East River and throw myself off."

Herf ran after him through the restaurant to the street. At the door he threw off his coat, at the corner his vest.

"Gosh he runs like a deer," panted Roy staggering against Herf's shoulder. Herf picked up the coat and vest, folded them under his arm and went back to the restaurant. They were pale when they sat down on either side of Alice.

"Will he really do it? Will he really do it?" she kept asking.

"No of course not," said Roy. "He'll go home; he was making fools of us because we played up to him."

"Suppose he really did it?"

"I'd hate to see him. . . . I like him very much. We named our kid after him," said Jimmy gloomily. "But if he really feels so terribly unhappy what right have we to stop him?"

"Oh Jimmy," sighed Alice, "do order some coffee."

Outside a fire engine moaned throbbed roared down the street. Their hands were cold. They sipped the coffee without speaking.

Francie came out of the side door of the Five and Ten into the six o'clock goinghome end of the day crowd. Dutch Robertson was waiting for her. He was smiling; there was color in his face.

"Why Dutch what's . . ." The words stuck in her throat.

"Dont you like it . . . ?" They walked on down Fourteenth, a blur of faces streamed by on either side of them. "Everything's jake Francie," he was saying quietly. He wore a light gray spring overcoat and a light felt hat to

match. New red pointed Oxfords glowed on his feet.
"How do you like the outfit? I said to myself it wasnt no
use tryin to do anythin without a tony outside."
"But Dutch how did you get it?"
"Stuck up a guy in a cigar store. Jez it was a cinch."
"Ssh dont talk so loud; somebody might hear ye."
"They wouldnt know what I was talkin about."

Mr. Densch sat in the corner of Mrs. Densch's Louis XIV
boudoir. He sat all hunched up on a little gilt pinkbacked
chair with his potbelly resting on his knees. In his green
sagging face the pudgy nose and the folds that led from
the flanges of the nostrils to the corners of the wide mouth
made two triangles. He had a pile of telegrams in his hand,
on top a decoded message on a blue slip that read: Deficit
Hamburg branch approximately $500,000; signed Heintz.
Everywhere he looked about the little room crowded with
fluffy glittery objects he saw the purple letters of *approximately*
jiggling in the air. Then he noticed that the maid,
a pale mulatto in a ruffled cap, had come into the room and
was staring at him. His eye lit on a large flat cardboard box
she held in her hand.
"What's that?"
"Somethin for the misses sir."
"Bring it here. . . . Hickson's . . . and what does she want
to be buying more dresses for will you tell me that. . . .
Hickson's. . . . Open it up. If it looks expensive I'll send it
back."
The maid gingerly pulled off a layer of tissuepaper, un-
covering a peach and peagreen evening dress.
Mr. Densch got to his feet spluttering, "She must think
the war's still on. . . . Tell em we will not receive it. Tell
em there's no such party livin here."
The maid picked up the box with a toss of the head and
went out with her nose in the air. Mr. Densch sat down in
the little chair and began looking over the telegrams again.

"Ann-ee, Ann-ee," came a shrill voice from the inner room; this was followed by a head in a lace cap shaped like a libertycap and a big body in a shapeless ruffled negligée. "Why J. D. what are you doing here at this time of the morning? I'm waiting for my hairdresser."

"It's very important. . . . I just had a cable from Heintz. Serena my dear, Blackhead and Densch is in a very bad way on both sides of the water."

"Yes ma'am," came the maid's voice from behind him.

He gave his shoulders a shrug and walked to the window. He felt tired and sick and heavy with flesh. An errand boy on a bicycle passed along the street; he was laughing and his cheeks were pink. Densch saw himself, felt himself for a second hot and slender running bareheaded down Pine Street years ago catching the girls' ankles in the corner of his eye. He turned back into the room. The maid had gone.

"Serena," he began, "cant you understand the seriousness . . . ? It's this slump. And on top of it all the bean market has gone to hell. It's ruin I tell you. . . ."

"Well my dear I dont see what you expect me to do about it."

"Economize . . . economize. Look where the price of rubber's gone to. . . . That dress from Hickson's. . . ."

"Well you wouldnt have me going to the Blackhead's party looking like a country schoolteacher, would you?"

Mr. Densch groaned and shook his head. "O you wont understand; probably there wont be any party. . . . Look Serena there's no nonsense about this. . . . I want you to have a trunk packed so that we can sail any day. . . . I need a rest. I'm thinking of going to Marienbad for the cure. . . . It'll do you good too."

Her eye suddenly caught his. All the little wrinkles on her face deepened; the skin under her eyes was like the skin of a shrunken toy balloon. He went over to her and put his hand on her shoulder and was puckering his lips to kiss her when suddenly she flared up.

"I wont have you meddling between me and my dress-makers. . . . I wont have it . . . I wont have it. . . ."

"Oh have it your own way." He left the room with his head hunched between his thick sloping shoulders.

"Ann-ee!"

"Yes ma'am." The maid came back into the room.

Mrs. Densch had sunk down in the middle of a little spindlelegged sofa. Her face was green. "Annie please get me that bottle of sweet spirits of ammonia and a little water. . . . And Annie you can call up Hickson's and tell them that that dress was sent back through a mistake of . . . of the butler's and please to send it right back as I've got to wear it tonight."

Pursuit of happiness, unalienable pursuit . . . right to life liberty and. . . . A black moonless night; Jimmy Herf is walking alone up South Street. Behind the wharfhouses ships raise shadowy skeletons against the night. "By Jesus I admit that I'm stumped," he says aloud. All these April nights combing the streets alone a skyscraper has obsessed him, a grooved building jutting up with uncountable bright windows falling onto him out of a scudding sky. Typewriters rain continual nickelplated confetti in his ears. Faces of Follies girls, glorified by Ziegfeld, smile and beckon to him from the windows. Ellie in a gold dress, Ellie made of thin gold foil absolutely lifelike beckoning from every window. And he walks round blocks and blocks looking for the door of the humming tinselwindowed skyscraper, round blocks and blocks and still no door. Every time he closes his eyes the dream has hold of him, every time he stops arguing audibly with himself in pompous reasonable phrases the dream has hold of him. Young man to save your sanity you've got to do one of two things. . . . Please mister where's the door to this building? Round the block? Just round the block . . . one of two unalienable alternatives: go away in a dirty soft shirt or stay in a clean Arrow collar. But what's the use of spending your whole life fleeing the City of Destruction? What about your unalienable right, Thirteen Provinces? His mind unreeling phrases, he walks on doggedly. There's nowhere in particular he wants to go. If only I still had faith in words.

"How do you do Mr. Goldstein?" the reporter breezily chanted as he squeezed the thick flipper held out to him over the counter of the cigar store. "My name's Brewster. . . . I'm writing up the crime wave for the *News.*"

Mr. Goldstein was a larvashaped man with a hooked nose a little crooked in a gray face, behind which pink attentive ears stood out unexpectedly. He looked at the reporter out of suspicious screwedup eyes.

"If you'd be so good I'd like to have your story of last night's little. . . . misadventure . . ."

"Vont get no story from me young man. Vat vill you do but print it so that other boys and goils vill get the same idear."

"It's too bad you feel that way Mr. Goldstein . . . Will you give me a Robert Burns please . . . ? Publicity it seems to me is as necessary as ventilation. . . . It lets in fresh air." The reporter bit off the end of the cigar, lit it, and stood looking thoughtfully at Mr. Goldstein through a swirling ring of blue smoke. "You see Mr. Goldstein it's this way," he began impressively. "We are handling this matter from the human interest angle . . . pity and tears . . . you understand. A photographer was on his way out here to get your photograph. . . . I bet you it would increase your volume of business for the next couple of weeks. . . . I suppose I'll have to phone him not to come now."

"Well this guy," began Mr. Goldstein abruptly, "he's a welldressed lookin feller, new spring overcoat an all that and he comes in to buy a package o Camels. . . . 'A nice night,' he says openin the package an takin out a cigarette to smoke it. Then I notices the goil with him had a veil on."

"Then she didnt have bobbed hair?"

"All I seen was a kind o mournin veil. The foist thing I knew she was behind the counter an had a gun stuck in my ribs an began talkin . . . you know kinder kiddin like . . . and afore I knew what to think the guy'd cleaned out the cashregister an says to me, 'Got any cash in your jeans Buddy?' I'll tell ye I was sweatin some . . ·"

"And that's all?"

"Sure by the time I'd got hold of a cop they vere off to hell an gone."

"How much did they get?"

"Oh about fifty berries an six dollars off me."

"Was the girl pretty?"

"I dunno, maybe she was. I'd like to smashed her face in. They ought to make it the electric chair for those babies. . . . Aint no security nowhere. Vy should anybody voirk if all you've got to do is get a gun an stick up your neighbors?"

"You say they were welldressed . . . like welltodo people?"

"Yare."

"I'm working on the theory that he's a college boy and that she's a society girl and that they do it for sport."

"The feller vas a hardlookin bastard."

"Well there are hardlooking college men. . . . You wait for the story called 'The Gilded Bandits' in next Sunday's paper Mr. Goldstein. . . . You take the *News* dont you?"

Mr. Goldstein shook his head.

"I'll send you a copy anyway."

"I want to see those babies convicted, do you understand? If there's anythin I can do I sure vill do it . . . Aint no security no more. . . . I dont care about no Sunday supplement publicity."

"Well the photographer'll be right along. I'm sure you'll consent to pose Mr. Goldstein. . . . Well thank you very much. . . . Good day Mr. Goldstein."

Mr. Goldstein suddenly produced a shiny new revolver from under the counter and pointed it at the reporter.

"Hay go easy with that."

Mr. Goldstein laughed a sardonic laugh. "I'm ready for em next time they come," he shouted after the reporter who was already making for the Subway.

"Our business, my dear Mrs. Herf," declaimed Mr. Harpsicourt, looking sweetly in her eyes and smiling his gray Cheshire cat smile, "is to roll ashore on the wave of fashion the second before it breaks, like riding a surf-board."

Ellen was delicately digging with her spoon into half an alligator pear; she kept her eyes on her plate, her lips a little parted; she felt cool and slender in the tightfitting darkblue dress, shyly alert in the middle of the tangle of sideways glances and the singsong modish talk of the restaurant.

"It's a knack that I can prophesy in you more than in any girl, and more charmingly than any girl I've ever known."

"Prophesy?" asked Ellen, looking up at him laughing.

"You shouldnt pick up an old man's word. . . . I'm expressing myself badly. . . . That's always a dangerous sign. No, you understand so perfectly, though you disdain it a little . . . admit that. . . . What we need on such a periodical, that I'm sure you could explain it to me far better."

"Of course what you want to do is make every reader feel Johnny on the spot in the center of things."

"As if she were having lunch right here at the Algonquin."

"Not today but tomorrow," added Ellen.

Mr. Harpsicourt laughed his creaky little laugh and tried to look deep among the laughing gold specs in her gray eyes. Blushing she looked down into the gutted half of an alligator pear in her plate. Like the sense of a mirror behind her she felt the smart probing glances of men and women at the tables round about.

The pancakes were comfortably furry against his gin-bitten tongue. Jimmy Herf sat in Child's in the middle of a noisy drunken company. Eyes, lips, evening dresses, the smell of bacon and coffee blurred and throbbed about him. He ate the pancakes painstakingly, called for more coffee. He felt better. He had been afraid he was going to feel sick. He began reading the paper. The print swam and spread like Japanese flowers. Then it was sharp again, orderly, running in a smooth black and white paste over his orderly black and white brain:

Misguided youth again took its toll of tragedy amid the tinsel gayeties of Coney Island fresh painted for the season when plain-clothes men arrested "Dutch" Robinson and a girl companion alleged to be the Flapper Bandit. The pair are accused of committing more than a score of holdups in Brooklyn and Queens. The police had been watching the couple for some days. They had rented a small kitchenette apartment at 7356 Seacroft Avenue. Suspicion was first aroused when the girl, about to become a mother, was taken in an ambulance to the Canarsie Presbyterian Hospital. Hospital attendants were surprised by Robinson's seemingly endless supply of money. The girl had a private room, expensive flowers and fruit were sent in to her daily, and a well-known physician was called into consultation at the man's request. When it came to the point of registering the name of the baby girl the young man admitted to the physician that they were not married. One of the hospital attendants, noticing that the woman answered to the description published in the *Evening Times* of the flapper bandit and her pal, telephoned the police. Plain-clothes men sleuthed the couple for some days after they had returned to the apartment on Seacroft Avenue and this afternoon made the arrests.

The arrest of the flapper bandit . . .

A hot biscuit landed on Herf's paper. He looked up with a start; a darkeyed Jewish girl at the next table was making a face at him. He nodded and took off an imaginary hat. "I thank thee lovely nymph," he said thickly and began eating the biscuit.

"Quit dat djer hear?" the young man who sat beside her, who looked like a prizefighter's trainer, bellowed in her ear.

The people at Herf's table all had their mouths open laughing. He picked up his check, vaguely said good night

and walked out. The clock over the cashier's desk said
three o'clock. Outside a rowdy scattering of people still
milled about Columbus Circle. A smell of rainy pavements
mingled with the exhausts of cars and occasionally there
was a whiff of wet earth and sprouting grass from the Park.
He stood a long time on the corner not knowing which way
to go. These nights he hated to go home. He felt vaguely
sorry that the Flapper Bandit and her pal had been arrested.
He wished they could have escaped. He had looked forward to reading their exploits every day in the papers.
Poor devils, he thought. And with a newborn baby too.

Meanwhile a rumpus had started behind him in Child's.
He went back and looked through the window across the
griddle where sizzled three abandoned buttercakes. The
waiters were struggling to eject a tall man in a dress suit.
The thickjawed friend of the Jewish girl who had thrown the
biscuit was being held back by his friends. Then the
bouncer elbowed his way through the crowd. He was a
small broadshouldered man with deepset tired monkey eyes.
Calmly and without enthusiasm he took hold of the tall
man. In a flash he had him shooting through the door. Out
on the pavement the tall man looked about him dazedly and
tried to straighten his collar. At that moment a police-
wagon drove up jingling. Two policemen jumped out and
quickly arrested three Italians who stood chatting quietly on
the corner. Herf and the tall man in the dress suit looked at
each other, almost spoke and walked off greatly sobered
in opposite directions.

V. The Burthen of Nineveh

Seeping in red twilight out of the Gulf Stream fog, throbbing brassthroat that howls through the stiff-fingered streets, prying open glazed eyes of skyscrapers, splashing red lead on the girdered thighs of the five bridges, teasing caterwauling tug-boats into heat under the toppling smoketrees of the harbor.

Spring puckering our mouths, spring giving us gooseflesh grows gigantic out of the droning of sirens, crashes with enormous scaring din through the halted traffic, between attentive frozen tiptoe blocks.

MR. DENSCH with the collar of his woolly ulster up round his ears and a big English cap pulled down far over his eyes, walked nervously back and forth on the damp boat deck of the Volendam. He looked out through a drizzly rain at the gray wharfhouses and the water-front buildings etched against a sky of inconceivable bitterness. A ruined man, a ruined man, he kept whispering to himself. At last the ship's whistle boomed out for the third time. Mr. Densch, his fingers in his ears, stood screened by a lifeboat watching the rift of dirty water between the ship's side and the wharf widen, widen. The deck trembled under his feet as the screws bit into the current. Gray like a photograph the buildings of Manhattan began sliding by. Below decks the band was playing *O Titin-e Titin-e*. Red ferryboats, carferries, tugs, sandscows, lumberschooners, tramp steamers drifted between him and the steaming towering city that gathered itself into a pyramid and began to sink mistily into the browngreen water of the bay.

Mr. Densch went below to his stateroom. Mrs. Densch in a cloche hat hung with a yellow veil was crying quietly with her head on a basket of fruit. "Dont Serena," he said huskily. "Dont. . . . We like Marienbad. . . . We need a rest. Our position isnt so hopeless. I'll go and send Blackhead a radio. . . . After all it's his stubbornness and rashness that brought the firm to . . . to this. That man thinks he's a king on earth. . . . This'll . . . this'll get under his skin. If curses can kill I'll be a dead man tomorrow." To his surprise he found the gray drawn lines of his face cracking into a smile. Mrs. Densch lifted her head and opened her mouth to speak to him, but the tears got the better of her. He looked at himself in the glass, squared his shoulders and adjusted his cap. "Well Serena," he said with a trace of jauntiness in his voice, "this is the end of my business career. . . . I'll go send that radio."

Mother's face swoops down and kisses him; his hands clutch her dress, and she has gone leaving him in the dark, leaving a frail lingering fragrance in the dark that makes him cry. Little Martin lies tossing within the iron bars of his crib. Outside dark, and beyond walls and outside again the horrible great dark of grownup people, rumbling, jiggling, creeping in chunks through the windows, putting fingers through the crack in the door. From outside above the roar of wheels comes a strangling wail clutching his throat. Pyramids of dark piled above him fall crumpling on top of him. He yells, gagging between yells. Nounou walks towards the crib along a saving gangplank of light "Dont you be scared . . . that aint nothin." Her black face grins at him, her black hand straightens the covers. "Just a fire engine passin. . . . You wouldn't be sceered of a fire engine."

Ellen leaned back in the taxi and closed her eyes for a second. Not even the bath and the halfhour's nap had washed out the fagging memory of the office, the smell of it, the chirruping of typewriters, the endlessly repeated phrases, faces, typewritten sheets. She felt very tired; she must have rings under her eyes. The taxi had stopped. There was a red light in the traffic tower ahead. Fifth Avenue was jammed to the curbs with taxis, limousines, motorbusses. She was late; she had left her watch at home. The minutes hung about her neck leaden as hours. She sat up on the edge of the seat, her fists so tightly clenched that she could feel through her gloves her sharp nails digging into the palms of her hands. At last the taxi jerked forward, there was a gust of exhausts and whir of motors, the clot of traffic began moving up Murray Hill. At a corner she caught sight of a clock. Quarter of eight. The traffic stopped again, the brakes of the taxi shrieked, she was thrown forward on the seat. She leaned back with her eyes closed, the blood throbbing in her temples. All her nerves were sharp steel jangled wires cutting into her. "What does it matter?" she kept asking herself. "He'll wait. I'm in no hurry to see him. Let's see, how many blocks? . . . Less than twenty, eighteen." It must have been to keep from going crazy people invented numbers. The multiplication table better than Coué as a cure for jangled nerves. Probably that's what old Peter Stuyvesant thought, or whoever laid the city out in numbers. She was smiling to herself. The taxi had started moving again.

George Baldwin was walking back and forth in the lobby of the hotel, taking short puffs of a cigarette. Now and then he glanced at the clock. His whole body was screwed up taut like a high violinstring. He was hungry and full up with things he wanted to say; he hated waiting for people. When she walked in, cool and silky and smiling, he wanted to go up to her and hit her in the face.

"George do you realize that it's only because numbers are so cold and emotionless that we're not all crazy?" she said giving him a little pat on the arm.

"Fortyfive minutes waiting is enough to drive anybody crazy, that's all I know."

"I must explain it. It's a system. I thought it all up coming up in the taxi. . . . You go in and order anything you like. I'm going to the ladies' room a minute. . . . And please have me a Martini. I'm dead tonight, just dead."

"You poor little thing, of course I will. . . . And dont be long please."

His knees were weak under him, he felt like melting ice as he went into the gilt ponderously ornamented diningroom. Good lord Baldwin you're acting like a hobbledehoy of seventeen . . . after all these years too. Never get anywhere that way. . . . "Well Joseph what are you going to give us to eat tonight? I'm hungry. . . . But first you can get Fred to make the best Martini cocktail he ever made in his life."

"Tres bien monsieur," said the longnosed Roumanian waiter and handed him the menu with a flourish.

Ellen stayed a long time looking in the mirror, dabbing a little superfluous powder off her face, trying to make up her mind. She kept winding up a hypothetical dollself and setting it in various positions. Tiny gestures ensued, acted out on various model stages. Suddenly she turned away from the mirror with a shrug of her toowhite shoulders and hurried to the diningroom.

"Oh George I'm starved, simply starved."

"So am I" he said in a crackling voice. "And Elaine I've got news for you," he went on hurriedly as if he were afraid she'd interrupt him.

"Cecily has consented to a divorce. We're going to rush it through quietly in Paris this summer. Now what I want to know is, will you . . . ?"

She leaned over and patted his hand that grasped the edge of the table. "George lets eat our dinner first. . . . We've got to be sensible. God knows we've messed things up enough in the past both of us. . . . Let's drink to the crime wave." The smooth infinitesimal foam of the cocktail was soothing in her tongue and throat, glowed gradually warmly through her. She looked at him laughing with sparkling eyes. He drank his at a gulp.

"By gad Elaine," he said flaming up helplessly, "you're the most wonderful thing in the world."

Through dinner she felt a gradual icy coldness stealing through her like novocaine. She had made up her mind. It seemed as if she had set the photograph of herself in her own place, forever frozen into a single gesture. An invisible silk band of bitterness was tightening round her throat, strangling. Beyond the plates, the ivory pink lamp, the broken pieces of bread, his face above the blank shirtfront jerked and nodded; the flush grew on his cheeks; his nose caught the light now on one side, now on the other, his taut lips moved eloquently over his yellow teeth. Ellen felt herself sitting with her ankles crossed, rigid as a porcelain figure under her clothes, everything about her seemed to be growing hard and enameled, the air bluestreaked with cigarettesmoke, was turning to glass. His wooden face of a marionette waggled senselessly in front of her. She shuddered and hunched up her shoulders.

"What's the matter, Elaine?" he burst out. She lied:

"Nothing George. . . . Somebody walked over my grave I guess."

"Couldnt I get you a wrap or something?"

She shook her head.

"Well what about it?" he said as they got up from the table.

"What?" she asked smiling. "After Paris?"

"I guess I can stand it if you can George," she said quietly.

He was waiting for her, standing at the open door of a taxi. She saw him poised spry against the darkness in a tan felt hat and a light tan overcoat, smiling like some celebrity in the rotogravure section of a Sunday paper. Mechanically she squeezed the hand that helped her into the cab.

"Elaine," he said shakily, "life's going to mean something to me now. . . . God if you knew how empty life had been for so many years. I've been like a tin mechanical toy, all hollow inside."

"Let's not talk about mechanical toys," she said in a strangled voice.

"No let's talk about our happiness," he shouted.

Inexorably his lips closed on to hers. Beyond the shaking glass window of the taxi, like someone drowning, she saw out of a corner of an eye whirling faces, streetlights, zooming nickleglinting wheels.

The old man in the checked cap sits on the brownstone stoop with his face in his hands. With the glare of Broadway in their backs there is a continual flickering of people past him towards the theaters down the street. The old man is sobbing through his fingers in a sour reek of gin. Once in a while he raises his head and shouts hoarsely, "I cant, dont you see I cant?" The voice is inhuman like the splitting of a plank. Footsteps quicken. Middleaged people look the other way. Two girls giggle shrilly as they look at him. Streeturchins nudging each other peer in and out through the dark crowd. "Bum Hootch." "He'll get his when the cop on the block comes by." "Prohibition liquor." The old man lifts his wet face out of his hands, staring out of sightless bloodyrimmed eyes. People back off, step on the feet of the people behind them. Like splintering wood the voice comes out of him. "Don't you see I cant . . . ? I cant . . . I cant."

When Alice Sheffield dropped into the stream of women going through the doors of Lord & Taylor's and felt the close smell of stuffs in her nostrils something went click in her head. First she went to the glovecounter. The girl was very young and had long curved black lashes and a pretty smile; they talked of permanent waves while Alice tried on gray kids, white kids with a little fringe like a gauntlet. Before she tried it on, the girl deftly powdered the inside of each glove out of a longnecked wooden shaker. Alice ordered six pairs.

"Yes. Mrs. Roy Sheffield. . . . Yes I have a charge ac-

count, here's my card. . . . I'll be having quite a lot of things
sent." And to herself she said all the while: Ridiculous how
I've been going round in rags all winter. . . . When the bill
comes Roy'll have to find some way of paying it that's all.
Time he stopped mooning round anyway. I've paid enough
bills for him in my time, God knows." Then she started
looking at fleshcolored silk stockings. She left the store her
head still in a whirl of long vistas of counters in a violet
electric haze, of braided embroidery and tassles and nastur-
tiumtinted silks; she had ordered two summer dresses and an
evening wrap.

At Maillard's she met a tall blond Englishman with a
coneshaped head and pointed wisps of towcolored mustaches
under his long nose.

"Oh Buck I'm having the grandest time. I've been going
berserk in Lord & Taylor's. Do you know that it must be a
year and a half since I've bought any clothes?"

"Poor old thing," he said as he motioned her to a table.
"Tell me about it."

She let herself flop into a chair suddenly whimpering,
"Oh Buck I'm so tired of it all. . . . I dont know how much
longer I can stand it."

"Well you cant blame me. . . . You know what I want
you to do. . . ."

"Well suppose I did?"

"It'd be topping, we'd hit it off like anything. . . . But you
must have a bit of beef tea or something. You need picking
up." She giggled. "You old dear that's just what I do
need."

"Well how about making tracks for Calgary? I know a
fellow there who'll give me a job I think."

"Oh let's go right away. I dont care about clothes or
anything. . . . Roy can send those things back to Lord &
Taylor's. . . . Got any money Buck?"

A flush started on his cheekbones and spread over his
temples to his flat irregular ears. "I confess, Al darling,
that I havent a penny. I can pay for lunch."

"Oh hell I'll cash a check; the account's in both our names."

"They'll cash it for me at the Biltmore, they know me there. When we get to Canada everything will be quite all right I can assure you. In His Majesty's Dominion, the name of Buckminster has rather more weight than in the U.S."

"Oh I know darling, it's nothing but money in New York."

When they were walking up Fifth Avenue she hooked her arm in his suddenly. "O Buck I have the most horrible thing to tell you. It made me deathly ill. . . . You know what I told you about the awful smell we had in the apartment we thought was rats? This morning I met the woman who lives on the ground floor. . . . O it makes me sick to think of it. Her face was green as that bus. . . . It seems they've been having the plumbing examined by an inspector. . . . They arrested the woman upstairs. O it's too disgusting. I cant tell you about it. . . . I'll never go back there. I'd die if I did. . . . There wasnt a drop of water in the house all day yesterday."

"What was the matter?"

"It's too horrible."

"Tell it to popper."

"Buck they wont know you when you get back home to Orpen Manor."

"But what was it?"

"There was a woman upstairs who did illegal operations, abortions. . . . That was what stopped up the plumbing."

"Good God."

"Somehow that's the last straw. . . . And Roy sitting limp over his damn paper in the middle of that stench with that horrible adenoid expression on his face."

"Poor little girl."

"But Buck I couldn't cash a check for more than two hundred. . . . It'll be an overdraft as it is. Will that get us to Calgary?"

"Not very comfortably. . . . There's a man I know in Montreal who'll give me a job writing society notes. . . .

Beastly thing to do, but I can use an assumed name. Then
we can trot along from there when we get a little more
spondulix as you call it. . . . How about cashing that check
now?"

She stood waiting for him beside the information desk
while he went to get the tickets. She felt alone and tiny in
the middle of the great white vault of the station. All her
life with Roy was going by her like a movie reeled off backwards, faster and faster. Buck came back looking happy
and masterful, his hands full of greenbacks and railway
tickets. "No train till seven ten Al," he said. "Suppose
you go to the Palace and leave me a seat at the boxoffice. . . .
I'll run up and fetch my kit. Wont take a sec. . . . Here's
a fiver." And he had gone, and she was walking alone
across Fortythird Street on a hot May afternoon. For
some reason she began to cry. People stared at her; she
couldnt help it. She walked on doggedly with the tears
streaming down her face.

"Earthquake insurance, that's what they calls it! A whole
lot of good it'll do 'em when the anger of the Lord smokes
out the city like you would a hornet's nest and he picks it up
and shakes it like a cat shakes a rat. . . . Earthquake
insurance!"

Joe and Skinny wished that the man with whiskers like
a bottlecleaner who stood over their campfire mumbling and
shouting would go away. They didn't know whether he was
talking to them or to himself. They pretended he wasnt there
and went on nervously preparing to grill a piece of ham on a
gridiron made of an old umbrellaframe. Below them beyond
a sulphurgreen lace of budding trees was the Hudson going
silver with evening and the white palisade of apartment-
houses of upper Manhattan.

"Dont say nutten," whispered Joe, making a swift cranking motion in the region of his ear. "He's nuts."

Skinny had gooseflesh down the back, he felt his lips getting cold, he wanted to run.

"That ham?" Suddenly the man addressed them in a purring benevolent voice.

"Yessir," said Joe shakily after a pause.

"Dont you know that the Lord God forbad his chillun to eat the flesh of swine?" His voice went to its singsong mumbling and shouting. "Gabriel, Brother Gabriel . . . is it all right for these kids to eat ham? . . . Sure. The angel Gabriel, he's a good frien o mine see, he said it's all right this once if you dont do it no more. . . . Look out brother you'll burn it." Skinny had got to his feet. "Sit down brother. I wont hurt you. I understand kids. We like kids me an the Lord God. . . . Scared of me cause I'm a tramp aint you? Well lemme tell you somethin, dont you never be afraid of a tramp. Tramps wont hurt ye, they're good people. The Lord God was a tramp when he lived on earth. My buddy the angel Gabriel says he's been a tramp many a time. . . . Look I got some fried chicken an old colored woman gave me. . . . O Lordy me!" groaning he sat down on a rock beside the two boys.

"We was goin to play injuns, but now I guess we'll play tramps," said Joe warming up a little. The tramp brought a newspaper package out of the formless pocket of his weathergreened coat and began unwrapping it carefully. A good smell began to come from the sizzling ham. Skinny sat down again, still keeping as far away as he could without missing anything. The tramp divided up his chicken and they began to eat together.

"Gabriel old scout will you just look at that?" The tramp started his singsong shouting that made the boys feel scared again. It was beginning to get dark. The tramp was shouting with his mouth full pointing with a drumstick towards the flickering checkerboard of lights going on up Riverside Drive. "Juss set here a minute an look at her Gabriel. . . . Look at the old bitch if you'll pardon the expression. Earthquake insurance, gosh they need it dont they? Do you know how long God took to destroy the tower of Babel, folks?

Seven minutes. Do you know how long the Lord God took to destroy Babylon and Nineveh? Seven minutes. There's more wickedness in one block in New York City than there was in a square mile in Nineveh, and how long do you think the Lord God of Sabboath will take to destroy New York City an Brooklyn an the Bronx? Seven seconds. Seven seconds. . . . Say kiddo what's your name?" He dropped into his low purring voice and made a pass at Joe with his drumstick.

"Joseph Cameron Parker. . . . We live in Union."

"An what's yours?"

"Antonio Camerone . . . de guys call me Skinny. Dis guy's my cousin. His folks dey changed deir name to Parker, see?"

"Changing your name wont do no good . . . they got all the aliases down in the judgment book. . . . And verily I say unto you the Lord's day is at hand. . . . It was only yesterday that Gabriel says to me 'Well Jonah, shall we let her rip?' an I says to him, 'Gabriel ole scout think of the women and children an the little babies that dont know no better. If you shake it down with an earthquake an fire an brimstone from heaven they'll all be killed same as the rich people an sinners,' and he says to me, 'All right Jonah old horse, have it your own way. . . . We wont foreclose on em for a week or two.' . . . But it's terrible to think of, folks, the fire an brimstone an the earthquake an the tidal wave an the tall buildins crashing together."

Joe suddenly slapped Skinny on the back. "You're it," he said and ran off. Skinny followed him stumbling along the narrow path among the bushes. He caught up to him on the asphalt. "Jez, that guy's nuts," he called.

"Shut up cant ye?" snapped Joe. He was peering back through the bushes. They could still see the thin smoke of their little fire against the sky. The tramp was out of sight. They could just hear his voice calling, "Gabriel, Gabriel." They ran on breathless towards the regularly spaced safe arclights and the street.

Jimmy Herf stepped out from in front of the truck; the
mudguard just grazed the skirt of his raincoat. He stood
a moment behind an L stanchion while the icicle thawed out
of his spine. The door of a limousine suddenly opened in
front of him and he heard a familiar voice that he couldnt
place.

"Jump in Meester 'Erf. . . . Can I take you somewhere?"
As he stepped in mechanically he noticed that he was
stepping into a Rolls-Royce.

The stout redfaced man in a derby hat was Congo. "Sit
down Meester 'Erf. . . . Very pleas' to see you. Where
were you going?"

"I wasnt going anywhere in particular." "Come up to
the house, I want to show you someting. Ow are you today?"

"Oh fine; no I mean I'm in a rotten mess, but it's all the
same."

"Tomorrow maybe I go to jail . . . six mont' . . . but
maybe not." Congo laughed in his throat and straightened
carefully his artificial leg.

"So they've nailed you at last, Congo?"

"Conspiracy. . . . But no more Congo Jake, Meester 'Erf.
Call me Armand. I'm married now; Armand Duval, Park
Avenue."

"How about the Marquis des Coulommiers?"

"That's just for the trade."

"So things look pretty good do they?"

Congo nodded. "If I go to Atlanta which I 'ope not, in
six mont' I come out of jail a millionaire. . . . Meester 'Erf
if you need money, juss say the word. . . . I lend you tousand dollars. In five years even you pay it back. I know
you."

"Thanks, it's not exactly money I need, that's the hell
of it."

"How's your wife? . . . She's so beautiful."

"We're getting a divorce. . . . She served the papers on
me this morning. . . . That's all I was waiting in this goddam town for."

Congo bit his lips. Then he tapped Jimmy gently on the knee with his forefinger. "In a minute we'll get to the 'ouse. . . . I give you one very good drink." . . . Yes wait," Congo shouted to the chauffeur as he walked with a stately limp, leaning on a goldknobbed cane, into the streaky marble hallway of the apartmenthouse. As they went up in the elevator he said, "Maybe you stay to dinner." "I'm afraid I cant tonight, Con . . . Armand."

"I have one very good cook. . . . When I first come to New York maybe twenty years ago, there was a feller on the boat. . . . This is the door, see A. D., Armand Duval. Him and me ran away togedder an always he say to me, 'Armand you never make a success, too lazy, run after the leetle girls too much. . . . Now he's my cook . . . first class chef, cordon bleu, eh? Life is one funny ting, Meester 'Erf."

"Gee this is fine," said Jimmy Herf leaning back in a highbacked Spanish chair in the blackwalnut library with a glass of old Bourbon in his hand. "Congo . . . I mean Armand, if I'd been God and had to decide who in this city should make a million dollars and who shouldnt I swear you're the man I should have picked."

"Maybe by and by the misses come in. Very pretty I show you." He made curly motions with his fingers round his head. "Very much blond hair." Suddenly he frowned. "But Meester 'Erf, if dere is anyting any time I can do for you, money or like dat, you let me know eh? It's ten years now you and me very good frien. . . . One more drink?"

On his third glass of Bourbon Herf began to talk. Congo sat listening with his heavy lips a little open, occasionally nodding his head. "The difference between you and me is that you're going up in the social scale, Armand, and I'm going down. . . . When you were a messboy on a steamboat I was a horrid little chalkyfaced kid living at the Ritz. My mother and father did all this Vermont marble blackwalnut grand Babylonian stuff . . . there's nothing more for me to do about it. . . . Women are like rats, you know, they leave a sinking ship. She's going to marry this man Baldwin who's just been appointed District Attorney. They're said to be grooming him for mayor on a fusion reform ticket. . . . The delusion of power, that's what's biting him. Women fall for it like hell. If I thought it'd be any good to me I swear I've got the energy to sit up and make a million dollars. But I get no organic sensation out of that stuff any more. I've got to have something new, different. . . . Your sons'll be like that Congo. . . . If I'd had a decent education and started soon enough I might have been a great scientist. If I'd been a little more highly sexed I might have been an artist or gone in for religion. . . . But here I am by Jesus Christ almost thirty years old and very anxious to live. . . . If I were sufficiently romantic I suppose I'd have killed myself long ago just to make people talk about me. I havent even got the conviction to make a successful drunkard."

"Looks like," said Congo filling the little glasses again with a slow smile, "Meester 'Erf you tink too much."

"Of course I do Congo, of course I do, but what the hell am I going to do about it?"

"Well when you need a little money remember Armand Duval. . . . Want a chaser?"

Herf shook his head. "I've got to chase myself. . . . So long Armand."

In the colonnaded marble hall he ran into Nevada Jones. She was wearing orchids. "Hullo Nevada, what are you doing in this palace of sin?"

"I live here, what do you think? . . . I married a friend of yours the other day, Armand Duval. Want to come up and see him?"

"Just been. . . . He's a good scout."

"He sure is."

"What did you do with little Tony Hunter?"

She came close to him and spoke in a low voice. "Just forget about me and him will you? . . . Gawd the boy's breath'd knock you down. . . . Tony's one of God's mistakes, I'm through with him. . . . Found him chewing the edges of the rug rolling on the floor of the dressing room one day because he was afraid he was going to be unfaithful

to me with an acrobat. . . . I told him he'd better go and
be it and we busted up right there. . . . But honest I'm
out for connubial bliss this time, right on the level, so for
God's sake dont let anybody spring anything about Tony or
about Baldwin either on Armand . . . though he knows he
wasnt hitching up to any plaster virgin. . . . Why dont you
come up and eat with us?"

"I cant. Good luck Nevada." The whisky warm in his
stomach, tingling in his fingers, Jimmy Herf stepped out into
seven o'clock Park Avenue, whirring with taxicabs, streaked
with smells of gasoline and restaurants and twilight.

It was the first evening James Merivale had gone to the
Metropolitan Club since he had been put up for it; he had been
afraid, that like carrying a cane, it was a little old for him.
He sat in a deep leather chair by a window smoking a thirtyfive cent cigar with the *Wall Street Journal* on his knee and
a copy of the *Cosmopolitan* leaning against his right thigh
and, with his eyes on the night flawed with lights like a
crystal, he abandoned himself to reverie: Economic Depres-
sion. . . . Ten million dollars. . . . After the war slump.
Some smash I'll tell the world. BLACKHEAD & DENSCH FAIL
FOR $10,000,000. . . . Densch left the country some days
ago. . . . Blackhead incommunicado in his home at Great
Neck. One of the oldest and most respected import and
export firms in New York, $10,000,000. *O it's always fair
weather When good fellows get together.* That's the thing
about banking. Even in a deficit there's money to be handled,
collateral. These commercial propositions always entail a
margin of risk. We get 'em coming or else we get 'em
going, eh Merivale? That's what old Perkins said when
Cunningham mixed him that Jack Rose. . . . *With a stein
on the tabul And a good song ri-i-inging clear.* Good con-
nection that feller. Maisie knew what she was doing after
all. . . . A man in a position like that's always likely to be
blackmailed. A fool not to prosecute. . . . Girl's crazy he

said, married to another man of the same name. . . . Ought
to be in a sanitarium, a case like that. God I'd have dusted
his hide for him. Circumstances exonerated him completely, even mother admitted that. *O Sinbad was in bad
in Tokio and Rome* . . . that's what Jerry used to sing. Poor
old Jerry never had the feeling of being in good right in on
the ground floor of the Metropolitan Club. . . . Comes of
poor stock. Take Jimmy now . . . hasnt even that excuse,
an out and out failure, a misfit from way back. . . . Guess
old man Herf was pretty wild, a yachtsman. Used to hear
mother say Aunt Lily had to put up with a whole lot. Still
he might have made something of himself with all his advan-
tages . . . dreamer, wanderlust . . . Greenwich Village stuff.
And dad did every bit as much for him as he did for
me. . . . And this divorce now. Adultery . . . with a prostitute like as not. Probably had syphilis or something. Ten
Million Dollar Failure.

Failure. Success.

Ten Million Dollar Success. . . . Ten Years of Successful Banking. . . . At the dinner of the American Bankers
Association last night James Merivale, president of the
Bank & Trust Company, spoke in answer to the toast 'Ten
Years of Progressive Banking.' . . . Reminds me gentlemen
of the old darky who was very fond of chicken. . . . But if
you will allow me a few serious words on this festive occa-
sion (flashlight photograph) there is a warning note I should
like to sound . . . feel it my duty as an American citizen,
as president of a great institution of nationwide, international
in the better sense, nay, universal contacts and loyalties
(flashlight photograph). . . . At last making himself heard
above the thunderous applause James Merivale, his stately
steelgray head shaking with emotion, continued his speech.
. . . Gentlemen you do me too much honor. . . . Let me
only add that in all trials and tribulations, becalmed amid the
dark waters of scorn or spurning the swift rapids of popular
estimation, amid the still small hours of the night, and in the
roar of millions at noonday, my staff, my bread of life, my

inspiration has been my triune loyalty to my wife, my mother, and my flag.

The long ash from his cigar had broken and fallen on his knees. James Merivale got to his feet and gravely brushed the light ash off his trousers. Then he settled down again and with an intent frown began to read the article on Foreign Exchange in the *Wall Street Journal.*

They sit up on two stools in the lunchwaggon.

"Say kid how the hell did you come to sign up on that old scow?"

"Wasnt anything else going out east."

"Well you sure have dished your gravy this time kid, cap'n 's a dopehead, first officer's the damnedest crook out o Sing Sing, crew's a lot o bohunks, the ole tub aint worth the salvage of her. . . . What was your last job?"

"Night clerk in a hotel."

"Listen to that cookey . . . Jesus Kerist Amighty look at a guy who'll give up a good job clerkin in a swell hotel in Noo York City to sign on as messboy on Davy Jones' own steam yacht. . . . A fine seacook you're goin to make." The younger man is flushing. "How about that Hamburgher?" he shouts at the counterman.

After they have eaten, while they are finishing their coffee, he turns to his friend and asks in a low voice, "Say Rooney was you ever overseas . . . in the war?"

"I made Saint Nazaire a couple o times. Why?"

"I dunno. . . . It kinder gave me the itch. . . . I was two years in it. Things aint been the same. I used to think all I wanted was to get a good job an marry an settle down, an now I dont give a damn. . . . I can keep a job for six months or so an then I get the almighty itch, see? So I thought I ought to see the orient a bit. . . ."

"Never you mind," says Rooney shaking his head. "You're goin to see it, dont you worry about that."

"What's the damage?" the young man asks the counterman.

"They must a caught you young."

"I was sixteen when I enlisted." He picks up his change and follows Rooney's broad shambling back into the street. At the end of the street, beyond trucks and the roofs of warehouses, he can see masts and the smoke of steamers and white steam rising into the sunlight.

"Pull down the shade," comes the man's voice from the bed.

"I cant, it's busted. . . . Oh hell, here's the whole business down." Anna almost bursts out crying when the roll hits her in the face, "You fix it," she says going towards the bed.

"What do I care, they cant see in," says the man catching hold of her laughing.

"It's just those lights," she moans, wearily letting herself go limp in his arms.

It is a small room the shape of a shoebox with an iron bed in the corner of the wall opposite the window. A roar of streets rises to it rattling up a V shaped recess in the building. On the ceiling she can see the changing glow of electric signs along Broadway, white, red, green, then a jumble like a bubble bursting, and again white, red, green.

"Oh Dick I wish you'd fix that shade, those lights give me the willies."

"The lights are all right Anna, it's like bein in a theater. . . . It's the Gay White Way, like they used to say."

"That stuff's all right for you out of town fellers, but it gives me the willies."

"So you're workin for Madame Soubrine now are you Anna?"

"You mean I'm scabbin. . . . I know it. The old woman trew me out an it was get a job or croak. . . ."

"A nice girl like you Anna could always find a boyfriend."

"God you buyers are a dirty lot. . . . You think that because I'll go with you, I'd go wid anybody. . . . Well 1 wouldnt, do you get that?"

"I didnt mean that Anna. . . . Gee you're awful quick tonight."

"I guess it's my nerves. . . . This strike an the old woman trowin me out an scabbin up at Soubrine's . . . it'd get anybody's goat. They can all go to hell for all I care. Why wont they leave you alone? I never did nothin to hurt anybody in my life. All I want is for em to leave me alone an let me get my pay an have a good time now and then. . . . God Dick it's terrible. . . . I dont dare go out on the street for fear of meetin some of the girls of my old local."

"Hell Anna, things aint so bad, honest I'd take you West with me if it wasnt for my wife."

Anna's voice goes on in an even whimper, "An now 'cause I take a shine to you and want to give you a good time you call me a goddam whore."

"I didnt say no such thing. I didnt even think it. All I thought was that you was a dead game sport and not a kewpie above the ears like most of 'em. . . . Look if it'll make ye feel better I'll try an fix that shade."

Lying on her side she watches his heavy body move against the milky light of the window. At last his teeth chattering he comes back to her. "I cant fix the goddam thing. . . . Kerist it's cold."

"Never mind Dick, come on to bed. . . . It must be late. I got to be up there at eight."

He pulls his watch from under the pillow. "It's half after two. . . . Hello kitten."

On the ceiling she can see reflected the changing glare of the electric signs, white, red, green, then a jumble like a bubble bursting, then again white, green, red.

"An he didn't even invite me to the wedding. . . . Honestly Florence I could have forgiven him if he'd invited me to the wedding," she said to the colored maid when she brought in the coffee. It was a Sunday morning. She was sitting up in bed with the papers spread over her lap. She was looking at a photograph in a rotogravure section labeled Mr. and Mrs. Jack Cunningham Hop Off for the First Lap of Their Honeymoon on his Sensational Seaplane Albatross VII. "He looks handsome dont he?"

"He su' is miss. . . . But wasn't there anything you could do to stop 'em, miss?"

"Not a thing. . . . You see he said he'd have me committed to an asylum if I tried. . . . He knows perfectly well a Yucatan divorce isn't legal."

Florence sighed.

"Menfolks su' do dirt to us poor girls."

"Oh this wont last long. You can see by her face she's a nasty selfish spoiled little girl. . . . And I'm his real wife before God and man. Lord knows I tried to warn her. Whom God has joined let no man put asunder . . . that's in the Bible isnt it? . . . Florence this coffee is simply terrible this morning. I cant drink it. You go right out and make me some fresh."

Frowning and hunching her shoulders Florence went out the door with the tray.

Mrs. Cunningham heaved a deep sigh and settled herself among the pillows. Outside churchbells were ringing. "Oh Jack you darling I love you just the same," she said to the picture. Then she kissed it. "Listen, deary the churchbells sounded like that the day we ran away from the High School Prom and got married in Milwaukee. . . . It was a lovely Sunday morning." Then she stared in the face of the second Mrs. Cunningham. "Oh you," she said and poked her finger through it.

When she got to her feet she found that the courtroom was very slowly sickeningly going round and round; the white fishfaced judge with noseglasses, faces, cops, uniformed attendants, gray windows, yellow desks, all going round and round in the sickening close smell, her lawyer with his white hawk nose, wiping his bald head, frowning, going round and round until she thought she would throw up. She couldn't hear a word that was said, she kept blinking to get the blur out of her ears. She could feel Dutch behind her hunched up with his head in his hands. She didnt dare look back. Then after hours everything was sharp and clear, very far away. The judge was shouting at her, from the small end of a funnel his colorless lips moving in and out like the mouth of a fish.

". . . And now as a man and a citizen of this great city I want to say a few words to the defendants. Briefly this sort of thing has got to stop. The unalienable rights of human life and property the great men who founded this republic laid down in the constitootion have got to be rein‐ stated. It is the dooty of every man in office and out of office to combat this wave of lawlessness by every means in his power. Therefore in spite of what those sentimental newspaper writers who corrupt the public mind and put into the head of weaklings and misfits of your sort the idea that you can buck the law of God and man, and private property, that you can wrench by force from peaceful citizens what they have earned by hard work and brains . . . and get away with it; in spite of what these journalistic hacks and quacks would call extentuating circumstances I am going to impose on you two highwaymen the maximum severity of the law. It is high time an example was made. . . ."

The judge took a drink of water. Francie could see the little beads of sweat standing out from the pores of his nose. "It is high time an example was made," the judge shouted. "Not that I dont feel as a tender and loving father the mis‐ fortunes, the lack of education and ideels, the lack of a loving home and tender care of a mother that has led this young woman into a life of immorality and misery, led away by the temptations of cruel and voracious men and the excitement and wickedness of what has been too well named, the jazz age. Yet at the moment when these thoughts are about to temper with mercy the stern anger of the law, the impor‐ tunate recollection rises of other young girls, perhaps hun‐ dreds of them at this moment in this great city about to fall into the clutches of a brutal and unscrupulous tempter like this man Robertson . . . for him and his ilk there is no punishment sufficiently severe . . . and I remember that mercy misplaced is often cruelty in the long run. All we can do is shed a tear for erring womanhood and breathe a prayer for the innocent babe that this unfortunate girl has brought into the world as the fruit of her shame. . . ."

Francie felt a cold tingling that began at her fingertips and ran up her arms into the blurred whirling nausea of her body. "Twenty years," she could hear the whisper round the court, they all seemed licking their lips whispering softly "Twenty years." "I guess I'm going to faint," she said to herself as if to a friend. Everything went crashing black.

Propped with five pillows in the middle of his wide colonial mahogany bed with pineapples on the posts Phineas P. Blackhead his face purple as his silk dressing gown sat up and cursed. The big mahogany-finished bedroom hung with Javanese print cloth instead of wallpaper was empty except for a Hindu servant in a white jacket and turban who stood at the foot of the bed, with his hands at his sides, now and then bowing his head at a louder gust of cursing and saying "Yes, Sahib, yes, Sahib."

"By the living almighty Jingo you goddam yellow Babu bring me that whiskey, or I'll get up and break every bone in your body, do you hear, Jesus God cant I be obeyed in my own house? When I say whiskey I mean rye not orange juice. Damnation. Here take it!" He picked up a cutglass pitcher off the nighttable and slung it at the Hindu. Then he sank back on the pillows, saliva bubbling on his lips, choking for breath.

Silently the Hindu mopped up the thick Beluchistan rug and slunk out of the room with a pile of broken glass in his hand. Blackhead was breathing more easily, his eyes sank into their deep sockets and were lost in the folds of sagged green lids.

He seemed asleep when Gladys came in wearing a raincoat with a wet umbrella in her hand. She tiptoed to the window and stood looking out at the gray rainy street and the old tomblike brownstone houses opposite. For a splinter of a second she was a little girl come in her nightgown to have Sunday morning breakfast with daddy in his big bed.

He woke up with a start, looked about him with bloodshot eyes, the heavy muscles of his jowl tightening under the ghastly purplish skin.

"Well Gladys where's that rye whiskey I ordered?"

"Oh daddy you know what Dr. Thom said."

"He said it'd kill me if I took another drink. . . . Well I'm not dead yet am I? He's a damned ass."

"Oh but you must take care of yourself and not get all excited." She kissed him and put a cool slim hand on his forehead.

"Havent I got reason to get excited? If I had my hands on that dirty lilylivered bastard's neck. . . . We'd have pulled through if he hadnt lost his nerve. Serve me right for taking such a yellow sop into partnership. . . . Twentyfive, thirty years of work all gone to hell in ten minutes. . . . For twentyfive years my word's been as good as a banknote. Best thing for me to do's to follow the firm to Tophet, to hell with me. And by the living Jingo you, my own flesh, tell me not to drink. . . . God almighty. Hay Bob . . . Bob. . . . Where's that goddam officeboy gone? Hay come here one of you sons of bitches, what do you think I pay you for?"

A nurse put her head in the door.

"Get out of here," shouted Blackhead, "none of your starched virgins around me." He threw the pillow from under his head. The nurse disappeared. The pillow hit one of the posts and bounced back on the bed. Gladys began to cry.

"Oh daddy I cant stand it . . . and everybody always respected you so. . . . Do try to control yourself, daddy dear."

"And why should I for Christ's sake . . . ? Show's over,

why dont you laugh? Curtain's down. It's all a joke, a smutty joke."

He began to laugh deliriously, then he was choking, fighting for breath with clenched fists again. At length he said in a broken voice, "Don't you see that it's only the whiskey that was keeping me going? Go away and leave me Gladys and send that damned Hindu to me. I've always liked you better than anything in the world. . . . You know that. Quick tell him to bring me what I ordered."

Gladys went out crying. Outside her husband was pacing up and down the hall. "It's those damned reporters . . . I dont know what to tell 'em. They say the creditors want to prosecute."

"Mrs. Gaston," interrupted the nurse, "I'm afraid you'll have to get male nurses. . . . Really I cant do anything with him. . . ." On the lower floor a telephone was ringing, ringing.

When the Hindu brought the bottle of whiskey Blackhead filled a highball glass and took a deep gulp of it.

"Ah that makes you feel better, by the living Jingo it does. Achmet you're a good fellow. . . . Well I guess we'll have to face the music and sell out. . . . Thank God Gladys is settled. I'll sell out every goddam thing I've got. I wish that precious son-in-law wasnt such a simp. Always my luck to be surrounded by a lot of capons. . . . By gad I'd just as soon go to jail if it'll do em any good; why not? it's all in a lifetime. And afterwards when I come out I'll get a job as a bargeman or watchman on a wharf. I'd like that. Why not take it easy after tearing things up all my life, eh Achmet?"

"Yes Sahib," said the Hindu with a bow.

Blackhead mimicked him, "Yes Sahib. . . . You always say yes, Achmet, isn't that funny?" He began to laugh with a choked rattling laugh. "I guess that's the easiest way." He laughed and laughed, then suddenly he couldnt laugh any more. A perking spasm went through all his limbs. He twisted his mouth in an effort to speak. For a second his eyes looked about the room, the eyes of a little child that has been hurt before it begins to cry, until he fell back limp, his open mouth biting at his shoulder. Achmet looked at him coolly for a long time then he went up to him and spat in his face. Immediately he took a handkerchief out of the pocket of his linen jacket and wiped the spittle off the taut ivory skin. Then he closed the mouth and propped the body among the pillows and walked softly out of the room. In the hall Gladys sat in a big chair reading a magazine. "Sahib much better, he sleep a little bit maybe."

"Oh Achmet I'm so glad," she said and looked back to her magazine.

Ellen got off the bus at the corner of Fifth Avenue and Fiftythird Street. Rosy twilight was gushing out of the brilliant west, glittered in brass and nickel, on buttons, in people's eyes. All the windows on the east side of the avenue were aflame. As she stood with set teeth on the curb waiting to cross, a frail tendril of fragrance brushed her face. A skinny lad with towhair stringy under a foreignlooking cap was offering her arbutus in a basket. She bought a bunch and pressed her nose in it. May woods melted like sugar against her palate.

The whistle blew, gears ground as cars started to pour out of the side streets, the crossing thronged with people. Ellen felt the lad brush against her as he crossed at her side. She shrank away. Through the smell of the arbutus she caught for a second the unwashed smell of his body, the smell of immigrants, of Ellis Island, of crowded tenements. Under all the nickelplated, goldplated streets enameled with May, uneasily she could feel the huddling smell, spreading in dark slow crouching masses like corruption oozing from broken sewers, like a mob. She walked briskly down the crossstreet. She went in a door beside a small immaculately polished brass plate.

MADAME SOUBRINE
ROBES

She forgot everything in the catlike smile of Madame Soubrine herself, a stout blackhaired perhaps Russian woman who came out to her from behind a curtain with outstretched arms, while other customers waiting on sofas in a sort of Empress Josephine parlor, looked on enviously.

"My dear Mrs. Herf, where have you been? We've had your dress for a week," she exclaimed in too perfect English. "Ah my dear, you wait . . . it's magnificent. . . . And how is Mr. Harrpiscourt?"

"I've been very busy. . . . You see I'm giving up my job."

Madame Soubrine nodded and blinked knowingly and led the way through the tapestry curtains into the back of the shop.

"Ah ça se voit. . . . Il ne faut pas trravailler, on peut voir dejà des toutes petites rrides. Mais ils dispareaitront. Forgive me, dear." The thick arm round her waist squeezed her. Ellen edged off a little. . . . "Vous la femme la plus belle de New Yorrk. . . . Angelica Mrs. Herf's evening dress," she shouted in a shrill grating voice like a guineahen's.

A hollowcheeked washedout blond girl came in with the dress on a hanger. Ellen slipped off her gray tailored walkingsuit. Madame Soubrine circled round her, purring. "Angelica look at those shoulders, the color of the hair. . . . Ah c'est le rêve," edging a little too near like a cat that wants its back rubbed. The dress was pale green with a slash of scarlet and dark blue.

"This is the last time I have a dress like this, I'm sick of always wearing blue and green. . . ." Madame Soubrine, her mouth full of pins, was at her feet, fussing with the hem.

"Perfect Greek simplicity, wellgirdled like Diana. . . . Spiritual with Spring . . . the ultimate restraint of an Annette Kellermann, holding up the lamp of liberty, the wise virgin," she was muttering through her pins.

She's right, Ellen was thinking, I am getting a hard look.

She was looking at herself in the tall pierglass. Then my figure'll go, the menopause haunting beauty parlors, packed in boncilla, having your face raised.

"Regardez-moi ça, cherrie;" said the dressmaker getting to her feet and taking the pins out of her mouth "C'est le chef-dœuvre de la maison Soubrine."

Ellen suddenly felt hot, tangled in some prickly web, a horrible stuffiness of dyed silks and crêpes and muslins was making her head ache; she was anxious to be out on the street again.

"I smell smoke, there's something the matter," the blond girl suddenly cried out. "Sh-sh-sh," hissed Madame Soubrine. They both disappeared through a mirrorcovered door.

Under a skylight in the back room of Soubrine's Anna Cohen sits sewing the trimming on a dress with swift tiny stitches. On the table in front of her a great pile of tulle rises full of light like beaten white of egg. *Charley my boy, Oh Charley my boy,* she hums, stitching the future with swift tiny stitches. If Elmer wants to marry me we might as well; poor Elmer, he's a nice boy but so dreamy. Funny he'd fall for a girl like me. He'll grow out of it, or maybe in the Revolution, he'll be a great man. . . . Have to cut out parties when I'm Elmer's wife. But maybe we can save up money and open a little store on Avenue A in a good location, make better money there than uptown. La Parisienne, Modes.

I bet I could do as good as that old bitch. If you was your own boss there wouldn't be this fightin about strikers and scabs. . . . Equal Opportunity for All. Elmer says that's all applesauce. No hope for the workers but in the Revolution. *Oh I'm juss wild about Harree, And Harry's juss wild about me.* . . . Elmer in a telephone central in a dinnercoat, with eartabs, tall as Valentino, strong as Doug. The Revolution is declared. The Red Guard is marching up Fifth Avenue. Anna in golden curls with a little kitten under her arm leans with him out of the tallest window. White tumbler pigeons flutter against the city below them. Fifth Avenue bleeding red flags, glittering with marching bands, hoarse voices singing Die Rote Fahne in Yiddish; far away, from the Woolworth a banner shakes into the wind. 'Look Elmer darling' ELMER DUSKIN FOR MAYOR. And they're dancing the Charleston in all the officebuildings. . . . *Thump. Thump. That Charleston dance.* . . . *Thump. Thump.* . . . Perhaps I do love him. Elmer take me. Elmer, loving as Valentino, crushing me to him with Dougstrong arms, hot as flame, Elmer.

Through the dream she is stitching white fingers beckon. The white tulle shines too bright. Red hands clutch suddenly out of the tulle, she cant fight off the red tulle all round her biting into her, coiled about her head. The skylight's blackened with swirling smoke. The room's full of smoke and screaming. Anna is on her feet whirling round fighting with her hands the burning tulle all round her.

Ellen stands looking at herself in the pierglass in the fitting room. The smell of singed fabrics gets stronger. After walking to and fro nervously a little while she goes through the glass door, down a passage hung with dresses, ducks under a cloud of smoke, and sees through streaming eyes the big workroom, screaming girls huddling behind Madame Soubrine, who is pointing a chemical extinguisher at charred piles of goods about a table. They are picking something moaning out of the charred goods. Out of the corner of her eye she sees an arm in shreds, a seared black red face, a horrible naked head.

"Oh Mrs. Herf, please tell them in front it's nothing, absolutely nothing. . . . I'll be there at once," Madame Soubrine shrieks breathlessly at her. Ellen runs with closed eyes through the smokefilled corridor into the clean air of the fitting room, then, when her eyes have stopped running, she goes through the curtains to the agitated women in the waiting room.

"Madame Soubrine asked me to tell everybody it was nothing, absolutely nothing. Just a little blaze in a pile of rubbish. . . . She put it out herself with an extinguisher."

"Nothing, absolutely nothing," the women say one to another settling back onto the Empress Josephine sofas.

Ellen goes out to the street. The fireengines are arriving. Policemen are beating back the crowds. She wants to go away but she cant, she's waiting for something. At last she hears it tinkling down the street. As the fireengines go clanging away, the ambulance drives up. Attendants carry in the folded stretcher. Ellen can hardly breathe. She stands beside the ambulance behind a broad blue policeman. She tries to puzzle out why she is so moved; it is as if some part of her were going to be wrapped in bandages, carried away on a stretcher. Too soon it comes out, between the routine faces, the dark uniforms of the attendants.

"Was she terribly burned?" somehow she manages to ask under the policeman's arm.

"She wont die . . . but it's tough on a girl." Ellen elbows her way through the crowd and hurries towards Fifth Avenue. It's almost dark. Lights swim brightly in night clear blue like the deep sea.

Why should I be so excited? she keeps asking herself. Just somebody's bad luck, the sort of thing that happens every day. The moaning turmoil and the clanging of the fireengines wont seem to fade away inside her. She stands irresolutely on a corner while cars, faces, flicker clatteringly past her. A young man in a new straw hat is looking at her out of the corners of his eyes, trying to pick her up. She stares him blankly in the face. He has on a red, green, and blue striped necktie. She walks past him fast, crosses to the other side of the avenue, and turns uptown. Seven thirty. She's got to meet some one somewhere, she cant think where. There's a horrible tired blankness inside her. O dear what shall I do? she whimpers to herself. At the next corner she hails a taxi. "Go to the Algonquin please."

She remembers it all now, at eight o'clock she's going to have dinner with Judge Shammeyer and his wife. Ought to have gone home to dress. George'll be mad when he sees me come breezing in like this. Likes to show me off all dressed up like a Christmas tree, like an Effenbee walking talking doll, damn him.

She sits back in the corner of the taxi with her eyes

closed. Relax, she must let herself relax more. Ridiculous to go round always keyed up so that everything is like chalk shrieking on a blackboard. Suppose I'd been horribly burned, like that girl, disfigured for life. Probably she can get a lot of money out of old Soubrine, the beginning of a career. Suppose I'd gone with that young man with the ugly necktie who tried to pick me up. . . . Kidding over a banana split in a soda fountain, riding uptown and then down again on the bus, with his knee pressing my knee and his arm round my waist, a little heavy petting in a doorway. . . . There are lives to be lived if only you didn't care. Care for what, for what; the opinion of mankind, money, success, hotel lobbies, health, umbrellas, Uneeda biscuits . . . ? It's like a busted mechanical toy the way my mind goes brrr all the time. I hope they havent ordered dinner. I'll make them go somewhere else if they havent. She opens her vanity case and begins to powder her nose.

When the taxi stops and the tall doorman opens the door, she steps out with dancing pointed girlish steps, pays, and turns, her cheeks a little flushed, her eyes sparkling with the glinting seablue night of deep streets, into the revolving doors.

As she goes through the shining soundless revolving doors, that spin before her gloved hand touches the glass, there shoots through her a sudden pang of something forgotten. Gloves, purse, vanity case, handkerchief, I have them all. Didn't have an umbrella. What did I forget in the taxicab? But already she is advancing smiling towards two gray men in black with white shirtfronts getting to their feet, smiling, holding out their hands.

Bob Hildebrand in dressing gown and pyjamas walked up and down in front of the long windows smoking a pipe. Through the sliding doors into the front came a sound of glasses tinkling and shuffling feet and laughing and *Running Wild* grating hazily out of a blunt needle on the phonograph.

"Why dont you park here for the night?" Hildebrand was

saying in his deep serious voice. "Those people'll fade out
gradually. . . . We can put you up on the couch."

"No thanks," said Jimmy. "They'll start talking psychoanalysis in a minute and they'll be here till dawn."

"But you'd much better take a morning train."

"I'm not going to take any kind of a train."

"Say Herf did you read about the man in Philadelphia who
was killed because he wore his straw hat on the fourteenth
of May?"

"By God if I was starting a new religion he'd be made a
saint."

"Didnt you read about it? It was funny as a crutch. . . .
This man had the temerity to defend his straw hat. Somebody had busted it and he started to fight, and in the middle
of it one of these streetcorner heroes came up behind him
and brained him with a piece of lead pipe. They picked him
up with a cracked skull and he died in the hospital."

"Bob what was his name?"

"I didnt notice."

"Talk about the Unknown Soldier. . . . That's a real hero
for you; the golden legend of the man who would wear a
straw hat out of season."

A head was stuck between the double doors. A flushfaced
man with his hair over his eyes looked in. "Cant I bring
you fellers a shot of gin. . . . Whose funeral is being celebrated anyway?"

"I'm going to bed, no gin for me," said Hildebrand grouchily.

"It's the funeral of Saint Aloysius of Philadelphia, virgin
and martyr, the man who would wear a straw hat out of
season," said Herf. "I might sniff a little gin. I've got to
run in a minute. . . . So long Bob."

"So long you mysterious traveler. . . . Let us have your
address, do you hear?"

The long front room was full of ginbottles, gingerale bottles, ashtrays crowded with halfsmoked cigarettes, couples
dancing, people sprawled on sofas. Endlessly the phono-

graph played *Lady . . . lady be good*. A glass of gin was pushed into Herf's hand. A girl came up to him.

"We've been talking about you. . . . Did you know you were a man of mystery?"

"Jimmy," came a shrill drunken voice, "you're suspected of being the bobhaired bandit."

"Why dont you take up a career of crime, Jimmy?" said the girl putting her arm round his waist. "I'll come to your trial, honest I will."

"How do you know I'm not?"

"You see," said Frances Hildebrand, who was bringing a bowl of cracked ice in from the kitchenette, "there is something mysterious going on."

Herf took the hand of the girl beside him and made her dance with him. She kept stumbling over his feet. He danced her round until he was opposite to the halldoor; he opened the door and foxtrotted her out into the hall. Mechanically she put up her mouth to be kissed. He kissed her quickly and reached for his hat. "Good night," he said. The girl started to cry.

Out in the street he took a deep breath. He felt happy, much more happy than Greenwich Village kisses. He was reaching for his watch when he remembered he had pawned it.

The golden legend of the man who would wear a straw hat out of season. Jimmy Herf is walking west along Twenty-third Street, laughing to himself. Give me liberty, said Patrick Henry, putting on his straw hat on the first of May, or give me death. And he got it. There are no trollycars, occasionally a milkwagon clatters by, the heartbroken brick houses of Chelsea are dark. . . . A taxi passes trailing a confused noise of singing. At the corner of Ninth Avenue he notices two eyes like holes in a trianglewhite of paper, a woman in a raincoat beckons to him from a doorway. Further on two English sailors are arguing in drunken cockney. The air becomes milky with fog as he nears the river. He can hear the great soft distant lowing of steamboats.

He sits a long time waiting for a ferry in the seedy ruddy-lighted waiting room. He sits smoking happily. He cant seem to remember anything, there is no future but the foggy river and the ferry looming big with its lights in a row like a darky's smile. He stands with his hat off at the rail and feels the riverwind in his hair. Perhaps he's gone crazy, perhaps this is amnesia, some disease with a long Greek name, perhaps they'll find him picking dewberries in the Hoboken Tube. He laughs aloud so that the old man who came to open the gates gave him a sudden sidelong look. Cookoo, bats in the belfry, that's what he's saying to himself. Maybe he's right. By gum if I were a painter, maybe they'll let me paint in the nuthouse, I'd do Saint Aloysius of Philadelphia with a straw hat on his head instead of a halo and in his hand the lead pipe, instrument of his martyrdom, and a little me praying at his feet. The only passenger on the ferry, he roams round as if he owned it. My temporary yacht. By Jove these are the doldrums of the night all right, he mutters. He keeps trying to explain his gayety to himself. It's not that I'm drunk. I may be crazy, but I dont think so. . . .

Before the ferry leaves a horse and wagon comes aboard, a brokendown springwagon loaded with flowers, driven by a little brown man with high cheekbones. Jimmy Herf walks round it; behind the drooping horse with haunches like a hatrack the little warped wagon is unexpectedly merry, stacked with pots of scarlet and pink geraniums, carnations, alyssum, forced roses, blue lobelia. A rich smell of maytime earth comes from it, of wet flowerpots and greenhouses. The driver sits hunched with his hat over his eyes. Jimmy has an impulse to ask him where he is going with all those flowers, but he stifles it and walks to the front of the ferry.

Out of the empty dark fog of the river, the ferryslip yawns all of a sudden, a black mouth with a throat of light. Herf hurries through cavernous gloom and out to a fog-blurred street. Then he is walking up an incline. There are tracks below him and the slow clatter of a freight, the hiss of an engine. At the top of a hill he stops to look back. He can see nothing but fog spaced with a file of blurred arclights. Then he walks on, taking pleasure in breathing, in the beat of his blood, in the tread of his feet on the pavement, between rows of otherworldly frame houses. Gradually the fog thins, a morning pearliness is seeping in from somewhere.

Sunrise finds him walking along a cement road between dumping grounds full of smoking rubbishpiles. The sun shines redly through the mist on rusty donkeyengines, skeleton trucks, wishbones of Fords, shapeless masses of corroding metal. Jimmy walks fast to get out of the smell. He is hungry; his shoes are beginning to raise blisters on his big toes. At a cross-road where the warning light still winks and winks, is a gasoline station, opposite it the Lightning Bug lunchwagon. Carefully he spends his last quarter on breakfast. That leaves him three cents for good luck, or bad for that matter. A huge furniture truck, shiny and yellow, has drawn up outside.

"Say will you give me a lift?" he asks the redhaired man at the wheel.

"How fur ye goin?"

"I dunno. . . . Pretty far."

THE END